THE MOTIVE WAS REVENGE ...

THE METHOD WAS A NIGHTMARE ...

PREY

A shocking and riveting novel of psychological suspense that takes you on a killer's terrifying and deadly quest for vengeance ...

"A REAL PAGE TURNER ... a gripping psychological drama ... the psychopath is truly scary. This is a good thriller!"

—*The Greenwich Times*

"HORRIFYING TENSIONS ... SCREAMING SUSPENSE."

—*Publishers Weekly*

"A POWERFUL STORY ... THE TENSION IS UNDENIABLE!"

—*Toronto Star*

PREY

A NOVEL BY

C. TERRY CLINE, JR.

A SIGNET BOOK

NEW AMERICAN LIBRARY

PUBLISHED BY
THE NEW AMERICAN LIBRARY
OF CANADA LIMITED

NAL BOOKS ARE AVAILABLE AT QUANTITY DISCOUNTS WHEN USED TO PROMOTE PRODUCTS OR SERVICES. FOR INFORMATION PLEASE WRITE TO PREMIUM MARKETING DIVISION, NEW AMERICAN LIBRARY, 1633 BROADWAY, NEW YORK, NEW YORK 10019.

ACKNOWLEDGMENT
Poetry selections from "A Shropshire Lad"—authorized edition from *The Collected Poems of A. E. Housman* © 1939, 1940 by Holt, Rinehart & Winston.
© 1967, 1968 by Robert E. Symons.
Reprinted by permission of Holt, Rinehart & Winston, Publishers.

First Signet Printing, October, 1986

2 3 4 5 6 7 8 9

To friends whose love has endured a lifetime:

Harry and Margaret Street
Rick and Patsy Street

1

He stood with a foot on the bumper of his twenty-year-old Ford, watching the elderly proprietor. This was one of those general stores once so common in rural America, now a vestige of the past. The gas pumps showed amber fluid in a globe with a tiny propeller which spun as fuel passed through on the way to the buyer.

The pistol was cold against his abdomen, covered by his shirt.

"Want me to check your tires?" the old man asked.

"Thirty pounds each."

The June heat was suffocating. Across the road, faded red letters of a sign wiggled in rising convective currents: "LAST GAS."

The old man tested a tire, examined his gauge. "Thirty pounds, you say?"

"That's right."

The nearest town east was fifteen miles. The next to the west was forty miles.

"Them's what I call 'maypops,' " he said. "May pop any minute under that load and in this heat."

"Do you sell tires?"

"Not this size."

"Not that it matters. Times are hard."

"They are that. Worst since the Great Depression hereabouts. Betwixt the drought and the government, everybody is suffering. Banks don't much care who you are anymore. Used to be, a man's character was his bond. But the big outta-towner banks been buying up the little ones and all they see is figures in a ledger. They foreclosed a few this year."

"Yeah."

The terrain was nearly flat here. To the south, dry fields, a dusty farm road; north, behind the owner's house, more of the same.

"Oil's okay." The elderly attendant held the dipstick at arm's length. "Needs changing, though."

"Where do you get enough business to survive out here?"

"That what is, finds me. Anything else?"

"My wife and son will want something."

"She got some groceries."

"She'll want more."

The man walked with shoulders rounded, knees bent. Inside, the store was cooler and dark. A refrigerated glass-front display case held loaves of sandwich meat and perishables such as butter. In a porcelain tray lay chocolate candy misshapen from melting. The soft-drink box was the old-fashioned kind with sliding top lids. It purred as the compressor labored against heat.

In the rear, in a rest room, he heard Bonnie admonish his boy, "Wash your hands, Chuck." The toilet flushed noisily.

There was a smell of sawdust, sprinkled on the wood floor to hold down dust when sweeping. The faintest scent of light machine oil blended with the aroma of dry goods. Shelves on the walls rose to the ceiling. Amidst foodstuffs, bolts of cloth, an outdated calendar with a pastoral scene, were relics of times past: a horse collar, trace chains, an adz, a rusting sledgehammer priced at one dollar.

"Don't you worry, stuck out here alone?"

"Worry?" The old man lifted shaggy eyebrows. "About what?"

"Oh—fire, for one thing."

"Only way to win in a fire is don't have one."

"—and robbery, for another."

A hint of wariness appeared in the pale gray eyes now. The owner rubbed his unshaven jaw, feigning a casual study of his wares. "Nothing much worth taking. Anybody did, though, where would he go? Miles of flatlands—they'd get him."

"I suppose so."

The commode flushed again, a water pipe thumping a gentle tattoo as a pump somewhere replenished the pressure. Bonnie was speaking to Chuck in low maternal tones.

"Long way to anywhere from here," the old man reinforced his point. "The state troopers would catch a body before he'd get away." He dabbed his tobacco-stained mouth with a checkered bandanna. "Besides," he said, "no need to steal when credit will do. It's available to folks for the asking."

"Well, I tell you"—he took a breath—"I need some credit right now."

"That so?"

"I lost my job about a year ago and we're trying to get to California so I can find work. How about it?"

The old man looked rueful. "I don't know you."

"I'm good for the money. Soon as I get settled in, I can get work. I'll send interest on the loan."

"Don't know that for sure, though—do I?"

Bonnie emerged from the toilet, holding Chuck's wrist so high the boy was on tiptoes.

"We need some more things, Truman."

"Get what you want, honey."

The old man blinked rheumy eyes, watching Bonnie walk the aisles.

"Toilet paper," Bonnie pondered. She took three rolls. "Can we have some luxuries, Truman?"

"Get what you want, honey."

"Ten percent interest fair enough?" the proprietor asked. His voice quavered. He was frightened. When they drove away, he'd call the law. It *was* a long way to the next town.

"Could you tell me where to find sanitary napkins?" Bonnie inquired.

"Yes, ma'am. Far wall."

The men were motionless.

"I'm going to get some candy, Truman."

"All right, Bonnie."

"What kind of candy do you want, Chuck?"

A drop of sweat hung on the old man's earlobe. The buzz of a trapped insect on a spiral of flypaper was like the drone of a B-29.

"I guess that's all," Bonnie said pleasantly. "I already got cheese and crackers and cold drinks."

"You want me to make a ticket on everything?" the owner asked.

Truman drew the pistol, held it lazily, muzzle pointed at the wide board floor.

When Bonnie and Chuck were outside, the old man croaked, "I won't tell anybody."

"Of course you would."

"You could lock me in the storeroom."

"Where the money?"

"Cash register."

"Open it."

The machine clanged, drawer ajar. Truman emptied the tray, lifted it. "Way out here with no banks—come on, old man, where's the money?"

"That's all. I swear it."

With his thumb, Truman cocked the hammer. The proprietor stepped backward.

"I swear before Jehovah, that's all."

He placed the muzzle against the man's forehead and said softly, "Where is it?"

"If I had more, I'd give it to you."

It was interesting the way different men faced this moment. Some wept and begged, some erupted furiously, others tried logic. The elderly, he had learned, would give up their lives before their cash. There was no point arguing. Even fear of death did not overcome a fear of old age without money.

"Last time," he said mildly.

"I swear, I swear, this is all!"

He squeezed the trigger and the old man's head jolted with the explosion. He crumpled into a fetal position, one frail leg extending slowly, quivering.

Truman took a carton of cigarettes from beneath the counter, tucked it under his arm. From the house out back he heard a woman calling, "Andy? Andy?"

The moment she entered a rear door, the dead man's wife knew. A bearded, deeply tanned stranger with a gun and a carton of tobacco could mean just one thing.

He raised the revolver, fired. She grabbed for support and canned goods rained around her as she fell.

An automobile passed them at high speed, the first they had seen since leaving the service station. Their tires sang on hot asphalt; their faces were seared by drying heat.

"I got to do number two, Mommie."

"You should've thought of that when you had a chance, Chuck."

"I got to now," the child insisted.

Truman drove absently, flicking ashes at the window, only to have the residue hurled back inside by wind. *How many times?* How many to come? His revolver was under the seat again, reloaded, ready.

"How much did you get back there, Truman?"

"Not much."

Bonnie burped, cheeks puffed. "I never saw so much grass. Is that grass?"

"Wheat." As far as the eye could see, gently rolling, endless fields of wheat.

Exhaust fumes rose from a faulty muffler, the uncarpeted floorboard hot and shivering underfoot. In the rearview mirror he saw Chuck's face, parched, rosy red. "Stop bouncing on the seat, son," he said.

Fifty-five years old, going where? Where had five decades gone? He felt empty.

"Wonder who owns all that wheat?" Bonnie squinted at the fields.

"Consortiums. Multinational corporations. No individual, you can be sure of that."

When he thought about his life, he was appalled by the uselessness of it. He had once aspired so grandly. What happened?

"Want a Pepsi, Truman?"

"No."

"They're hot anyway," Bonnie said. "Want a Pepsi, Chuck?"

"I have to poot, Mommie."

"Truman, you might as well stop."

"Momentarily."

"Daddy says in a minute, Chuck."

He had made a list as a youth: *Climb mountains.* He

had never climbed a mountain. *Fly an airplane. Paint a picture . . .*

"I bet it's fun to lie on your back out there," Bonnie mused. "Look up at the clouds changing shapes. Probably makes you itch, though. You think it would, Truman?"

"Would what?"

"Make you itch—the wheat."

He nodded, pulled on his cagarette. He flicked the ashes and watched Chuck blink rapidly in the back seat.

Never climbed a mountain. Never studied music. He'd gotten swept up by life. By events. By the military. He'd spent twenty-five years in the Army. Korea, then Vietnam. Three marriages . . .

"I gotta pee myself," Bonnie said.

He glanced at her. Bonnie Blue-eyes he called her, sometimes.

The boy looked like her. His other marriages had produced four children, and they, none of them, favored him. *Weak genes*, and just as well.

"Truman, can we stop someplace before Chick poots in his pants?"

He glanced in the rearview mirror—no traffic. When they reached the crest of the next hill they could see for miles—nothing. He pulled over. The highway fell toward the horizon as a manmade ribbon of tar and gravel.

"Where the hell am I?" Truman murmured.

"Kansas, I think." Bonnie pawed through the map compartment.

"Where am I going?"

"To your mother's!" Bonnie cried. "Isn't that what you said? To California." She unfolded a map. "Yep— see, we're in Kansas."

"It isn't the government," Truman said.

"What isn't?"

"I've been angry for years," he said. "I watch TV and scream at politicians. I listen to the news and my belly knots up—furious with the system—but it isn't the system."

"What isn't?"

"I thought you had to go to the toilet," he snapped.

"Oh. Okay. Come on, Chuck, we'll walk out in that field so nobody can see us."

"Who?" Chuck asked.

"Your daddy and God—come on, we'll lie down and look at the clouds."

What had happened to those dreams? He twisted in place, anguished. Here he was, five years past half a century, and none the wiser for it. If there was a hell, he was going there.

He'd been there already.

Bonnie's laughter rode the still air as she galloped through wheat with Chuck unseen at her side.

Who was to blame for his failures, for this emptiness—for everything in his life—who was to blame?

Son of a bitch. Papa, that's who.

He should be going to South Georgia, not California. He should track that son of a bitch—make him pay for all these years of futility and failure.

He conjured the most vivid recollection of his childhood, the moment that had haunted him a thousand times in his life.

He remembered the wallpaper, a pattern of ivy gone yellow with age. They could hear roaches rustling in the walls, the scratch of rodents making plaster fall.

He closed his eyes tightly, perspiration trickling into his beard. Remember?

Yes. He remembered.

Lana, weeping beyond the wallpaper, the roaches

and crumbling plaster—begging Papa to stop, but he didn't stop. Her childish cries muffled, nobody to hear but Truman—Mama worked nights.

When it was over, Papa always put Lana in the bed with Truman, where she lay crying, hurt, cold, and rigid to his touch.

When Mama discovered the blood, she blamed Truman. Screaming accusations, she demanded punishment. Papa beat him unconscious that night. Years later, taking a routine X ray, a technician noted three broken ribs that had healed poorly. It was hard to mend a fracture broken again and again. . . .

Through all of that, Lana said nothing. Papa had told her the police would come and take them away. Neighbors would spit on them as they walked the streets. Besides, Papa had said, it was Lana's fault—not his.

As he remembered, sweat oozed between his fingers, locked to the steering wheel.

He was twelve when it came to a head. He had gone to a trusted teacher and she called in Lana for confirmation. But Lana said no, it wasn't Papa—it was Truman.

The teacher told people. The other children ostracized him with angry silence. And Papa—beating, beating, beating—

"Truman? We need some tissue."

He opened his eyes to brilliant blinding sunlight. A cloud brought shade and relief. In the distance, thunderheads roiled, going black from the bottoms up. Crooked legs of lightning walked flatlands below.

"Truman! Chuck has worms."

And Chuck was the son of the son who should never have been begot. The result of twisted genes and a warped personality, the product of poverty and paternal abuse. *Papa* was the man who had caused it all.

"Truman, precious—we need a roll of toilet paper. Do you hear me?"

He pushed aside articles in various sacks, seeking the tissue.

He should be going to Georgia. He should end this!

"Are those worms, Mommie?"

What would Chuck recall of these days? Did he know about the robberies, the killings?

The air freshened. Thunder grumbled.

Bonnie knew. Her insouciance was not an act. She had neither the intelligence nor the fortitude to resist the truth. If caught, she'd tell the law and the law would be upon him.

Truman stepped out of the car.

All these years he had fumbled and faltered. So many times in the stockade he'd lost count. Dishonorable discharge. Worthless then and dangerous now.

And for what? He searched his mind for a single constructive act, the glimmer of any dream still alive. But he could find none.

He got the pistol from under the seat and shoved it into his belt. Bonnie's laughter came in musical notes as she and Chuck squatted unseen in the wheatfield.

What his father had done to him he now did to Chuck, and surely, someday, Chuck would do the same to his children.

It was Papa who should be suffering. As Lana the whore suffered yet. As Mama suffered in alcoholic stupor.

He could do one constructive act before it was over. As for Bonnie and the boy—it should end here.

He found them in the wheat and Bonnie took the tissue, tearing away wrapping. "Truman, look at Chuck's poot—he has worms."

The boy gazed up with blue eyes wide, fearful until he knew the reaction to such a condition.

Bonnie stood, pulled up her panties, flexing her knees to get them right. "Bend over, precious, so Mommie can see."

"Why did you marry me, Bonnie Blue-eyes?"

She hesitated, as if to remember. "Because I loved you, Truman. See there—aren't those worms?"

"It's normal in a child."

"It's disgusting. We have to stop someplace and get some bitters, okay?"

"You married me because I'm a provider, wasn't that it?"

She glanced at him, uncertain. Beyond her, clouds rose in angry boils, a hiss of electrical discharge bringing ozone to the air.

"Is something wrong, Truman?"

"I'm not sure you'll understand, Bonnie," he said. "Even though, intellectually, I see what's happened to me, I am incapable of altering it. I was abused, and so abused is Chuck."

"Ah, phooey," Bonnie laughed. "We love you. Don't we, Chuck?"

The boy was mute, mouth agape, sensing violence. He'd seen it before.

"The genesis was my adolescent suffering, Bonnie."

"Please don't use big words, Truman."

He pulled the pistol from under his shirt.

"Everything is going to be okay when we get to California, Truman. You said so, remember? There's work out there; Lana and your mama told you that."

"If it chance your eye offend you, Pluck it out, lad, and be sound."

"No," Bonnie screamed. "No poems! Talk plain to me, please."

" 'Twill hurt, but here are salves to friend you, And many a balsam grows on ground."

"Truman . . ." Bonnie seized Chuck's hand and tried to pass, but Truman shoved her backward.

"And if your hand or foot offend you, Cut it off, lad, and be whole; But play the man, stand up and end you, When your sickness is your soul."

"Why?" she wailed. "I haven't been much trouble, have I? I never complained. Truman . . . why?"

He raised the gun and she wheeled to flee, skirt flouncing as her knees rose high to gain momentum. He fired and she catapulted forward. He watched her claw the loam, struggling to rise, moaning. He aimed more carefully . . . fired.

The boy stood as stone, waiting his turn. His shoes were on the wrong feet. No socks. Face crimson from exposure, he put a thumb in his mouth and began sucking.

"It has to end here, Chuck," Truman said tenderly. "I don't know any other way to change things."

He stroked the boy's head and stepped back. The gun recoiled, the child fell.

The son of the son who should not have been.

2

Her world was changing. Denise could see it as they passed beach property under development. She could feel an even more pervasive change in Brad, driving with a wrist hung over the steering wheel, his mind elsewhere. *Nothing is forever,* he was fond of saying.

Nothing.

They had taken the coastal highway from Pensacola, a favored route, at her insistence. Since they were here last, the area had been transformed. No cattle egrets stalked the byways in search of food. Gone were the flocks of migratory fowl which once covered the hummocks like a million brilliant, moving blossoms. In their place stood rows of identical condominiums.

"Look what they've done to the beach." She sighed.

Brad nodded automatically. Where was he? The past? Future?

A stroke, Mother Taylor had first reported. The doctors were "cautiously optimistic," she had said. An hour later, *heart attack.* Father Taylor was dead.

She had never seen Brad weep before. Thirty-four-year-old cop, detective, homicide division, Mobile, Alabama—Brad was not an emotional man. But he wept last night, his broad shoulders racked with sobs.

Denise had read somewhere that after the death of his father, a man was immutably a man. Never again would he be a boy. The thought filled her with sadness.

"I wonder who is taking the Spanish moss?" Elaine asked from the rear seat.

"Nobody is taking it," her brother, Jeffrey, responded. "There's a disease killing it."

"That's awful." At thirteen, Elaine bore such news poorly.

"Also," Jeffrey informed her, "the carbon monoxide from the traffic is deleterious to epiphytics."

"Deleterious?" Elaine wailed. "Epiphytics! Are these your new words for the day, Jeffrey?"

"Knock it off," Brad said.

"Want some advice, Elaine?" Jeffrey asked *sotto voce*. "With your looks, get all the education you can."

Two years younger than his sister, Jeffrey bore a burden of a different sort. A teacher had recently informed him of his score on an intelligence test.

"My I.Q.," Jeffrey had announced, "is one hundred forty-seven. That is proof at last, I am officially a genius."

"They were probably referring to the specific gravity of your brain," Elaine had countered.

This had been going on for weeks.

Denise slipped nearer to Brad, stroking his leg. "What's on your mind?"

"Dad." He gazed away a moment. "I feel as if a part of me went with him."

"It did, Brad. But a part of him goes with you, too."

"I'm not a philosopher, Denise."

Her attempt to comfort was irritating him. His jaw clamped, lips compressed, a barrier formed between them. He had shut her off. The first few times that happened, years ago, she had taken it as a personal affront. Now it was as natural as his unruly hair and deep brown eyes. She had finally decided the invisible wall was a protective device, required by his profession and, unfortunately, brought home to their private lives.

"Spanish moss is related to pineapples," Jeffrey went on.

"That's absurd, Jeffrey."

"They're both bromeliaceous."

"Jeffrey," Elaine replied wearily, "what good is such information? I mean, who *cares?*"

"Botanists care. Agronomists care . . ."

As they passed through Tallahassee, Denise pointed to the red-brick library of Florida State University. "That's where your daddy and I went to school."

"Mama, you tell us that every time we pass here," Elaine said.

Denise noted another landmark, ". . . and that is where we spent our honeymoon. It was a weekend between classes, wasn't it, Brad?"

"You spent your honeymoon in a service station?"

"It was a small motel then."

Thirty-four miles to Thomasville. Denise said, "I'll bet there's a crowd at your mother's house."

"Probably."

"I look a fright."

"It isn't formal."

"Stop someplace and let us get decent, Brad."

As he pulled into a service station, Brad warned,

"No running, no shouting, no nonsense—you hear me?"

"Yes, sir."

Denise stood outside the rest-room door waiting her turn. She could see Brad, car door ajar, sitting behind the steering wheel. They were so different, he and she. Distress made her talkative. "Nervous chatter," Brad called it. When things went badly, she needed companionship and a sympathetic ear. Brad, on the other hand, withdrew behind his invisible wall, silent, brooding.

For fifteen years she had been observing the Taylor family. The three sons, of which Brad was youngest, were as different as day from dark. Brad was the one most like his father—the son of Sheriff Bo Taylor had embarked on a career in law enforcement as if it had been preordained and he was cut from his father's silhouette. Muscular, two hundred pounds, tall and handsome men, they wore the paraphernalia of their profession as if born to it. Both men were every inch the law officer, commanding in demeanor, intimidating when necessary.

She had seen Brad sit with his father for hours, neither man speaking. They didn't need conversation, Brad once said. If they had anything to say, they said it. He once mentioned Father Taylor had never uttered the word "love." Yet, as closely as a man can emulate his sire, Brad had fulfilled the shadow cast by his father.

But the two men parted ways when it came to criminology. Brad's education included forensic sciences, unknown to Sheriff Bo Taylor when he took office nearly forty years ago. Law enforcement was a matter of practical experience to the senior lawman. He had little patience with "classroom crap" about criminals. Bo Taylor saw the criminal much as prehistoric man must have viewed the saber-toothed tiger—a deadly threat requiring a response in kind. He was not the least interested in why a man was driven to commit a crime. To the bad guys, Bo Taylor was the enemy. To the good guys, he was a protector. Like a shield, he was unbending.

Denise was surprised to learn that Father Taylor had attended college, nights and summers and by correspondence courses. He had received his bachelor's degree from the University of Georgia while serving as sheriff of Thomas County. Some years later, she had discovered a transcript from Father Taylor's college days. It came as a shock to discover his major was psychology! Only his second minor related to peacekeeping. How, then, could he be so deaf to Brad's interest in the motives of the man who had produced the crime itself?

"Okay, Mama." Elaine emerged from the rest room. "Have at it."

"Hold on, Elaine. Let me see you."

Her round face was sunburned, but clean. Elaine's blond hair fell in soft natural waves. It looked especially soft now.

"Mama, really," Elaine said. "Do you know how mortified I feel, standing like a simpleton while you check me over in public?"

"I'm sorry, darling. Go keep your daddy company."

"He doesn't want my company. He doesn't hear me. He doesn't see me."

"He's preoccupied, Elaine. Have patience. Go sit with him."

"Mama." Elaine's sea-green eyes clouded. "Do I have to go to Granddaddy's funeral?"

"I think you should."

"Do I have to look at his body?"

"Not if you don't want to."

"I want to tell you why—okay?"

They were both in the rest room now, Elaine's voice magnified by tiled walls. "When Grandmama called to tell us Granddaddy died," the girl said, "I shut my eyes and tried to make a picture of him. The one I saw was Granddaddy laughing. That's how I want to think of him. If I saw him dead, it might erase that picture."

"Yes, that could happen."

"I don't want to remember him dead."

"Very well, Elaine. I think everyone will understand that."

"It has nothing to do with loving Granddaddy. I loved him."

"We all did."

"Do you think *he* would understand?"

"I feel sure he would. . . . Elaine, I need privacy in here."

With her daughter gone, Denise examined her reflection under godawful blue fluorescent lights. Pale, drawn, cheerless—Elaine had inherited the flat cheekbones, small lips, and tiny nose. "Cute snoot," Brad sometimes teased. Denise smiled at the reflected image and miraculously it assumed character and . . . charm.

"Personality, sweetie," she whispered. "It's your saving grace."

Driving toward Thomasville, Jeffrey asked, "Who inherits all of Granddaddy's stuff?"

Denise shot a glance at Brad. "Grandmama, Jeffrey."

A moment later Jeffrey asked, "Do you think she'll want it all?"

"Jeffrey, this is *not* the time for this conversation."

"Okay, I'm sorry. But what is Grandmama going to do with a pistol?"

"It probably has sentimental value, Jeffrey," Elaine said.

"A pistol? Bullets? Handcuffs?"

"Knock it off, dammit," Brad said.

Denise turned to face the rear seat. "I don't want any talk along these lines while we're at Grandmama's. Is that clear?"

"Okay," Jeffrey said. The boy twisted his lips, eyes darting behind spectacles that seemed too heavy for such a delicate face. "I wasn't asking for myself. I was thinking about Daddy."

"Then let your grandmama bring it up—not you. Do you understand, Jeffrey?" Denise asked.

"It shows a distinct lack of tact, Jeffrey," Elaine added.

"Aw, shut up."

"Knock it off, both of you!" Brad said.

"Yes, sir."

Brad drove through town on back streets, avoiding places and people. His mood darkening, he seemed almost fearful as they approached the family home.

"For God's sake," he said, "look at the crowd."

Vehicles lined the curb, bumper-to-bumper under the trees on either side of the driveway.

"I wish I could sneak in and sneak out," Brad said. "I hate this kind of thing."

Even as he parked, people were moving toward them.

After a series of tearful embraces, Mother Taylor allowed everyone to find the way to bedrooms, food, and other guests. She sat in the dining room, the traditional meeting place for this family. Father Taylor's usual chair was vacant and remained that way.

"He was on the telephone when it happened," Mother Taylor said. "I heard him ask who was calling—it was long distance, collect. I heard Bo say, 'Yes, I'll accept the charges, operator.' I was paying close attention because I worried it was about you, Brad, or Denise, or one of the children."

Brad sat beside her, holding her hand, listening with tears in his eyes.

"Bo said, 'How did you get this number?'" Mother Taylor dabbed her eyes with a paper napkin. "Then he said, 'I wouldn't do that, if I were you.'"

"Who was calling, Mom?"

"I don't know. Bo turned as if to speak to me. He was ghostly pale and shivering. I saw something was wrong. His mouth twisted down, he took a step, stumbled . . . then he fell."

The room was full of people, silent, listening. Outside, laughter in the yard, the shrill of Elaine playing with her cousins.

"I grabbed the telephone to ask the caller to hang up so I could call a doctor," Mother Taylor related. "I said, 'Sheriff Taylor is ill—please clear the line.'"

She pulled her hand from Brad's grasp, blew her nose gently, regaining composure.

"He laughed," she said.

"The person calling laughed?"

"Yes. Laughed."

"A man?" Brad asked.

"I think so."

"Son of a bitch. It was probably somebody Dad had thrown in jail at one time or another. I wouldn't dwell on it, Mom."

"I was so shocked—I said, 'Get off this line at once!'"

"Did he?"

"No. I hung up, but the call wouldn't disconnect. I slammed down the receiver again and again and I was screaming. Bo reached up—his fingers wouldn't straighten out . . . I fell on my knees beside him . . . It was terrible, Bradley. There was nothing I could do but go next door and leave him."

"Mom, those few seconds didn't matter—"

"When I came back, Bo had crawled to the telephone. There was still no dial tone. Oh, my God, the ambulance took forever getting here."

Brad pulled her into his arms, rocking gently.

"The thing of it is," Brad's oldest brother said, "I had just gotten a similar call a few minutes before."

"Who was it?"

"I don't know. I didn't accept the charges. I heard him ask the operator if I was the sheriff and I said, 'No, that's my father.' I'm afraid I was the one who gave him the telephone number."

"It makes no difference," Brad said. "People like that get to drinking and thinking, and with a thousand miles between them, they decide to call and bolster their egos with a few choice words."

"It killed him," Mother Taylor said.

"No, Mom—the heart attack happened to coincide with the call. The call didn't cause it."

"I think it did."

"Dad may have been upset," Brad said. "He may have been angry. But you don't kill somebody with words."

"The last thing Bo said . . ." Mother Taylor hesitated, shook her head.

"What did he say, Mom?"

"Now is not the time."

"Mom, what did he say?"

"He said, 'Boy . . . look out . . .' "

"Boy? One of us?"

"I don't know. He could barely talk."

"Well, we're attaching too much importance to the call. Hey, don't I see some of Minnie's chickens on the sideboard?"

Every visitor had brought a covered dish, then stayed to sample what others had prepared. To local palates, the cook was known by her recipe. Brad had gone for "Minnie's chicken," and knowing it by sight was the highest compliment he could bestow.

With each new arrival, Mother Taylor rose, embraced, wept briefly, and recounted Father Taylor's final moments. The telephone call mesmerized her listeners, and Mother Taylor's account varied not one syllable in the retelling.

"What do you think, Brad?" his brother Bob asked.

"The call was a coincidence."

"Probably."

Denise hovered, as did the wives of the other brothers. To these women, related by marriage, fell the task of supporting the hostess. They would clear the table a dozen times, carry out garbage, wash glasses and cups continually.

"I suppose you and Brad will be coming home to Thomasville now," Bob's wife, Vera, commented to Denise in the kitchen.

"Uh . . . no, I don't think so."

"Don't say that," Vera said. "Bob told me it was settled—well, almost settled."

"What is settled?"

"They've offered the job of sheriff to Bradley! He hasn't told you?"

"We've been so busy—"

"Oh, my, I've stuck my foot in my mouth."

"Which is a testament to the size of both," Lanita,

Jack's wife, said sweetly. She handed Vera a dish towel. "Do something productive, dearie."

"I am sorry, Denise," Vera said. "We were just so excited about having the whole family in the same town again."

Lanita led Denise away by an arm. "That's bullshit. If you come back here, Vera will go crazy. She's been trying to write for Bob's newspaper and so far she hasn't had so much as a line in print."

"What has that to do with me?"

"Oh, now I've done it too." Lanita shooed children away from the porch swing and sat down. "Bob is hoping you will come to work with *Rose City News*. He's doing a good job there—business revenues are building, subscribers are coming aboard nicely."

"But no writers," Denise guessed.

"None as good as you. He'll try to be casual about it, but believe me, he wants you on his staff. I think you could name your terms, within reason."

This was her favorite sister-in-law. Pert, pretty, practical Lanita. With Vera, Denise had to second-guess every statement. But what Lanita said was what she meant.

"Brad and I haven't talked about this," Denise said helplessly.

"I'm not surprised. He's just like his father. I'd been married to Jack two years before I heard Father Taylor say three connecting sentences. I suppose you can thank Vera that you are at least forewarned."

"The fact that Brad hasn't mentioned it," Denise said, "probably means he isn't considering coming back here."

Lanita pursed her lips and looked mischievous. "Let's go at it this way," she said. "What do *you* think about moving to Thomasville?"

"There are so many considerations," Denise said. "Elaine and Jeffrey are in classes for exceptional children. I don't know where they got the brains, but they both have too much."

"Kids are adaptable," Lanita said. "What do *you* think?"

"I . . . It would depend on Brad, of course."

"*Rose City News* needs a sharp editor, a feature writer."

"I can't do both."

"Pick one—what do you think?"

Denise laughed. "I have to admit, it has appeal."

"Aha." Lanita tossed her reddish hair, hazel eyes aglow. "In which case, Bradley Taylor will soon be sheriff of Thomas County."

"Doesn't the sheriff have to be elected?"

"They plan to appoint Brad to serve out the balance of Father Taylor's term. Then comes the election."

"Suppose he loses?"

"What!" Lanita stopped the swing. "A Taylor running for sheriff? It's a case of royal descent, from father to son. Believe me, if Brad wants it, he will be sheriff."

"Sheriff, publisher, and mayor." Denise pondered the professions of the Taylor sons.

"Sounds exciting," Lanita said, "but it isn't. That's the good part and the bad part all rolled into one. Nothing ever happens in Thomasville."

3

All afternoon and into evening, Denise subdued her irritation with Brad. Why hadn't he mentioned the offer to serve out his father's term as sheriff? She planned to confront him at bedtime, but the family outlasted her. After performing as scullery maid, cook, and keeper of children—her own, Vera's four, Lanita's three—she went to bed, exhausted.

She awoke to the soft murmur of voices downstairs, a sound reminiscent of water over stones in a brook. The smell of ripening pears came through an open window, the curtain gently wafting with a soft breeze.

She sat up, still groggy.

"Mama?"

Elaine sat across the room, hands between chubby knees, watching.

"We went to the funeral home this morning, Mama."

The girl's face was a pale moon against stained oak wainscoting. Denise blinked away sleep.

"I told Daddy I didn't want to go in. Jeffrey wanted to go, but I didn't."

"Did you?"

"I had to cry before Daddy would agree."

"Elaine, I didn't have a chance to tell your daddy how you felt."

In the darkened room, the child seemed far away and small.

"Jeffrey said Granddaddy looked like he was sleeping. He was cold. Jeffrey touched him."

"Come sit beside me, darling."

But she didn't move. "Jeffrey said he felt like wax paper."

"Elaine—"

"He said the undertaker pumps formaldehyde through the veins to wash out the blood so the body won't rot. He said they put paraffin in Granddaddy's mouth to keep his face from sagging."

"Elaine, come here."

The girl spoke as she stood up. "Jeffrey said he flexed one of Granddaddy's fingers and it was like hard rubber."

Damn that boy.

"Now Daddy is mad at me. When I refused to go inside, he told me to sit in the car and not to play the radio. I think I embarrassed him."

"I'll talk to Daddy."

"I'm not going to the funeral, Mama."

"Elaine . . . sweetheart, funerals are designed to comfort the people left behind. People come to the services and send flowers to show that the deceased person was loved and respected. It's our way of assuring the family that Granddaddy was important to us." Denise felt a thumping temporal artery warning of a headache-to-be.

"I hate this town," Elaine sniffled. "I hate the people here."

"Elaine, don't overreact."

"Aunt Vera's children are snobs. Robbie said I was pie-faced."

"Children are . . . children."

"They're crass and moronic! You would think with a father who's a publisher, they would have good vocabularies. But they don't."

The bedroom door opened and Elaine whirled away as if caught in a tryst.

Brad's silhouette loomed in the bright hallway. "People are asking for you, Denise."

"Brad, come in. I need to talk to you."

"It'll have to wait, honey. Hurry down."

"Bradley—"

The door closed. Laughter rose from the dining room, directly beneath the bedroom.

Elaine moved toward the door, her shoulders lifting. "Men are difficult," she observed. "Particularly the Taylor men."

Denise laughed, despite herself.

Of the three brothers, Bob Taylor was the oldest, most successful, and most cosmopolitan member of the clan. His wife, Vera, bought only designer originals and imported shoes. She wore diamonds even with blue jeans and spent more on her coiffure than Denise lavished on her entire wardrobe.

Bob met Denise at the dining-room door, escorting her into the circle of the immediate family. "We've been waiting for you," he said. "We have something to discuss."

"Oh?"

Jack Taylor, realtor and town mayor, was the quintessential salesman. His garb was not cheap, but garish, like that of a peacock ready to spread his feathers for attention. Jack sat next to Brad, his Dacron sport coat unbuttoned, lavender shirt and tie loosened around a thick neck that flowed into sloping shoulders.

"While you were sleeping," Jack said, "we've been working out the rest of your life."

"I need all the help I can get," Denise said with a smile.

"The county commissioners met this morning," Bob said. "If Brad agrees to serve out Dad's term of office, they'll vote unanimously to appoint him."

"It'll be two years before the next election," Jack said. "By the time that comes around, opposition will be minimal. What do you think, Denise?"

Vera sat across the table from Denise, examining her manicured nails. Through the kitchen door, Denise could see Lanita trying to appear busy, but listening. When their eyes met, Lanita winked.

"Uh . . . what do I think?" Denise said. "It would take some thinking, wouldn't it, Brad?"

Bob was standing, every inch the newspaper mogul, presiding officer, and chairman. "I don't know what a homicide detective earns in Mobile, Alabama," he said. "But there are benefits to the office of sheriff here which don't meet the eye. And, I want you to join me at the newspaper, Denise. I've kept up with your work in Mobile and I need your talents as writer and editor."

"Coffee?" Lanita delivered a steaming cup.

"I'll establish a profit-sharing plan for you," Bob continued. "I'll give you the option to buy stock on a periodic basis. It means that, eventually, you and I could be full and equal partners."

"That's very generous, Bob."

Mother Taylor gazed wistfully past Denise. "It would

make me happy to have all of you in Thomasville again."

She was being manipulated, and yet . . .

Denise turned to Brad for a clue to his thoughts. He sat with thumbs hooked in his belt, leaning back in his chair.

"We have to consider Elaine and Jeffrey, Brad."

"They'll love it here!" Bob interjected. "Especially when they see the house we found for you. Tell her, Jack."

"It's the old Reinecke house," Jack said smugly. "The kind of place most people can't afford until after the youngsters are grown and gone. Swimming pool, tennis court—when the kids see that, they'll be happy enough."

"That's a huge house," Denise said.

"It is." Jack chortled. "I've dickered with the estate and the price is now right, an excellent value which is sure to appreciate." Jack leaned nearer, voice now lowered to confidential tones. "When Brad goes on duty in Mobile, you worry, right? Of course you do. Homicide division in a big city like that—his safety concerns you—right?"

"Yes—"

"Thomasville is bucolic." Jack turned pink hands palm up. "People leave their doors unlocked. They walk the streets without fear. The sheriff here is a *peace*keeper, not a warrior on the front line."

"Maybe Brad would be bored with serenity," Vera suggested.

Bob waved away his wife's words. "Okay," he said, "so Brad is taking a slight reduction in pay. But, Denise, with you at the newspaper, your income will more than compensate for Brad's personal reduction in salary."

"It sounds good."

"Think of it." Vera buffed her nails. "Publisher, mayor, sheriff—that's a lot of power in a town this size."

"That isn't our motive at all, Vera," Bob said. "We're trying to put together a deal that's good for everybody. This isn't a sneaky coalition. We had the same situation when Dad was alive. If Denise and Brad agree, nothing has changed in the power structure."

Denise turned to Brad. "What do you think?"

"It's worth considering."

"You will have absolute editorial autonomy at the newspaper," Bob said. "My job becomes handling the advertising, exclusively. Yours will be to corral good writers, oversee reporters, and set the tone and personality of the paper."

"Your generosity is obvious, Bob."

"It is," he agreed. "But if *Rose City News* is to advance any further, I have to divide responsibility. Sales require my full-time attention and I don't enjoy the editorial end of publishing, anyway. So I need you. We need one another."

"How soon do I—we—have to make a decision?"

"The sooner the better," Bob said. "Jack will take you by the Reinecke place and show you the house."

"Can we afford that, Brad?" Denise asked.

"We could sell the house in Mobile, I suppose."

"That could take a while."

"Price it right and it'll sell," Jack declared. "I'll handle all that."

Everyone was looking at her, waiting for a decision. The issue seemed a foregone conclusion, except for her vote. Suppose she voted "No"—what would Brad do then?

Lanita arrived to refill Denise's cup. Another wink and a grin.

"Yeah, okay, so we're making a pitch here," Bob conceded. "Vera is right, this is good for us as a family. But where could Thomas County get a better man than Bradley? He's educated, experienced, capable . . ."

That was all true, of course. And Denise did worry when he came home late. Mobile was destined to be a city of a million, undergoing all the pains associated with rapid growth. Thomasville today was fundamentally as it had been fifteen years ago. There was security in that.

"Wait until you see inside the Reinecke house." Jack put a soft arm around Denise's shoulder. His breath smelled of mouthwash and the fibers of his jacket held the summer scent of trapped perspiration despite dry cleaning.

"Six bedrooms, four baths, walk-in pantry . . ."

She had been working with a Mobile newspaper seven years. The bureaucracy was maddening. She had seen good work discarded to make room for advertising. Periodically they cut the most popular features, leaving readers to fume over incomplete columns. Too often, they didn't edit—they printed. A change in the old guard was still a long time to come. Her heart was hammering. Editor . . . autonomy! She had hundreds of ideas she'd like to implement. Articles, series, public-service features . . .

"You'll own more than a quarter of a city block, completely fenced . . ." Jack continued. "The cabana serves both the swimming pool and tennis court. Hell, it's such a good deal, I'd made up my mind to buy the property if you didn't." Jack gave her a flabby squeeze, his face glowing. "You're going to love the place," he promised.

Across the table, Vera looked up. "You *will* love

it," she predicted. "Another one of those invisible benefits."

More than two hundred people attended the graveside services for Bo Taylor. While the family sat sheltered by a canvas canopy with scalloped trim, the public and friends stood in blistering heat as the minister delivered a eulogy which made heads nod drowsily.

Denise concentrated on the speaker's Adam's apple, bobbing in contrapuntal harmony to the monotone of his words. Her thoughts kept slipping away to the newspaper.

Elaine had stayed at Grandmama's, helping prepare for the onslaught of visitors sure to come after the funeral. Thus far, Brad hadn't noticed the girl's absence and Denise had warned Jeffrey to remain silent. When someone inquired about his sister, Jeffrey replied with masculine disdain, "Indisposed."

When the formalities were over, cliques and clusters formed around relatives, lingering to chat. Denise drove toward Mother Taylor's with Jeffrey at her side.

"What do you think about moving to Thomasville, Jeff?"

"Elaine won't like it."

"What about you?"

"I have a problem or two, but I can handle it."

"Oh?"

"Robbie is testing me. He called Elaine pie-faced and he said I was four-eyed." Jeffrey adjusted his spectacles with a delicate finger. "I'll just have to stomp his butt," he said.

"He's four years older and considerably larger than you, Jeffrey."

"True," Jeffrey acknowledged. "But I'm banking

on surprise and I intend to do the job adequately, so a second confrontation will be less likely."

Denise patted his leg. "I love you, toughie."

"Yes," he sighed. "I'm the kind of child a mother would love."

Laughing, she gave him a hug.

Undressing for bed, Denise said, "We made the decision to move her by default, didn't we?"

"Did we?" Brad tossed his shirt on a chair.

"I didn't hear you say anything."

"It was an offer we couldn't refuse."

"Suppose I had refused? What would you have done?" she asked.

"Given in."

"You would?"

"We're just supposing, aren't we?"

"Well . . . yes . . ."

"Then let's suppose I would have given in." He pulled covers around his shoulders and turned on his side away from her.

"In other words, you might not have given in?"

"It was your decision, Denise."

"Mine? You didn't even discuss it with me!"

"What was there to discuss?"

She slapped his shoulder and Brad chuckled. "Are you going to be mean?" he asked.

She leaned over and bit his arm, but he didn't move. After she withdrew a moment later, he said, "Oww."

"We may have a problem with Elaine," Denise said.

"She'll be all right. Turn out the light, will you?"

Denise lay on her back in the dark, eyes open. Somewhere afar she heard the clatter of an overturned garbage can, an angry human voice. Car tires rumbled on brick streets as vehicles passed.

"Can we afford the house Jack was talking about?" she asked.

"He says we can."

"That's a lot of house."

"Yep."

A commode flushed across the hall. The pad of slippered feet made Denise think of Elaine. It had never been easy for the child to make friends.

"The newspaper can be a real force in this area," Denise said absently. "It's already good—it could be excellent."

Brad's response was a whispery snore.

She set her mental alarm and drifted to sleep.

Denise awoke before anyone else. She dressed quietly, went across the hall, and gently shook Elaine awake. "How about you and I going downtown for breakfast alone?" Denise offered.

"Sure!"

"Don't wake anyone," Denise cautioned. "Or we'll have to invite them along."

"Okay," Elaine said gleefully. "I'll be dressed in a minute."

Downstairs, Denise set up the coffee urn so it would percolate on command. She stood at the kitchen window gazing past a magnificent Japanese tulip tree in the yard. Thick green foliage, pecans, and magnolias—this was the true South, this town. Bob and Jack were right—this was serenity.

Elaine appeared, bright with adventure. "Do I look all right, Mama?"

"Beautiful. Come on, let's go."

The telephone rang and they hesitated. It rang

again. "If I don't answer that," Denise said, "everybody will be awake."

Running on tiptoes, she grabbed the telephone on the fourth ring. "Hello?"

"Let me speak with Bo Taylor."

"He isn't . . . who's calling?"

"Is he there?"

Something—the intensity, perhaps—made Denise press the receiver to her ear, listening for sounds beyond the man himself.

"Is he there?"

Who would not know Bo Taylor was dead? Denise said, "Where are you calling from?"

Click. The dial tone burred. When Denise turned, Mother Taylor stood in her bedroom door, nightgown rumpled, gray hair askew.

"Who was calling, Denise?"

"He didn't give his name."

The matriarch's deep blue eyes widened. "It was him," she whispered.

4

Sitting with Elaine at the Plaza Restaurant, Denise confessed a need for advice. Thrilled with her role as confidante, Elaine ordered coffee, which she didn't like, and listened with feigned nonchalance.

"They're offering your daddy the job as sheriff, serving out Granddaddy's term of office," Denise said. "Uncle Bob and Uncle Jack believe that in two years, when an election is held, your daddy will win."

"What does Daddy think about this?"

"You know your father—he never says what he's thinking."

"Why is Daddy like that?"

"Maybe he's afraid he'll look weak. Or maybe he just doesn't know how to put his thoughts into words."

"Or maybe he doesn't trust you with knowledge that could be used to hurt him."

Slightly stunned, Denise said, "Oh, I doubt that."

Elaine gazed away at other patrons, green eyes troubled. "Is this job so important to Daddy?"

"There's more to it than that," Denise said. "Uncle

Bob wants me to work with him at the newspaper. He's offering a partnership. It looks good, Elaine. But then, can I do the job?"

"Sure you can."

"I would need help."

Incredulous, Elaine lifted her eyebrows. "Me?"

"I need your youthful view," Denise said. "Which comic strips should we carry? Should we feature a crossword puzzle? What about the *Jumble* or cryptograms?"

"It doesn't take long to make those decisions."

The waitress brought more coffee and Elaine diluted hers with milk.

"The future of any newspaper depends on today's young people," Denise said. "We need to encourage them to read the paper—it's a lifelong habit, once acquired. I thought about a weekly page of young peoples' news. I would need advice: How good are the articles? Will it be interesting to people your age? I'll need you to proofread and edit that section."

The concept kindled a glint in Elaine's round eyes.

"If you would act as a junior editor," Denise went on, "learn layout and paste-up—"

"I could do all of that." Elaine twisted her lips thoughtfully. "There were three typographical errors on page one yesterday."

Denise sat back and sighed. "We have another decision to make, too. Uncle Jack has a house he wants us to buy. It's got six bedrooms, four baths— just cleaning the swimming pool would take time each week."

"Swimming pool?"

"And a tennis court."

"It sounds . . . wonderful."

"We'd be leaving our friends in Mobile," Denise said. "It won't be easy. If we don't come here as a strong family unit, acting together, I worry that we won't be happy. Of course, if we all agree . . ." It was naked propaganda, blatant parental psychology.

Elaine put another dollop of milk in her coffee, weighing the conversation. "You want to do it, don't you?" she asked.

"I think it might be the opportunity of a lifetime. What do you think?"

"I don't like this town, Mama."

"I suspect your feelings would change, Elaine. We're here because of Granddaddy's death, and the family is in turmoil. A town is what we make of it."

"What about Jeffrey? Have you discussed this with him?"

"No."

Elaine lifted her chin, looking down her nose at the coffee cup. "Oh, well, Jeffrey will agree. He'd adapt to a tree house if you put him in it. All he wants to do is read, anyway. Fantasy is his escape. That's why he shows off all that stupid, useless information he accumulates. He's very insecure, you know."

Denise was taken aback by her daughter's insight. "That . . . that's very astute, Elaine."

Elaine crumpled her napkin and put it beside her plate. "All right, Mama. I see what you're doing. I guess this must be pretty important to you and Daddy. We may as well go look at the house."

They drove to the Reinecke house and strolled the wide porch from one window to another. Peering through wavy panes of glass, they saw the potential— and the labor that would be required to attain it.

Pushing through a tangle of shrubbery gone wild, they came to the swimming pool. It was half-filled with stagnant water, clogged with leaves. The tennis court was covered with a crawling vine, bound by a high masonry wall that secured the rear of the lot. The cabana's doors were off their hinges, its shingled roof collapsing.

Elaine turned full circle, hands on her hips. "I can see that it was once beautiful," she said. "I guess it can be again. But it's going to take a bunch of money."

Dismayed, Denise agreed, "Yes."

They left, no closer to a resolution than before.

The next four days were a flurry of activity, as if events were water and they the flotsam swept here and there in response to currents. Brad was interviewed by the county commissioners, rushed from one meeting to the next as politics and personal goals were aligned.

Jack took Denise, Elaine, and Jeffrey through the Reinecke house, pointing out its attributes. While the flooring creaked underfoot, he stroked the marble fireplace surrounded by an Italian fresco.

"It's the kind of house a man would work a lifetime to acquire," Jack said. "Eight thousand square feet of living space. Returned to its original grandeur, every dollar spent will be worth twice that amount in appreciated value."

"But can we afford this?" Denise asked.

"Hell, you can't afford to let it get away, Denise! I'll have the place declared a historic site—you'll be able to borrow what it takes to do the work."

"It had better be a big loan," Elaine said.

Jack patted her head as if Elaine were an overgrown dog. "Don't anybody fret the little stuff," he said. "Leave the financing to Brad and me. That's my business and I know what I'm doing. The basics are here—good foundations, safe wiring, adequate plumbing—"

"Arachnids, *Periplaneta americana*," Jeffrey intoned.

Jack affected a laugh. "These kids of yours, Denise. Precocious, precocious."

"Not to mention perceptive, perceptive," Jeffrey countered.

"Let's go out and look at the things these youngsters care about," Jack said. "The pool!"

"As in cess," Elaine murmured.

"Jack," Denise asked, "how much do you think it will cost to get the place renovated?"

"That depends . . . Watch your step, some of these planks are slippery." He helped Denise cross the back porch and opened a rotted screen door. "What's acceptable to one person might be less acceptable to another. I'd say fifty thousand would make this a showplace again."

"Fifty thousand—"

"Thirty-year amortization and low interest . . ."

She watched the children, Jeffrey walking with his hands shoved in pants pockets, Elaine beside the boy as they stopped at the pool.

"Look at these magnificent oaks," Jack said. "What would you say, Denise? A hundred, two hundred years old?"

Jeffrey and Elaine looked at one another, then into the pool again.

"What does Brad think?" Denise asked.

"Hell, honey, if you're happy, he's happy. Let me tell you something—even without the lot, this is a steal at eighty thousand."

"What lot?"

Jack's smile went stiff over his perfect teeth. "I told Brad I would buy the east third of the property," Jack explained. "I'll pay twenty thousand for it. That's more than enough to provide the down payment, right? I admit, the lot is worth thirty thousand, but God knows how long it would take to sell it. So, as family, I'll buy it and you will have the money for your investment. I've got it all worked out, honey. Just leave it to me."

"Jeffrey, Elaine? What do you think?"

"Dee-neese . . ." Jack wailed softly. "This isn't a decision for children!"

"They have to live here, Jack."

"Mama, if you're working at the newspaper and Daddy is working as sheriff," Jeffrey asked, "who's going to get everything done?"

"The contractors," Jack said. "By the time you folks are ready to move over here, the work will be well under way. A crew will come in—professionals. I'm not trying to deal you a handyman's special. Believe me, everything will be done right. I'll see to it."

"Including the pool and cabana?" Elaine asked.

"Including the pool and cabana." Jack jiggled coins in his pocket, looking past Denise as if in pain.

"Well, Mama," Elaine said, "I don't see how you can turn it down. Do you, Jeffrey?"

"Unless something is happening that we don't know about," Jeffrey said solemnly, "we don't need this much space."

"There's always you and me," Elaine suggested. "We could fill the extra bedrooms with grandchildren."

Jack walked off toward the house to lock up. Denise pulled Jeffrey and Elaine to her. "What *do* you think?"

"It's terrific," Jeffrey whispered.

"Then why are you giving Uncle Jack a hard time?"

"He's making a good deal for himself, too!"

"There's nothing wrong with that."

Jeffrey peered through his glasses at the garden. "The ornamentals should be cut back severely."

"Fine, that's your department."

"Really?"

"Absolutely." Denise grinned. "Elaine and I will decorate the interior. You see to the yard."

"Uncle Jack!" Jeffrey called. "We've decided to take this turkey."

"Have you indeed?"

"And we thank you for your help," Jeffrey said.

Suddenly animated, Elaine and Jeffrey ran around the house together.

"Lovely children," Jack said. "So bright."

As Brad loaded their luggage into the car, Bob and Jack tied up loose ends to the visit.

"I'll have a reporter call you next week, Brad," Bob said.

"For what?"

"I'll break the story then. Front page. You will have resigned by then, won't you?"

"Yes, but why the reporter?"

"Comments," Bob said. "Quotes give the breath of life to a story—right, Denise?"

"That's right." She hugged Mother Taylor. "If you need anything, call us."

"I'm so pleased you're all coming to Thomasville."

Jack was next in line to embrace. "Don't forget, you have to contact the Mobile realtor and sign a sales agreement," he said. "I've already arranged it."

"I will."

In the rear seat, Jeffrey was working a crossword puzzle, the magazine propped against his knees. Elaine was presenting herself for a last round of good-bye hugs and kisses.

"Before long," Mother Taylor said, "you'll be bigger than me, Elaine."

"Size thirty-two-A bra," Jeffrey called.

"Knock it off, wise guy," Brad said.

Finally they were pulling out of the driveway. Bob, Jack, and Mother Taylor waved. Denise saw Jack steal a glance at his wristwatch.

Turning south toward Tallahassee and Interstate 10, Brad drove past the Reinecke place.

"What did you think of the layout, Brad?"

"I didn't see it."

"You didn't see it! Brad, didn't you go inside?"

"Jack said you liked it. That was good enough for me."

"Are you telling me we bought a house you've never been to?"

He looked at her. "Did you like it?"

"Yes, but—"

"If you liked it, fine. Jack says it's sound."

"That house is very large, Brad. And so is the mortgage!"

"Jack says we can handle it. He knows how to figure things like that."

They crossed the Florida state line, the two children silent in the rear seat. Denise spoke softly. "I can't believe you signed a purchase agreement on that house without looking at it, Brad."

"The home is your business."

"It's *our* business!"

"Jack says it's a solid buy," Brad said mildly. He spoke over his shoulder. "Did you kids like the house?"

"Yes, sir."

"Okay, then." Brad smiled. "That settles it."

They were home by dark. *Home.* After eleven years, the dwelling suddenly seemed alien. Heat and humidity had given the rooms the dank smell of a cellar. Denise's plants were exhausted, thirsty, and she couldn't muster energy to tend them. Most would be left behind when they moved. She opened doors and windows as Brad sat before the television set sorting mail.

"Are you hungry, Brad?"

"No."

Good. She felt wrung out, suddenly depressed with the weight of impending obligations. She'd have to submit her resignation to the newspaper tomorrow.

"Mama," Elaine asked in a low voice, "may I spend tomorrow night with a friend?"

"I don't think so, Elaine. We have a lot to do."

Elaine threw herself on the couch and sat with arms folded. "I guess I'll just disappear and none of my friends will even know I'm gone, until school this fall."

"If then," Brad said.

"It isn't funny, Daddy!"

He winked at Denise.

"It isn't so important to you two," Elaine accused. "You don't have many friends."

"We have friends," Brad said gruffly. "By this time next year, you'll have as many new friends as old ones. Denise, did you pay the Visa bill?"

"I thought I did."

He tossed the statement in her lap. "It says we're overdue."

"Are we going to slave twenty-four hours a day until we leave?" Elaine demanded.

"Probably."

"Could we at least have a going-away party?"

"Elaine, knock it off."

"Yes"—Elaine jumped to her feet—"I'll knock it off! You wouldn't be interested in my opinion of anything, would you? You don't care about the house we're moving into, or who we're leaving behind, or anything—"

"Elaine . . ."

She ran down the hall and slammed her bedroom door. An instant later she emerged and banged on Jeffrey's door with both fists. "Turn down the stereo, Jeffrey!"

Slam! Back in her bedroom again.

Brad shuffled mail. "Tension," he said. "It must be contagious."

"She's at a difficult age, Brad."

"Thirty-four is difficult too," he said.

"They're growing up."

"That's the way it works."

"Eventually," Denise said, "you're going to have to extend your communication beyond 'Knock it off.' Elaine and Jeffrey aren't little kids anymore. They want to be treated more like grown-ups."

He placed the tips of his fingers together and contemplated her with sleepy eyes. "All right," he said finally.

"Elaine and I had breakfast alone the other morning," Denise said. "She's really perceptive for her age."

"Jack says she's precocious. What he means is, she's rude."

"She *is* precocious; they both are. They're intelligent. I think we should respect their opinions."

His face colored, the pyramid of fingers touching cleft chin. "I'm not much for the modern-day approach to children, Denise. 'Spare the rod and spoil the child' is still a good adage."

"That's a strange thing for you to say. How many times have you ever spanked those children?"

"None, and maybe you should remember that. I can tell you, my father wouldn't have permitted that outburst a moment ago. He never coddled us and we did all right."

"That's a matter of opinion."

The flush deepened. "Would you like to explain that remark, Denise?"

"Elaine made the comment that you didn't see her, didn't hear her, and didn't want to."

"I'd have to be stone deaf not to hear their racket."

"The sounds, yes. But do you hear the meaning?"

His glare was discomfiting. His face had become that nonexpression she associated with policework.

"When we get to Thomasville," he said, "I'll try to be better. You know why I didn't go see the house, Denise? Because I didn't care what it was. I'm so goddamned glad to be quitting my job, getting away from here—"

"I didn't . . . You never told me that—"

Elaine spoke from the hallway, her voice a contralto. "Mama, Daddy, I'm sorry I lost my temper."

"Forget it," Brad said. "Come here, Elaine."

She came, hesitantly, as if to pull away even as she advanced. "I'm sorry, Daddy."

He pulled the girl into his lap and held her head to his chest. "Your mama says I don't listen. From now on, I'll try to do better."

Elaine burst into tears, clutching his arm. Brad stroked her hair, soothing. "You want to know what makes me happy, darling? Your happiness and Jeffrey's and Mama's. But sometimes I'm so unhappy myself, I am blinded and maybe a little bitter that everyone else is so happy."

"You are?"

"I'll tell you," Brad said, "I've had a job that I hated so much, for so long—a pressure-cooker job. I've had to look at and think about horrible things done by terrible people. Things I wouldn't want any of you ever to see or think about."

"Bodies," Elaine said. "Blood and gore."

"Blood and gore is right. I've gone for days so

nauseated I couldn't keep food in my stomach. I've come awake in cold sweats, dreaming about cases I couldn't solve."

He pushed Elaine up to a sitting position on his lap. "Well, that's behind us now. I'm going to be a rural county sheriff with nothing much to worry about but processing court subpoenas and delivering writs. I'll toss the riffraff into jail and be home for lunch every day. We'll have plenty of time together to communicate more. How does that sound?"

"Sounds good, Daddy."

He kissed her forehead, then the tip of her nose. "My first communication is this," he said. "You're breaking my leg."

"I'm fat."

"No you aren't. You are endowed. There's a heap of difference."

Elaine withdrew, giggling.

Brad pulled Denise to his lap.

"What a relief it'll be," he said, "not to think about murder."

5

Truman selected Cuero because it was several hundred miles from the last hit. But mostly because there were so many routes for escape— west to San Antonio, southeast to Victoria, north to Austin, east to Houston—with a web of secondary roads connecting major arteries.

He had been here two days, waiting. Across the street a neon sign faltered: "FAMILY—STEAKS." Friday was their busy night, a waitress had said.

Naked, sitting in the dark, he could see the motel entrance and the steakhouse. True to the girl's word, they had been busy.

His bed was a thin cotton mattress over steel bands which yielded only slightly. The room had been powdered with insecticide to kill fleas and bedbugs. His nostrils had dried, making his nasal membranes itch.

Before him lay all the cash he'd acquired—currency soft as chamois, limp from handling and moisture absorbed. *Four thousand dollars.*

When he reached Georgia, there could be no robberies. There would be no means of increasing his wealth. When he arrived, it must be as a specter unencumbered.

In the room next door, a Mexican woman berated her companion with a staccato of vulgarities which needed no translation. Their radio blared joyfully, Tijuana Brass, Spanish guitars, the clickety-click of castanets.

Truman drew on his cigarette. In the mirror, his features appeared as a crimson mask before the glow subsided.

From here he could see the dark-skinned motel clerk, feet on his desk, reading *Playboy*. Across the road, the last customers were finishing their dinner.

A security light cast an amber circle over the few cars in the motel lot. Drawn by the beacon, insects swirled, undulating; the air was scented with a stink of crushed chitin from their fallen comrades. The odor conjured images of thatched huts, vegetation rotting in dried rice paddies, a stench of nocturnal creatures underfoot.

"What is yoah task?" He heard the instructor's voice as if yesterday. "Yoah task is terrah!"

He remembered the way burning huts had cast shadows on the officer's freckled face. "A dead man is meat!" he'd drawled. "Terrah is not *this*." He indicated the village with a sweep of an arm. "*This*"— he'd sneered—"is disgustin'. . . . Terrah is the result of anticipation. Dreaded anticipation! Terrah is achieved not by what you do, but by what you do not do. . . ."

Truman drew on his cigarette; the bloody mask in the mirror returned his gaze with narrowed eyes.

"Terrah"—the Southern instructor touched thumb to forefinger—"is finesse. There ain't no finesse in *this*."

Tangled bodies, the crackle of flames, grotesque and obscene. Death.

"Y'all tell me which one of these folks is afraid now?"

It had been Truman's first commando raid. From hut to hut they were to go, killing one—only one—and then withdrawing. But somebody screamed and in unison they had panicked. The muzzles glowed red hot, the ground littered with cartridges, the sick sput-sput as shells struck flesh.

"Terrah," the officer repeated, "is the result of dreaded anticipation. Not realization, gentlemen—an-ti-ci-pa-tion."

The Cong were masters—like shadows through the trees they infiltrated a village. Birds hushed, animals froze, and yet, faintly, the tiniest sound possible, bells tinkled as they came unnoticed.

They came to indoctrinate and impress. They needed havens for men and material. In a land where fealty is assured only by fear, they came to teach a lesson.

They gathered the children for propaganda. They chastised elders for aiding their foes. Then they chopped off one arm of every child. Next time, they would come for the other arm. . . .

That was terror.

For as long as any witness lived, he would be subconsciously attuned to the tinkle of a bell. An ox snorting in the field, clapper to bronze—the musical peal of wind chimes—the tinkle would bring a nameless, numbing terror.

Truman had learned his lesson. He knew the methodology. Psychological warfare was—as the instructor said—a matter of finesse. The object was to produce a Pavlovian response which rendered a man helpless to resist, even if death were imminent.

It took time. He needed money.

He heard laughter, a thud of car doors, customers departing across the road. A waitress was sweeping under empty tables. The youthful cook had carried garbage outside to a dumpster, where he paused for a quick smoke before continuing his chores.

Truman gathered the sticky currency and put it in his suitcase. It would take more than he had found in rural grocery stores and late-night service stations. That was why he'd been here two days—waiting for Friday, waiting for their busy night.

He watched the young cook stare away dreamily, apron rolled around his waist, smoking the cigarette. The scene altered. Light from the motel office became yellow honey, the sky deepened to cobalt, the cyclone of insects a groan in slow motion—*surreal*. A jungle cat must experience this, this warp of time and motion, this acuity of perceptions in the last moments before the strike.

He dressed slowly. A few customers lingered at their tables. The cashier had not yet begun to tally the day's receipts.

To presage his arrival in Thomasville he had used the telephone. His first call was a token of things to be.

I have a collect call for Sheriff Bo Taylor—will you accept the charges?

"Who is calling?" The voice had been deep, resonant.

He had spoken past the operator. "The son of Renee and brother of Lana."

Silence.

The operator said, "Sir, will you accept the call?"

"Yes, I'll accept the charges, operator."

"Where is my papa?" Truman had questioned.

"How did you get this number?"

"I'm on my way there," he'd said. "I'm coming for my papa."

"I wouldn't do that if I were you."

"Mother is an alcoholic," Truman said. "Lana is a whore. That is my papa's legacy."

Strung by an electronic umbilical, each of them hung on opposite ends of the line; the telephone bumped, a woman shouted, "Bo . . . Bo!"

He'd held the phone to his ear so hard the cartilage burned from pressure. "Sheriff Taylor is ill," a woman cried. "Please clear this line."

In that Kansas telephone booth, he was shivering, nauseated.

"Please clear the line—this is an emergency."

He had laughed.

He heard a gasp, then an angry command: "Get off this line at once!"

She slammed the receiver. Slammed it again. But in her excitement, she did not leave it down long enough to sever the connection.

Truman dressed with deliberation, remembering:

"Bo . . . the phone . . . I'll have to go next door."

He had heard footsteps receding, the bang of a door. For a moment, he thought it was ended, but no—heavy breathing, the telephone bumping.

"Truman—"

"Tell me my papa isn't there," Truman dared. "Tell me he is no more."

"Truman . . . don't come."

"For all the years of suffering he has caused, he will suffer," Truman growled. "For the destruction he has wrought, he will be destroyed."

"Truman, my God . . ."

"Does anybody know the truth?" Truman taunted. "Do they know, Sheriff Bo Taylor?"

Throat constricted, quivering with emotion, he'd

given warning. They knew he was coming. As it should be, must be. . . .

He laced his shoes. Closed his suitcase. Across the street, the last automobile turned to depart. Both waitresses were sweeping now. The youthful cook was going inside.

Truman took his luggage to the car, placed it in the trunk. He felt for the pistol, hidden behind a spare tire. He shoved it under his belt. He wore a sweater to hide the instrument. He saw lights go out in the room with the Mexican couple. They turned down their radio.

He walked past the motel office, smiling upon the clerk.

You smile upon your friend today. Today his ills are over . . .

He crossed the road to the restaurant. When he looked back, the motel manager was still there, feet propped up on a desk, facing away from the entrance, reading his magazine.

You hearken to the lover's say, And happy is the lover . . .

They had hung a sign on the front door of the restaurant: "Closed. Sorry . . . Come again."

He didn't go to the front door. He followed the path taken by the cook a few minutes before.

'Tis late to hearken, late to smile, But better late than never . . .

He let himself in, easing shut the screened door. Pans clattered, cleanup in progress.

I shall have lived a little while, Before I die forever . . .

When he appeared, the cook stepped back, startled. "We're closed, mister."

"Yes, I know. Show me your freezer."

"What?"

He drew the pistol. "Show me the freezer."

"Hey, hey . . . yessir . . . here it is."

"Get in."

"Yessir."

Truman waggled a finger. "Don't make any noise and don't try to get out—understand?"

"Yessir."

He closed the heavy portal, pinned it so the prisoner couldn't trip the lock from inside. Then quickly he went to the swinging double doors opening into the dining area. Two waitresses—there they were—and the cashier, busy counting bills.

He stepped into the dining room and lifted his voice. "Hello—may I have your attention?"

Slow motion. They turned from their chores, obediently silent.

"There are three of us," Truman advised. "One out front, the other out back. Nobody will be hurt if you do exactly as I tell you. Come into the kitchen, please."

Nobody moved. Truman cocked the pistol. "Come into the kitchen."

"Do it, do it," the cashier instructed. Then, to Truman, "Do you want me to bring the money?"

"I'll get the money. Come into the kitchen."

Eyes wide, the waitresses eased past him, the cashier following. "There you go," Truman said amiably. "Now, into the freezer with your friend."

Nobody resisted. Their breath came in plumes of moisture, cold air flowing around Truman's ankles until he closed the door, all of them in the freezer together. "Face the wall and get on your knees."

"Mother of God, most Holy Savior . . ."

"Now, now," Truman soothed. "Nobody will get hurt."

The younger waitress prayed over clasped hands, her eyes closed, "Forgive us for our sins, forgive us for—"

He fired from largest male to smallest female, the praying girl.

"Oh, oh, please—no!"

Cook . . . cashier . . . waitress . . .

The praying girl had turned, one hand extended as if her palm were a shield, wailing in Spanish now.

He pushed aside her hand and pulled the trigger.

He stepped out of the freezer, closed the door, pinned the lock. Before entering the dining area, he stood at the swinging door, assessing the empty parking lot, the motel across the street.

It took only a moment to get the cash—a brown paper sack ready for bank deposit, a few cents in the till.

He extinguished the lights.

When he reached the motel office, he leaned near the window, smiling, tapping glass with a knuckle.

"Yes, sir?"

"Cigarettes?"

"Oh, yes, sir."

The clerk unlocked the door, stood aside to admit his customer.

Truman pulled the pistol. "Get behind the desk, son. Lie flat on the floor."

"Are you going to hurt me?"

"Not if you do as I tell you."

"The money is in the desk."

"Face down on the floor."

There was no suffering. This was not an exercise in terror. This was quick-hit-and-withdraw, mission accomplished.

The boy jolted, whimpered, lay still.

Truman crossed the lot to his car, opened the trunk, and threw in the money bag. He pulled out of the parking lot—no traffic.

He turned east, toward Houston.

A few more times like this and he'd be ready. He lit a cigarette, trickled smoke between his lips. A fender rattled in sympathetic response to the reverberations of unbalanced wheels and the untuned motor. The floorboard shimmied beneath his feet, growing warm as the engine heated.

He had called Thomasville twice. After the first call, Bo Taylor refused to come to the telephone again. But that was all right—they knew he was coming. Hiding behind others would not prevent his arrival.

He inhaled deeply, slowing the pump of adrenaline, bringing his responses under control.

He would stop next in Louisiana—somewhere along Highway 90. Hammond, perhaps, or Covington. He'd been through there years ago and he remembered the swampy terrain, the isolated pockets of humanity that clung to roadways traversing the bayou country.

Then, north into Mississippi for another strike.

That would be his last move; then he must quit and be content with whatever he had. There was no hurry. No witnesses were left behind to help assimilate a composite of the criminal. The chance of mass alarm was slim—the strikes had been carefully spaced, no two in a given jurisdiction. The news would stay localized, sensational but unworthy of national attention.

He smoked the cigarette, lulled by heat from the bare floorboard, the whumpity-whump of tires against the roadway. Texas was huge. He'd struck here three times.

He was tired, but not sleepy. In fact, he felt better than he had in some time, with the same nervous flow that kept him going when he crossed battle lines to create havoc and strike the enemy with terror.

Psychology. It was all psychology. Craft a nightmare, create the illusion, instill an awareness of approaching peril—and the human mind would fuel its own panic.

Would Sheriff Taylor warn anybody?

Truman doubted it.

People would ask: Why? Papa would be exposed.

Sheriff Taylor might issue vague statements to be cautious. He might imply a threat existed. But he wouldn't tell the whole story, Truman was sure of it.

But Papa would know. He would know the seriousness of the danger, the imminence of it. His nightmares would pierce the night, he would hesitate before entering a dark house, he would pause when the wind made shrubbery move in the shadows. A few more telephone calls and Papa would become positive: Truman was approaching.

Papa would know, and yet . . . what did he know?

It had been forty-three years since he beat his son without mercy, molested his daughter, coerced his wife into sneak retreat.

Truman had often wondered if they favored one another, he and Papa. He had no photographs to study; Mama had destroyed those in an attempt to erase the past.

But then, in the spring of 1968, a sensational murder in Thomasville, Georgia, had brought international notoriety to the City of Roses. A deputy director of the CIA had shot one of the wealthiest men in America at his Thomasville plantation. The trial was a media event.

Newspapers and magazines sent journalists, the networks featured interviews with attorneys, prosecutors, judges—and Sheriff Bo Taylor.

Truman read the articles in *Time* magazine, sitting in a PX in Saigon. He had followed the reports over armed-services telecasts.

Bo Taylor. Eyebrows shaggy, rugged and official—a graduate of the University of Georgia, lawman of the year twice. . . .

Truman bit the filter of his cigarette, reliving his emotions at the time.

Father of three sons, town elder and linchpin of law—this man knew Papa as Truman knew him. Sheriff Bo Taylor was a respected man, described in *Time* as dedicated, a servant of the people, a diplomat who had survived the turbulence of Southern integration years with the respect of blacks and whites alike. But he shared Truman's secret, the son of a bitch.

Seething, he threw the cigarette butt out the car window. Easy . . . easy . . . take a breath . . . easy . . .

When he heard that voice, that deep baritone drawl, Truman's response had shocked him. He was frightened! The unexpected fear had stunned him. It was he who held control, he who had instigated the call—but suddenly, he was fearful. It was the residue of childhood, an exaggerated sense of size. Papa would be an old man by now. As his life expectancy waned, so too his courage would have diminished. He would no longer be the brute in his prime who whipped a boy senseless.

The tables were reversed now! He, Truman, was the man. Papa, the child. It was Papa who was the weaker and more defenseless.

Where was Papa?

Sheriff Bo Taylor knew. No matter his disguise, or by what name he was known, Papa was still there.

Truman knew it. Sheriff Bo Taylor knew it.

Off to his left, he could see the lights of Houston. It was after midnight. Warm air through his window brought the sweet scent of crude oil. Somewhere out there the pumps rose and fell like prehistoric monsters seeking greasy remnants of their ancestors—the fiery combustion of an internal engine their ultimate pyre.

One or two more hits like tonight, and he'd be ready. Once or twice more, calls to Bo Taylor as the man cowered behind the woman who answered the phone . . .

He was coming, and Papa knew it!

Before it ended, Papa would tell the world what he was. He would confess his crimes and present himself for public condemnation. He would beg for mercy and there would be no mercy, no atonement.

When shall I be dead and rid/Of the wrong my father did?

He must be calculating, unemotional, detached. He was coordinator and perpetrator of this mission.

How long, how long, till spade and hearse/Put to sleep my mother's curse . . .

Analytical.

Otherwise—he inhaled—otherwise, he would fail.

He remembered the final admonishment from that drawling freckled instructor teaching commandos their grisly duties. "If yoah enemy captures you," he'd intoned, "all you have done will be compounded in retribution. Death will be slow to come and yoah pain will exceed the pain of their dreaded antici-pation."

Professional. Methodical. Cold-blooded.

It would not be Truman who disgraced him. Papa must disgrace himself. The unbelievers must know.

But for now, it was their secret. And Bo Taylor was the man who would expose it.

6

Forty years.

Annette Taylor stood in the center of her bedroom. Bo was everywhere. His hairbrush on the dresser held strands of gray in soft bristles; his workshirt hung on a clothes tree; his nail clippers and pocketknife lay in a brass tray with loose change.

A lifetime.

His shoes were under their bed, his uniforms in the closet. The service revolver and badge were on a shelf in the bathroom foyer. What to do with such things? The thought of giving anything away was painful.

His portrait gazed at her from the wall. The photographer had caught the solemn mien, but a twinkle in the eye suggested reserved humor. He peered at her from beneath thatch eyebrows, his expression seeming to question: What now, Annette?

What now, indeed?

She had retired early, with a book. Dozing, lights burning, she'd awakened to the ring of the telephone. The old instant fear leapt in her chest—

hurt, dead—lawmen and their wives lived with that possibility.

But that was not nature of the call.

"Mother Taylor?"

"Hello, Vera."

"Bob wanted me to call you. Are you all right?"

Why didn't Bob call for himself? "I'm fine."

"Do you need anything?"

Yes. Bo. "No, nothing."

"Don't hesitate to call us, will you?"

"I would, Vera. Thank you."

Then came the call from Lanita—same song, second verse. *Everything fine.*

Finally, long distance, Bradley and Denise, with Elaine behind them, begging for a chance to talk to Grandmama.

"I'm so tired my bones feel like jelly," Denise laughed. "We've been packing and packing and packing."

"Tell Jack the house sold today," Bradley said. "We got our price, and cash."

"Oh, wonderful, Bradley."

"Mother Taylor"—Denise pretended exasperation— "Elaine is standing on one foot and then the other. Here she is."

"Hi, Grandmama!"

"Hi, yourself."

"Jeffrey says hi."

"Hi to Jeffrey."

No talk of death. No platitudes by rote. Just verbal sunshine and the melody of Elaine's giggles.

But when she hung up, Annette felt drained, the house all the more empty. She returned to bed, reading. Dozing. Again, the telephone.

"May I speak with Bo Taylor?" The male voice was deep, soft-spoken.

"Who *is* this?" Annette demanded.

"Ask Bo."

"If you refuse to identify yourself," Annette said, "I will not talk to you."

"Give him a message, please."

"What is it?"

"Have you a pencil?"

"Yes," she lied.

He murmured a poem:

> *None will part us, none undo*
> *The knot that makes one flesh of two,*
> *Sick with hatred, sick with pain,*
> *Strangling—When shall we be slain?*

She hung up, trembling. With a hand on the receiver, she waited, anticipating the next ring. But it didn't ring.

Anger and loneliness teamed to steal her sleep. She wandered through the house, turning on lights until every room was ablaze. She washed a cup and saucer, her only soiled dishes. She went into the pantry and prepared a grocery list. But for whom would she be buying now?

She washed a load of dirty clothes and as she moved them to the dryer, one of his socks appeared amid lines. She clasped it to her chest, weeping uncontrollably.

Desperately she sought activity. It took will to keep her thoughts neutral.

The death certificates arrived today. Name: ROBERT BEAUREGARD TAYLOR; age: 71.

Cause of death: CORONARY.

There were copies for probate, for insurance companies, for governmental agencies.

They were delivering the headstone to the grave

tomorrow. The bill, for eight hundred dollars, was on her desk. She wrote a check to pay for it, addressed an envelope for mailing.

Had Bo occupied so much of her life that this emptiness was justified? He worked every day—he went fishing on weekends and holidays with Judge Felder Nichols! She had spent a lifetime alone—but never so alone, so completely alone as now.

The sense of void angered her. She was manufacturing his presence needlessly. Bo had never been a homebody. Except for nights, and sometimes his duties took nights as well, Bo went about his profession, and she . . . did what?

Whatever it was, she seemed to have more time for it.

She was glad Bradley and Denise were moving to Thomasville. She felt a special rapport with Elaine and Jeffrey—her favorites among the grandchildren. Both treated her as equal—not older, not younger, but a friend. Elaine chatted gaily about things a thirteen-year-old girl cared to discuss. But she also listened raptly, responding to her grandmother with wit, sometimes teasingly—but always as a friend.

And Jeffrey—such a serious little boy. He rarely laughed, his world a somber one. But under that droll exterior there was a boy who loved his grandmother's attention! She always had chocolate-chip cookies or his beloved pineapple upside-down cake when Jeffrey was expected.

The lad loved crossword puzzles and Annette was sure it was because of her. She had taught him the key to working the *Jumble*—word roots, prefixes, and suffixes—and they enjoyed stealing off together to solve the more difficult Sunday *Jumble* with seven-letter words and tricky resolutions.

The bedroom. *Again.*

Wandering like a lost child, clad in a nightgown and terrycloth robe, she stood where she'd been an hour ago, staring at things reminiscent of Bo.

She would clean out the closet—tomorrow, perhaps. Somebody would use the clothing, surely. Send it to the Salvation Army, or to Goodwill Industries.

Annette struggled with an overwhelming desire to weep. There had been enough weeping. Her eyes burned with it, her body ached from it. *No more!*

She went into the closet and got out a scrapbook. Sitting on the edge of their bed, she turned pages and tears spattered on paper brittle with age. The sepia photos, and the images, were haunting moments from the past. Bo, in 1945, when they met. Like Jeffrey, he had been such a solemn person—as if his soul were etched with the acid of remorse.

She remembered the dress she wore. Full sleeves, puffed at the shoulders, her hair the style of wartime, postdepression women. She still had the barrette, somewhere. In the attic, most likely.

He had been married before. A miserable union, he'd said. He had feared another marriage because of it.

But she overcame that.

She turned pages of the scrapbook. Their first automobile. First home. Bo and Judge Nichols grinning, showing off a string of fish they had caught in Lake Miccosukee.

The ring of the telephone made her cry aloud.

Ring—

She wouldn't answer.

Ring—

Suppose it was an emergency? Or Bradley with second thoughts and another message for Jack or Bob?

Ring—

It was him. Damn him!

Ring—

Annette lifted the receiver. "All right," she said evenly, "let's get this over. It's obvious you are emotionally disturbed. Tomorrow I will change this number and you won't be able to call again. So, here's your last chance. Say what you wish."

"Did you give Bo Taylor my message?"

"No, I did not."

"Will he talk to me?"

"No, he won't."

"He's afraid."

"If you knew Bo Taylor, you'd know better."

He laughed—as if genuinely amused.

"Say what you have to say," Annette commanded. "Then let's both get some sleep."

"I'm on my way."

"You're in for a surprise."

"Tell him I'm coming."

She forced her voice to level tones. "What do you expect to accomplish?"

He laughed, hung up.

Why didn't she tell him: *Bo is dead!*

To punish him for this childish prank? To retaliate in the only way she could—withholding information because he wouldn't reveal his identity?

Her hands felt cold. What had he said?

None will part us, none undo . . . The knot that makes one flesh of two . . .

She remembered the harrowing months of integration. Midnight calls, whispery voices, intimidating Bo, threatening the children. Bo had shrugged it off, changed their telephone number. Still the calls had come—menacing, vulgar, assaulting her senses with omens of death and worse.

This caller was nothing to compare with that. The male voice threatened only with innuendo.

Yet, as if by sixth sense, this caller frightened her more than any other.

The big difference between years past and now—Bo was gone. She was alone.

Where was he calling from?

He could be down the street, around the corner. Maybe he *knew* Bo was gone.

She checked the bedroom windows, locked them, twisting the hasps as tightly as she could. She drew the drapes more securely.

The telephone—damn the man!

She would have the number changed. Do that tomorrow. But even as she thought it, she resisted. She'd have to tell her friends—the children would know, and the grandchildren. The telephone was her link to everyone she loved.

She was having trouble breathing. Into the hallway, check the doors—double-check the doors!— locked.

She turned off lights as she progressed, room to room, throwing back curtains to feel the locks, twisting them, trying to lift the sash to be certain—locked.

Ring . . . ring . . .

"Damn you," she muttered.

Off with the dining-room lights. The house was dark now. The burr of the telephone seemed magnified . . . pulsing in the night.

It stopped.

The room felt smaller. The house larger. The clock ticked in a cadence which seemed too slow.

Tick . . . tock . . . tick . . .

Bo's revolver was in the bathroom foyer. She detested the thing. Only once had she touched it, and the pistol seemed to emanate an ugly violence.

"It's no better or worse than the man holding it," Bo claimed.

What, then, would it be in her hands?

"I'll teach you to fire it, Annette," Bo had offered.

No. No, she didn't want that.

Suppose her imagination had gone awry. Suppose one of the children were playing a game, ready to jump out and cry "Boo!"

No, the gun was a tool of Bo's trade, not a device for reassuring herself in the dark. When Bradley arrived in Thomasville, she would give it to him, along with his father's badge. It was only fitting, bestowing them to his successor. She didn't need the gun, didn't want it.

Yes, the walls seemed to be surging, glowing blue and black, blue and black. She stood as if rooted, incapable of movement, suffocating and unable to rise . . . holding her breath, immersed in liquid.

Blue and black . . . blue and black . . .

The house shrilled—the bell—

The door reverberated with pounding . . . the shrilling bell stabbing at her—the walls blue and black . . . blue and black . . .

"Mrs. Taylor!"

"Yes?" she called.

"This is Deputy Smitherman, Mrs. Taylor—are you all right?"

"Yes . . ." *Thank God.* "Yes, I'm all right."

"Will you come to the door, please?"

Her knees buckled. She had to force the joints to lock upright. "Coming," she said. "I'm coming."

She turned on the porch light, unlocked the door.

"We came by on patrol and saw all the lights burning," the deputy said. He was looking past her, his flashlight poking into dark corners. "When we telephoned, there was no answer," he said. "I hope we didn't disturb you."

"No." *Thank God.* "No, I appreciate your concern."

"We drive by here several times every night," the young deputy reported. "We're keeping an eye on you."

The rotating blue lights atop the deputy's car threw alternating strokes of blue and dark . . . blue and dark . . .

"I couldn't sleep," she said.

"But you are all right?"

"I've been getting crank telephone calls."

"You ought to change your number, Mrs. Taylor. That kind of thing is one of the drawbacks to our work. The telephone company will do it for you immediately, if you ask."

"I will. Tomorrow. Thank you for coming to see about me."

He was still looking past her, checking the house. "Is there anyone who could stay with you?"

"I'll see about that, too, tomorrow."

But she wouldn't. Marie, Bo's cousin, had offered. Lanita and Vera had offered. Better to be alone with her demons than to stay the devil with idle chitchat.

"Good night, then," the deputy said.

She closed the door, locked it. Halfway down the hall, she hesitated. Returning, she checked the lock again.

If Bo were here, he would assuage her fears with subdued humor. He would treat her like a child, deliberately and teasingly condescending. "See, there's nothing in this closet—nothing under this chair, or that one."

She could almost feel his burly arm around her shoulder as he took her from stairwell to alcove, peeking behind pictures. "Nothing there. . . ."

She bit her lip.

"Under the carpet, maybe?" He would drop to all fours, a ridiculous sight, lifting one corner of the rug as if certain he would be attacked. "Aw, phoo—nothing there, either."

Then he would hold her—Annette wrapped her arms around herself, squeezing her body, eyes closed.

"I'll look after you," Bo would murmur. "I'll keep the bad guys away."

He always had.

"Oh, Bo," she moaned. "I miss you, Bo. . . ."

Ten o'clock. Promptly. Vera was at the door not by choice, but because Bob had sent her. Annette allowed herself a rare obscenity. She had dressed to go out.

"My, you look nice," Vera declared.

"I was about to go downtown," Annette said.

"Well, good for you! I'll take you."

"No, I can drive, but thanks."

Vera's manner was irritating, walking through the house as if inspecting the premises.

"Why don't we have lunch together?" Vera suggested.

"I'm sorry, Vera. I've made other plans."

Her carefully plucked eyebrows arched. "Now, that's the way! Good for you."

"I'm in a bit of a rush," Annette said.

Vera sat at the dining-room table. She crossed her legs and placed her matched handbag beside one high-heeled foot.

"Bob wanted me to take you to lunch," she said. "The garden-club luncheon is at noon. We're having Mrs. Rostow speak on her new roses."

"I appreciate the invitation, but I just don't want to go."

Vera picked a piece of lint from her skirt and glanced about for a receptable in which to place it. "She won best of show with her latest hybrid," Vera noted. "She's having it patented. This is her fifth one, you know."

Annette was still standing, struggling with impatience.

"I told the girls you might be coming," Vera said. "They were so pleased. It's just what you need these days."

"I despise gardening, Vera."

Another mote of lint. Vera rolled it between her fingers and placed it on the table. "You seem to think we get on our hands and knees to till the soil, Mother Taylor! Most of the ladies hire gardeners."

"It isn't for me."

Vera pursed rouged lips. "You must tell Bob I did my best and you were adamant."

"I'll tell him." Annette took a step toward the door, hoping to draw Vera with her. But Vera sat there gazing from wall to wall.

"Vera, I must hurry along."

"Yes, of course. Actually, I hate to burden you . . ."

But? With Vera, anything relevant always followed "but."

"But," Vera said, "I wanted to ask a favor."

Annette waited, hands clasped.

"You know that Bob is offering Denise a job at the newspaper."

"A partnership, I thought."

Vera fluttered a hand. "That's a possibility, if things work out. The most optimistic moment in any business is the very beginning."

"I think Denise will do quite well."

Vera flicked at her skirt with the backs of her

fingers. "And she probably will. She seems to make up in energy what she lacks in experience."

"Seven years with a newspaper in Mobile, Vera."

"I know, I know."

"The favor?" Annette asked pleasantly.

"This puts me in an awkward position, Mother Taylor. I've been working with Bob since he bought *Rose City News*. Now, of a sudden, I find myself the boss and the employee at one and the same time."

"How's that?"

"Bob and *I* own the paper—and Denise assumes she will be over all personnel. I assume she assumes that."

"I assumed that."

"What I need is an intermediary," Vera said. "Somebody who can make my feelings evident without bruising Denise's pride. Do you see what I mean?"

"That isn't something I can do, Vera."

"I see."

"Denise would feel I'm meddling. Bob, too, for that matter."

"Bob and I have worked very hard to build up the business," Vera said. "I'm not altogether sure I like giving away the fruits of our labor."

Annette walked to the table and sat down. After a moment she said, "Vera, writing is a hobby with you. Denise studied journalism, she worked for a county weekly, then the Mobile daily paper. She's had articles published in *Southern Living*. She writes because it's her career."

"She's obviously made some good contacts."

"Her writing has made the contacts. Denise can show you drawers full of rejection slips. She knows her craft, and her experience can be very beneficial to Bob. To you too."

"That girl." Vera laughed caustically, standing up.

"She has winsome ways, I'll give her that much. Bob, Lanita, and Jack—and you—everybody loves her."

"She's a lovable person," Annette acknowledged. "But so are you, Vera. The job at the newspaper isn't the result of a personality contest. Bob needs Denise. If she's moving to Thomasville, they can serve one another's needs nicely."

"Of course"—Vera pulled on a cotton glove—"you are absolutely right, Mother Taylor. Perhaps it would be best if I just withdrew from the paper and let them have their reins."

Annette ushered Vera to the door and watched her depart. Vain and jealous, Vera was not likely to yield any ground. But a frontal assault wasn't her style, either.

Psychological warfare, Annette thought. That was Vera's style.

7

Parking at the post office, Annette sat in the car, dreading human interaction. She and Bo had lived in Thomasville all their adult lives and yet the most familiar face now seemed that of a stranger. Businessmen coming and going, the workaday routine of commerce and social contact— which of them was calling her?

She forced herself to go inside. She felt eyes upon her.

"I was so sorry to hear about your husband, Mrs. Taylor."

"Thank you, Mrs. Dean."

"I'll remember him in my prayers."

"Thank you."

"Is there anything I can do? Anything you need?"

"No, my sons are looking after me quite well. Thank you for asking."

"It seems to be nature's way to take our menfolk."

Repeatedly. Each new condolence became more difficult to bear. She wished they would ignore her.

"I lost my Harvey six years ago come May," Mrs.

Dean rasped. "How he suffered. Cancer of the colon. You can bless your stars that your husband didn't linger and linger."

"I suppose so."

The postmaster spotted Annette and opened another window to serve her.

"Sorry about Bo, Annette."

"Thank you."

"Good sheriff. Good man."

"Thank you."

She found herself analyzing his inflections of speech, listening to other voices in other lines: deep, baritone, softly spoken words . . .

Her mouth was so dry, the stamp stuck to her tongue. She felt as if everyone were staring.

"I hear Bradley is stepping into Bo's shoes," the postmaster said. "Any truth to that?"

"I think it's under consideration."

There were no secrets in a town this size. Her reply was practiced politics—wait for the formal announcement.

"Brad would make a fine sheriff for Thomas County."

"I'll tell him you said so."

She gave her envelope to a postal clerk, dispatching payment for Bo's headstone. Self-conscious, she walked outside into searing heat. She was tempted to drive straight home and shut out the world, hide from reality. No, that was foolish. But what to do with herself?

In her sleep last night, she'd decided not to change her telephone number—not yet. A new unlisted number would complicate things. Bradley and Denise would be here next week; she would do it then. They might need to reach her. Besides, she didn't

feel like writing her friends to tell them. If she inadvertently omitted someone, the act of changing her
number might be construed as a gesture to exclude
that person from her life.

Across the street, half a block away, she could see
the courthouse. On benches beneath live oaks, the
elderly and idle swapped tales and watched pedestri-
ans pass. *One of them?*

It could be anybody. An employee from the drugstore, someone working with the utility company. Or
the telephone company!

A man in Bo's position made enemies with every
arrest. It could be someone related to such a person. . . . Annette saw a minister parking his car. She
wasn't up to Baptist intonations. She moved away,
unconsciously approaching Jack's real-estate office.
Lanita would be there. Lanita was a good excuse to
sit a minute.

Jack had been the difficult son. Annette had read
somewhere that the middle child of three was always
troublesome. Overshadowed by Bob, editor of the
high-school newspaper, outshone by Bradley, athlete
and family baby, Jack had quit school a year before
graduation.

He seemed doomed to the rut so many men trod—
manual labor, drinking too much, squandering money
on cars and girls. Finally he stood before his father,
arrested for driving under the influence of alcohol.

Annette had been there, summoned to witness the
sorry state of their flesh and blood.

"Your goddamned license is revoked," Bo declared.

"That the way it works?" Jack had asked. "You just
snatch my license because you're my daddy?"

"You damned right, boy. And because I'm your
daddy I'm not going to throw you in the can with the
other drunks. But next time . . ."

Except, the next time, Jack was driving drunk and didn't even have the license. The time after that, he was in a friend's automobile—taken without permission. In frustration, Bo threw him in jail, threatened to beat him.

"Maybe that's part of the problem," Bo had said. "I never spanked those boys—not once."

"Your score is pretty good," Annette had said. "Two out of three on the straight and narrow."

It had been Lanita who saved Jack from himself. She'd finished college in Valdosta, returned home to Thomasville because her father was ill, and married Jack. She was licensed to sell real estate and she had tutored her husband. Annette had been awash with relief as Lanita enticed Jack into the role of responsible citizen.

Sassy, petite, and headstrong, Lanita helped Jack become a broker and then they bought a colonial-style home which they converted to offices. To the world, Jack became the flamboyant civic leader, easily elected mayor, tithing time and money for community good. But those who knew them well knew Lanita was the leveling force in Jack's life.

Annette entered the office; Jack's voice boomed from somewhere in back, lecturing his sales staff. "Listings," Jack insisted, "listings are the key to everything! When somebody drives through town, I want them to think we're the only game there is."

Lanita looked up, a grin bringing dimples to her cheeks. "Ten Commandments," she advised. "Moses will be down momentarily. "How about a cup of coffee?"

"That would be nice."

Annette could see Jack in the conference room. He hacked at an open palm, using his other hand as a cleaver. "When we make a sale, don't wait for the closing—get out there and hang a *sold* sign. Nothing sells like a sold sign."

Lanita caught his eye and made a rolling motion with a forefinger. "Enough—hurry and end it."

"That's it." Jack shuffled papers into a folder. "Hit the streets and bring in those listings."

As his salespeople departed, Jack bent to kiss Annette's forehead. "How ya feel?"

"Bradley sold his house. He got his price, and cash."

Jack rubbed his hands briskly. "We get a referral fee on that."

"That means they'll be moving next week," Annette said. "Will their new house be ready?"

"They're working on it. Few problems, but nothing insurmountable."

"Will it be habitable?" Annette asked.

"Better than a tent, and appreciating with every hammer-fall. What's on my agenda, Lanita?"

"A closing at two."

"Commercial." Jack beamed. "Ten percent, that one."

He touched a finger to his forehead, bidding goodbye, and breezed out, whistling.

"What's wrong, Lanita?"

"Termites and borers. The whole house has to be encased in a plastic cover and fumigated. It's expensive."

"Oh, dear."

"It's still a good buy, Mother Taylor. Otherwise, the work is proceeding nicely. They're doing tile work in the baths today and tomorrow. It's looking good."

Annette sipped coffee.

"Now, then." Lanita pulled her chair nearer. "What's wrong with you?"

"I'm fine."

"Nope, you aren't. What is it?"

"Doldrums mostly."

"Secondly?"

"I've been getting calls from the same man who killed Bo."

"Mother Taylor, the call didn't do it. Bradley was right—words don't kill. What did he say?"

"He quoted poetry." Annette took a breath. Her chest felt heavy, as if she had congested lungs.

"You should change your number, Mother Taylor. I'll call the phone company for you."

"No. I've decided to wait until Bradley and Denise get here."

"Then at least let me tell them you're being bothered. Maybe they can trace the call."

"When I change the number it'll be over, anyway. Besides, he doesn't say anything obscene. He isn't even threatening, at least not overtly. He's just . . . ominous."

"How about my staying with you overnight?"

"I don't think so. I'm being silly. Blowing this thing out of proportion, probably."

"All right," Lanita concurred, "but remember what they say about such things—don't encourage him by listening to him. When you hear his voice, hang up."

"I should. I haven't, but I should."

"Have you considered going to visit someone for a few days?" Lanita asked. "If he gets no answer for a night or two, he'll get discouraged."

"I should, maybe. I can't, though. I . . . Oh, damn, Lanita, I don't know what I want to do. I want him to stop calling, but I don't want any more changes in my life right now."

She stood up to leave. "Don't worry about me, Lanita. You're right, words can't hurt me."

"Poetry, you said?"

"A limerick—doggerel. He breathes in my ear and talks from deep in his chest. He says he is coming here, and to tell Bo."

"Tell the jerk that Bo is dead."

"I should."

"Say . . ." Lanita brightened. "Want to have some lunch with me?"

"No, thank you, Lanita. I'm going to the cemetery. They're delivering Bo's headstone today."

She left the office, angry with herself. What had that conversation accomplished? She had burdened Lanita with her problems. She *knew* she should hang up, she shouldn't talk to him—yet she had. She sounded like a helpless old woman who complains, but resists moves to correct her situation! "Professional martyrs," Bo called such people. "Like a bluetick hound sitting on a cactus—yowling, but too lazy to move."

She encountered the Baptist minister in spite of everything.

"Mrs. Taylor, Mrs. Taylor, how ah you?"

"Doing fine!" She walked on and he fell in step beside her.

"The ladies of the Bible-study class were talking about you," he said sonorously. "I suggested they stop by for a visit and share a prayer or two."

"Not this month, please. I'm terribly busy. But thank the ladies for remembering me."

"May his soul rest in peace," the minister said. "May God forgive him his sins."

Annette halted, facing him. His voice was the same timbre—rich, deep—but the caller had no Southern drawl. It hadn't struck her until this instant. He spoke with the broader inflections of a person from the West, perhaps.

The minister was holding her hand now, head down, murmuring a prayer. Annette gazed past his shoulder, remembering the sounds of the words spoken last night.

The poem.

That cadence, so rigidly structured, so tightly metered . . .

The minister clung to her hand during his supplications to God.

The poetry wasn't a limerick at all! It wasn't doggerel, either. Annette patted a foot, humming the cadence: *hm-hm-hm-hm-hmmm-hm* . . .

The minister continued, head down, but he was peering up at her through his eyebrows.

Seven or eight beats to a line, four lines to a stanza: *hm-hm-hm-hm-hmm-hm* . . .

"Amen," the minister concluded.

Annette patted his shoulder. "Thank you." She got into her car, humming the beat, that strictly metered beat—and what were the words?

None will part us, none undo . . . The knot that makes one flesh of two . . .

She circled the block to CoCroft Music Store. She could visit the cemetery later.

"May I help you, Mrs. Taylor?"

"Yes," she said. "I'd like to buy a tape recorder. I want the kind you use to tape a telephone call."

"Yes, ma'am. The new G.E.'s are excellent . . ."

Annette ate fried chicken from a fast-food restaurant. The telephone was ready. The salesman had shown her how to place a small suction cup on the receiver, which buttons to depress, and it worked! She'd recorded Vera's call, then Lanita's. Their voices on the recording tape were as natural as they had been over the telephone line.

"Come on," she said, "call me."

Minutes ticked away, the house growing darker. Impatiently she vacuumed the floors, her hair bound in a kerchief, wearing old shorts and tennis shoes.

Maybe he wouldn't call tonight. Perhaps he'd tired of his silly charade. The thought was disappointing— as if they had played a game and she'd lost before she learned the rules.

She sorted clothing from the closet, selecting certain items for one charitable organization, other pieces for another. She put Bo's revolver and badge in a dresser drawer and locked it.

Passing Bo's portrait, she said, "We're going to get him if he calls again."

"You can't play with psychopaths," Bo had once said. "They don't think like rational people."

She responded as if spoken to. "Well, two can play that game, Bo."

His photograph seemed more concerned, the twinkle in his eyes less humorous.

"Hey, you," she said fiercely, "I'm not going to become a professional martyr! If a dog snaps at me, I'm going to snap back. You mind the ether and I'll tend the telephone."

Midnight. Then, two A.M. She had worked herself to nervous exhaustion—too tired to sleep. Annette made hot tea, ate the last of cold French-fried potatoes.

Ring . . .

She giggled nervously, waiting.

Ring . . .

Let him think he'd awakened her. She made sure the tape recorder was plugged in, tugged the suction cup that would pick up a voice by conduction.

Ring . . .

Her hands were perspiring as she answered. "Hello?"

"Let me speak with Bo."

"Bo says, 'Go to hell.'"

"Tell him to come to the phone."

The reel revolved in the machine. Annette adjusted her glasses to peer down at it. What a marvelous contraption!

"He says no," Annette reported.

"Did you give him my message?"

"You know, I completely forgot it. What was your message?"

A long silence. Annette heard background noises. A truck stop, maybe, or bus terminal.

"I'm listening," she said.

"Is Sheriff Taylor there?"

"I can't wake him."

"I don't think you're taking me seriously."

"It's difficult to take you too seriously," Annette said. "Frankly, your effort to upset anyone is failing. That is your intent—to upset somebody?"

"Tell Bo Taylor I'm coming."

"I'll repeat anything you say."

Another silence. She heard him sigh. "It would not be wise to get between us, lady."

"Is that your message?"

He hung up.

Annette rewound the tape and listened to the call again. He had sounded less sure of himself tonight. Her own voice carried a note of gaiety, as if she were enjoying the exchange. *Good.*

Ring . . .

She made the tape run forward, little peeps of sound coming from the machine, as if she had a nest of baby birds.

Ring . . .

She set the machine for recording, lifted the receiver. "Hello there," she said pleasantly.

"A word to the wise—stay out of my way."

"Let me ask you a question," Annette said sharply. "Do you think a professional lawman is awed by crude threats? Bo Taylor endured the Ku Klux Klan, black militants, rednecks, and the Mafia."

"Don't get between us, lady."

"Quote your damned poem, why don't you?"

" *'When shall I be dead and rid/ Of the wrong my father did?/ How long, how long, till spade and hearse/ Put to sleep my mother's curse?'* "

He was breathing harder. Maybe she had carried this as far as she should.

"Is that all?" Annette asked.

"Bitch," he said, and hung up.

8

Annette sat in a rocking chair on the back porch. She sipped hot tea, nerves already frazzled from too much tannic acid. She had gone to bed, tossing fitfully, dreaming that Bo was calling her name. The effort to rest was more exhausting than arising. She took a prolonged shower to ease the tension; her muscles felt as if the tissue were embedded with granulated blood.

A mockingbird ran its repertoire, a lonesome melody announcing dawn. Annette watched the graying sky, the Japanese tulip and pecan trees etching a tatted border against the horizon.

She had listened to the tape-recorded call again and again, analyzing the timbre and pattern of speech. He was not trying to disguise his voice, Annette was sure of it. He spoke distinctly, voice unmuffled, undistorted.

The background sounds she had detected seemed to be the rumble of diesel engines and she thought she had heard a hiss—air brakes released. A truck stop, possibly. Maybe he drove a truck.

Earlier, she had taken boxes of Bo's clothing to her car. This morning she would deliver them to welfare agencies. Then she would go to the cemetery and inspect the headstone. Finally, when the business day began, she would take her tape recording to Bob down at the newspaper. Maybe he would recognize the voice.

Possession of the tape made her feel more secure, as if she had captured a piece of the caller himself. He was mature, middle-aged or older—the delivery as much as the depth of tone assured her of that. When he recited his poetry it was more than the flat reading of a passage. His voice had the quality an actor gives his lines in a performance.

She wished she had a cigarette. She and Bo quit smoking at the same time, fifteen years ago—it had been a grueling exercise. She'd caught him in the attic, smoking on the sly, and there they had sat, laughing at themselves, baked in the heat of that lofty aerie—smoking away the last of his hidden pack.

Annette drew a breath, as if inhaling—blew the "smoke" toward the yard.

Now that Bo was gone, perhaps she should get a cat. The thought of fur balls and flea collars staved the impulse. Who would care for the creature when she went away?

To where?

They talked of going to Europe, Mexico, Canada— but they never had. Time tends to jade such youthful aspirations. When finally you can, you no longer wish to.

The tea was cold. She sipped it anyway, listening to the mocker's song.

Five o'clock.

Grief had made taffy of time, each second thicker, endlessly drawn. Her thoughts had become introverted. She reflected more upon the past than the present, and upon the future not at all. It was a deadly warning of encroaching age and she struggled to fight it off. The caller had inadvertently given her more to consider than herself.

As she listened to his voice, a premonition of tragedy mounted. His poem gathered a sense of foreboding with each new examination. *How long, how long, till spade and hearse . . . Put to sleep my mother's curse?*

Annette remembered her father holding her in his lap more than half a century ago. His breath smelled of tobacco, his handlebar mustache mesmerized her as he recited the words of Edgar Allen Poe. *To the tintinnabulation that so musically wells from the bells, bells, bells . . .*

The sound of the words enthralled her. Like the beat of a primordial drum, her father's voice a metronome: *From the jingling and the tinkling of the bells.*

Ultimately, she had learned the agony of Poe. His writing never seemed joyful again. The morbidity of *Annabel Lee* and the dark passages of *The Raven* cast a pall over all else he composed. The torment of his personal life made mockery of the melody of *The Bells.*

The same forbidding cloak rode the shoulders of the caller. "You aren't taking me seriously," he had said.

She wasn't then. More so now.

Her frivolous responses had angered him. "Don't get between us, lady."

She went into the kitchen, the lights off, to boil more water for tea. Waiting, she stood at the window, listening to the mockingbird.

She had once met a survivor of Nazi atrocities, an elderly rabbi who lived near Apalachicola, Florida.

Bo and Judge Felder Nichols had gone there to fish. Annette was left at the dock to while away her day and there she encountered the rabbi who had shed his faith.

He had lost his belief in God, he said, because no Supreme Being would permit a Hitler to live. He could believe God might resist striking the despot down, but he couldn't believe a just deity would thwart the serious attempts to assassinate Hitler.

The rabbi's eyes remained alight, his lips suggesting amusement as he recalled God's fall from grace. But behind the words, beneath the practiced elocution, she felt immense agony.

The same sense of agony lay behind the recorded voice. As if his suffering were oatmeal bubbling in a pot, the tinkling of the lid a warming promise of a hot meal to come—and the porridge itself ready to scald any finger which tested it.

Agony. That was a good word. The deep suffering of which he spoke—implying that Bo had been a part of the cause.

Something clattered in the yard. Annette stiffened. The mockingbird was silent; a veil of ground fog shrouded the shrubbery beside the driveway. She turned her head, straining to hear . . .

Footsteps.

She latched the screen, thinking: The screen wouldn't stop him!

A shadowy form came across the neighbors' backyard. So still was the scene, she could hear the swish of the man's trousers as he walked. Behind her, the teakettle shrilled and she dived for it, moving the pot from the flames.

Back at the door, watching, waiting, she'd lost sight of the intruder. Her heart thumped, her ears throbbed.

A scraping noise—a bump of metal to metal. She ran on tiptoes to her bedroom, peeked through the curtains.

"Dear God," she said. *The garbage man.*

Feverishly she dressed, raking at her damp hair with a comb. She had deluded herself. She was not blasé, not calm as she would have believed. She had tempted fate and his telephone response was, "Bitch!"

She grabbed the tape recorder and electrical cord. The first rays of sunshine pierced the shaded lot, the lawn beaded with dew. She could see the dark spoor of the garbage man, his path marked across grass by moisture disturbed.

The time: *six*. Bob wouldn't be in his office until eight.

Had she shut the back door?

To hell with it.

Better to drive around town than stay here. Go where people gathered, the Plaza Restaurant for breakfast. She fumbled the keys into the ignition, turned the motor. The windshield and rear window were veiled by condensation. She flicked a switch to activate the wipers and the blades flung moisture with a single swipe. Backing up, she heard a yell and jammed the brakes.

The garbage man circled from the rear, grinning, a hand lifted in mock fear. Little did he know.

This was irrational. She'd invited this—foolishly imagining things.

How secure was she? She should have someone come and examine the locks. Have an alarm installed, perhaps.

Watching the garbage man jump on his truck, Annette remembered something Bo once said, arguing against burglar alarms and electronic devices. "If a man can crack a safe, he can get into a house."

She drove downtown to the Plaza Restaurant and parked near the entrance. A man delivering milk was unloading crates, oblivious of his surroundings, loudly singing, "Welcome to my world . . ."

Silly woman. Silly!

Bob's office was a glassed-in cubicle overlooking the desks of sales and editorial staff. The smell of pulp paper and the clack of typewriters were a thing of the past. He had recently installed a computer system. Each reporter worked with a silent keyboard, the words appearing on a green-tinted TV screen.

Sitting at his desk, Bob cupped his forehead in one hand, concentrating on the mellifluous voice from Annette's tape recorder reciting poetry. Vera poised beside him, expression intent.

When the call ended, Bob turned off the machine and rocked back in his chair. "Vera, call the telephone company and have Mother's number changed, today."

"Do you know the voice?" Annette questioned.

"No."

"I recorded the call in hopes somebody might recognize him. I hadn't changed my number partly for that reason. I worried that people who count couldn't reach me."

"People who count know how to find you, Mother."

Vera spoke into the telephone, "Customer service, please."

"It sounded as if he were calling from a truck stop," Annette said. "I thought I heard trucks and air brakes."

"Mother, why are you playing with this man?"

"I wasn't playing with him, Bob. I was trying to find out who he is."

"It doesn't matter who he is. He's a nut. You

should have hung up immediately. You should have told him Dad is dead."

Vera advised, "The phone number will be changed this afternoon."

"Mother, I want you to come stay with us awhile."

"I'm not going to do that."

A youthful employee tapped on the door and Bob motioned her in.

"Mr. Taylor, somebody dumped the computer." She blushed. "We've lost the national news."

"F'chrissake! I've told everybody to stay off the computer terminals until after the national news is locked in."

"I'll take care of it," Vera said, rising.

When the door closed, Bob massaged his brow. "That's what Vera does best. It isn't what she wants to do, but she knows that computer. It saves me hours of correcting editorial problems when I should be out selling." He stared at the tape recorder. "Mother, how about going to stay with Aunt Marie?"

"I don't want to listen to her sniffle and weep— which she'll do. She called me twice to sympathize and I ended up consoling her."

"Go to our condo down at the Gulf, then."

"Bob, I'm all right!"

"Sure you are. I saw your face when that guy was talking. You're frightened. There's no need staying there alone."

Vera came in, shut the door, and stood with her back to the pressroom. "Gerald did it. This is the second time, Bob. Not only has he lost the national news, he broke the security code and lost the classifieds."

"Goddammit!"

"I want to fire him immediately. He thinks a synonym is a social disease and antonyms are the injec-

tions to cure it. He creates horrible headlines . . ."
Vera directed her words at Annette. "You remember
the controversy over a lady firefighter who was breast-
feeding her infant at the fire station? This man's
headline was 'BREAST FEEDING CAUSES BIG FLAP.' "

"He's a good reporter, Vera," Bob said. "Let Denise handle him when she gets here."

"Have you calculated the hours-to-cost ratio in this?"
Vera demanded. "I'll spend all afternoon restructur-
ing the classifieds and if you were paying me by the
hour—"

"Vera, please, just do it!"

She pulled the door closed with a yank, her posture and expression suggesting mayhem for the outer
office.

Annette retrieved her tape recorder, winding the
electrical cord.

"Denise has been a bone of contention since I
offered her a partnership," Bob said. "Vera resents
it. I've tried to explain, if Denise had fifty percent of
this newspaper tomorrow, our personal income would
rise because I would be free to concentrate on sales.
But I've also explained, Denise will be the boss around
here. I can imagine how it will be if Vera persists in
playing stockholder."

He opened the door for Annette. "Mother, go to
the Gulf for a few days, will you? Relax and catch
your breath." He kissed her brusquely. "I'll have
Vera call you later."

Vera and three employees were huddled around a
computer terminal, sorting reams of copy.

"Mother, forgive me," Bob said. "I have to go
supervise this mess."

When she reached the door, Annette looked back.
Bob had pushed Vera aside, taking the task in hand.
Annette stepped out into hot sunshine. Her car was

like a broiler. She rolled down the windows, reviewing the scene she had just witnessed.

She had tried to help Bo, years ago. He'd chosen his cousin, Marie, instead. Hurt, Annette had resented it. As if she hadn't been worthy or adequate.

Chauvinist.

So was Bob.

At least Vera was fighting it.

With a tremendous sense of loss, Annette delivered Bo's clothing to the Salvation Army. Then, with aching heart, she went to the cemetery to visit his grave.

Each headstone gave the sum of a life in a sentence: *name, birth and death dates.*

"I'm not going to be the kind of widow who comes to weep over you every few days, Bo," Annette said. "You always told me not to do it, and I won't."

She couldn't bear the thought of him lying below, arms crossed, cold and dark. She wished she could lie beside him, feel his chest rise and fall in peaceful slumber.

"I love you, you old goat."

So many friends. So many loved ones. Annette returned to the car and sat with the door open, gazing at nothing, staring past dogwood trees and marble markers—so many lives, reduced to a sentence: name, birth, death.

Bo wasn't here. He was at home! What spirit would stay in a place so devoid of life?

She drove to the billiards academy for hot dogs and stood at the sidewalk window waiting for her order.

The husky attendant leaned through the window. "Want a cool brew, Mrs. Tee?"

"Uh . . . yes. That would be good."

As if smuggling contraband, the young owner put

a can of beer in a paper sack, transporting it at his side until he handed it, and the dogs, to Annette. "No charge for the cold drink," he said. "Bo did me a favor more than once."

At home, she poured beer in a wineglass and sipped it. She had never understood Bo's affinity for the stuff. But then, he didn't like poolroom hot dogs.

She examined her mail as she ate. Sympathy cards, each requiring a response. The task of thanking people for flowers, food, and letters—Annette pushed them aside.

She opened the telephone bill and saw calls made by Bo: to Brad and Denise; to a company that sold parts for an outboard motor Bo was trying to repair.

There was one collect call . . . the evening Bo died.

Annnette read the time of day. The call had seemed so much longer—only twelve minutes total. *From Garden City, Kansas.*

It had been about this time of day—four-thirty. Suppose she called this number and he answered? She would know his voice for sure.

She dialed the area code, then the number. It rang, rang, rang again . . .

"Yeah?"

"With whom am I speaking, please?"

"Who you calling?"

"Somebody there telephoned me," Annette said. "I'm returning their call."

The male voice spoke aside, "Anybody make a call on this phone?"

He returned, voice lower. "Sorry, nobody here."

"Where . . . where is this telephone?"

"Spur 83. Lady, I got customers waiting."

"What city? What state?"

"Garden City, Kansas. Hold the line . . ."

She could hear automobiles, the ring of a cash

register, people talking. Minutes passed. Annette waited.

"Who's on the phone?" somebody yelled. A gruff voice spoke in her ear. "Who you calling?"

"Sir, my name is Annette Taylor. I'm in Georgia."

"Long distance? Kee-rice!" He bellowed at somebody, "Who's on the phone?"

"Sir? I wanted to—"

"Lady, we're busier than hell. Who you calling?"

"Nobody, I was . . . If I played a recording for you, I wonder if you might identify—"

He slammed the receiver.

She hung up, sipped the beer. All right, no more calls, no more games. "Leave the detective work to Bradley," Bob had suggested.

It was good advice.

Bradley would be here next week.

9

Damned car.
     This one was a whore. Burning oil. Hiccuping fuel. Driven too slowly, the radiator boiled. Too fast and it convulsed, the seizure lasting until pistons cooled. The mere sight of a garage produced a tubercular cough and vulgar black farts.

He'd been lucky last night. The sign read: "FISH FRY—BINGO. *Annual building fund.*"

A boyish minister and his chubby wife were keepers of the coffers—buckets filled with coins, a box full of paper currency.

Truman had peeled crawfish until his fingers were sore, eating his fill of the Cajun delicacy. A local hillbilly band provided entertainment before the bingo began. Church affair or not, people drank themselves giddy. Two fistfights erupted. All the while, Truman had watched the flow of cash. The money funneled down to two caretakers—the minister and his wife.

The last patrons were departing in pickup trucks with rifles in racks across the rear windows. The pastor and his wife were loading money into the trunk of their vehicle. In that crucial instant of final decision, Truman had discovered he had a flat tire.

He still planned to go through with it. The unwitting pastor helped him wrestle with a locked lug and an ill-fitting wrench. The pistol was in Truman's waistband.

At that moment, a police car came to investigate.

"Got a problem, preacher?"

"One of the flock with a bad tire."

Cicadas whirred, mosquitoes droned. Truman kept his back to the lawman.

"Need a hand?" the policeman asked.

"I think we can manage," the minister said. "God bless, though."

The patrol car circled away slowly and the cop threw a light on Truman's car tag. That ended any chance to strike.

God saved the churchman and his money.

Driving south, swearing at the coughing vehicle, Truman felt it twitch, then quit. He'd spent the night sweltering behind closed windows to ward off mosquitoes that sounded like vultures in the dark. At dawn, a farmer helped him get under way again.

Off to his right now was the Gulf of Mexico and a crescent of white beaches. He hoped to get to Georgia before buying another car.

At thirty miles an hour, the engine quit. Truman depressed the clutch, swearing, and coasted to a halt in a parking bay. Children shrilled in the surf. A calliope played at a nearby wharf.

It could be worse. A motel. Restaurant. He lifted the hood and a malodorous mist of burnt oil and rusty steam rose in his face.

The reflective sands were blinding. The beaches

were a Monet impression of candy-striped umbrellas and enticing bikinis.

Assessing his troubles, he bent over the engine. Busted hose, the patter of oil underneath. This time it appeared to be over. He wouldn't be going anywhere.

Suddenly he felt relieved, as if a dreaded obligation had been postponed. He took his luggage and walked across four lanes of traffic to the motel. Rest and recreation. He could use it. A decent meal, a hot shower, a pleasant room for a change. So, okay, for a day or two—why not? He would resist the temptation to strike. He would forget Thomasville and that bitch—she would pay for her insolence, toying with him.

The motel receptionist was young, her short shorts revealing a peek of cheek when she turned away from the desk. Her hair was bleached blond by summer sun, her teeth made whiter by a deep tan.

"How long will you be staying?" she asked.

"That's up to my jalopy. It's across the street. I think it just died."

"Your luck isn't all bad." She read the name under which he registered. "The restaurant next door is the best on the Gulf. You can walk to town from here. There'll be dancing at the wharf tonight, and there's always a shortage of"—she paused for effect—"mature men."

"Sounds a lot like heaven."

"It can be."

The room was spacious, clean, well-insulated against the sounds of neighbors. Palm trees shaded the grounds and the sweet perfume of oleanders evoked images of tropical isles. Around a pool, women more his age watched him through sunglasses.

He telephoned a garage. They agreed to haul away

his car. It was the nature of such places to procrastinate with tourists. Truman would protest their prices, refuse to pay—and thereby forfeit the car in a way that would not bring it to police attention.

In the meantime, with the world at play, he showered, shampooed his hair and beard, and fell across the bed. He hadn't realized how tired, how exceedingly tired he had become.

The money was in his luggage. Over six thousand dollars. The pistol was there too. He had to buy more cartridges.

The bed felt as if it were moving, swinging to the pulse of his body. He heaved a sigh, closed his eyes.

Tomorrow, and tomorrow, and tomorrow, Creeps in this petty pace from day to day . . .

He missed the theater. He opened his eyes, staring at the low ceiling. He might have flourished as a performer. Never a big star, possibly, but a steady player—they liked his voice, even when his body did not conform to the requirements of a role. It wasn't a real world, the theater, but he had found nothing in the real world anyway.

Another heavy sigh.

He shouldn't have attacked the director. He was young, volatile—the director had pushed him too far, that was all. It was only a community playhouse, but people had been discovered there. Who knew what course his life might have taken? But the director pressed charges. Mama had begged the bastard to forget it. She had offered to pay for the orthodontist and facial surgery—but no, he pressed charges.

It had been Truman's first time in jail. Twenty years old. The judge gave him a choice: prison or military service. Six months later he was paying his dues in Korea, wishing he'd killed that pansy director.

Dozing now . . . a loud crack, like a rifle shot, and he sat straight up. Easy . . . lie back.

As a youth, when that happened, it sometimes brought him out of a sound sleep, positive he'd heard a gunshot. It took years to identify the source—his own spine cracking as muscles relaxed, the vertebrae slipping back into alignment.

Another sigh. *Creeps in this petty pace . . .*

Nothing separated the generations like music. Truman sat at a small table by a window overlooking the marina. The band made up in volume what it lacked in melodic nuance. The sound was deafening, and to Truman, discordant. The girl from the motel was right—there were more women than men. Any steady gaze brought an encouraging smile. But he didn't feel like making the effort. He didn't want to dance to cacophony. Those who did seldom embraced—so why did they do it? *Calisthenics.*

He remembered the last concert he'd attended, in Los Angeles with Lana. A road company of the Boston Pops orchestra. Arthur Fiedler had soothed his soul with a Viennese waltz, electrified him with the *1812 Overture*, complete with cannon booms which shook the walls. Stars and Stripes was the finale.

"Another drink?"

The waitress presented an expanse of bare bosom as she bent to speak.

"No. I'm too old for the noise."

His own words shocked him. He'd never referred to himself as aging before.

She laid a hand on his shoulder, put her lips close to his ear. "What kind of music do you like?" He could feel her breath when she spoke.

"Softer . . . sweeter."

"Pete Fountain is in town."

"Not jazz."

She shrugged ruefully. "Sorry."

He walked out onto the pier. Cut bait and the lap of waves against pilings assured him this was the seashore. Lovers walked hand in hand. Crab fishermen tested their nets—chicken necks the lure. An elderly man greeted Truman with a toothless grin.

"Catching anything?"

"A cold, maybe."

Truman leaned on the rail, the moon reflected below. "What do you use for bait?" Truman asked.

"Money."

"Money—what do you mean?"

"This is where they come, see." The man spit into the brine. "Girls, I mean. You stand here long enough and one'll get you."

"For money."

"Old's I am," the man said, "looks don't count." He cackled softly, leaned to spit.

"I assume you mean hookers."

"Nothing's free, m'boy. My first three wives cost money."

"I'll buy that."

"I certainly did. Where you from?"

"Oh, here and there."

The man crooked a finger at a girl and she continued to walk as if she hadn't seen. "Get what you pay for," he said. "Sometimes you don't get that. Here and there where?"

"All over. You live here?" Truman inquired.

"Sixty-two years. Here comes another." He hissed at her. She ignored him.

"Maybe you should try showing the money," Truman suggested.

"Can't do that." He blew between rubbery lips and winked at another girl.

"I'm not much of an authority," Truman said, "but hookers would respond better to cash than foreplay, it seems to me."

They talked about pompano and mackerel and the way the weather seemed to be changing. Truman listened to a colorful description of the last hurricane to maul the area. Throughout, the old man made kissing sounds, wiggled his hips, and murmured at the women who passed. Finally one responded.

"How much, m'darlin'?" he asked, straight out.

"Twenty dollars."

"Before or after?"

"Before."

He pulled out a money clip, peeled off a bill, and gave it to her. "Could I get a receipt?"

"Are you kidding me?"

"I get it back from Medicare."

She tucked the money in her brassiere, took him by the arm. Immediately, two women stepped from the shadows. "Under arrest—soliciting."

Stunned, Truman listened to them read the prostitute her rights. He slipped down the rail to pass by, and the old man called, "Take care—enjoy your stay."

He tried to remember the policeman's questions. "Where are you staying? What kind of work do you do? How long will you be here?"

He walked the beach toward his motel, sand crunching beneath his weight. Murmuring silhouettes passed him; foaming waves were effervescent on the shore.

He sat on a sea wall and lit a cigarette, shaken by his encounter with the vice cops. He had to stay alert, remain aloof. He couldn't afford a mistake. Suppose they had discovered Bonnie and the boy? It wasn't likely they could identify the remains, but suppose they had?

Bonnie would have enjoyed this place. Bonnie Blue-eyes—she found childish pleasure in simple . . .

He turned his head aside, eyes shut. *She would have talked!* She hadn't the wit for subterfuge. He couldn't just abandon her.

He dispelled the images and threw off remorse, peering at the shimmering reflection of a full moon. In a hundred years, what difference would anything make? He'd forfeited his youth and any opportunity for immortality. There would be no great performances on film, no books at the Library of Congress. He had outlived his chance to make anything of himself.

He was lonely. Not for sex, although it would be nice, but for a woman who cared about him and who listened because she cared. He had a fantasy that had endured most of his adult life. A vision of himself in a tuxedo with a woman in evening finery. Her face had never been clear—it was the persona he envisioned. She would be witty but not caustic, caring but not clinging. She would appreciate Housman when he quoted it, helping pick up the lines when they slipped his memory. They would flow like mercury, across a stage to the musical theme from a film adaptation of his latest novel. . . .

"Hi, want some company?"

The girl from the motel. He stood up.

"I saw that the music drove you away from the wharf," she said. "To tell the truth, they aren't that good. Could I have a cigarette?"

He lit it for her, the flame flickering in her eyes before she blew out the match.

"I know your name is George," she said. "Mine is Peggy. I was fifteen before I realized they weren't calling me 'Piggy.' "

She sat beside him. He could smell coconut oil in her tanning lotion.

"Let's see," she said, "I'm twenty-four, studying medicine at the University of South Alabama in Mobile—my uncle owns the motel and he raised me. I take the pill but I can't remember why."

Truman laughed.

"I like anchovies, jalapeño peppers, olives stuffed with pimentos, and little green onions. That may be why I can't remember. My breath is terrible."

"Smells good to me."

She leaned away. "Sorry."

Truman lit a cigarette from the butt of his other, self-conscious under her scrutiny.

"Now then," she said, "let me hear your capsulated biography."

"I don't condense well."

"All right. Give me the long version."

"You wouldn't want me to lie," Truman said.

"Not unless you want to."

"There's nothing to tell."

"I love a mystery," she said. "But okay. Some guys are turned off by frontal assault. Are you?"

"Is this a frontal assault?"

She puffed her cigarette, holding it between thumb and forefinger, not inhaling.

"You're not a heavy smoker," he observed.

"No, but Lauren Bacall sold me on this approach in a movie I once saw. Actually, she taught me two things."

"The other?"

"Men who won't talk about themselves are usually worth the effort. Humphrey Bogart."

"It could be a cover for low intelligence," Truman said.

"Somehow I doubt that. Do you mind if I put this out? My tongue is on fire."

"I like Strauss—Johann, not Richard—and Sousa, the conductor as well as the composer."

"Well, well," she said. "A kindred spirit. I've been missing that."

"Me too."

The moon made a halo of her hair. "Do you like anchovies, jalapeño peppers, and stuffed olives?"

"Yes."

"How would you like to share a pizza at a terrific little place near here? The music is Glenn Miller and Tommy Dorsey. Only the locals go there. If you're under forty you aren't admitted."

"How do *you* get in?"

"Emotional index, not chronological. How about it?"

"I have no car."

"I do. Come on."

Truman awoke to the hum of an air conditioner. He turned, expecting Bonnie, stroking her thigh.

" 'Morning," Peggy said.

"What's your uncle going to think if he finds you in bed with a customer?"

She put her arms around his neck and kissed Truman's nose. "He'll say, 'Peggy, you are giving me gray hair.' "

She kissed his lips and snuggled nearer. "He's bald."

They had danced the old-fashioned way, in unison, her head against his shoulder. It was past midnight when they returned and without discussion entered his room. In the dark, undressing, there had been no unpleasant change of personality as happened with so many young women these days—shedding good taste as they dropped their clothing.

She'd allowed him to lead, taking over only after he thought they were through. "Just lie here," she had whispered. "Let me do the work. It's my turn."

He hadn't slept so soundly in years.

"When will you be leaving?" she asked.

"Depends on my car."

"Stay as long as you can."

"A few days."

She wrapped a leg around him, drawing him nearer.

"I don't know that my system allows this," Truman cautioned.

"Let me do the work," she said. "I'll take care of your system."

He rolled onto his back. Her lips were warm. Her tongue touching here, there . . .

"Relax, George."

"Believe me, I'm trying."

Maybe age was a state of mind after all. Not arteries, but a condition of the mental process.

His body surprised him, but the time of reaction was a shock.

"There," she said. "I told you I could handle your system."

She was prettier than he had thought.

"I have to watch the desk this afternoon," she said. "But I'm off as of eight o'clock tonight."

"I don't want to impose."

She cut her eyes impishly. "No imposition."

"Why me, Peggy?"

"If you mean, how many before you, not many."

"Why me?"

She stroked his body, sitting on the side of the bed. "I don't know. Why me?"

"I wouldn't have had the nerve to try, if you hadn't led the way."

She put a finger on his sternum. "See—*that* is why."

He watched her dress.

This was the way it could have been. If the director had not pressed charges. If Papa hadn't sent them into social and financial exile.

"Gotta go," Peggy said. "See you tonight."

"Thank you, Peggy."

She halted at the door and turned, expression quizzical. "That's a strange thing to say."

"I had a pleasant evening."

"We'll do it again tonight. 'Bye."

It could have been this way. Truman sat up and reached for his cigarettes, but the pack was empty.

Papa—the son of a bitch. The thief who stole childhood away. Over there in Georgia—was he sitting on the side of his bed worrying because Truman was coming? Pray God so.

Truman stared at his feet. The veins were broken in his ankles, the flesh had a sheen. In the mirror he saw the darkly tanned face, neck, and arms, the rest of his body stark white by contrast.

He needed to trim his beard. Take better care of himself. Had he suspected he would live this long, he might have done better with his diet and physical regimen.

But his torso was solid, the muscles firm. Except for the creases of weathered neck and face, he didn't look bad.

Why me?

Maybe the girl sought a father figure. Her uncle reared her, she had said.

She had listened. When he recited Housman, she'd savored every syllable. She was intelligent, seeking a medical degree. She didn't ply him with questions, even at his most vulnerable moment.

This was how it could have been.

A tap on the door brought him to his feet.

"George?"

Peggy opened the door and extended a mug of coffee. "Get some rest," she urged. "Save your strength!"

He watched her walk away briskly, flashes of fanny punctuating each stride. A bald-headed man spoke to her and she entwined her arm with his, laughing.

Truman tasted the coffee. *Perfect.* He returned to sit on the bed again.

But for Papa, this was how it could have been.

Should have been.

10

Denise stood in the living room. The house seemed cavernous, sound reverberating from wall to wall. Sandblasting of the exterior had powdered every surface with dust. There were plumbers in the bathrooms, but no water. Electricians had reduced the wiring to exposed spaghetti, yet there were no lights.

"What a place," Jack said. "It's looking good, isn't it, Denise?"

"I'm having trouble visualizing it."

Moving men were delivering their household goods. In Mobile they had been crowded. Here every article seemed smaller, more battered than Denise remembered.

"Child's bedroom number one?" the foreman asked.

"I'm child number one," Elaine said. "I've selected a room. Come with me and I'll show you."

Jeffrey observed, eyes magnified, spectacles smudged. "Are we sleeping here tonight?"

"I don't know, Jeffrey. Stay out of their way."

"What a beauty this is going to be," Jack persisted.

"Look at that crown molding, Denise. You don't find workmanship like that anymore. The marble on the fireplace is going to polish nicely, too."

Brad had gone to Judge Felder Nichols' chambers. He was to be sworn in tomorrow and assume his duties immediately. That left Denise to supervise this chaos.

"Child's bedroom number two?" the foreman inquired.

"I am the secondary consideration in this family," Jeffrey said. "Follow me, please."

The workman chewed a cigar. "Follow the midget," he instructed a helper.

"Master bedroom?" another mover hollered.

"Upstairs, first door to the right," Denise called. Jack followed her into the kitchen, spouting figures relating to capital investment, depreciation, and appreciation.

"The interest comes off your taxes and Uncle Sam is shouldering the burden . . ."

The kitchen Congoleum was slippery; a workman under the sink was replacing a drain.

"We can't stay here in this mess," Denise said. "We'll have to go to a motel."

"Mother is expecting you to stay with her," Jack said. "In a few days everything will settle down and you'll be here."

"It doesn't seem nearly finished to me, Jack."

"But it is. We're on schedule."

She had told Bob she would report to work at the newspaper on Monday. She wouldn't be there in a week!

"Where do you want the telephones?" a serviceman asked.

"Telephones," Denise said numbly. "Master bedroom, the kitchen and den ... the living room, I suppose."

"How about child's bedroom number one?" Elaine suggested.

"No."

"Which automatically precludes child two," Jeffrey remarked.

"Want to show me where in each room?" the telephone man asked.

An electrician presented a gadget for Denise to inspect. "These should be replaced. The whole panel should be replaced. The service ought to be upgraded, and if it were me, I'd go for breakers, not fuses."

Jack steered the man away.

"Mama," Jeffrey said, "there's a dead dog in the swimming pool. He's bloated and his hair has fallen off."

"Oh, gore!" Elaine shrieked.

Lanita's voice rang out from the porch. "Yoo-hoo!"

"We're in the kitchen, Lanita."

She stepped over boxes, around electrical cable being drawn through a wall socket. "What a mess!"

"Everyone seems to have arrived at once."

Lanita spied the telephone man. "Hey," she said, "no phones until next week."

"The work order says today."

"No phones until next week! They don't know how the furniture will be arranged yet. Where's Jack?"

He leaned around the pantry door. "Hey, darlin'."

"What's the end date on the contracts?" Lanita demanded.

"Yesterday, but—"

"Penalties?"

"Lanita, they ran into unexpected—"

"Penalties?" Lanita said.

"We can't threaten them with that, Lanita."

"Can and will," she replied. She collared an electrician. "How soon done, my man?"

"Couple of days."

"Today."

"We can try."

"Today," Lanita said. She marched upstairs for inspection. When she reappeared, she wiggled a beckoning finger at the paint contractor. "How can you paint in all the dust?"

"We're still scraping and sanding, Mrs. Taylor."

"How much longer?"

"God knows."

"No painting until the place is dusted and cleaned. Get a crew over here this weekend and do it. Start painting the interior on Monday. I want it completed by the end of next week."

"If the weather stays dry and—"

"Edward." She smiled, but her eyes were flint. "This takes precedence over the apartment contract. Over everything else. So bring in those crews and get it done."

"Mrs. Taylor . . ." He looked to Jack, then nodded grimly.

"There," Lanita said pleasantly. "Let's get out of here, Denise. Mother Taylor is expecting Elaine and Jeffrey for lunch."

"What's on my agenda this afternoon, darlin'?" Jack asked.

"This house," Lanita said firmly. She smiled at Denise. "How about lunch?"

"Dare we leave?"

Lanita winked at the painter. "Remember, cleanliness is next to payday."

"Yes, ma'am."

"Come on, youngsters, Grandmother is waiting."

*   *   *

Mother Taylor had arranged the food buffet style—
potato salad, condiments, sandwich spreads, and cold
cuts. The bedlam of children subsided as cousins
and siblings withdrew to the wide back porch. The
swing creaked, youngsters shrieked and Mother Taylor sat down at last. Vera ate sliced salami with a
fork, her mood heavy with resentment.

"I told Bob I'd start work Monday," Denise said. "I
don't think I'm going to make it."

"He shouldn't be surprised," Vera said.

"I'm sure he knows it will take a few days to get
settled in," Mother Taylor said. "I believe the ham is
a bit salty, Denise, what do you think?"

Lanita was on the telephone, contacting a company that provided commercial cleaning for offices.

"Denise," Mother Taylor said, "I have a tape recording I want you to hear."

Vera waved a hand impatiently. "Must we, again?"

"I want Bradley to hear it too," Mother Taylor
said. "It's the voice of a man who was calling me
until we changed my telephone number."

"She has played that for everybody under the sun,"
Vera said. "Bob and I have insisted she should put it
out of her mind, but no, she keeps playing the voice
as if a reward were posted for identifying it."

"He quotes poetry," Mother Taylor continued as if
Vera weren't there. "I thought you might find it
interesting, anyway, and I do hope somebody might
recognize the voice."

Lanita returned, began constructing a sandwich.

"Do you mind hearing it, Denise?" Mother Taylor
asked.

"No, of course not."

"Now?" Vera asked. "Must we?"

"When is a better moment than this, Vera?" Mother Taylor set up the machine, plugged it in.

The voice on the tape recorder caught Denise by surprise. It was the same man who had called the morning she and Elaine were going out alone for breakfast.

He recited his poem, ending the call with a hissing, "Bitch!"

It was Mother Taylor's expression which held Denise. She was bent as if to hear better, eyes narrowed, facial muscles drawn. Her tension was almost contagious.

"Have you ever heard that voice, Denise?" Vera asked.

"Yes. He called here one morning after the funeral."

"I knew it!" Mother Taylor said. "I knew it was him."

"So what?" Vera snapped. "Once an obscene caller finds you, he isn't likely to go away. But now the phone number is changed and the matter is ended. Why dwell on it?"

"He sounds educated," Lanita remarked, "and he has a nice voice if you can forget what he's saying."

"It is a nice voice," Mother Taylor said. "He speaks with emotion, too. As if he feels every word."

Vera patted her mouth with a napkin, irritably, then took her paper plate to the kitchen trash receptacle.

"He's quoting A. E. Housman," Denise said. "I had a course in college under a professor who loved the man's work. He thought Housman was the most perfect poet he'd ever encountered."

"Housman?" Lanita lifted her eyebrows. "The man that wrote 'When I was one-and-twenty'?"

"Yes."

"What difference does it make?" Vera asked. "The

creep is obviously disturbed. He's probably quoting poems to some other unlucky listener these days."

"I just can't figure what connection such a man might have to Bo," Mother Taylor said.

"Oh, for God's sake, Mother Taylor." Vera threw her napkin on the table. "Surely you can find better things to occupy your mind. We've listened to the tape, we've listened to the guesswork, and we've milked this thing for all it's worth. But, really! Enough is enough."

"Bo was married before," Mother Taylor said.

"What?"

"Bo had been married when I met him," Mother Taylor said. "I don't know if I ever mentioned it."

"No," Lanita said with amusement, "I don't believe you did."

Mother Taylor massaged her fingers. "It wasn't something Bo would discuss. He once told me the marriage was a bad one and that it ended bitterly. He never heard from the woman again, as far as I know."

Conversation lapsed around the dining-room table. In the backyard the children were playing, their voices audible.

"And this man," Denise said. "You think he's connected to that first marriage somehow?"

"I'm just trying to consider every possibility," Mother Taylor said.

"Were there any children in the first marriage?"

"I don't know," Mother Taylor whispered.

"It would be easy to find out, wouldn't it?" Denise asked.

"I don't know. Who could we ask?"

"Mother Taylor"—Vera spoke as if to a child—"why are you doing this to yourself?"

"His poem refers to 'the knot that makes one flesh

of two,' " Mother Taylor said. "He says, 'When shall I be dead and rid of the wrong my father did?' "

"The creep is a creep!" Vera cried. "They say creepy things!"

"I went through our scrapbooks," Mother Taylor continued, "and all our old address books—there isn't one thing relating to that first marriage, not one thing. I can't remember Bo ever talking about it. He never told me his first wife's name."

"Never mentioned children?" Denise asked.

"Never."

"There probably weren't any," Lanita said. "If there had been, Father Taylor would have faced child support, wouldn't he?"

"Maybe. I don't know. I wish I knew."

Denise and Lanita looked at one another and Lanita lifted her shoulder in silent frustration.

"Suppose the caller *is* a son—how would that affect the execution of Father Taylor's will?" Lanita asked.

"I hadn't thought of that," Mother Taylor said.

"Maybe *that* is why he's calling," Lanita suggested.

"Assuming there is a son at all," Vera said. "I think we have little to do if we speculate on things like this."

"There should be records at the courthouse," Denise said. "Did they get married in Thomas County, Mother Taylor?"

"I don't know, Denise. I don't know any more than I've said. It's been worrying me ever since I thought about it."

"Is this going to be a surprise to Jack and Bob and Bradley?" Lanita asked.

"I expect so."

"Dear me." Lanita sighed.

Denise tried to dispel the gloom. "Well, I'm pretty

good at investigative reporting—I'll see what I can find out."

"Should I tell the boys about this first marriage?" Mother Taylor asked at large.

"I think you should, Mother Taylor," Denise said. "They ought to know because it's a part of Father Taylor's past."

Mother Taylor exhaled tiredly. "I wish Bo had done that."

Brad stood at the bathroom sink, brushing his teeth vigorously. Denise leaned against the doorjamb, arms crossed over her bosom. "Wouldn't it be something if there were another part of the family out there somewhere?"

"Umm."

"Who knows what they have become?" Denise speculated. "They might be rich or famous—as unaware of you as you were of them until tonight."

Brad shifted his reach, cheeks jiggling.

"On the other hand," Denise went on, "they could be a very unpleasant discovery. Especially if it *is* a half-brother calling Mother Taylor with those spooky poems."

"I'm not going to worry about it." Brad dried his face with a towel. "Are you ready for bed?"

"Aren't you curious?" she asked.

"Not really. Do I have a suit over here, Denise?"

"In the closet. Bradley . . ."

He examined the garment, hung it again. "That's not my favorite suit, but all right. Do I have brown shoes?"

"Yes. Bradley, what do you think about me tracking down this other family?"

"Leave it alone, Denise."

"Mother Taylor is obviously worried about it."

"That will pass. How about tan socks?"

"In your suitcase. Listen to me . . ." She preceded him to the luggage. "I can ease Mother Taylor's mind about this man if I learn about the other family. It doesn't mean you have to invite them in for a reunion."

"Denise, if Dad married some woman and divorced her, it's like it never happened. He didn't tell any of us and I suspect there was a reason for it. Leave it alone."

"What about Father Taylor's will?"

"Mother gets everything anyway." Brad reclined on his back, hands clasped behind his head. "It doesn't make any difference."

"When your mother dies, what then?"

"I'm not an attorney, Denise. Are you ready for bed? I have a busy day tomorrow."

She sat beside him, leaned over his body, using one arm as a prop on his far side. "I think it's interesting that this has come up," she said, looking down. "Here's a closet full of old bones, a genuine skeleton, and you are ho-humming it away as if it didn't exist. Seems to me it would be, at the very least, *interesting* to know the whole story."

"Writers do weave fantasies." Brad sighed. "Have you stopped to think how old Dad would have been when he was married to this hypothetical woman? He was a kid! If they had a child, the child would be older than Bob, and Bob is thirty-eight. That means Dad fathered a child when he was a child himself."

"People married young in those days."

He pushed a wisp of hair from her forehead. "The house is a mess. I went by this afternoon."

"It sure is."

"I'm being sworn in tomorrow and then I'm up

to my eyeballs in work that has waited for my appointment."

"I'll worry about the house. Lanita is helping me hurry things along."

He touched the tip of his nose. "You're going to work at the newspaper right away, aren't you?"

"In a week. I talked to Bob tonight."

"So, then, when are you going to have time to chase phantoms?"

She kissed him, drew away with lips pursed, then bent to kiss him again.

"If you get into bed sometime before daylight, I'll play a little game with you," he said.

She crawled over him in the dark and he grabbed her, held her atop himself. "You're losing weight."

"Wait until you see the house payments," Denise said. "You'll lose weight too."

He resisted when she tried to move off.

"When was the last time we did something different?" he asked. "Something wild and awkward?"

"When we were younger and more supple."

He kissed her shoulder, blowing warm breath on her breast. "I'm young," he said. "I'm supple."

"You're flat on your back. What's to bend?"

Denise could hear Elaine gargling in a bathroom across the hall. Downstairs, a clock pealed the Westminster chimes, the four notes of a quarter-hour.

She stroked Brad's chest, hair running between her fingers. Incongruously, she had a mental image of their new master bedroom—placing furniture first here, then there.

"Denise?"

"What?"

"Would you rather wait?"

"What's wrong?"

"If we were wrestling, you'd win the fall—I'm pinned."

She lifted her body and he groaned. "I lied," he said. "You haven't lost an ounce."

11

"This is an awful lot of work for a ten-minute ceremony," Jeffrey complained. "Who invented ties, anyway? They impede the flow of blood to the brain and that affects the ability to think clearly."

"The same person who invented high-heeled shoes," Elaine responded. "Why are you blushing?"

"I'm not blushing," Jeffrey said, "I'm suffocating."

"Knock it off." Brad spoke from the bedroom. "You don't have to go if you don't want to."

"I want to go," Jeffrey said. "I just don't want to walk around hung while I'm there."

"You can take off the tie after the swearing-in," Denise said. She adjusted Jeffrey's coat, looked him over. "Brush your hair."

Elaine sat on the bed, her hands folded in the valley of her skirt between plump legs. "What are the duties of a sheriff?"

"He's the chief executive and administrative officer of the county," Jeffrey said.

"Thank you, Jeffrey." Elaine sneered. "I know so much more than I did."

"He's a process server," Jeffrey elaborated. "He summons the jury. He holds judicial sales when people don't pay taxes. He is in charge of the prisoners at the county jail."

"Daddy?" Elaine asked skeptically.

"He got it right," Brad said. He turned to Denise. "How do I look?"

His trousers were too short. "You look fine." Denise smiled.

"The sheriff is primarily there to serve the court," Jeffrey continued. "He attends to the grand jury, serves subpoenas—the job is quite a responsibility, actually," Jeffrey pressed his point. "Dad had to post a bond. He isn't as fortunate as Granddaddy was in the old days—he's on salary. The fee system was a license to steal."

"Jeffrey," Brad said, "your grandfather was a good lawman and an honest one. Now, knock it off."

"Good and honest has nothing to do with the potential income," Jeffrey said.

"Jeffrey!"

"Yessir." The boy walked out, tugging his collar.

Brad kneaded his hands nervously. "I don't feel as if I look right."

"But you do," Denise said.

"Except for the pants," Elaine noted. "They're too short."

Denise withered the girl with a glare.

"They are too short," Brad said. "Do I have another suit?"

"Elaine"—Denise lowered her voice—"go downstairs and wait for us." To Brad she suggested, "Push your trousers down slightly. See if that helps."

"Judge Nichols has sworn in my father six times," Brad said. "Now me."

"I'm looking forward to meeting him."

"He's crusty. He's a tough judge. Seventy-four years old, he told me. Still sharp, though. Denise, if I shove these down any further, they'll fall off."

"That looks good."

Brad appeared . . . *country*. Denise felt responsible, as if she had tailored the suit herself. She turned before a mirror, wondering if he thought the same of her.

"Do I look like a country girl?"

"If you do, God bless America."

"Do I?" she insisted.

He laughed, kissed her. "I'll be downstairs."

I do, she thought. And now there wasn't time to make amends. Her best clothes were at the new house. Her best shoes . . . *Dammit!* There went the clasp on her bra. She stared at her reflection in dismay.

She remembered one of her mother's favorite adages, "A winning smile is the best accessory any dress ever had."

Dead. And father. All her family, in fact—her brother missing in action in Vietnam, a sister killed in an auto accident. The only family remaining was hers by marriage. Except for Jeffrey and Elaine, of course.

"Mama," Elaine said at the door, "everybody is waiting."

"I'll be down in a minute, Elaine. Close the door."

"Grandmama said I look like a bouquet." Elaine beamed.

"Yes, you do. Shut the door, please."

Quickly she stripped to underclothes and replaced the defective brassiere. Wrong cup size, but all right.

At least she didn't look as if she were transporting stolen melons.

Everyone would be there—commissioners from county and city, representatives of all the courts, family and friends. Denise raked at her hair—frizzy.

"How about it, Denise?" Brad yelled at the bottom of the stairs.

She grabbed her pocketbook and hurried to join the others.

"My goodness," Mother Taylor said bravely, "you look like a bouquet, too."

Judge Felder Nichols described himself to Denise: "Georgia-born, Harvard-educated, a child of the Depression, and a New Deal Democrat."

The judge's guests flowed from den to dining room, through French doors out onto a patio at poolside. Cocktails had worked their magic; laughter and conversation flowed as afternoon gave way to evening. Servants were setting up tables for a buffet.

"I presume you knew Bo Taylor quite well," Denise said to the judge.

"Well, God, I'll say so," he said. "We grew up here. His daddy and my daddy fished the holes we fished in years to come. I miss him."

"Good friends," Denise said.

"Like brothers. I used to accuse Bo of having scars on his ass from smoking on a commode." Judge Nichols laughed heartily, head back. "Throwing away the lighted butts," he explained. He cleared his throat in one fist. "Fact was, though, Bo was plenty smart. Knew people. Knew what made them tick. More important, knew what made himself tick."

"Bradley is like his father," Denise said. She accepted a drink from a tray as a uniformed waiter moved through the crowd.

"He is," Judge Nichols concurred. "But Bo was one of a kind. He weathered some easterly blows in his day."

"Easterly blows?"

"Wind from the east is good for neither man nor beast," Judge Nichols said. "Mariners' saying—east wind is bad for fishing."

"You grew up together?"

"Went to school in the same one-room schoolhouse—grades one through ten and a single teacher. Down at Metcalf. You know Metcalf?"

A village southeast of Thomasville. "Yes," Denise said.

"We plowed many a furrow, milked many a cow, chopped many a stand of tobacco, and picked our share of cotton. I was lucky—got away to college, Harvard at that. In those days you had to earn your way in. Nowadays you can get in if you're a female, black, from poverty-stricken rural Southern parents. Which I personally think is the way it should be—but it wasn't that way when I went there."

"What brought you back to Thomasville?"

His watery eyes gazed past her, head wobbling on neck muscles weakened by time. "I don't know," he said.

The conversation was interrupted by newly arrived guests. The judge greeted them without standing, his cane leaning against a wall by the fireplace. Denise had seen so many politicians, she recognized the subtle shift in tone of voice, the practiced banter—saying little, imparting nothing.

When he returned his attention to Denise, Judge Nichols lowered his wild eyebrows and his voice. "Where were we?"

"Talking about Bo."

He drew a deep breath and exhaled loudly. "Bradley has some big shoes to fill, but he can do it. If he wishes, he can be sheriff here until he dies, just like his pappy."

Denise circled the rim of her glass with a fingertip. "Did you know Bo's first wife?"

She could feel a sudden chill; his guard went up so fast it seemed to alter the man's features.

"I've forgotten her name," Denise lied.

"I don't think you knew," he said.

"Mother Taylor told us, yesterday. She said Bo had been married before—that's all she knew."

He twisted, in search of his cane.

"She has become worried about it," Denise said.

"Fifty years ago—no worry." The judge positioned the cane to give himself leverage.

"Mother Taylor is concerned about the legal ramifications," Denise said. "Other children . . . legal heirs . . . Bo's will."

"No need for concern." Judge Nichols rose to his feet, back bent, a three-legged stand. He looked down on Denise; *coldly*, she thought.

"Some things are best left buried, young lady. All that nonsense is one of them. The buffet is ready—may I escort you?"

In slow, short steps they moved toward the terrace. Denise spoke in a low voice. "We have reason to believe there may be a son, Judge Nichols. We think he may be coming to Thomasville."

He halted. She could feel a tremor in his arm. Then, as if from due consideration, "That won't happen."

"He says he's coming."

He turned to look at her, eyes as hard as coal. "Who says he is coming?"

"We presume it is a son, Judge Nichols. He's been telephoning Mother Taylor—he called Bo the day he died, collect. From somewhere in Kansas, Mother Taylor said. He hasn't been overtly threatening, but he reads or recites poems by A. E. Housman—by innuendo, by the poems, we think he is Bo's son."

The cane quivered, the judge glaring at Denise. "There was a boy," he said. "His name is Truman."

"It isn't idle curiosity which prompts these questions," Denise explained. "I love this family. I want to protect them."

"You feel they are threatened?"

"That's precisely what I want to know."

"Dredging up the past won't serve that purpose, girl."

"Suppose I agree that anything you tell me will be held in strictest confidence," Denise said. "I could tell you what we know and you could help me determine whether the matter should be pursued."

Someone spoke to the judge and instantly it was the politician and public figure who responded. "Get out there and get yourself a drink, boy! Try that ham—former Governor Talmadge sent that down."

Her jerked his head toward a darkly stained door. "Let's go to the den."

She held his arm, inching across the room. Inside, he spoke brusquely. "Shut the door and lock it."

He went to a desk, sat in a high-backed chair, and placed his cane across his lap. "There's some whiskey in the credenza. Pour us a drink."

She did, following instructions—"Two ice cubes." On the walls hung signed photographs of former governors and Presidents Roosevelt, Truman, Eisenhower, and Kennedy. Scrolls and awards, accolades of a lifetime—the kind of place a man creates to bolster his self-image.

The judge held out his glass to admire the liquid and exhaled appreciatively. "Tennessee Walking Horse

Whiskey," he said. "Too expensive to put out to the public. Not that what they're drinking is rotgut."

He sipped again, swallowed, eyes closed. "Some souls come like putty to the cast," he said. "Others come kiln-dried and hardened. A judge has to learn that. We can daydream about remedial psychology and we can swear we're going to construct penitentiaries which rehabilitate the criminal mind—but some souls are born fired and glazed."

He opened his eyes, staring at Denise. "You old enough to know what constitutes a man, young lady?"

"I don't know."

"Nobody does," Judge Nichols said. "Your husband—you know him, do you?"

"I think so."

"The key word is 'think.' You don't know him. He doesn't know you. No goddamned body knows anybody, if the truth be known. I've seen mothers weep at the bench, swearing on the virtue of sons headed for the electric chair. I've heard ministers with their hands on the Good Book testify to the character of a man who has raped and killed in cold blood. The mother knew her son. The minister knew his parishioner."

He held out his glass. "About twice the shot and half the ice this time."

He waited for his drink, peering at the far wall as if absorbed in thought. When Denise sat down again, he swiggled the drink by rotating a wrist.

"Robert Beauregard Taylor was a good man," the judge said.

"Yes, he was."

"He married Annette, and look what their seeds brought in fertile soil—a publisher, a mayor and successful realtor, and Bradley the new sheriff. Not one among them ever got in trouble—except Jack when he was sowing his wild oats, but that was just a phase. He was from good stock and came down on both feet."

"Yes," Denise said.

"Truman. Jesus . . ."

Denise watched his expression flow to pain. "Truman was a mean little bastard even when he was in elementary school. He was about twelve when I last saw him."

"Truman is the son," Denise said.

"Firstborn." Judge Nichols sighed. "Lana was his sister."

Two children.

"Mother's name was Renee," Judge Nichols said. "That was Bo's first wife. She was in her twenties; Bo was a farmboy about sixteen years old with Georgia clay between his toes. Hell, he'd never seen an escalator and couldn't imagine how stairs could be made to move. He was pure—gullible."

"When he married Renee?"

"When he married Renee." Judge Nichols took another swallow, winced, and coughed.

"Renee wasn't a bad woman," he said finally. "She could have made a good wife. Far as I know, she went on to marry again and *did* make a good wife. But the chemistry was wrong. With Annette, Bo was a good father and husband. With Renee—*to* Renee—Bo was the scum of the earth. I don't know why such things happen, but they do. A man is a good lover to one partner and cold as a walrus's tusk to another woman. It just happens."

"What do you know about Truman?" Denise asked.

"Like I say, mean as hell. Cruel. Sly. He had the meanness of a grown man about him. He tried to destroy Bo in this town. Spreading malicious lies, defaming Bo to the teachers at the school. If Bo had been less the man than he was, he would have been driven away by all that."

"What kind of lies, Judge Nichols?"

"That's not important!" He raised his hands and shoulders in concert, yielding. "Lies about Bo within the family. He accused Bo of mistreatment."

"I see."

"Abuse."

Nodding, Denise waited. Judge Nichols sighed again.

"After the divorce, he grew up. He met Annette and married her."

Happily ever after.

"Now, then," Judge Nichols said, "you tell me what has been going on."

Denise recounted the telephone calls, the poems, Mother Taylor's tape recording. Judge Nichols listened, reared back in his chair, his whiskey untouched while Denise spoke. His hard penetrating glare must appear overpowering to a man on trial, Denise thought. Not a muscle moved as he took in her "testimony," unblinking.

"He doesn't know that Bo is dead?" Judge Nichols asked.

"Mother Taylor said she didn't tell him."

"She should have told him."

"She wasn't sure—still isn't sure—it was Truman."

"It was Truman," Judge Nichols said hoarsely.

"I sensed that it might be."

"Truman," he said. "If he's coming here, you can bet it is for no good."

"Then what do you suggest we do, Judge Nichols?"

He sipped his drink now, staring beyond her. Denise saw one finger quiver until he clamped it, holding the glass with both hands. "There's no law says he can't come to Thomasville."

"If he would walk up and identify himself, that would be one thing," Denise said. "But the late-night phone calls and those eerie poems . . ."

Judge Nichols seemed lost in thought.

"I would hate to see any trouble," Denise said. "Mother Taylor doesn't need any more emotional strain."

"It isn't Annette," Judge Nichols said. "Truman isn't after her."

"Would he be 'after' somebody?"

"Might be." Judge Nichols laughed unexpectedly. "Bo, maybe."

"Mother Taylor told him he was in for a surprise."

"Yes," Judge Nichols murmured. "A surprise."

12

They had stayed at Judge Nichol's party until nearly midnight. Now, with Bradley sleeping late upstairs, Denise helped Mother Taylor wash dishes.

"Elaine and Jeffrey would enjoy the Y," Mother Taylor said. "They can walk there from your new house. The facilities are marvelous, I'm told."

"I'll look into it," Denise said.

Whom did Truman favor? A boy Judge Nichols had described as cruel and sly, "with the meanness of a grown man."

Tracing the genetic flow of the Taylor family was easy. Jack was "mama's boy." Short of stature, eyes quick like restless bluebirds—when Jack and his mother were in the same room, comparisons were obvious. Bob was a blend of mother and father—tall, rugged, more of his mother's temperament; he seemed to have taken the strongest attributes of both parents.

It was difficult to believe Mother Taylor had contributed a single gene to Bradley.

"Vera and Bob will want you to join Glen Arven Country Club." Mother Taylor scoured a pot. "They're golfers, but their membership is mostly for business purposes. Does that appeal to you?"

"Not really."

Truman. Would he have Brad's sleepy brown eyes? Would he be as deliberate in gesture, as sparse with words?

"Vera tries to get me in the garden club." Mother Taylor laughed softly. "Ladies dressed for tea and talking about compost . . ."

Denise stood at the kitchen door looking at Jeffrey. Elaine, ever the bored one, had gone to Vera's to visit her cousins. Jeffrey sat on the back-porch swing, reading. He was not a child who required entertaining. *Like his father temperamentally.* When Denise studied the boy she had a strong sense of Bradley as a child. Jeff kept his swing in motion with lazy kicks of one foot, unaware he was being observed.

"Thomasville is a good place to grow up," Mother Taylor said. "Simple pursuits and good influences for children."

Denise heard a bump upstairs. Brad getting dressed.

"When I was a girl," Mother Taylor reminisced, "coming to Thomasville was 'going to the city.' "

"You grew up on a farm?"

"Well, everything here was a farm in those days. I never thought of myself as a farmgirl, although we had livestock. My father was a broker, buying and selling cattle. He did quite well investing in futures— wheat, corn, that kind of thing."

Denise put away a cleaned pot. "Father Taylor grew up in Metcalf. Did you know one another then?"

"Gracious, no. I was a student at Vashti, which was a boarding school for young ladies; then I went to Rollins College in Florida. I met Bo when I came

home in 1945, at a cotillion at the Whitney plantation. Cotillions in those days were a must for every
debutante."

"It sounds like high society."

"Oh, it was! During quail season, the plantation
owners would return to Thomasville with an entou-
rage of friends and business acquaintances—some
famous people, too. Jock Whitney owned the film
rights to Margaret Mitchell's book, *Gone with the Wind*.
He knew Margaret Mitchell and Clark Gable and
Vivien Leigh. When you went to his place, you were
liable to meet actors and actresses, senators and
congressmen—that was where I met Bo."

"Judge Nichols indicated that Father Taylor was a
country boy—naive."

For an instant Mother Taylor seemed hurt. Then,
lifting her head, she smiled. "It was Felder who introduced us. Felder was a fancy young Harvard lawyer.
He'd just been appointed a judge by President Roosevelt. Compared to Felder, I guess Bo was naive."

She dried her hands. "I'll never forget how uncomfortable Bo was, standing there in new shoes
that squeaked. A *very* eligible bachelor, Felder whispered in my ear. Bo couldn't dance. He sat like a
stone unless spoken to, but I saw him as mature and
strong. I think I fell in love with him immediately."

Brad entered, interrupting. " 'Morning."

Mother Taylor turned, and seeing him, put a hand
to her chest.

"You all right?" Brad questioned.

"Yes, I . . . Goodness, Bradley, this is the first time
I ever saw you in uniform. Bo's badge and gun—the
resemblance is . . . you look like your father standing
there."

"Any coffee?"

Mother Taylor fumbled with the percolator and nearly dropped it.

Watching, Brad said, "Want me to do that?"

"I'll get it. Do you want breakfast?"

"Just coffee." He walked to the back door. " 'Morning, Jeff. What are you doing?"

"Reading."

"I see that. What are you reading?"

Jeffrey turned his book to display the title. *"Prisoners of Childhood,* by Alice Miller."

"What kind of book is that?"

"It's one of Grandaddy's. It's about child abuse."

Brad turned to Denise sourly. "I'll be glad when that boy discovers girls."

"Bite your tongue," Mother Taylor warned. "Go sit down and I'll make toast."

"Coffee, Mom. That's all."

Denise went out on the back porch and sat in the swing with Jeffrey. He placed his book against his abdomen, meeting her gaze.

"Do you feel abused?" Denise teased.

"Everybody is abused. That's what the book is about. None of us can escape parental influence."

"Your father would enjoy your company—want some toast?"

"No, thanks."

"Come on in, why don't you?"

"Mama, don't let the book give you a complex."

"I'm not suffering any guilt, Jeffrey—get your little butt in there and visit with the family for a while."

Jeffrey closed his book. "Abuse, abuse," he said.

Denise drove to the Reinecke-Taylor house. The aroma of fresh paint wafted through open doors and windows. Cleaning crews were scrubbing and waxing floors. Lanita came downstairs, her hair bound in a scarf, wearing work gloves.

"It will be next Friday before you can move in," she said.

"Do you have to take part in the labor?" Denise asked. "I feel as if I'm shirking my duties."

"Nonsense. I need to trim these thighs." Lanita pinched herself for emphasis. "Besides, nothing motivates the workmen like a boss setting the pace."

"Would you like me to pitch in?"

"Dressed like that? Go away, Denise. The pacesetter does not need a pacesetter."

"Actually, there are a couple of things I need to do."

"Then go in good conscience."

"Lanita, where does Aunt Marie live?"

"Metcalf. Why?"

"I thought I'd stop by and visit."

Lanita mopped her brow with a sleeve. "Anyone in Metcalf can tell you where to find her. She isn't well, you know. Father Taylor's death really hurt her."

"A good reason to drop in."

"That's more than anybody else has been willing to do. Aunt Marie was never close to anybody but Father Taylor."

Denise surveyed the exterior of the house. "It's looking better."

"We'll be down to final touches by Wednesday."

As Denise got into her car, she leaned through the window. "Did anyone take care of the dead dog in the swimming pool?"

"Yes, Denise. Go away!"

The drive from Tallahassee to Thomasville gave a deceptive impression of working plantations. Stately pines and tended grounds left a passerby with the belief that all had been well since the Civil War.

But going south toward Metcalf, the terrain was a truer legacy of slave days. Denuded of topsoil by the single-crop planting of cotton, ruts and gullies carved ugly scars in the earth. For a century, nature's effort to replenish topsoil had failed. The pines and oaks were scrub, the undergrowth stunted.

Metcalf had been the cotton-gin center, close to the Florida state line. Rusting equipment and abandoned buildings were all that remained of a once bustling little town. Only a few homes remained.

Seeking directions, Denise selected a house with ivy-shaded porches, a trellis of hog wire forming a framework for the vines.

"I'm looking for Marie Taylor."

"Was," the woman behind a screen door said. "She ain't no more."

"What do you mean?"

"Taylor was her name before she married. When it didn't take, folks went back to calling her Taylor like always."

"Can you show me where she lives?"

The spring on the door screeched and a finger pointed. "That way. Second house past the crick."

"Past the creek?"

"That's the one."

It was hotter here than it had been in Thomasville. By the time Denise located the house, she was slick with perspiration. She parked under a monstrous oak tree. The front screen door opened, but nobody emerged.

"Aunt Marie," Denise called. "I'm Brad Taylor's wife, Denise."

"Come in here, child!"

She climbed the steep wooden steps.

"Look at you!" Marie said, an arm outstretched. "Come in here where the horseflies can't get us."

The woman was a first cousin to Bo, a first cousin once removed to his children, but everybody called her "Aunt Marie." Ten years older than Bo, she had once been a heavyset, no-nonsense woman with a barbed tongue.

"Sit yourself down, child. Would you like a glass of iced tea? I just plucked the mint this morning."

"That would be nice."

Backlighted by the brighter kitchen door, Aunt Marie's legs were an X-ray vision in a thin cotton skirt. She threw her weight in a lurching gait, arthritic joints making her moan with every step.

Denise heard her muttering, "Lemme see, lemme see, tea, tea, tea—and sugar." She lifted her voice. "You take sugar, child?"

"Yes, I do."

"Sugar, sugar . . . hmm . . . oh, yes, sugar."

The lid to the sugar bowl chattered as her shaking hands prepared the refreshments.

"You look more and more like Bradley," Aunt Marie said.

"I'm Bradley's wife, Aunt Marie."

"I know that! But you sleep with a moose and you get horns, they say. How is he?"

"Brad is fine. He sends love."

"New sheriff." Aunt Marie extended a teaspoon and the sugar bowl. "Bo was about his age when he became sheriff."

Denise heard an emotional swallow. Tiny leaves of mint made the beverage aromatic. She stirred in sugar, smiling.

Aunt Marie massaged an emaciated leg. "You have what?" she asked. "Two or three children?"

"Elaine and Jeffrey—just two."

"Two's aplenty."

The furniture was of an era even before Marie—an overstuffed couch and chairs, little round tables with fluted legs. The walls were plain except for faded photographs and a postcard hung by a thumbtack. The card read: "RATTLESNAKES—Silver Springs, Florida."

Seeing Denise read it, Marie said, "Bo and I went down there to get a woman prisoner once. We had to wait a day or two, so we went to see the sights."

"You grew up with Bo, didn't you?"

"Right here in this house. My parents got took by the fever, and Bo's mama—God rest her good soul— she took me in. I changed that boy's diapers when they were feed sacks boiled in lye water. That's how we sterilized things in that day. Every Monday, out in the backyard, boiling a caldron of lye water. It could skin you."

"I'll bet it could."

"When they invented Ivory soap, we thought it was a miracle. Soft—and it floated."

"I remember."

"Pshaw! You're not that old."

"We used Ivory, though, when I was a child."

"I still do—got a cake in the kitchen. It has a groove in it, so you can make two bars out of one— that way you could take it to the tub and have a piece for a bucket out by the pump."

They contemplated one another pleasantly.

"Times were hard, though," Marie said. "The good old days weren't so good."

"I don't suppose they were."

"Except for friends. That's what made them good."

Denise added more sugar, stirred the tea.

"I can't imagine the world without Bo." Marie tuned up. "I worked with him thirty-five years."

"I know you did."

"Secretary and number-one pillbox, he called me."

"Pillbox?"

"I knew you weren't so old." Marie laughed. "In World War II, pillboxes were little round concrete fortifications where the Japanese had machine guns. It was the first line of defense. They looked like old-fashioned pillboxes, I reckon."

Marie fingered the fabric of her skirt, fretting with a loose thread.

"Worked with Bo," she said, "until it got to where I couldn't get there. But never a day passed that he didn't send a deputy down to see about me. Or called me."

Marie wiped her nose with her free hand. "We weathered some easterly blows. You old enough to know what that means?"

"Wind from the east, good for neither man nor beast."

"Bad for fishing. I heard Bo say it a hundred times."

As a reporter, Denise had learned to interview diverse people in different ways. For some, isolation was a dam, the need to talk building in a massive reservoir waiting to be released. She responded only enough to encourage conversation, and Marie opened the floodgates of her mind.

". . . his mother said, 'Beauregard, did you feed them chickens?' Nobody but his mother could get away calling Bo 'Beauregard.' She got the name from a rich uncle and we always thought she hung it on Bo hoping there'd be mention of it in a will. Never was, though."

Twice she went to a family Bible to remember a name. Twice she said, "I never thought I'd forget that name."

In the peculiar and endearing way of the aging mind, Marie could recall a moment as if viewing it afresh: the whir of a "button buzz saw" spun on a string, snatching hair from the head of a young girl. She rocked gently to and fro, rambling over eight decades, bouncing from one period to another in her recollections.

"Bo had to give the heifer a pill . . ."

Marie held her bony knees, tilting back, feet lifting from the floor.

"Put the hose down the cow's throat and put the pill in the hose and blow it past her tongue . . ."

She described Bo's father, a rugged, harsh disciplinarian with a domineering wife, Bo's mother.

"The heifer coughed . . ."

Marie clapped her hands like a child, laughing. "Bo swallowed that pill in the wink of a gnat's eye!"

Shadows grew long through the windows. Denise would have to leave soon. She listened to tales one upon the other; memories bittersweet, the dearer to recall, the more painful to recount.

"I had to lead the mule because he was blind. Bo held the plow . . ."

Marie wept . . . laughed . . . looked away sadly for prolonged moments of silence.

"Did you know Renee?" Denise asked.

"Much to my sorrow."

"What kind of woman was she?"

"Renee was no good—never was. She married Bo for somebody to look after her. Her and the children."

"Bo's children?" Denise asked.

"Renee claimed they were. I never thought so. There was none of Bo in Truman. Lana was the biggest flirt ever put on a skirt by the time she was nine—she took after her mama, that girl. Truman—what a foul boy he was."

"How long were they married, Aunt Marie?"

"Thirteen years. It was like thirteen years in prison, Bo said. Renee was twenty-two when Bo was turning sixteen. Claimed she was pregnant. It was the only honorable thing he could do, Bo said."

"So he married her."

"She claimed she had a miscarriage. Then she came up sure enough pregnant a month or so later. She ran around every night, leaving Bo to feed and bathe those youngsters. He was scarce more than a boy himself."

Marie glared at Denise. "I'm telling things Annette never knew."

"I won't repeat it."

"Makes no never-mind to me if you do. Except for Bo's sake. He made a mistake and paid with thirteen years married to that woman. He was just a big old lovable fellow who had tried to do what was right. If either one of those children were out of Bo, I couldn't see it."

"What can you tell me about Truman?"

"In the sheriff's office, you see little boys like that. Conniving—street-wise—they look you in the eye and lie through their teeth, begging for a second chance."

"Is that the way you view Truman?"

"That's the way he was! You couldn't believe a thing he said—vicious lies, some of them. One thing Bo detested was a liar."

"Can you give me an example?"

"If Truman claimed it was raining, you had to look to be sure. He lied about everything. He once accused a teacher of stealing from a grocery store. Another time he said the same teacher was having an affair. Lies aimed to hurt folks."

"Was Lana the same way?"

"About lying, I don't recollect. But she was fast. In

those days people thought such things were beyond a child. They know better now."

"What kind of lies did he tell about Bo?"

"Tongue-of-satan lies. When Bo found out, I thought he'd kill that boy. He beat him so bad it scared Bo about himself. Not long after that, Renee took the children and left. Thomasville drove them off, and good riddance. They knew better than show their faces again."

"Where did they go?"

"Never cared to know."

Aunt Marie rubbed her legs with both hands, trapped in thought. "Bo nearly lost his job as deputy over all that. Hadn't been for Felder, he would've lost it. He worked as deputy twelve hours a day and went home to that pigsty house to cook and wash clothes. Then that terrible little boy tried to destroy him."

Denise stood up. "I've enjoyed our visit, Aunt Marie. The tea was superb."

"It's the mint that does it."

Denise walked onto the front porch. Marie halted inside the door, latching the screen. "I'm mighty proud of Bradley," Marie said. "If you want to see Bo Taylor, look at Bradley. Two of a kind and just alike."

"Yes," Denise said. "I guess they are."

13

Cumulus clouds gathered at sea; lightning leapt from one dark column to another, too far distant to produce thunder.

"We can use the rain," Peggy said.

Truman sat in a lawn chair, his expression concealed by dark glasses. Bees hovered under a date palm, seeking juice from ripe fruit.

"What's on your mind, George?" Peggy asked Truman.

"Business."

"You haven't told me the business you're in."

"At the moment, sales."

"Selling what?"

"Dollar bills and goodwill."

"Really—selling what?"

"At the moment, serendipity."

"Not going to tell me," she said amiably. She lay on her back, her body glistening from tanning lotion.

"My uncle would hire you to do maintenance, if you're interested."

"I think not. But thanks."

He watched her abdomen rise and fall with easy breathing. A pale hairline ran from the top of her skimpy bikini to her navel.

"Will you be gone long, George?"

"A while."

"What about your car?" she asked.

"I told the mechanic it's his now."

A faint rumble of thunder rode a freshening breeze. On the beach, bathers began to gather their belongings.

"How will you get where you're going?" she asked.

"By bus, I suppose."

"Do you mind telling me where you're headed?"

"South Georgia."

An insect sampled her toe and she wiggled it away. She had shapely feet, high arches. "I'll buy a car when I get there," Truman said.

She took a deep breath, eyes closed. "I don't want you to go, George."

"Come with me."

"July Fourth is a busy time at the motel."

"You could drive me over in your car," Truman suggested. "Drop me off and come back."

She had accepted him on his terms this past week. His evasions were met with aplomb. She never persisted, never insisted. He hated to give up what he'd enjoyed here.

"Where does a motel clerk go for vacation?" Truman asked.

"Not to the beach," she said.

"Georgia is not the beach. Would your uncle object?"

"Not if I can be back by the Fourth."

"Do as you wish," he said. "I'd like you to go. I would enjoy relaxing—your uncle makes that difficult."

She laughed softly. "He's a pretty understanding fellow."

The heavens grumbled, the sea became choppy. Truman had planned this moment—he needed her. To avoid the discomfort of a bus trip, to make inquiries when he arrived there—and she was good in bed.

"Okay." Peggy turned, raised her sunglasses to look at him. "I'll do it."

"Good. That settles that."

Rain fell in torrents, blown in lateral patterns; palms flung like dwarfs with plaited hair.

"Wouldn't it be wiser to wait for the weather to clear?" her uncle worried.

"We'll drive out from under it, Uncle Zachary."

"This mess could ruin the Fourth," he said. "Even if the sun shines here, people inland will stay home if it storms." He turned to Truman. "You know, the worst days for travel are New Year's, Memorial Day, Labor Day, and the Fourth of July."

"We'll be careful."

Uncle Zachary stroked his bald pate, brow furrowed. "Well, let's eat breakfast. Sit down, George."

Awkwardly they ate in silence.

"When you leave me," her uncle said to Peggy, "I suffer some old pains—you can understand that."

She smiled tightly. "Of course I can."

"Donna went out for a loaf of bread, no more than ten blocks," he said. "Who would have thought anything could happen in ten blocks?"

"Accident?" Truman asked.

"She walked into a grocery store where she'd been a thousand times," he said. "A hoodlum, a worthless hoodlum, was robbing the place."

The egg in Truman's mouth congealed to rubber. He stared at his plate, chewing.

"Murdered the young clerk, just a boy in high school, then shot my Donna."

"Uncle Zachary—"

"For sixty dollars," the uncle whispered. "I'd have given all I possessed and ever hoped to have to keep my Donna."

"Now, Uncle Zachary . . ."

"My life ended that morning," he said hoarsely. "Then Peggy's parents were in an accident, and here God sent this child to me. Folks thought I was crazy to take a baby. God knew I needed her."

Uncle Zachary and Peggy held hands, eyes moist.

"Take care of my girl, George," he said.

"Yes, I will."

Through the windshield, blue with an oily film, they watched vehicles ahead of them churn plumes of water from wet pavement. Peggy sat next to Truman, her arm linked in his.

"Did they catch the man who shot your aunt?"

"No."

"Curious how fate decrees," Truman murmured.

"I don't even remember Aunt Donna. That was twenty years ago."

Twenty years.

He was in Vietnam twenty years ago. It was raining. Litter floated from sewage ditches; rats swam amid the debris. Old men pushed bicycles, their baggy trousers pinned above knobby knees. Prostitutes promised warm drinks and welcome relief.

"It doesn't matter that they didn't catch him." Peggy interrupted his thoughts. "He'll pay when his time comes. It will be a punishment equal to the crime."

"In hell." Truman caught sarcasm in his own voice. If the thought gave her comfort, why destroy it?

"I guess you're right," he amended. "God will get him."

"I see you don't believe that." Peggy hugged his arm. "But I do. I think a man determines the extent of his own retribution. What we do to others comes back to us. In this life or the next one—sooner or later we reap what we sow."

"Does that mean your Aunt Donna deserved being shot? How can that thought be comforting?"

"I didn't say it was a comforting thought."

He straightened his back. "If I had to pay an eye for an eye," he said, "I'd be in trouble."

They drove around Mobile, into a tunnel, and as if into a new world. The sky cleared, the sun shone.

"Let's take the coastal highway through Pensacola and Panama City," Peggy suggested. "Maybe we can spend the night in a sleepy little fishing village and eat oysters on the half-shell."

"It's the wrong time of year for oysters."

"Scallops then," she said.

He quelled irritation, following the interstate for speed.

"We're in no hurry, are we?" Peggy asked.

"Except to get you home by the Fourth."

He'd been thinking about a day from his childhood, a rare happy moment at a miserable time in his life. It had happened at a place south of Tallahassee, a town called Panacea.

They had gone to a state park, pitched a tent, built a campfire. Mama and Lana waded in the shallows, poking horseshoe crabs, which scurried away in clouds of silt. He and Papa had unloaded the boat, rowing out to catch their supper. Mullet leapt and others followed, ripples interlocking on waters otherwise placid.

They had seen a school of porpoises, first lolling carelessly, then cavorting in awesome jumps. Papa laughed. So rare was the occurrence, the sound of it was still vivid in Truman's memory.

"George, I'm getting hungry. How about you?"

He drove another mile before answering. "There's a place in Panacea. The food is excellent. I'd like to eat dinner there."

Peggy consulted a map. "That's a long way to go, George."

He picked up speed, watching for state policemen.

"Why don't we stop and let me go to the potty," Peggy suggested. "I'll get some crackers and a cold drink. That will hold us until dinner."

He used the opportunity to buy gasoline. Irritated, he watched Peggy wander the aisles of the convenience store trying to make her selections.

He wasn't sure he could relocate that scene from forty-six years ago. His impression of it was that of a boy—things would not be so far distant as he recalled them, nor as large as his child's eye saw them.

"A picnic!" Peggy jumped into the front seat, a paper sack between them. "You want chocolate milk or Pepsi?"

"Either one."

"I got both so you could have a choice."

He pulled into traffic, picking up speed.

"George, which is your preference?"

"I said, I don't give a damn."

When they reached Panacea, the western horizon was a bloody glow behind moss-draped cypress trees. Ospreys wheeled, soaring toward their nests. Sandpipers raced beside waters as motionless as they were forty-six years ago.

"Alligator Point," Peggy mused. "What an interesting name for a place. Do you suppose we'll see any alligators?"

Pelicans skimmed so low their mirrored images appeared to be flying beneath them, bottom-side-up. Muskrats rustled in the sea oats.

Was this the place?

He hesitated at a fork in the road. There had been no paving back then. He turned right, barely moving, following some instinctive pull.

"George, are you all right?"

"Yes."

"You don't look all right." She slipped nearer, holding his arm protectively. Truman felt light-headed, swallowing saliva that seemed to gush as if a warning of nausea to come.

"I spent a happy day here once," he said.

"One happy day can be a lot."

"One day," he said.

But he couldn't be sure. The parking areas had not existed, the trash receptacles weren't here. Aimlessly he wandered through the park, then back to Panacea.

They ate dinner in a restaurant overlooking the Ochlockonee River. The motel had no vacancy and it was getting late.

"How far to anywhere from here?" Peggy asked peevishly.

"Tallahassee. About twenty-two miles."

A man flirted with her and Peggy responded with a grin.

It didn't matter. Truman ate food because his body required fuel. He had no taste for it. *Exhausted.* Physically, from driving all day; emotionally, because of his stupid hope of finding a lonely camping area where he'd been happy for a day.

"I need a shower," Peggy said. "When you're ready, let's go, George."

Passing the flirt's table, she traded smiles with the man, preceding Truman to the door. Her goddamned shorts were too short for public decency.

Driving to Tallahassee, neither of them said a word.

They stayed the night in an economy motel. A vibrator connected to the bed delivered ten minutes of muscular relief for a quarter. Somewhere past seventy-five cents, Truman dropped off to sleep.

When he awoke, Truman heard Peggy singing softly to herself, nude before a mirror, brushing her hair. Sunshine burned the edges of the closed curtains.

Today was the day.

He'd been through Thomasville four times as an adult, the last time fifteen years ago. He'd spent the night there, trying to gain the courage to look up Papa. But he hadn't. After a tormented evening in a small motor court, he'd arisen before dawn, stealing away like a cowardly pup.

This time would be different. This time he would be master.

"Good morning!" Peggy bounded onto the bed, kissed him. "How about some breakfast? There's a restaurant up the street."

He dressed without bathing. Peggy prattled like a child. "I nearly came to Tallahassee to go to college," she said. "Florida State has a student circus and I fancied myself flying from trapeze to net."

In thirty minutes he could be across the Georgia line and into Thomasville. His chest hurt. Tension.

"Did you ever want to join a circus, George?"

"Yes."

"What did you want to be—a clown, or what?"

"A star."

After breakfast they drove north. Nothing was as it had been. The trees seemed to have less moss. The plantations were giving way to housing developments. Lake Iamonia was the site of a television tower, relaying microwave transmissions where once frogs and snakes had reigned.

Crossing the Georgia line, Peggy said, "Make a wish, George. I always make a wish when I cross a state line."

Wish? *That he's there. Terrified. Waiting.*

Pecan groves had been fenced as yards. Horses grazed among Black Angus and whiteface Herefords— people playing rancher, a hobby rather than dead-earnest necessity.

From this plantation they had bought dairy products. From that one he'd stolen melons one day, pedaling his Western Flyer bicycle as if the devil himself were in hot pursuit.

The railroad depot. The restaurant was closed. The benches were empty. Truman had a powerful olfactory memory of coal smoke puffing, steam spewing. He had been enthralled by strangers who came from romantic faraway places, their luggage carried by black men wearing red caps. He would sit on their back porch watching the engines idle, waiting for the moment when the wheels would spin, sparks flying, the chug-a-chug-chug quickening his young heart. *Deserted now.*

"What are we doing?" Peggy asked.

He'd been sitting here ... how long? Truman passed through the lot, circled the building, turning past a wholesale grocer's warehouse.

The icehouse.

The bays were boarded, docks rotting. Two floors high; he had once known every inch of the place. The house they lived in lay in the evening shadow of the structure. He had worked there as a boy. His wages were penny tips and tiny chips of crystal-clear ice, a treat on hot summer days.

An old delivery truck with flat tires was backed to a loading platform as if still waiting for the three-hundred-pound blocks of ice to slide out of the building. They had insulated their cargo with burlap sacks, going forth to cool the wares of merchants and homes in a day before electric refrigerators were common.

"Brick streets," Peggy marveled. "Isn't that quaint!"

The courthouse. Truman rounded the square. Two cars marked "SHERIFF" were at the curb. The old post office was now the library. The new post office was a block away. Things had changed, and yet everything was the same.

The atmosphere seemed leaden. He had to suck for oxygen, chest hurting.

"George, are you ill?"

"No."

"It could be the heat. Do you want a cold drink?"

"No."

He couldn't take any more. He turned south, crossed the railroad tracks, picking up speed. The people seemed odd, like mechanical toys wound too tightly or footage from a silent film.

"Are you going back to Tallahassee?" Peggy recognized the return route.

"No."

"Hey, don't let me keep you from what you have to do."

"No," he said. "I won't."

He turned toward Metcalf.

"George, you're driving too fast."

He had to force his foot to lift. His leg shook, his mouth was dry, throat searing.

"Thank you," Peggy said.

In fifteen minutes he was there, crossing a creek and into an area that was as it had been and might be forever.

He remembered the oak tree. Suspended on a thick sisal rope there had been an old tire, which they used as a swing.

Truman circled back, creeping past the same house.

"What're we looking for?" Peggy asked.

"I once knew somebody who lived here."

"Why don't you stop?"

He turned around, going by again. Flowers with tiny red petals grew in pots upon the porch banister. The screen door was a dark rectangular eye, watching them.

"George, why don't you stop and ask if they're still here?"

"I wouldn't know what to say."

"I'll do it, if you want."

He turned, approaching the house.

"Want me to go up and ask?" Peggy asked.

The inquiry would find its way to Papa. Mystified, the caller would say, "Mississippi car tags . . ." But Papa would know who.

Yes. It was a good ploy.

He pulled in the yard, beneath the oak tree. The screen door opened, but nobody came out.

It suddenly occurred to him: *Papa could be here!* He would have fled, but Peggy was out of the car now, leaning to speak through the window.

"Who do I ask for, George?"

"Ask if they know where to find Bo Taylor."

"Bo Taylor," Peggy repeated. She walked toward the open screen door. When she reached the top step, she halted, talking, her voice too low to be heard. Truman's heart was slamming his ribs like a hammer.

Peggy waved a hand, descended the steps. She was practically skipping, returning.

The moment she was in, Truman threw the car into reverse, the tires spinning, dust rising around them.

"Well?" he demanded.

"George, I hope he isn't a good friend . . ."

"What?"

"He's dead, George. The lady said he died a few weeks ago."

"It's a lie!" he cried. "It's a goddamned lie!"

14

For several miles he drove at an alarming speed. Then, recklessly, George turned into a dirt lane and stopped. He sat at the wheel, staring straight ahead. "Who told you he's dead?"

"The woman in the house, George."

"How old a woman?"

"Seventy. Eighty, maybe."

"Aunt Marie," he snarled.

Peggy touched his arm. "George, I'm really sorry about your friend."

"Friend, shit."

He glared at her, dark eyes intense. "What did she say, exactly—word for word?"

"Well, I asked her if she knew Bo Taylor. She said yes. I asked if she knew where I could find him and she said, 'Who are you?' "

"What'd you say?"

Peggy shrugged her shoulders. "I said, 'I'm Peggy Ellis.' "

"Son of a bitch."

Peggy moved toward him, smiling. "George, what is it?"

"What else did she say—word for word?"

"She asked me who you are."

"And?"

"I said, 'George Killdeer'—was that all right?"

"What else?"

"Then she said he died. She said he died a few weeks ago."

"Why would she say that?"

"Why? Well, George, if he's dead—"

"No, goddammit, he is *not* dead. Now, why would she say that?"

Helplessly Peggy lifted the palms of her hands.

"Wait a minute!" His voice rose. "Wait a god-damned minute! Now, that was stupid of me." He laughed mirthlessly. "He's thinking like he thinks I'm thinking. Of course—where would I go first? To Aunt Marie."

"She's your aunt?"

"That's it!" He yanked the car into gear, shoved the accelerator. They catapulted into motion. "Okay," he crooned. "The son of a bitch told Aunt Marie to lie—pretty smart, he thought. Well, it isn't smart. Only an idiot would accept that at face value."

"George, we're going very fast! Would you slow down, please?"

But he didn't. The car rose to the top of a hill and Peggy's stomach floated as they descended the other side. He slapped the steering wheel with the flat of a hand, laughing.

"So now we begin," he said.

She sat with her back pushed into the seat, legs ramrod straight. "George, please slow down!"

He topped the next hill, and with a giddy sensation, Peggy's insides rose. But he eased his foot on the gas pedal and the speedometer fell from ninety to eighty to seventy . . .

"You have to forgive me, Peggy." He grinned at her. "For years I've been waiting for this day. I must seem like a maniac to you."

"No."

He reached over and shook her leg playfully. "Look, let's go back to Tallahassee, find a nice motel, and have a good meal and a few drinks. What do you say?"

"Sounds good to me."

"Yeah." He beat a tattoo on the steering wheel now. "I'll have to explain all this to you. I hope you can bear with my tawdry tales of woe."

"Sure."

He turned on the headlights, driving toward a dusky horizon. Peggy shivered with tension, surprised at the depth and tenacity of it. *What am I doing here? What did she know of this man?*

But he was humming now, turning to smile, reaching over to pat her leg reassuringly. "If you could have anything you wanted to eat," he asked, "what would it be?"

"I don't know—what appeals to you?"

"You decide."

They hurtled through the tunnel of overhanging branches and shrouds of Spanish moss on either side of the Tallahassee road. The headlights caught the leap of a deer and George said, "Did you see him?"

"Yes, beautiful."

He was humming, keeping cadence with a hand tapping the wheel. His mood of a few minutes ago had completely vanished—yet the glimpse of it gave her pause.

From where? Selling what? He'd paid for his lodging at Uncle Zachary's motel with cash—prepaid, actually.

The night air through the open windows brought the scent of virgin woodlands and damp humus. Traffic was sparse. *Florida line.*

"Make a wish!" George laughed.

That all is well, Peggy thought.

She had assumed he was married. Most men his age were, or had been, and reticence was surest proof of it. He might have a son or daughter older than she was and feared admitting it. Male ego—but she hadn't cared. Nor did she now. She'd made all the advances, hadn't she?

The thought was reassuring. He hadn't come on to *her.* She'd been manipulating him.

In fact, his stolid refusal to discuss himself was precisely the reaction she preferred. There would be no serious sticky attachment. It would be a summer fling and be done. He would return to his life and it would be over.

She'd grown so weary of immature, uneducated, and insensitive men. Boys, really. They assumed she was on the pill, taking from her but seldom giving—with the staying power of a rubber band over an open flame.

"You didn't answer me," George said pleasantly.

"About what?"

"What do you want to eat?"

"How about steak?"

"Umm. Okay."

"Would you prefer something else?"

"Steak is all right."

"It's difficult to decide when you aren't hungry," Peggy said. "Tonight is your night—you pick the fare."

"Fare" was a cue for a homophonic response: "'When first my way to fair I took/ Few pence in

purse had I,/ And long I used to stand and look/ At
things I could not buy.' "

Housman again. Peggy listened to the sonorous delivery, the second stanza so true to life: " 'Now times
are altered: if I care/ To buy a thing, I can;/ The
pence are here and here's the fair,/ But where's the
lost young man?' "

She heard him sigh. A subtle shift in humor.

"That says it all," he said softly.

She'd heard dozens of poems since she met him.
He must have memorized everything A. E. Housman ever wrote. But it was *A Shropshire Lad* which
seemed to affect him most. Quoting the lines, George
was not himself—more a reincarnation of the poet
than a reciter of the works. His voice took on a slight
British accent, the names of places rolled from his
tongue in musical tones—Thames, Ludlow, Severn,
and Shrewsbury—as if the sites were home turf.

The first night they went out together, to eat pizza
and dance, he'd spoken of "Alfred Edward Housman" as though the Englishman were a close friend.

"Elegiac pessimism in simple form," George had
described the man's work. "He loathed paleographi-
cal probability!"

She hadn't understood it, but the mastery of language was a joy, the melody of his observations cap-
tivating to the ear.

George had sat, his beer mug between his hands,
proving point after point with line upon line from
Houseman. " '. . . malt does more than Milton can
. . . To justify God's ways to man . . .' "

He described Housman's personal ordeals and sexual preferences as if defending a friend. Then, with
a final accolade, summed up the man he so admired:
" 'His poems are as romantic as ballads and as classi-
cal as the Greek anthology.' That's what *Encyclopaedia*

Britannica says of him. Less than a hundred poems and his mark was made forever."

She knew when George was born by an allusion he made to Housman's death. "He died six years to the day after the date of my birth," George reported. "April 30, 1936."

Then, sitting there coddling his beer, tears had rolled down George's cheeks. He made no effort to apologize, mourning for a man he never knew.

They entered Tallahassee mute, each immersed in thought, and without further discussion, George selected a Mexican restaurant.

"You love jalapeños," he reminded Peggy. "Here's a chance to sate yourself."

They sat in a far booth, shielded from other customers, the flicker of a candle giving his eyes the elliptical glint of a cat.

"I was a ward of the state," George said softly. "The woman I call Aunt Marie was my foster parent— she and her brother, Bo Taylor. He was a deputy sheriff. Foster homes are paid a certain amount a month. I don't know how much—not much. To make a profit, the trick is to feed cheap and cut corners."

Peggy took his hand and held it.

"He sodomized me."

"Dear God . . . who?"

"Bo Taylor. He was huge. Hairy. The bastard nearly killed me."

"Jesus, George . . . how old were you?"

"Six. Seven. He said if I told anybody, they would have to operate on me—he said they would sew up my anus."

"Oh, George . . ." She gripped his hand.

"And Aunt Marie," he rasped. "She woke us at daybreak—me and my sister, Lana. She had a garden. She said tomatoes weren't good unless picked with the dew on them. She made us gather okra—I can still remember the way my arms stung."

George shook his head, eyes sleepy, his voice a monotone. "She was a lesbian, I guess. She hated Lana. Aunt Marie beat that girl unmercifully. She made her wash dishes, scrub floors, until Lana's knees would be bleeding—she had to do it naked, so she wouldn't soil her clothes, Aunt Marie said. I can remember Lana crying, the sound of those brush bristles hitting that wood, the lye searing her skinny little legs. . . ."

"George, did anyone ever report them for this?"

"We were children. We were at their mercy. Oh, there was an investigation after Lana died—"

"Died?" Peggy recoiled.

"I guess Bo got tired of me and took Lana."

"Oh, my *God*!"

"Aunt Marie helped him. She said it was Lana's due. She'd send Lana into the bedroom with him—I would lie there rigid with fear, utterly helpless."

"I can't stand this." Peggy turned aside.

"I swore I'd punish them."

"I'm sure you did!"

"Bo Taylor was a powerful man—he became sheriff. You know those horror stories about law officers in the rural South—arresting people, sexually molesting the women. People actually disappeared from those jails—and God help black people who came afoul of the law."

"But you tried to take action?"

"Oh, I tried. Yeah, I tried. I sat behind bars with Bo Taylor looking in on me. He said, 'Okay, keep on now and see what happens.' He and one of his ghouls worked me over. I had to crawl to my car to leave town. They broke two ribs—you saw those scars on my back and legs?"

"The shrapnel wounds?"

"I lied—Bo did that. He beat me within an inch of my life, using a bicycle chain."

"He's still there? Still sheriff?"

"Still there, still sheriff."

"Did you go to the state's attorney?"

"Peggy, I tried everything. But you have to remember, it was my word against theirs. Forty-three years have passed—the statute of limitations expired long ago. I've devoted a lot of my life to this. I've been obsessed by it."

"What did you intend to do this time, George?"

"I was going to kill them."

"Oh, George . . . my God, George, that isn't the answer."

"What is, then?"

"I don't know. But to destroy your life—forget it."

"I wish I could. Sometimes months go by and I don't dream about it. Then I dream I hear Lana— that piteous voice, like I remember it when she was in the next room with Bo Taylor—calling my name, pleading for help."

Peggy covered her eyes with a trembling hand. "Well," she said finally, "I'm glad you didn't kill anybody."

"If I thought like you," he said, "I might go on, get married, settle down, raise a family. But I can't believe God is going to do what the legal system hasn't done. They've gotten away with murder, Peggy—they killed my sister!"

"And scarred you physically and emotionally."

"I can tell when the barometer falls." He smiled cynically. "My legs begin to hurt. When I was in the Army, they took X rays and found hairline fractures dating from childhood."

"George, I know it's impossible to forget, but try—

let's go back to Mississippi and think this through. I have a friend who is a criminal lawyer. We'll talk to him. Maybe even that isn't the way to go—maybe public disclosure would do more damage to these people than actual prosecution."

"Nobody would believe it."

"You tell the world, just as you told me—they'll see the sincerity in your face, George. Accusations of this nature have a lingering effect. Their lives will be blighted."

"No, Peggy. I've thought about it. I want to do something that's ludicrous."

"What?"

"You'll laugh ... but I swear, I believe I could purge my soul if I did it."

"What?"

"I want to rape Aunt Marie. I want to beat Bo Taylor with a switch, as if he were a child. That's all."

"No rape, George. You mustn't do that."

"Okay, maybe I should whip the both of them."

They ordered two more margaritas and George licked salt from the rim of his glass before every sip. As if revealing his past in layers, he droned on dispassionately—tied to a bedstead for days, forced to drink vinegar when he wept for water. Almost without rancor, he told Peggy incidents of abuse more psychological than physical, giving credence to the story with wry wit.

"The law was on their side, don't you see? By law, a minor cannot run away. He must attend school. Finally Lana and I decided we'd risk reform school— anything had to be better than the situation we were in. So we gathered our belongings—Lana took a wooden doll that our father gave her before he died ..."

"What happened to your parents?"

"My father—you aren't going to believe this."

"Tell me."

"He got drunk and Bo Taylor arrested him. They threw my dad in jail, where he passed out. Sometime during the night he vomited, choked—they found him dead the next morning."

"The same man, George?"

"Mama died in Warm Springs—you know, where President Roosevelt went?"

"No."

"That dates me," he said. "It's a place where President Roosevelt went because he suffered from polio. Warm baths, massages—the treatment was mostly passive, but it eased the pain, I guess. Mama was confined to an iron lung. They had auxiliary power, but something went wrong—she suffocated during a thunderstorm when the lines went down."

He smiled at her and shrugged. "Sounds like a soap opera, doesn't it?"

"It . . . it is astounding, George."

"They said she clawed the inside of the iron lung so desperately it shredded the bedding and marked the stainless steel."

"George?" Peggy cocked her head skeptically.

He laughed uproariously. "Mama shot herself," he said. "After my father died, she couldn't cope. When Bo Taylor told the court he felt a responsibility for Lana and me, they made Aunt Marie a foster parent."

"Is all this true, George?"

He raised one hand solemnly, sipping his drink. He exhaled. "I so vow," he said.

A moment later, George sighed, frowning. "You know, Peggy, I don't know how much of my story is true anymore."

"How can that be so?"

"A child's perception is . . . a child's perception. I can't honestly say that every mishap was intentional abuse. There are parents who sincerely believe that the rod saves the child."

"We aren't discussing corporal punishment, George. Sexual molestation of children—that is not a disciplinarian act."

"No," he said darkly. "No, it isn't."

When they left the restaurant, George passed motels, taking the highway north toward Thomasville again.

"Where are we going?" Peggy questioned.

"To get this over, Peggy. Tomorrow you'll have to go home. I'm going back to Aunt Marie's."

"For what? It's almost midnight."

"She woke *me* plenty of nights."

"George, what are you planning to do?"

"I'm going to find out where Bo Taylor is."

"No violence—"

"No, no, I wouldn't do that to you, Peggy. But I'm going to find out where he is. You can stay in the car."

"I don't think so, George. I'd better go in with you."

He turned off the main highway, approaching Metcalf from a different direction. Frightened, Peggy debated alternatives: get out, stay away from this, call the police—but the sheriff was the crux of the problem!

The town was poorly lighted.

"Now, listen to me, Peggy," he said. "I'm going to act mean to her—I won't actually hurt the bitch, but she'll think I'm going to."

"What if she has a gun, George?"

"I don't intend to knock on the door and announce my presence." He turned off the headlights and put the car in neutral, coasting toward the house. The wheels crunched debris, rolling to a stop beneath the large oak tree.

"I'm going in the back way," George said. "When you see lights come on, you'll know I'm in there."

"I'm going with you."

"No." He grabbed her wrist firmly. "Stay here until you see the lights. Then you can come inside."

She peered into the shadows. Crickets chirped, the howl of a dog came from afar. George shut the car door, pushed gently, and it latched.

"Wait until you see the lights," he said.

She couldn't believe this was happening! Sitting here, waiting as he forced entry.

There . . . lights!

Peggy jumped out, ran to the porch. She looked through the glass of the front door. The light was in the kitchen. She saw the old woman in her night-gown, George talking, his stance threatening.

Peggy ran down the steps, rounding the house. A neighbor's dog barked as if unsure of himself. The rear door was open.

"Where is he, God damn you?"

The woman's rejoinder was so calm, the scene seemed unreal. "He's dead, Truman."

"You're lying."

"That's your specialty."

He shoved her backward and she stumbled, grabbing the wall for support. Quickly she wheeled to face him again, frail legs spread for stability.

"If he's dead," George demanded, "where is he buried?"

"Laurel Hill Cemetery in Thomasville."

"You're lying to me, you bitch. I ought to knock your head off."

The old woman lifted a fist and shook it at him. "Come on, try, you gorilla."

He swatted her hand aside, advancing.

"George, take it easy," Peggy said.

He took another step and the old woman faltered, backing away. She turned jerkily, as if to run, and George grabbed her from behind.

She screamed and he yanked her to him, his arm around her neck.

"George, please, be careful—she's old!"

She kicked at his legs and he lifted her bodily, arms flailing.

"One last time," George warned. "Where is he?"

"Dead!"

Peggy moved toward them to calm George. He lifted the woman higher. Then, with a precision that was stunning, he jerked her head one way as his arm clamped the neck in an opposite direction. A sickly crack and the old woman's fingers extended, quivering, her legs going limp.

Peggy gasped, stumbling backward. George held the woman, his teeth bared, as if to savor a moment of triumph.

Peggy ran to the sink and vomited.

15

Denise opened her eyes, lying on her side. Brad snored in resonant inhalations. The windows were gray with the coming of dawn, the clock dial glowing faintly: *5:30.*

A tapping on the door, Mother Taylor's voice from the hallway. "Bradley?"

Denise put on robe and slippers. When she stepped into the corridor, Mother Taylor took both her hands.

"Aunt Marie is dead."

"Oh, no."

"Bradley's office is on the telephone. A neighbor found her a few minutes ago. Apparently she got up during the night and fell down the back steps. They want Brad to tell them what to do."

"I'll wake him."

Returning to the bed, Denise had a mental image of the woman as she had been seven days ago—reminiscing, lonely, frail. "Brad?" She shook his shoulder. "Brad, your office is calling."

"What is it?"

"A neighbor found Aunt Marie dead."

"Damn."

"They want to know what to do."

He sat up. Seeing his mother at the bedroom door, Brad said, "Tell them not to touch anything. I'll drive down there."

Denise showered in one bathroom as Bradley bathed in the other. Downstairs, Mother Taylor was pouring coffee into thermos bottles.

"Mom," Brad said, "there's nothing you can do. Wouldn't you rather stay here?"

"I feel I should go."

Brad turned to Denise. "What about Elaine and Jeffrey?"

Elaine was still in pajamas, her face pale. "We can take care of ourselves, Daddy. Are we going to move into the new house today, or not?"

"Get your things ready," Denise said. "We'll start moving when I get back."

Brad telephoned his office. Denise heard him say, "Have Smitherman cordon off the house and keep people out until I get there."

He then called the funeral home and spoke to the elderly coroner. Preparations concluded, Brad said, "If we're going, let's go."

Driving toward Metcalf, Mother Taylor lamented, "Trouble comes in cycles, doesn't it?"

"Old people die," Brad said.

Neighbors stood in the yard in front of Aunt Marie's house. Deputy Smitherman's patrol car was in the driveway, one door open wide, the shortwave radio crackling sporadically with messages broadcast from the office back in Thomasville.

"It looks like an accident," Smitherman said as he led them around the house.

Aunt Marie was sprawled facedown, head twisted,

one leg still on the steep rear steps. An overturned bucket lay a few feet away.

"The kitchen light was on," Smitherman reported. "She must've come out in the dark, stumbled over the bucket, and pitched forward. What do you think, Sheriff?"

Brad knelt, examining Aunt Marie. He felt her jaw, without turning her, then flexed a finger and watched it slowly fall back into place. He moved to a bare foot, squeezing the calf, twisting the ankle, flexing a toe.

"When Earl Hurley gets here," Brad said, "I want him to look her over."

"We don't usually call Hurley for accidents," Smitherman replied. "If he came to look over every accident—"

"I called him," Brad said.

"Yessir."

Mother Taylor reached for the bucket and Brad said, "Don't touch it."

"I was going to put it on the porch, Brad."

"Don't touch anything."

"Sheriff"—Smitherman was almost reproving—"it's only an accident, right?"

"Until that is confirmed, never disturb the scene."

The deputy smiled condescendingly.

"Has anyone been in the house?" Brad asked.

"The man who found her—to call us. I went inside to call you."

"What was he doing here so early?"

"He said she always woke early and he was going to pick blackberries. He intended to ask if she wanted some."

Brad had been talking as he stood over the body, all the while staring down at her.

"That was about five o'clock," Smitherman added.

His mouth was too small for a face so large, the words squeezed to a tenor. "He said he saw the kitchen light and worried when she didn't come to the door. He came around back and there she was."

Denise tried to see what Brad saw. A fly buzzed Aunt Marie's face. "Brad, what is it?"

"Do you want a quick course in forensic science, Denise? This isn't the time for it."

Mother Taylor asked, "May we cover her, Bradley?"

"Not yet." He stooped, staring at her face. When he stood up, he said, "Smitherman, clear the area and keep it cleared."

The deputy turned to neighbors, "Okay, everybody, out front, please."

Denise followed Brad up the steps. He turned and looked down from that vantage. Then, carefully, as if afraid he'd step on something, he scrutinized the porch, the kitchen floor, the room at large, before entering.

Denise had never seen him work before. Brad didn't talk much about his job. He knelt, touched something on the floor, and lifted it, massaging the substance between his fingers.

To her eye, the room seemed normal. Dirty dishes in the sink, furniture in place, the light burning.

"Brad, is something wrong?"

"I don't think she fell down the steps," he said.

"Why not?"

He circled the room slowly, peering at the floor. "She may have fallen inside, crawled outside—but that doesn't make sense either. Hurley will know."

"What makes you think that?"

He reached the sink and stared at the dishes. "You were here a few days ago, weren't you, Denise?"

"Yes."

"Was she ill?"

"She didn't say so. The infirmities of age, of course. She was arthritic, I think."

He bent and sniffed the sink, then stood again.

"Ho, Sheriff!" Smitherman called. "Hurley is here. You want him to take her?"

Brad warned Denise, "Don't touch a thing." He walked to the back porch, spoke to the funeral director, who doubled as country coroner.

Denise looked into the sink. *Vomit?* The odor seemed to confirm it.

Mother Taylor stood where she'd stopped, hands clasped, distraught, but composed. Brad and the coroner were both kneeling at Aunt Marie's head now.

"Earl," Brad said, "look at her color."

"Good for you," Earl Hurley murmured. He felt Aunt Marie's neck. As Bradley had done, he felt here, there, working his way to feet and ankles, finally flexing a toe.

"What do you make of it?" Brad inquired.

"Five, six hours maybe. It was about seventy degrees last night. At this age, arthritis is a complicating factor." The coroner retraced the exercise, flexing, squeezing flesh.

"I guessed six hours," Brad said.

The coroner was a thin man, about as old as Bo Taylor had been. He sat on his haunches, staring at Aunt Marie.

"First guess is," he said, "she didn't fall and then die. The body is inclined toward the head. If she'd had a coronary . . . But her color . . ."

Both men stood up.

"Let me get my kit," Hurley said. He spoke to an assistant. "Put that bucket in a plastic sack for dusting."

"Bradley," Denise said, "I don't want to bother you—but what is it?"

"If she'd lived for even a few moments, she would've

had some discoloration. She was dead when she fell there."

"But how—?"

Brad spoke to his deputy. "The fellow that found her—ask him if he threw up in the kitchen sink."

Meticulously Earl Hurley and Brad moved Aunt Marie one appendage at a time. With a magnifying glass Hurley examined her fingernails, cleaning several, dropping microscopic bits into small bags, which he and his assistant labeled.

"Brad, look here." Hurley held a pair of tweezers up to the morning sun.

"Too dark to be hers," Brad said.

"But long enough to be. That's a bit of luck." Hurley put the strand of hair into another plastic bag, tagged it.

Together the two men went up the steps one at a time, examining tiny pieces of debris, selecting some, ignoring others. On their hands and knees they went through the kitchen door, each with a strong flashlight, inch by inch.

The coroner's assistant took photographs with an old-fashioned press camera, then duplicated the shots with an instant Polaroid, in color.

Watching, Denise saw Brad and Hurley at the sink.

"There's some in a cup," Brad noted.

"We'll take apart the drain," Hurley said.

"How long to analyze it?" Brad asked.

"If we send it to Atlanta, a few weeks. If we run it down to Tallahassee—which costs the county money— a day or two."

Two men in white smocks lifted Aunt Marie without turning her, as the coroner's assistant directed. They placed her on a stretcher and enveloped her with a plastic sheet. When Hurley's aide came to say they were leaving, the coroner said, "I want you to look for urine and fecal matter. Document what you can—it's the flow we're after."

"Legs and garments," the assistant said.

Alone with him, Denise asked, "Do you suspect foul play, Bradley?"

"I do until I know better."

Hurley supervised the disassembly of the drain in the sink, pouring the smelly mess into yet another container. Brad had a small vacuum now, spot-cleaning the floor. He bent low and sniffed the linoleum. He called Earl Hurley and both men performed the same act. The coroner blotted a sticky liquid, scraped the floor with a scalpel, cataloged the find.

"The man who found her didn't vomit," Deputy Smitherman reported.

"Did you?"

"No, sir—I've seen worse than this."

As if only now realizing his mother and wife were present, Brad drew them to him, an arm around each. "Take my car and go home," he said. "There's no point staying here."

As Earl Hurley walked past, he patted Brad's back. "It's a pleasure to work with a pro," he said.

Lanita and Jack formed a two-person welcoming committee at the Reinecke-Taylor house. Elaine raced inside, up the stairs, while Jeffrey went to inspect the swimming pool.

"The place is beautiful, Lanita," Denise said. Even the furniture had been more or less arranged.

"Look how the marble fireplace finished up, Denise," Jack said.

"And the floors," Lanita added.

"You've done a wonderful job." Denise walked through slowly, happily. The kitchen was gleaming, appliances in place, refrigerator humming. Even with a chest freezer in the pantry, the larder seemed vacant.

Jeffrey met them at the back door. "The pool is nice," he said. "It has lights underwater, Mama."

The cabana had a new canvas awning, the walks were pressed pebbles in concrete, everything was freshly swept.

"I love it!" Elaine hugged Lanita gratefully.

"So do I," Denise said.

"The microwave oven is a housewarming gift," Jack said magnanimously. He stroked the woodwork, following the tour.

"Now that it's done," Lanita said, "I think Jack wishes he'd kept the place."

"I'm glad he didn't." Denise turned impulsively and kissed him with tears in her eyes. "It's grand, Jack—it really is grand."

"It's a fine investment," he said.

They were in the master bedroom when Bradley arrived. Brad sent the children to the pool before speaking to the adults. "We're fairly sure it was murder."

"Good God!" Jack cried.

"Her neck was broken. At death, the muscles relax, the sphincter and bladder give way. There was urine in the kitchen, across the floor to the porch, and Hurley found traces down the leg, as if she were standing when she died."

"Godamighty," Jack said.

"We think she was carried from the kitchen and dropped down the steps. Hurley found hairs which he believes are male Caucasian—they're being examined in Tallahassee and we'll know for certain by evening."

"Was she robbed?"

"We found no indication of it," Brad said. "There was forty dollars on her bedside table."

Denise shuddered and Brad put an arm around her.

"Also," Brad added, "somebody vomited in the kitchen sink. It's being analyzed, too—the initial report is what made me come home."

"What?" Lanita said.

"The lab says the contents were tequila, lime, peppers, ground beef, lettuce, and cheese. What does that suggest to a cook?"

"Mexican food," Denise and Lanita spoke as one.

Brad released Denise. "And the nearest Mexican restaurant is in Tallahassee."

"People eat Mexican food at home, Brad," Denise said.

"We'll know more in a couple of hours," he said. "Hurley asked them to look for monosodium glutamate, which he says restaurants favor but housewives rarely use. Would that be right?"

"It would be right with us," Denise said.

"Anyway," Brad said, "we're going to have to skip a housewarming party tonight, Denise. I want to stay on this every second. The holiday weekend will delay us several days. What I uncover this afternoon will be all I'm going to get until after the Fourth."

"Since that's so," Lanita suggested, "let's have the party tomorrow night. The funeral won't be until next week—dammit, Brad, we've all had our share of grief."

"Tomorrow night is fine," he said. "If you folks will excuse me, I feel a need for a bath."

Jeff appeared in the doorway.

"May we go swimming, Mama?" he asked.

"Yes. So long as both of you are together. No carelessness—understood?"

"We both swim very well," Jeff said.

"Be careful," Denise said. "All mothers say that," Jeffrey said.

Brad was stretched full length in a tub of steaming water. When Denise shut the bathroom door, he spoke with eyes closed. "This is what I call a tub."

"Brad, may I talk with you about your investigation?"

He opened his eyes, almost amused. "Now you want the course in forensic sciences, right?"

"I'm guessing," Denise said worriedly, "but you do think the murderer was a male, a white man, and you think he may have been in Tallahassee for dinner last night. Is that correct?"

"It's the supposition we're following."

"Which brings us to a motive, doesn't it?"

"Could've been a transient." Brad laved water up his chest.

"Could've been surprised by Aunt Marie, and killing her was an overreaction."

"That's true," Denise said. "Or it could have been a deliberate act."

"What are you getting at, Denise?"

"I had planned to talk to you when I had some answers," she said. "But now, with Aunt Marie . . . I feel I should tell you some things I've learned recently."

He wiggled his toes, staring at them.

"You have a brother, a half-brother," Denise said. "His name is Truman. There's a sister, too. Lana. Father Taylor had a first wife named Renee."

Now she had his attention.

"I spoke to Judge Felder Nichols about it and I went to Aunt Marie to talk to her."

"Why did you do that?"

"Because, Brad, Mother Taylor was worried about the phone calls and the man did say he was coming here. Besides, why not? You're a man who wants all the answers to every little development—this was a development that begged for answers."

"Okay. Go on."

"Both Judge Nichols and Aunt Marie described Truman as a cunning and cruel boy. A pathological liar, evidently."

"Their perspective is jaundiced, Denise. But go on."

"Aunt Marie was particularly acerbic. She said Truman was evil. Even after all these years, she disliked that boy."

"You started out with the word 'motive,' Denise. What would be the motive?"

"I don't know."

"After so many years?"

"I don't want to sell you on this," Denise said. "But some things take time to develop, Brad. Hatred can simmer and intensify over the years. As I said, this is guesswork."

He sighed, brow furrowed, wiggling his toes again.

"I thought it might help." Denise stood up to leave.

"Wait a minute, Denise. Don't misconstrue my reaction. I'm just weighing the idea." He looked up and smiled. "That's pretty good investigating you were doing. All these years later, in a week or so, you learned things about my father that I never knew. I was thinking about that. I don't know much about his youth, except what I've overheard from Mom and Aunt Marie. I don't think Dad ever discussed it."

"He certainly didn't discuss his first family."

"The question is," Brad said, "why?"

"Ashamed of them, obviously."

"Or of himself."

"Yes, I thought of that. I thought of the book Jeffrey was reading at Mother Taylor's—*Prisoners of Childhood*—about child abuse. His job didn't entail child abuse, did it?"

"Except as an officer of the court, no."

"Brad, would you say your father had ever been abusive to you or Bob or Jack?"

"Never. He growled and threatened, but he never touched a one of us. We've all commented on that."

They gazed at one another a long moment. "Murder takes passion," he said. "The premise is weak, but it is a thought. I'll see what I can find out."

"Truman would be about fifty-four or fifty-five now," Denise said. "He'd have a family, most likely. He'd have a job record, military record, possibly."

"That's true."

"Even if the investigation reveals his presence elsewhere, it would be interesting to know how he turned out, wouldn't it?"

"Maybe. Get me a towel, will you?"

Having done this, Denise went into the bedroom to see if he had a fresh uniform. Through the door she saw him stand up, drying himself.

She knew him so well. By his movements and nothing more, she knew he was taking the existence of Truman seriously.

She had dreaded telling him. She'd begun dreading it even as she uncovered the existence of Truman, Lana, and their mother.

But how could a half-brother be all bad, if the same good blood flowed through the veins of Bradley Taylor?

"Denise?"

"Yes?"

"Call the FBI, honey. Get their local agent on the line for me."

"All right."

"And, Denise . . . call Judge Nichols. I want to see him right away."

"Yes, I'll do that."

Dialing the phone, Denise looked down through the window at the children splashing in the pool. Jeffrey's voice came to her, although he spoke in a normal low tone.

"This is really living," he said.

16

Denise listened as Brad asked the FBI agent what he would need to lend assistance.

"A possible murder suspect," he said, as if repeating the agent's reply.

Denise changed clothing, listening as he talked.

"I did call Albany," Brad said. "They say they can't come down until after the holiday. Look, I need the kitchen dusted at the very least. I have reason to believe the suspect may still be in the vicinity. If there are prints, I want them today."

He hung up, face flushed. "After the holiday," he fumed. "Damned federal people have good working hours."

"Brad, I could ask Mother Taylor to come for the children."

"Why?"

"I could go with you. Take notes. I might catch something in a statement that you didn't interpret that way."

Brad looked at his watch. "Eleven o'clock. Seems later."

"You said yourself," Denise argued, "I did a good job uncovering the information about Truman, Lana, and Renee."

He fumbled with his tie, then snatched it into place.

"Unless you forbid it," Denise persisted, "I'd like to go with you."

"I think you've been bitten by the bug that pulls people into policework, Denise."

"I'm a reporter," she said. "This could lead to a story. It'll help me understand your work better."

He met her gaze with amusement. "All right," he said. "I could use some help. But it's not the kind of help you have in mind."

"What?"

"Go to the courthouse and look up the marriage license. Look for birth certificates on this guy Truman and his sister. Go to the elementary schools and try to dig up school records—a yearbook with a photograph would be a bonus. They may have transfer records—where did the family go from here? While you're at it, see what you can find about Dad, too. Assume that everyone involved is a stranger, that everything must be confirmed with hard data."

"All right." Her tone reflected disappointment. "I'll do that, Bradley."

"If you do," he said seriously, "it would help move things along. That's where I would send a new man on the force—it's the tedious accumulation of facts that makes a case."

Denise encountered the lunch hour at the courthouse, then drove to Eastside elementary school.

"We don't keep those records here anymore," the secretary said. "You'll have to go to the main office of the Board of Education. They may not have them either."

Back to the courthouse. At the counter she met Troy Bacon, a lawyer and lifelong resident of Thomasville.

"You won't find those things here, Denise," he said. "Some years back, everything was transferred to microfilm and sent to the state offices. What do you need it for?"

"Bo Taylor was married twice," Denise explained. "We're trying to learn the name of his first wife and any children."

"Wife's name was Renee," Bacon said. "The boy was Truman, the daughter Lana."

"You knew them?"

"Briefly." He turned ledger sheets, tracing columns with a finger.

"May I speak to you in confidence, Mr. Bacon?"

"Certainly."

"Truman may be a suspect in a homicide."

"That so?"

"Bradley's Aunt Marie was murdered this morning."

"What makes you think it could have been Truman?"

"We're only supposing—"

"Ah."

"But we think he might be in the vicinity. He may have been making threatening calls to Mother Taylor."

The attorney pursed his lips, inhaling. "Truman Taylor," he mused. "The wheel comes full circle, doesn't it?"

"I don't understand."

He tapped the counter for a clerk, returning the ledger. "I'll be back later for this," Bacon said. He smiled at Denise. "Let's go to my office."

Whistling softly, Bacon escorted Denise down the

street to the Neel Building. They took an elevator to
the third floor. "Never moved my office," he remarked, unlocking his door. "The rent stayed rea-
sonable and I feel comfortable here. Come in, Denise."

1:05. Denise accepted a chair as he hung his hat
on a clothes tree and went to a file. "What have we
here?" he asked himself, thumbing indexed folders.
"Ah!"

He sat behind his desk and donned glasses with an
apologetic shrug. "Last we heard of Renee, she was
in Los Angeles, California," he said, peering through
the lower half of his bifocals. "That telephone number is so old the prefix is a name, but I can try it if
you wish."

"I'm not sure what to say," Denise said, flustered.

"I'll say, 'Hello,' " Bacon rehearsed, dialing one
slow digit at a time. "I'll say, 'How's tricks?' I'll say,
'How's Truman—and where is he?' "

He rocked back in his chair, letting the long-distance
call go through. "Ah," he said. He hung up. "She
doesn't speak Spanish so far as I know, and the
person who answered did. Let's see here . . ."

Back to the folder again, thumbing pages. "Renee
Taylor . . ."

He dialed again, whistling softly. Once more he
rocked back, only to end the call with, "Ah!"

He moved with excruciating slowness, licking a
finger, turning pages. Then, once more, he dialed a
number.

"Speak to the counselor," Bacon said into the phone.
"This is Troy Bacon in Thomasville, Georgia."

A moment later, "Hello there, you old fraud. This
is Troy Bacon!"

He laughed hard, wiped an eye with a finger, and
traded queries about weather, fishing, politics and
their respective wives.

"Say, listen." Bacon changed gears. "What do you hear from Renee and her family?"

He winked at Denise. "Ah," he said. He made a note. "Aha," he said. Another memorandum. "Pity," he said. "Um-mm-mm . . . tragic . . ."

Bacon cupped the receiver, inquiring of Denise, "The county will pay for the call?"

"If they don't, I will."

He screwed up his face. "Aha," he said. "Well, well, well. How about Lana?"

He scribbled, doodled, listening. Denise could hear the voice on the phone all the way across the desk.

"Whatever happened to Truman?" Bacon asked.

2:00. Her hands perspiring, Denise blotted the palms on her slacks.

"Any idea where?" Troy Bacon asked. More doodles, a cryptic list of numbers. He checked one and underlined it.

"No, no, nothing special." Bacon rocked back in his chair again. "At my age, now and again I get to wondering what happened to somebody. A name pops in the mind and interrupts the toilet or coffee or what-have-you. It's the what-have-you part that makes me take action."

When he disconnected, all humor vanished.

"Renee is in an institution for the mentally disturbed—alcoholic. Lana has an extensive record of arrests, well known to the Los Angeles police as a prostitute. Truman was, last we know, dishonorably discharged from the military service"—he adjusted his bifocals for clarity, reading—" 'Special Forces, Vietnam, 1974.' "

"Who were you talking to?" Denise asked.

"The husband of my son's ex-wife," Bacon said. "He's an attorney with the City of Los Angeles, but we once did a bit of legal jousting over Renee and

Lana and Truman. That was a few years after Bo
sent Renee away. She heard he'd become sheriff and
wanted to attach his salary. The court disallowed
that—the divorce settlement ended any chance of
alimony at the time of execution."

"Did he know where Truman is?"

"No, but he'd like to." The attorney shook his
head, eyes down. "Two weeks ago they found his
wife and son in a Kansas field. They were shot dead."

"Oh, dear God."

"Where's Bradley, sugar?"

"I'm not sure." Nausea made her swallow repeatedly.

Bacon telephoned the sheriff's office. "Get the sheriff on the radio—tell him to call Troy Bacon immediately. It's urgent."

When Bacon hung up, he said. "He's gone to
Tallahassee, Denise."

"If we only had a picture . . . anything!"

Bacon dialed another number. "Felder? This is
Troy Bacon."

Again, maddeningly, Denise listened to talk of fishing before the issue at hand was broached. "Say,
Felder," Bacon said, "you remember Truman Taylor, Bo's firstborn?"

Denise watched Troy's eyes harden. He stared at
her, but as if he didn't see.

"It's a mite more serious than that, Felder," Bacon
said softly. "I just talked to a contact in Los Angeles.
They found Truman's wife and young son shot dead
in a Kansas field. Look here, Felder, can you twist a
tail or two at the Federal Building?"

Denise watched Bacon's country-lawyer facade melt
away. His words carried an edge now. "Impress them
with the urgency of it, Felder."

He hung up, then gazed at his window a moment.

"Felder was way ahead of me. They're trying to locate the man's military record. Wish we could reach Bradley."

"Earl Hurley may know where he is."

"He does," Bacon murmured. "They're together."

Denise felt sick. "I'm going home," she said. "If you learn anything, will you call me?"

"Is there someplace else you might go, Denise?"

"Why?"

Bacon tapped his notes with a pencil. "Just a precaution," he said. "You have a couple of children—weren't there two children at the swearing-in?"

She couldn't breathe. She tried to respond, but no sound came.

Annette fussed with her hairdo irritably. *One damned thing after another.*

She enjoyed the children, relished time with them, but she felt put upon at the moment. She hadn't bought groceries in a week, the laundry was piling up. She yanked at her comb and nearly cried as a tuft of her hair came with it.

First Bo, now Marie.

She looked a fright. The only good thing to be said was that she had lost some weight, but even that had occurred where she needed it least. In the mirror her face looked older, gaunt and tired.

She tried to remember whether she had the makings of pineapple upside-down cake.

The telephone rang and Annette grabbed it. "Yes?"

"Mrs. Taylor?"

"This is she."

"Mrs. Taylor, I'm the custodian out at Laurel Hill . . ."

Oh, the cemetery.

"Yes," Annette said.

"I'm sorry, Mrs. Taylor, but there's been some vandalism."

"Yes?" Annette asked.

"Somebody defaced Mr. Taylor's grave. They broke the marble headstone, I'm afraid."

Oh goddammit. Annette nearly wept.

"I thought you'd like to know, ma'am. We try to keep an eye on things, but this place has growed to twice the size since I first started here. I barely manage to keep it mowed now'days."

"Thank you," she said.

"Want I should leave it be until somebody comes to see about it?"

"Have you reported this to the police?"

"No, ma'am, I haven't."

"I'll tend to it," she said. She hung up, furious, and dialed Bradley's office.

"Sheriff's department."

"This is Annette Taylor. I just had a report that my husband's grave was vandalized. I want Bradley to look into it immediately."

"Mrs. Taylor, that's city property."

"I know that! But it is Bradley's father."

"You want me to report it to the city police?"

"I want *you* to tell my son to call me."

"He's in Tallahassee and—"

Annette slammed the receiver, trembling. She dialed the city police. "This is Annette Taylor. Let me speak to Chief Madison."

"Hello, Annette!"

"Walt, I've just received some distressing news."

"I heard about Marie, Annette—I'm so sorry."

"Yes, that too. But I'm calling about a different matter. Somebody vandalized Bo's grave." She burst into tears.

"Annette, I'll see about this myself. Where are you?"

"I'm at home."

"I'll come by and get you. Have you seen the damage?"

"No."

"Maybe it isn't as bad as it sounds. Let me call a friend at the monument company. He'll meet us at the cemetery. He might be able to repair it."

"Thank you." She hung up and sank to a chair, crying.

Two o'clock.

She had to think of Elaine and Jeffrey. Sobbing, she struggled to regain her wits, going to the bathroom, splashing her face with water. Now her hair was wet as well as tangled.

She sat on the edge of the tub, crying hard and loud.

The doorbell. Knocking.

"Annette? It's Walt Madison . . . Annette?"

Sobbing, she walked down the hallway, unlatched the screen door, and went into the arms of an old friend. He patted her back tenderly.

Numb with shock, Peggy sat in the front seat of the car, as Truman slept behind her. The hands of the quartz clock read: *2:00.*

She knew from her medical training that she was in shock, emotional if not physical. As if her limbs were weighted, she sat with mosquitoes assaulting her, no longer able to fight them off.

How many lies?

The scars on his torso were shrapnel wounds. "Reminders," he'd described them the first night they made love. Then yesterday, in Tallahassee, he told her that was a lie—Bo Taylor had beaten him with a bicycle chain.

That too was a lie. The wounds were deep punctures, not the lacerations that would be caused by a chain. But what was truth? Dazed and muddled, she had been trying to guess.

She couldn't rid herself of images from last night. Truman carrying the dead woman to the back steps, where he cast her headlong into the dark. He'd kicked a bucket after her.

"They'll think it was an accident," he'd said. "Country bumpkins—it'll look as if she fell."

But later, anguished, he questioned his luck. "If they recognize murder," Truman had pondered, cigarette glowing in the dark, "it'll be the end of me. I'll be right where Bo Taylor always wanted me. A dead man. Unless . . ."

She remembered the instant leap of her heart with that word "unless." Was there a way out of this?

Everything seemed out of focus. The chirp of birds, the chatter of squirrels. Sunlight cast shafts of illumination through the foliage.

She sat without motion, for fear she'd awaken him. Twice she had tried to get out and both times he had awakened and seized her arm, saying, "Where you going, Peggy?"

"To the bathroom."

He'd waited in the dark, watching. He mentioned snakes.

His name had been a lie.

"She called you Truman," Peggy had said.

"That's my name."

Later, in this same wooded retreat, he had chain-smoked, weeping, begging forgiveness from a God he'd earlier ridiculed.

"It happened so fast," he'd said. "I didn't go in there to hurt her. I swear to God I didn't, Peggy."

But he had. With the ease of an executioner he had snapped that woman's neck. *Learned it in Vietnam,* he'd said, as if the explanation were an excuse. It was an automatic response, he claimed. Danger—attack! *Snap.*

It was so loud, so . . . brittle.

He'd clung to Peggy like a child, holding her hand as he talked through his situation—*their* situation, he'd termed it. "But don't you worry about that," he'd soothed. "I'll tell them what happened. You were not morally culpable, Peggy, remember that. Legally, yes, but morally, no."

She'd had visions of the news stories. What would Uncle Zachary think?

"Unless . . ." Truman had said.

Her head was throbbing. She hadn't eaten since last evening and she'd lost that in a violent upheaval. Her mouth tasted awful.

"Babe?"

Peggy tensed, eyes straight forward.

"What time is it?" Truman asked.

"Little after two, George."

She heard him yawn, ending with *um-mm-mmm.* "I could use a cup of coffee and some victuals," he said.

A wasp darted against the windshield, momentarily trapped.

"Are you hungry, Peggy?"

"A little."

Unless, he'd said, they could make Bo Taylor confess to his crimes.

Somehow, in the predawn darkness, with the blood running cold in her veins, the idea had seemed perfectly lucid. Only with daylight had the whole thing become so maniacal.

"That's it," Truman had exulted. "If Bo Taylor confesses what he did to Lana and me, no jury in the world will convict us!"

Us.

Peggy's stomach wrenched. How in God's name had she come to this? Who would believe such a bizarre story? How could *she* have believed it?

"I don't know about you"—his hand was on her shoulder now—"but I need a bath."

Her nostrils still burned from the stench of vomit and urine. She felt as if scales had formed on her flesh. "Yes," she said. "I could use a bath myself."

He crawled out of the rear, yawning repeatedly, and urinated against a pine tree. "I love the woods," he said. "I never really feel free except when I'm out in the wild."

He started the motor but sat there bemused. "Lana and I used to go to Colorado and shoot the rapids. Did you ever do that?"

"No. Never have."

"It's perfectly safe. They give you life jackets to wear."

Lana—who died at the hands of Bo Taylor and Aunt Marie—shooting the rapids in Colorado?

Was he insane, or was she?

Leaving the dead woman's house, he'd driven as fast as her car would travel, to Thomasville, through town at seventy miles an hour, through traffic lights—to a cemetery!

He had prowled one lane after another, reading inscriptions by the headlights. Finally he'd found it.

Dead. Just as the woman said. Dead!

He'd thrown dying flowers aside, then smashed the headstone with part of a smaller marker. "He *isn't* dead!" he'd screamed. . . .

"George, where are we going?"

"First a bite to eat, then a motel and a shower. How does that sound to you?"

"Good. But where?"

"Oh"—he hunched a shoulder—"back to the scene of the crime, I guess. Thomasville has a couple of fine motels."

17

Brad was inside a walk-in closet, undressing for a shower. In their bedroom with the lights off, Denise stood at a window watching traffic pass on the street below. She remembered evenings in Mobile when Brad would come home to shower, scrubbing his hands with a brush, only to bathe again at bedtime and yet again upon rising the next morning.

"We were lucky," Brad said from the closet. "A thousand police officers would have assumed it an accident. Especially considering Aunt Marie's age. Sometimes the heart stops and death is instant. But Hurley and I suspected more. Even when I wasn't sure what, something kept niggling at the back of my brain. Intuition. I don't know what else to call it."

Intuition. She believed in that.

A slow-moving vehicle passed, the blood-red flow of taillights first dim, then bright as the driver applied brakes. Denise could hear a radio, a woman's voice.

"If Hurley weren't the man he is," Brad said, "if I

hadn't the experience and training ... Denise, are you there?"

"Yes, I'm here."

Another automobile, slowing for the intersection. Denise heard a ping of loose rods, motor palpitating, faulty muffler puttering. From here she could not guess at the make or model. The car tag was illegible.

Elaine and Jeffrey were in their rooms, asleep. Brad had come home late, exhausted.

"The autopsy confirmed a broken neck," Brad had reported. "But it didn't happen in a fall. The vertebrae were wrenched, the nerves torn, the carotid paralyzed. The bastard knew how to do it."

Down the street, a vehicle rounded a corner. Was it the same one from a moment ago? Denise leaned near the window, listening for loose rods, leaky muffler.

She had resisted the urge to pour out the trauma of her own afternoon, racing from Troy Bacon's law office to Mother Taylor's house. Her spirits had lifted—the car was there!—then plummeted when she found the house deserted. The children should have been with Mother Taylor. Denise had run around the porch peering through windows with her hands cupped to glass to reduce the glare. She'd banged on doors, calling their names, terrified by visions of violence.

Consumed with dread, she'd rushed home, trying to purge her panic with cold logic. How would Truman know that Elaine and Jeffrey even existed? And if he did, what would he have against them? Truman would be a stranger in Thomasville. How could he possibly know where they lived on this, their first day in residence?

Elaine and Jeffrey were swimming in the pool, happily unaware and carefree.

"Look at you!" she'd screamed at Elaine. "You didn't use lotion. You're burned! Tonight you'll be whimpering and whining about your peeling skin. Get out of there this instant!"

Confused, Elaine had stood before Denise with toes pointed inward, knees knocked, drying her hair. "If you don't care about yourself, at least be considerate of those who have to care for you," Denise yelled. "If you're too damned lazy to protect yourself with lotion, stay out of the pool altogether."

"It's shady here, Mama," Jeffrey had intervened.

Denise threw a towel at him. "You too, young man!"

"I don't sunburn, Mama."

"There's more to exposure than burned skin, Jeffrey—skin cancer for one. Just because you can't see the damage doesn't mean you're immune. A tan doesn't make you safe."

But they were safe. No harm done. Into that idyllic childhood scene she had charged with unexpected fury. She should have been relieved, grateful; but anxiety turned to scalding rage and she had invented a reason to accuse them of wrongdoing—as if it had been their fault.

Suddenly, seeing herself in their eyes, she'd grabbed them to her. "Oh, children, forgive me."

Stiff in her embrace, Jeffrey had asked, "Is something wrong, Mama?"

"It isn't you. I'm sorry. It has nothing to do with you. I was mean."

Elaine put a wet cold arm around Denise's neck. "You're aren't mean, Mama."

"But I am."

And she was.

Later, she'd located Mother Taylor weeping over Father Taylor's broken headstone. Their grandmother had forgotten about the children after the trip to the cemetery with Chief of Police Madison.

What kind of man was this? Killing Aunt Marie. Defiling a grave.

"Has the FBI agreed to help you, Brad?" she asked from the bedroom window.

"Yes, thanks to Felder Nichols and Troy Bacon. They used the Kansas police reports about Truman's wife and son. Kansas has a warrant for his arrest as a suspect. They told us the family may have been involved in a robbery-murder about fifty miles from where they discovered the bodies of the woman and child. The woman had articles in her possession which made the police believe they could have been at a country store where the crime took place. The first suspect is always the spouse in cases like that. The truth is, Truman may be dead too, and undiscovered."

"Maybe Truman was the robber?"

"That's possible. I keep asking myself why a man would rob and murder a grocer, then slay his own family. Truman may have been slain along with his wife and son by the robbers. They said the bodies were found when a machine clogged on one of them. Truman could be a thousand yards or a mile away and not yet found."

He's out there.

Another automobile passed. Across town, a diesel locomotive droned in the dark, shunting cars on the rails, the link of couplings as distinct as if the freight train were a block away.

"Now what, Brad?" Denise questioned.

"Until the holiday is over, all we can do is wait. These things take time."

"I think I'll look in on the children," Denise said. "I'll be back in a minute."

Because the house was new to them, they had left

night-lights burning in the hallway and bedrooms. Denise went to see Elaine first. The girl was curled in a tight fetal position. Denise adjusted the bedsheets, stroking Elaine's back, murmuring assurances. The girl turned restlessly, her face hot from too much sun.

Across the hall, Jeffrey sprawled naked and un-covered. Denise pulled a sheet over him—he looked so small in this room. The book he'd been reading had fallen to the floor. She picked it up. *Prisoners of Childhood.*

She went into his bathroom and thumbed through the book. *113 pages. Translated from the German by Ruth Ward.* Disturbed, Denise read the contents: "The Drama of the Gifted Child and the Psychoanalyst's Narcissistic Disturbance."

Chapter 3. "The Vicious Cycle of Contempt."

She read the first sentence of the foreword: "If a fool throws a stone into the water, even a hundred sages can't bring it back."

A moment later, she understood. If a child has been warped by his upbringing, how can the damage be undone when the child has become an adult?

Denise stared into the bathroom mirror, arms down, the book at her side. She was a good mother. She wanted to be, tried to be.

What kind of thing was this for Jeffrey to read? What manner of child actively sought ammunition against his parents? Was she supposed to feel guilty? Wait until he was grown, wait until he had children, then see how well her errors were corrected with the grandchildren?

She remembered a half-joking remark her mother once made. "Just wait until you have children, they'll pay you back for what you do to me."

Denise returned the book to Jeffrey's bedside table, then snatched it up again. Taking it with her, she left the room.

Brad was lying on their bed, a towel across his stomach.

"Do you think I'm a good mother, Brad?"

"You know you are."

She sat on the bed and held up Jeffrey's book. "This is what our son is reading."

Brad grunted, fanned the towel over his abdomen.

"I'm offended by it," Denise said. "This is any child's dream—a psychiatrist who reinforces the child's concept that he is being mistreated."

"I don't see how reading that can hurt Jeffrey," Brad said.

Denise told him about the incident at poolside, the guilt she felt for railing at Jeffrey and Elaine.

"That's only human, Denise."

"But it isn't forgivable."

Brad stood up and began toweling his hair. "Do you feel inadequate as a parent?"

"At the moment I do."

"Don't worry, Denise. I don't think anyone could accuse you of child abuse."

"Abuse can be emotional as well as physical," she said softly. "I'm not sure which is worse. The way we criticize a child, the choice of words as well as tone of voice, can mold a child's perception of himself. Today I implied that Elaine was deliberately making things difficult by getting a sunburn. That is abusive."

"That isn't you or me," Brad scoffed.

"But we don't see ourselves objectively," Denise said. "That's what I was telling you in Mobile. The way you dismiss the children so gruffly. You're seldom affectionate in a physical way. You don't compensate by telling them you love them."

"A parent doesn't have to talk about love to love,

Denise. Love is food on the table, a stable environment, the security that results."

"It doesn't replace the need for touching, Brad. *That* is what you don't do."

Brad wrapped the towel around his body. "Since this is the second time you've brought this up, I assume you consider it a major problem."

"Not actually. It's the final tiny flaw in your relationship with the children."

"It isn't necessary to be perfect parents to bring up healthy, well-adjusted children. If my dad had come home and scooped me into his arms, I'd have thought he'd gone crazy. I can't remember him ever hugging, much less kissing."

"Would you have liked it?"

He dismissed the question by turning to comb his hair.

"Physical contact in a relationship is like yeast in dough," Denise said.

"Dear God, another writer's simile."

"The bread will bake, with or without the yeast," Denise persisted, "but it makes a different loaf."

She followed him to the closet. He flicked on the light.

"It isn't a lack of touching that's the real issue," Denise said. "It's your lack of desire to do it."

"It isn't my nature, Denise."

"*That* is the issue."

"You're saying I should be a father as described by a psychologist. If other fathers play handball, so should I."

"If handball doesn't appeal to you, how about checkers or chess, or just holding one of them on your lap for no reason at all?"

"I can imagine Jeffrey's response to that! Denise, why are we fighting over this?"

"This is not a fight. It is fine-tuning."

He searched her face for a moment. "You're having an affair, aren't you?"

"Don't be absurd."

"You're *thinking* about having an affair."

"Bradley, that's ridiculous."

"You are discontented, unfulfilled by my performance as a lover—that's why you're making a big deal out of this."

"Brad, the children may not be asleep."

He unfurled his towel with a matador's flourish and faced her naked. "You went out and got your adrenaline going, didn't you?" He advanced one foot before the other, catlike. "Now the excitement has passed and you feel a vague longing, a sense of restlessness—"

She slapped at the air between them, backing up, laughing.

"You think because I'm a cop I don't know about female libido and alter egos. You women get to growing hair on your chest and you start to crave the feminine equivalent of football. You want to pat your teammates on the ass . . ."

"Now you're being insulting."

"You have a fantasy"—he stalked her, blocking her escape with arms extended—"you wish I'd grow a mustache, become a contortionist."

"Stop walking that way, it looks threatening."

"How about a one-and-a-half gainer with a double twitch at the climax?"

The telephone rang.

Brad grabbed her, sweeping her into his arms. He growled into her neck and tossed her onto the bed.

It rang again.

He turned off the light and she could hear him

breathing in the dark, standing over her, debating. *Another ring*.

"Hello," Brad snarled into the telephone.

A moment passed. "Why did you do that, Jack?" Long pause. "Okay. Thanks." Brad hung up.

He stretched out beside her, lying on his back. "Damn," he whispered.

"What is it?"

"That was Jack. Have you seen the newspaper?"

"No."

"He says there's an article in it about this house."

Her chest constricted painfully.

"I guess he was trying to generate publicity for his business and the fine job they did here," Brad said. "Jack says there are photographs."

She heard a car passing, the hum of tires. *Any one of them could be him.*

She shivered and Brad pulled her to his chest. His voice sounded hollow. "Pictures of the kids," he said, "of you and me. Jack thought we'd be proud."

His palm was moist as he stroked her shoulder. "Whoever killed Aunt Marie is far away," he said. "We're creating needless fear with supposition and circumstantial evidence."

But it was too late for assurances. *Now he could know.*

"It was probably a vagrant who thought he had an easy victim," Brad said. "He went in to rob, became frightened when she resisted—you know what a feisty old girl Aunt Marie was."

Denise listened to his heart betray his concern, its beats ascending, stronger, faster.

"Next week we'll have the FBI reports. They'll find Truman's body, possibly. In any event, this has nothing to do with us, Denise. Not us." Brad held her more tightly, squeezing, murmuring.

Denise could sense an ominous presence. Her ears burned with a whisper of her name on strange lips. Her image, Brad and the children in a man's eyes—a madman who did not look upon them with favor.

Brad shook her roughly. "Come on, baby, stop it! Everything is all right."

She knew him too well. He was worried too. Considering possibilities, wondering how secure the house was.

"Sh, sh," he soothed.

What kind of man would slay a feeble old woman? Desecrate a dead man's grave?

Brad was wrong. She didn't understand why or how, but this man was stalking them.

He knows.

Brad clutched her to him.

He knows we're here.

18

When they arrived in Thomasville, Truman circled several motels without stopping. He selected the Holiday Inn. When he went in to register, he left Peggy in the car, but took the keys.

She watched him purchase out-of-town newspapers from racks in the foyer. Without sleep, drugged by the events of the night before, she sat there dumbly, sweat streaming down her face and legs.

When Truman returned, he tossed the motel receipt and room key into her lap.

He gave her the newspapers: Jacksonville, Tallahassee, the Atlanta *Constitution*.

Their room was on the second floor at the corner of the building. Standing in the window, she could see the parking lot, a shopping center across the street, traffic on the four-lane bypass.

From room service Truman ordered two steaks, two buckets of ice, and six soft drinks. "Don't forget the steak sauces, I want them all. Don't forget the silverware. Don't forget salt and pepper."

He turned to Peggy. "What kind of dressing on your salad?"

"Anything, George."

"Baked potato or french fries?"

"I . . . Baked."

"Butter or sour cream?"

"Jesus Christ, George! I don't give a damn!"

He motioned her down, voice mellow as he concluded his order over the telephone. Then, solicitous and fatherly, he took her in his arms. "You've had a rough night, baby. Take a hot bath, why don't you?"

He undressed her, placing her clothes in a pile near the bathroom. He ran a tub of water as she waited, naked. *Naked.* To preclude escape?

"Come on, m'love," Truman said. "This will make you feel better."

"I have to call my uncle, George."

"There's plenty of time for that after we eat. Come get in the tub."

"He expects me home for the weekend rush."

He put an arm around her, drawing her to the bath. "We'll work something out, Peggy. Give me a little fuel to fire the brain—we'll talk it over after we eat."

As she started to close the door, he blocked it. "Let's leave it open," he said. "It will be cooler for you."

As she sank into the fiberglass tub, her arms trembled with muscle spasms. The warming liquid eased the sting of insect bites covering her body.

"If you need anything, call me," he said.

She heard the TV, volume subdued. She heard Truman make another call to room service, ordering a carton of cigarettes. She thought back to a few minutes ago, the way he'd parked the car, backing it to a retaining wall to cover the license tag. This room was the last in a line, at the very corner. This tub was built against the outside wall—no neighbors adjoining.

"How does it feel, Peg?"

"Feels good."

She heard him turning pages of newspapers, the TV so muted nothing was intelligible. *Looking for the news.*

The news was: the sheriff was dead!

"George?"

"Yes?"

"Why don't we get out of this town?"

Long pause. "Well," he said, "do you want this hanging over your life? Or would you rather resolve it and get it behind us?"

"How can we resolve it?"

"I have a plan."

If the sheriff was dead—there seemed no doubt of it—Truman's fear of the authorities died with the man.

"What do you plan to do, George?"

"We'll talk after we eat, Peggy."

Her body felt like a balloon, pulsing with every heartbeat as if it were pumping to stay ahead of a slow leak. Her legs throbbed, abdomen taut.

Uncle Zachary would be near the motel desk now. Tourists arriving, the load increasingly difficult for a single clerk, he would consult his watch repeatedly, more often with each passing hour. He would stare at the highway, alert for cars like hers. She had learned as a child that her tardiness created absolute fear in the man's heart. Because of Aunt Donna, slain by a stranger.

Truman was on the telephone again, asking when the local newspaper would be available, ordering a copy to be delivered to their room.

The volume of the TV rose sharply. *News.* It was

WCTV in Tallahassee. But there was no mention of murder. Maybe they hadn't found the old woman. Such people were often reclusive. It might be days, a week or more.

The tub was too shallow, the water quick to cool.

"George, you know the sheriff is dead, don't you?"

"No, he isn't."

He was demented.

"George, who do you think is buried in that grave?"

"We'll talk after we eat, Peggy."

"Do you think the marker was an elaborate ruse to fool you?"

Truman loomed in the door, his sudden appearance making her suck in a short breath. "You think I'm crazy." He smiled down at her, hair disheveled, beard littered with bits of lint.

"It's all right to say that," Truman said amiably. "If you think I'm crazy, say it."

"I'm having difficulty with one or two things, George. I keep asking myself what you think is in that grave, if it isn't Bo Taylor?"

"This is what the shrinks call the instant of recognition," Truman mused. "There is a gravesite, there is a monolith which identifies the occupant, but the question is, *who* is buried there, not *what.* Do you understand?"

"Then who?"

He held up a finger. "That is the question. When that is answered, we'll be free."

"Maybe I'm missing something, George."

"Please, do not condescend. If you suspect something—lunacy—then pray, girl, speak it!"

The smile was gone, eyes piercing.

"I'm trying to understand," she said.

"And I'm trying to explain. But not well, obviously. May I make a suggestion—for the third or fourth time?"

"Yes."

"We will talk," he said harshly, "*when* you are out of your bath. *When* we've had something to eat!"

A tap on the motel door altered his mood. "Food." He smiled. "Come along, we need it."

She heard a male voice, Truman giving instructions. Then, angrily, "Young man, I specifically requested steak sauces, all of them, salt and pepper, and silverware. I don't see sauces or steak knives."

"I'm sorry, sir. I'll get them."

"*What* are you going for?"

"Steak knives and sauces."

"All of the sauces. That includes Lea and Perrins, A-1, Heinz Fifty-seven, and catsup."

"Yessir."

Truman's voice fell to a growl. "Do it instantly. Do not tarry, do not be delayed. If you return within ninety seconds this crisp five-dollar bill is yours. Fair enough?"

"Yes, sir!"

Was this the manner of a man who hoped to keep a low profile? He had imprinted his face on the waiter acting like that.

"Looks pretty good!" Truman called. "Come on, Peggy."

She scrubbed her legs hurriedly, her appetite responding to the aroma of the meal. A tap at the door, and Truman laughed, giving the waiter his tip.

"Peggy!" he roared. "Let's eat!"

After they ate, Truman put the refuse outside the door. "My turn for the tub," he announced. "Do you mind reciprocating?"

Peggy rinsed the tub, ran warm water. All the

while, he stood behind her, dropping his dirty clothes on hers.

"Mind keeping me company?" He placed a folded towel on the lid of the commode.

"I'd like to lie down, George."

"I thought you wanted to talk."

"I do. But I'm exhausted."

"Sit with me." He held her arm a bit too tightly. "I'd like to ease your mind. The rest of your life depends on it. Surely you can find the energy to listen."

She sat on the commode, watching him sink into the tub with a sigh. He closed his eyes. Peggy leaned toward the door, assessing the room. Their luggage was next to the dirty clothing. The car keys—

"I know what you're thinking," Truman said.

She sat upright. His eyes were still closed.

"You're thinking I'm a madman, out of touch with reality. You think I've embroiled you in something so terrible that I must be a threat to you."

She debated a response, but he continued without it.

"You've never met anybody like me, so you have no basis for judgment."

"That's true," she said.

"Your parents are dead," Truman said.

"Yes."

"Do you remember them—anything at all?"

"Not really."

"I know your parents."

He was mad.

"I can't be sure which is which," Truman said. "But one of them had gray eyes, the other probably had green. Or maybe green and brown, but that's not important. That's the tint of the paint on the piece, not the piece itself. Your mother had a certain way of lifting her eyebrows when she was puzzled about something. She walked with a saucy bounce to her step. She had a wonderful laugh. Your father—"

"George, what is this!"

He looked up without humor. "I know you," he said. "Hence, I know your parents. Has your uncle ever made the comment that you remind him of your mother"

"Yes."

"You didn't know them, but you are them."

"All right, point taken. Who the hell is buried in Bo Taylor's grave?"

"Not the man they think."

"Jesus," she said.

"Hey!" He jolted upright, washing water over the lip of the tub. "Give me the goddamned benefit of the doubt, will you? You want to be free of this unfortunate situation?"

"How?" she screamed.

He lunged, grabbed her arm, snatching her to her knees beside him. "Listen to me," he said, voice low. "Do not yell. Do not fall to pieces, or I will have no further use for you."

"George, you're hurting me."

His grip tightened. "One of the things that drew me to you," he said, "was your intelligence. In battle, I've seen intelligence succumb to brute stupidity. Now, if you will grant me an open mind and clear thinking, I will prove to you I am not crazy."

"All right."

He pulled her wrist to him, kissed it. "I shouldn't have done that," he said. "Please sit down and let me tell you what I have to say."

He waited until she sat down.

"Nothing is as it seems," he said calmly. "I think part of the problem is, you are thinking about survival. I, on the other hand, am thinking about how to accomplish what I came for—and walk away free at last. And if I walk away free at last, you will be allowed to return home. All of this can be put behind you."

"Is that possible now, George?"

"Positively. I came here with a plan."

He eased down in the water again. Minutes elasped.

Peggy said, "I'm listening, George."

"The man in the grave was a respected citizen. He was revered by his neighbors, held in high esteem by his family. He was sheriff of this county for thirty-eight years, and to accomplish that, he had to keep being reelected by a majority of the voters, so they too respected him."

"But he is Bo Taylor," Peggy said.

"The name is not to be confused with the persona, Peggy. The man they buried, by whatever name, is the man who took my sister! He is the beast—the son of a bitch—who made me what I am!"

"Okay," she said.

"Without his confession, who would believe me? Who believed me while it was happening? I went to my teachers in school and told them—they ignored it. The other kids ridiculed us—I was taunted and tormented as a liar, as if it had been my crime, not his. He beat me—God, that man beat me! He terrorized me, both of us! Lana lies to this day, refusing to admit it."

"You said she was dead."

"I said that to enlist you. Now is the time for truth."

"Let's begin with your name."

"Truman Taylor."

"So many lies, George . . ."

"Lies," he said. "The dross and not the gold. The slag and not the coal. The patina and not the silver. Nobody ever thinks to ask, 'Why the lies?' "

"Why the lies?" she asked.

"Now, for expediency. My name, to conceal my identity. In my childhood, before I even thought, the damnable words poured out—so extravagant, so preposterous I could see in the listener's eyes they *knew* the lies."

"Then why didn't you stop lying?"

"I asked myself that. I even went through a phase of telling people I met: I lie a lot. I could not help it. I would hate myself for it, but I couldn't stop. It was like a conditioned response, a knee-jerk reaction. I'd hear my own words and recoil. I claimed, sometimes, I'd dreamed it and the dream seemed so real I thought it so."

"You know what that's called, don't you?"

"Certainly. Pathological liar."

"Which you blame on Bo Taylor and Aunt Marie?"

"You're mighty damned right I do. It *was* their fault. I was a child, for God's sake! But having made me, they punished me for what I became. The abuse . . . the utter destruction of my opinion of myself . . . the mental agony I suffered—they did that to me, Peggy."

"Okay, George."

"Lana is a whore. She's never been able to form a bond with any living creature except me . . . and her poodle. She sells herself because she has no respect for the wares she offers. Then she loathes the men who pay her. Her life has been a daily, hourly denigration; she thinks she deserves the punishment, and if all else fails, she will flagellate herself. Mother is in an institution. Alcoholic."

"Could she have been a factor in all this, George?"

"Without a doubt. I don't excuse her. She's a selfish bitch who used us to pander to her needs. But she couldn't help it. She was a victim of her own parents. We all are, you know."

"So you want to kill Aunt Marie and Bo Taylor?"

"Death ends torment."

"He's already dead, George."

"The body is there. The heart beats not. But he isn't dead, Peggy. He lives in the minds and imaginations of his sons and their families. He lives in the voters who respect his name. He lives . . . the bastard *lives*."

"How can you change anything?"

"He must confess. Publicly."

"But you already said, who will believe?"

"They must believe."

"I don't see how this will get us free, George. Unless you mean 'free' in a philosophical sense."

"For me. For you—complete freedom. Look at us, Peggy. You aren't chained. You are here, nearly twenty-four hours after what happened. Who will believe I held you captive?"

"Am I a captive?"

"You are. But the tie that binds is of the mind, not the body. If you didn't believe I could set things right, you'd have run in the night, or while I was checking into this motel."

Had she imagined his grasp? No, even now, she sat here nude, the car keys nowhere in sight. Bondage. She didn't have the courage to argue—better that he believed she stayed of her own free will. *Did she?* Peggy watched him bathe, assessing his use of peripheral vision. Suppose she dashed for the door this moment—would he pursue her?

She was certain of it.

"How long do you think this will take, George?"

"The entire operation, a few days possibly. A week maybe. That depends on Bo Taylor."

"He . . . is . . . dead," she enunciated.

Truman shook his head wearily. "I don't think you understand even yet."

Somebody knocked on the door. Truman said, nonchalantly, "See who it is, will you?"

She grabbed her blouse and skirt, calling, "I'm coming!"

But when she reached the door, Truman was behind her, nude, dripping water.

"Who is it?"

"Newspaper, ma'am."

She opened the door to the length of the safety chain and a porter pushed it through. Closing it, locking it, she turned to Truman and he smiled.

"Let's see what they say." He took the paper. His eyes darted over the front page and a scowl creased his brow. "Nothing here."

He turned the pages, scanning the text and photos. The *Rose City News* unfolded from national to state and local to society events. "Nothing here," he said again.

She removed the soiled clothing, put her bag on a shelf to seek more. *Running out of underwear.* She hadn't come for a long stay.

Truman laughed and threw himself backward, naked, on the bed.

"The comics?" she asked.

He turned on his side, supporting his head with a

hand, elbow deep in the mattress. "Sarcasm," he said. "That's a healthy sign."

"I need to wash some clothes."

"Come here, Peggy."

She stood at the suitcase, angrily pawing through the few items remaining.

"Come here, Peg. I want to show you the last proof required. I'm not crazy. Come here."

Begrudgingly she walked to the bed and he pulled her down beside him. "Look at that article," he said.

The headline read: "HISTORICAL REINECKE HOUSE RESTORED."

"So what, George?"

He touched a photograph and she leaned nearer to better see.

Sheriff Taylor . . . his wife and children.

"We came by that house today," Truman said.

"What is your point!"

"Him." Truman's eyebrows rose as he touched the man's photograph. "That's him!"

"That's who, George?"

"That is Bo Taylor exactly as I remember him. I've seen that goddamned expression in my nightmares. I've seen those sleepy eyes, that nose—"

"George, he's younger than you are. He can't be Bo Taylor."

"Just as I remember him," Truman growled. "And he will confess."

19

Truman sat very close to her, the room phone in his lap. "Now, what are you going to say?"

"We had car trouble."

"Where are we?"

"Key West, Florida."

Truman shook his head sadly. "If anything happened to you, your uncle wouldn't get over it, would he?"

"No," Peggy said.

"Well, nothing is going to happen," he said. "We're doing this because we can't afford to have your car listed as missing. The Mississippi police would put it on the national crime computer. Some hick cop could stop us for any minor infraction, and he'd feed the tag number into the computer. There we'd be, nailed. Understand?"

"Yes, George."

"We want to reassure your uncle. He must be sick with worry. So, lift your voice, be lighthearted, but sorry you're letting him down. He's a perceptive man. If he detects a hint that something is wrong, you explain it by saying you're worried about the car. He's going to ask you what's wrong with it, and what do you do?"

"Give the phone to you."

"Give the phone to me. I'll explain. Take a deep breath, smile—a smile can be heard in the voice. Smile, Peggy."

"I'll try."

He was right. If anything happened, Uncle Zachary wouldn't live through it. Peggy watched Truman, his lips forming numbers as his finger dialed.

"It's ringing." He cupped the phone in a hand. "Remember what we decided. Say what we rehearsed."

She put the receiver to her ear and Truman pressed near, listening.

"Uncle Zachary?"

"Peggy . . . darling—I expected you yesterday."

"I'm sorry, Uncle Zachary."

Truman sat back, pulled the corners of his mouth, miming, "Smile!"

"Is something wrong?" Her uncle's voice trembled.

"Oh," she almost choked, "we have car trouble."

"Where are you, Peggy?"

Truman had unfolded a map, plotting distances, teaching her names of towns where she'd never been.

"We broke down on a long stretch of bridge between a town called Layton and a place named Key Colony," Peggy said. "We spent the day and night stranded. I only now found this telephone."

"Where is that?"

"Near Key West, Uncle Zachary."

"Florida? I thought you were going to Georgia."

"The weather was so nice—it was a foolish impulse and here I am. I've let you down."

"Let's worry about you, not me. Would you like me to wire money?"

"George has money."

"George. Yes. All right. What's involved in making repairs?"

"I don't really know, Uncle Zachary. I'll let George explain it."

She thrust the phone at Truman, and he took it, grinning. "Hello there, Zachary. Listen, hell, I'm sorry about this. I assume full responsibility. I convinced Peggy she could run away to Key West for a couple of days and still be home in time to help with the holiday load. But like she said, here we are."

As he spoke, he held Peggy by the wrist.

"We gathered driftwood, watched the pipers and gulls," Truman lied. "The buoys on crab pots are bobbing in water so beautiful you wonder if it's real."

So glib. So smooth.

"We thought we'd run down here and back. So far we've had superb key lime pie and horrible coffee as a reward."

She listened to the details, the tiny colorful indicators which cemented Uncle Zachary's image of their predicament. Truman commented on sea oats, pelicans, the price of a Florida lobster dinner. He joked about mosquitoes "the size of B-29's" and sand fleas on the beaches of the keys. Like an artist putting strokes on a painting, he completed the scene.

A long pause as Truman listened. Then, sadly, "It'll be Wednesday before we can expect repairs, Zack."

He sighed as if resigned. "No, the damage is minor. We burst a radiator hose and lost our coolant. But because of the holiday and the remote location, they say it will be next week before a hose can be sent from a town north of here. Hey, listen, if it weren't for worrying about you, we'd be okay. If you have to be trapped, what a place to be!"

Peggy shifted her weight and Truman's grip tightened. He laughed into the receiver, joked about the brevity of Florida island attire, then reassured Uncle Zachary that they had good accommodations.

"Except," Truman added, "no TV, no phones . . ."

Another lapse, Uncle Zachary talking. Then Truman pushed the receiver into a pillow, whispering, "He's doing fine. He wants to assure you he is all right. He's now urging you to take advantage of this and have fun. Respond regretfully, but assure him *you* are all right too."

She took the receiver, visualizing Uncle Zachary, alone with rooms to tend, overflowing with guests.

"Peggy?"

"Uncle Zachary, I'm so sorry."

"Nonsense, girl. I can manage this place alone. I want you to eat a lobster for me, and don't worry."

"Uncle Zachary," she sobbed, "I love you."

Truman pulled the phone away from her ear, listening.

"Darling, other than the automobile, is everything all right?"

Truman held her arm, a finger on the phone's cutoff button.

"Except for the car, we're fine."

"You know, I could shut down this joint and come get you. Or you can junk that car and—"

"No, no." She tried to laugh. "It hurts me that I let you down, that's all. You've always done so much for me."

Truman squeezed her wrist angrily.

"All right, Uncle Zachary," Peggy said. "Let me get off the phone—we're wasting George's money."

"Since you're there," Uncle Zachary responded, "enjoy it!"

"I'll try. I *love* you."

"Yes," he said softly. "Well . . . you are my life and you know it."

Truman took the phone and hung up, glowering. "Overall," he said grimly, "you did pretty good. At least we don't have to worry about a missing-persons report."

And if she were missing, they'd begin in Key West, Florida. Peggy sat with her hands at her sides, weeping.

Truman put an arm around her. "I know this is tough, baby. But we're going to get out of it. You'll see, everything will be fine. Your uncle isn't going to be disgraced by terrible publicity—you aren't going to be blamed for anything. Trust me, Peggy."

He wiped tears from her cheeks.

"I need you, Peggy. A little while longer—I need you. Then it will be over and forgotten."

Over? How could she forget?

"Let's take our things to the car," Truman urged. "Please help me, Peggy. A day or two more—by Wednesday at the latest—everything will be all right. I swear it. Okay, baby? Okay?"

"All right, George."

"Good. Be brave, now. Bear with me."

"I don't want anybody else hurt, George."

"No, no, none of that. That would be counterproductive."

"Don't hurt that sheriff and his family."

"Good God, no. I'm after Bo Taylor—not them."

"He is *dead*, George!"

"When the truth is known," Truman said, "that will be so. Come on . . . let's go."

Truman wore a plaid short-sleeved shirt which hung outside his trousers. His shoes were military boots, an oddity Peggy had not noticed before. But there were many things about him she had ignored until now. The way he paused entering a room, surveying all others casually but warily. He always selected remote tables in restaurants, with a chair that placed his back to a wall, his view of the entrance unimpeded.

She remembered tales of people under attack in public places: strangers watched but did nothing to help. Would that happen to her, if she resisted?

They ate breakfast in a McDonald's, coffee and "Egg McMuffins." There were only two other patrons at this hour, both elderly. Their car tag indicated they were from Michigan. The employees were young, three females, one male. Peggy saw no public telephone.

"Eat hearty, Peggy," Truman advised. "It's going to be a long day."

"What are we going to do?"

"Today we commence in earnest," he said. "I know you're growing short on patience, so we may as well begin."

"Begin what, George?"

He patted her arm. "Everything is fine. Will you stop worrying?"

A police car drove by and George watched it without turning his head, eating as if fully occupied. As the patrol car disappeared, he relaxed perceptibly.

How could she have missed such telltale signs? Thinking back to the first night they met, she remembered the sense of tension she'd felt. At the time, she had misinterpreted that as sexuality. God, *so stupid!*

"I refuse to compound our problems by breaking the law, George."

"I keep telling you, no such thing will happen. Trust me, please. Trust me and we'll be all right. But if you lose your composure, do something idiotic, *that* will compound our problems."

"George, if I got up and walked away, would you try to stop me?"

He grimaced painfully. "If that is a rhetorical question, why ask it?"

"I want to know."

"I don't know what I would do, Peggy." He looked into his cardboard coffee cup a moment. "Don't do it," he said.

As they left the restaurant, Truman stopped in the middle of the parking lot and stretched, arms overhead, turning full circle, eyes squinted against the glare. The attempt to seem casual was so theatrical it defeated his purpose—scanning the terrain. "It's going to be another scorcher," he said.

He drove through town as if he did it daily. One arm hung out the window, as he tapped his fingers against the door to the tune of a song on the radio. At the corner of Broad and Jackson, he peered both ways down the bricked main street, humming with the melody.

Crossing Broad, following West Jackson Street, the nature of the businesses and their clientele changing. Near the railway depot, the community shifted to commerce catering to a black population. Used-furniture stores, pawn shops, a pool hall, right up to the railroad yard, where Truman turned. When they first came here, she remembered, Truman had stopped at the railway station, staring at space as if lost in thought. Now, driving by, she recognized the icehouse where he'd also lingered.

Truman circled the brick building and halted. He pointed at a partially burned dilapidated wooden structure nearby. "I lived there as a child." A sign on the burned building advertised "RED BARN."

Truman pulled into the parking lot of the ice-house. On concrete loading docks, rusting iceboxes were the bones of a mechanical graveyard, relics of times past. Windows were knocked out, the office sign declaring, "Ice—25 cents" with tiny heaps of snow drawn on each red letter.

"Mind if I look around, Peggy? I worked here many an hour when I was a boy."

They got out and Truman led her onto a platform under a sheet-metal roof which crackled as it expanded to morning heat. He touched a contraption with a long hose. "Snow machine. It was used to blow ice over cargo."

A delivery truck with a broken windshield was backed to the dock. Litter gave mute testimony to the long disuse of the premises. Truman strolled past rectangular openings, now boarded. "This is where the ice blocks came out of storage areas. They weighed three hundred pounds each. I think I weighed less than ninety, but I could slide them around when I had to."

She heard him chuckle, stooping to retrieve an object against a wall. He held up a two-tooth article. "Tongs." The wooden handles had rotted away.

He took her arm, helping her step over debris. Then, in a cool dark corner, he wheeled to survey the partially burned building, and beyond, up the street, drab unpainted structures which poorer people called home. *Nobody in sight.*

Truman turned to a padlocked door, and with the tongs he snatched a hasp from decaying wood, its rusty screws scattering around their feet.

"George, dammit, I'm not going in there."

He reached beneath his shirt and pulled out a gun. "Now, Peggy," he said, "you must not lose your composure. We've come too far to quit. A day or two more and it will all be over."

Stupefied, she stared at the weapon. He took her elbow, pulling her with him.

"In battle," he said, "the commander must be firm. Can't allow defection in the face of the enemy. Discipline, Peggy. Discipline."

The depth of the darkness was almost liquid. Dim illumination from the torn door seemed absorbed by the interior. Stumbling, dumb with fear, she allowed him to half-support, half-haul her into blinding blackness. He moved as if he knew his steps, as if in a familiar room at home during the night.

"Stand still," he said. His voice had a slight echo. "Stand very still."

"Don't hurt me, George . . . please."

The reply was a dull thud. *Silence.*

"George?" She reached out, feeling nothing. "George, are you there?"

She heard nothing.

"George!"

She thrashed the air, turning, petrified. "George!" she screamed. Her voice echoed as if into the down of a pillowed cave. Then, silence.

"George!" She faltered first this way, then that. *A wall. Steel.* She ran her hand over the surface and a silken silt slithered between her fingers, the aroma musky.

"George, please . . . God, George, please . . ."

She found a door. She thought it was a door. It was wood amid metal, scarred and splintered at the bottom, a metal plate like the kind found on swinging doors in public places—a round hard object: *a handle, a plunger!* Yes, like in a freezer, push it and the door opened from within.

She shoved it and it held fast. She shoved again, with all her strength. Locked. He'd locked her in.

Her ankle turned, her foot slipped, and she felt water. *Calm. Be calm.*

"George, if you let me out, I'll help you. I promise I will."

The lack of sound was deafening.

"George"—she softened her tone—"come on, now, okay? I get the point. We'll work it out together. Open the door, will you?"

She touched her lips, then spit dryly. The silky silt had the smell of powdered mushrooms.

"I'm afraid of the dark, George."

Calm. Stay calm.

How long had she been here? A minute? Ten? She felt her wrist for a watch—she'd left it in her pocketbook and that was on the front seat of her car.

"George," she shouted. "Open the damned door, George!"

Shuddering, she clamped her teeth. She had an eerie sensation of turning, as if cartwheeling, and slammed both hands to the wall for support. She reached overhead, feeling the air—nothing. The wall and the door were her only points of reference. The floor was uneven. It took a moment to identify the problem. She was standing on a slat upon concrete, a small walkway designed to keep a person an inch or so above water. There had to be a drain, a window, other doors.

"Help me!" Peggy screamed. "Somebody, help me!"

But she knew by the muffled dullness of her voice that nobody could hear.

Weeping, she knelt, feeling around her feet. The water was slimy. The wooden walkway became slippery when her wet fingers touched it.

If she wandered, how would she return to this

place? But if she did not move, she was trapped here by the fears of her imagination. She felt with a foot, tracing the wall, arm outstretched. Moaning, fighting panic, she began to map the limits of her enclosure.

Peggy awoke with a start, clawing the dark, positive she had felt something crawl over her leg. Rigid, she held her breath, listening.

She couldn't be sure how much time had passed. She had discovered many rooms. Several she dared not enter, frightened by the drip of water. Suppose it were a well, the depth over her head. . . .

"Peggy?"

Brilliant light pierced the dark.

"Here!" Her voice was a whisper, hoarse from screaming.

"Peggy!"

She heard the splash of feet in water, saw the light probing like a laser in an adjoining area.

When he found her, Truman took her in his arms, crooning, "Oh, my baby . . . pretty baby . . . I had to leave you for a while. I'm back now. Don't cry, I'm here now."

She clung to him, sobbing. He lifted her. "It won't be much longer," he said.

"Don't leave me. Please don't leave me."

The light revealed pitted concrete floors, the endless dark of an old freezer.

"Come and see what I brought," he said gaily.

With the guiding light, he escorted her through a maze of cubicles, then flashed the beam over a pile of articles in the center of the most cavernous room. Sleeping bags, a folding cot, foodstuffs. "For you," he explained.

Enough to last days. "George, don't leave me here. Please don't. I'm no good to you in here."

"We also serve who stand and wait, Peggy. It won't be long. We're on the downhill run now."

"I can't stand it, George."

"You're a brave girl. Look, I brought sandwich meats and bread. Here's mustard and mayonnaise."

She scratched at his face, snatching his beard, and he shoved her backward. The light went out.

"George!" she croaked. "Oh, Jesus . . . George, please!"

He spoke at a distance. "I don't want to hurt you, Peggy. But if I must, I will. If you try to hurt me, then I will."

"I won't. I swear I won't."

She heard noises, the bump of wood on concrete. He turned on the flashlight again. The cot was set up. "Sit down, Peg."

He sat beside her, holding her to him. "You're perfectly safe here," he said. "The only harm you need fear is of your own making."

"Don't leave me, George."

"I didn't want to do this," he said. "But you give me no alternative, Peggy. You must think I'm a moron. I could see in your face what you were considering. If you ran, where would we be then?"

"Don't leave me, please."

"You won't be alone for long, I swear it. I want you to lie down and relax. I'll put everything within easy reach."

She listened to the disembodied voice reciting a list of goods he'd purchased. "Don't lose the can opener." Then, fatherly, "Be spare with the water, and yet, drink some now and then to avoid dehydration." He comforted her. "I'll always be near. Nothing can happen to you." Then, threatening: "There are places you must not enter. If you hurt yourself, you would lie here injured until I return, because nobody can hear you. The walls are a foot thick."

She couldn't stop shivering, but he ignored her distress.

"I didn't plan on having you along, Peggy. Your presence is a fortuitous happening. This doesn't have to be an ordeal unless you make it one."

She felt filthy, smudged by dust, damp from falling in slippery puddles.

He gave her a plastic cup of water. "Drink it, baby. Wet your lips. It'll ease your throat."

Then, in a more businesslike tone, "You must ration the ice—it's in the thermal cooler. There's milk in there also, other perishables. Be spare with the ice. When you close the lid, do it firmly."

"I can't stay here, George. I won't."

He seized her, shaking her shoulders. "You will," he seethed. "You will because you must! Now, damn you, do as you're ordered and this will end quickly. You force me to lock you up—do you think I'm a fool? I wanted to trust you and it became obvious I couldn't."

"You can. I'll help."

He shook her again until her neck snapped. "You are stronger than you know," he said. "I've seen people endure the unendurable. You'll come out of this better for it, I promise you."

"Stop," she whimpered. "I'm hurt."

He shoved her away and she fell from the cot.

"I expect you to do your duty, Peggy," he said. "You will do it—by choice or coercion. You will do it."

"I'll try, George."

"You have provisions adequate to see you through this."

"How long, George?"

"That's beyond my control."

"May I have a flashlight?"

"When I come again, if you have been a good girl, I may bring a light."

"I . . . I need a toilet."

"Toilet," he said. "Of course you do. Very well, I'll see what I can find."

"The food will spoil."

"No, goddammit, it won't! The temperature remains a steady seventy in here. If you close the lid to the thermal chest firmly, ration your ice . . ."

She found the cot by touch, climbed onto it.

"I'm not a cruel man," he said. "But I expect loyalty and obedience. Is that clear?"

"Yes."

"I didn't hear you."

"Yes!"

"Good girl." He threw the light on her face. "Pay attention," he said. He placed the cooler, the food, the sleeping bags, naming them in their order.

"I won't be gone any longer than necessary," he said.

"Until I return, stay put. There's no way out of here, so stay where it's safe and dry."

She heard the dull thud of the closing door.

Silence.

She refused to pray. God would sneer if she prayed at a time like this.

She found the ice chest, plunged a hand into cubes. She put one in her mouth, sucking.

What if Truman did not return? What if he were killed or frightened into escape? Peggy rolled the ice over her tongue.

Her foot bumped a rolled sleeping bag bound with twine. *More than one.* Then he planned to be here. She fumbled with the knotted string. She placed the bag upon the cot, sat on it. No, *lie down.*

She would conserve her strength, sleep as much as possible. If he planned to come here in retreat, *he* must sleep.

Be strong.

Not for herself.

Be strong!

For Uncle Zachary.

20

Elaine spread strawberry jam from crust to crust over toast. Jeffrey watched as if it were a laboratory experiment.

"You know why you do that?" he said.

"So I won't taste burned bread."

"You do it," Jeffrey said, "because you're afraid of making a mistake. To avoid criticism, you become excessively meticulous. Every little thing in its every tiny place."

"I'll be glad when you're through this psychology phase," Elaine said as she munched toast. "You've found something Freudian in every move I make."

Brad burst into the room with a grin. "Good morning, family. Good morning, lovely children!" He kissed Elaine and drew back with crumbs on his chin. "Ohhh, that's my sweetie." He rounded the table and kissed Jeffrey on the lips, then cuffed the boy's shoulder with a gentle fist. "What say, big guy? Want to arm-wrestle?"

"No, thanks."

"Denise, Denise, Denise . . ." Brad embraced her, swaying, patting her fanny. "Beloved wife . . ."

"Speaking of Freud," Jeffrey murmured.

"What a joy, and how I love you all." Brad turned to encompass Elaine and Jeffrey. Then, lightly, he nearly skipped from the room, going back upstairs.

"Mama," Jeffrey said, "we need to talk."

"Your daddy is being silly."

"Mama, are you aware of the influence of fathers on the ultimate sexual preferences of male children?"

"Brad!" Denise hollered. "You win!"

She heard him laugh at the top of the stairs.

"When does the housewarming begin?" Elaine asked.

"Three this afternoon, and there's a lot to do." Denise gathered dishes from the table. "Mother Taylor will be by to get both of you right after lunch. She wants help with the side dishes and some of the shopping."

"When an adult undergoes a radical change in behavior," Jeffrey said, "it shouldn't be dismissed. It could be a glandular thing, or an emotional crisis."

"Your daddy is playing with us, Jeffrey."

"That isn't the question, Mama. It's the game he selected that we need to discuss."

"Go sweep the cabana and patio."

The doorbell rang and Elaine leapt to her feet. "I'll get it!"

"Sometimes these things can be corrected by a change in diet."

"Cabana," Denise commanded. "Patio."

"You might try potassium, Mama."

"Jeffrey, out!"

He threw up both hands. "Okay. But if he starts smooching with the cousins, don't say I didn't warn you."

Elaine returned. "It's a man from the FBI. Daddy is with him."

"Do your work, Jeffrey. Elaine, help your brother."

Reluctantly Elaine and Jeffrey walked out the back door.

Brad entered with a stranger. "Denise, this is Darrell Ashe of the local FBI office. Any coffee?"

The agent shook her hand, sat at the table. He waited as Denise poured coffee, a briefcase in the chair beside him.

"I'm afraid I have bad news." Ashe withdrew a manila folder from his attaché case. "We have a pretty unsavory character on our hands."

The man shuffled papers to his satisfaction as Denise sat down beside Brad.

"You know he's your half-brother on the paternal side?" Ashe said.

"The rest of the family doesn't know, but we do," Brad replied.

"I think you'll have to advise them, Brad. This fellow is going on our most-wanted list as of Tuesday."

The agent pushed a glossy black-and-white photograph across the table.

An officer. He wore a beret. His nose was straight, eyes deeply set in folds of flesh which gave him a sleepy expression. A tiny cleft in the chin produced a strong masculine appearance.

"Brad, he looks like you."

"He does, doesn't he?"

"I'd know the man in a crowd of a thousand! Even his ears—see how the lobe is shaped?"

"Handsome dude," Brad joked weakly.

"He is," Denise whispered. "He really is."

"Fortunately, the similarity stops there," Ashe noted. "Ballistics tied the murder of the wife and son to the murder of an elderly couple in Kansas. When that

went into the computer, the modus operandi revealed other robbery-connected executions, and we
now believe the same pistol was used in incidents
over a twelve-state area. The pattern of crimes indicated a westerly movement from Pennsylvania to
Kansas, where he apparently killed his wife and son.
This morning, ballistics linked the same gun to the
murder of four young people in a Cuero, Texas,
steakhouse. They were herded into a freezer—you
may have read about it."

"I remember," Brad said.

"There's reason to believe he came east from there,"
Ashe said. "There were two similar crimes in Louisiana, two more in Mississippi—but always in different
jurisdictions. If it weren't for this new NCIC data
bank chasing down serial murderers, it might have
been months before we linked these."

Denise stared at the photograph. If his face were
fuller, his hair cut not so close, it could be Brad.

"We've issued a general alarm," Ashe said. "Since
you brought the matter to us, I decided I'd better
get over here with what we have so far. You suspect
he's in the vicinity, is that right?"

Brad summarized the suspicions regarding Aunt
Marie and the supposition that Truman may have
called Mother Taylor. He concluded with a question.
"He's a psychopath?"

"I'll tell you what the Bureau uncovered and you
decide." Ashe turned pages of teletyped information.

"He served in Korea with decorations for bravery
under fire. Battlefield promotion. Demoted for incit-
ing a riot while on leave. Promoted again, busted
again."

Denise took Brad's hand.

"He was accepted for special training in the early
sixties. Hand-to-hand combat, in which he excelled.

Infiltration techniques, paratrooper, demolitions expert—he became a member of an elite strike force which went behind enemy lines in Vietnam for the purpose of sabotage and something they call 'political expediency.'"

"Which is what?"

"Assassination, creating fear in the enemy—psychological warfare."

She could feel perspiration in Brad's palm. His expression was stoically professional, but she felt a tremor in his fingers.

"He was court-martialed," Ashe said. "Accused of teaching terrorist tactics to the enemy."

"Why wasn't he shot, then?"

"We don't have the full story yet. But evidently Taylor was working with paramilitary groups behind enemy lines. He was chosen for the job based on his 'unique psychological profile.' Which is to say, he was a career military man who couldn't adapt to military discipline. He was the kind of man they felt could be trained to perform duties many people would call murder. If I understand this correctly, he wears no uniform, works with local guerrillas who wear no uniforms, and the tendency is to create strong personal attachments with one's companions. The result was, when the Vietnamese decided to fight for the other side, Truman Taylor shifted with them. His loyalty was to them, not his own nation. The military court found themselves with a man they euphemistically called 'a convert,' meaning 'brainwashed,' and they didn't know what to do with him. The war was lost before it began, the media were digging up horror stories for public consumption. So they settled the matter by offering him a dishonorable discharge and he agreed to forfeit all pay and pensions."

"That *is* a horror story," Denise said.

"Part of the agreement required Taylor to stay in a psychiatric hospital, but it was voluntary. He was there six weeks before he left. He married a woman much younger than himself—it was his third marriage, actually—and they had a son. He worked in the steel mills near Pittsburgh, but lost his job during the recession. Apparently that is when the crime spree began."

For a long time they said nothing. Brad looked at the photograph.

"He's intelligent," Ashe said softly. "He can be ruthless. We are urging extreme caution."

"The FBI will continue to investigate?"

"Yes."

"I want someone to interview his sister, Lana, and his mother, Renee. Troy Bacon believes they're in Los Angeles."

"It's being done. If it weren't for the holiday weekend this would be hitting newspapers and TV news today. The Bureau believes we'll get better coverage by waiting until Tuesday, the fifth. We learned the value of intense publicity with the sex slayer Christopher Wilder—the race-car driver who grabbed beauty contestants from shopping malls."

"I remember."

"Truman Taylor will get the same blitz—bulletins daily, his photograph on TV, reports tracing his known movements. Nobody can endure such exposure for long."

"We're in for some uncomfortable attention," Brad said to Denise.

"I suggest you inform your family." Ashe stood up. "I'll leave that to you, Brad. Mrs. Taylor, thank you for the coffee."

He hadn't touched it. Denise sat with the photograph as Brad escorted the agent to the front door.

How could this man be what they said? His likeness to Brad and Father Taylor was at odds with all she'd learned.

When Brad returned, he took the picture. "My father's son. My brother. God . . ."

"This is going to be a shock to the family, Brad."

"I know."

"What do you think we should tell the children?"

"I don't know, Denise. We can't shield them for long. This man looks so much like Dad . . ."

"Should we cancel the party this afternoon?" Denise asked.

"Dad's death," Brad recounted, "then Aunt Marie, the vandalism at the cemetery—this family needs some relief."

"Yes, we do."

"All right. Everyone will be here this evening. I'll save this mess until the end of the party. How about calling Vera and Lanita—tell them we want the children to stay overnight for a slumber party. The kids will go upstairs and we adults can stay down here to debate whatever we have to debate. I wish the bastard had changed his name."

Brad heaved a sigh. "Until then, let's go along as always, Denise."

Through the back door, she saw Elaine sweeping the patio, Jeffrey using a long filtered hose to vacuum silt from the bottom of the swimming pool. *Eight weeks until school.* What would this scandal invite from other students? For Elaine, especially, making new friends seemed so difficult. What would the notoriety do to Brad when the election came around in two years?

"Denise"—Brad broke her train of thought—"I

wish you'd reconsider going to work at the newspaper until this thing is settled. It would be wise to stay out of the public eye, and the children will need emotional support."

Thinking as she thought. "All right, Brad."

"I wish we'd stayed in Mobile," he said. "What have I gotten us into?"

"You don't believe that! Neither do I." Denise stood up angrily. "If you're looking for easy street, get out of policework! This man, this monster, would have surfaced sooner or later no matter where we were. At least here you have a direct hand in the hunt for him."

He wasn't appeased, nor less anguished. Brad lowered his fist to the photograph. "Why?" he asked. "Why?"

Annette drove from the grocery store, Jeffrey and Elaine in the front seat beside her. "What do you think of your new home, children?"

"I like it," Elaine said.

Annette patted Jeffrey's leg. "Your mother says you're responsible for the yard."

"In the same way Elaine is responsible for the interior," the boy replied. "I suspect a more equitable arrangement will be forged."

She laughed, turning into her street.

"Actually, that would be good for Elaine," Jeffrey said. "She's developing the classic female self-concept that has retarded women throughout history."

"What in the world does *that* mean?" Elaine scoffed.

"It means you should broaden your horizons. Stop thinking a girl is confined to playing dolls. Take on pursuits you consider a man's job."

"We've been going through this for days, Grandmama," Elaine complained. "I wish you hadn't lent

Jeffrey those books on psychology. He thinks he's Freud."

"I don't adhere to everything Freud believed."

As she entered the driveway, in her rearview mirror Annette saw a car stop out front. She realized she had seen it several times since picking up the children at Brad's house. "Who could that be?" she asked.

As the children carried in groceries, Annette waited to see if anyone came forward. The car remained parked, tinted glass hiding its occupant.

"Want me to go see who it is?" Jeffrey asked.

"No. If they're coming here, they'll come on. We'll only be a few more minutes, anyway. Jeffrey, did you take in the sack with the hot-dog buns?"

"Yes, ma'am."

"Bring them back, please. Put them in the trunk."

Inside, Elaine helped organize items required for the cookout and chattered to Annette.

"I try to indulge Jeffrey," Elaine said. "He has an identity problem, and despite what he says, he needs someone to talk to."

Annette scanned the kitchen to be sure everything was secured. *Stove off, percolator unplugged.* Nearly three o'clock. They were running late.

"Be sure the doors are locked, Elaine."

Carrying a bag of food, Annette called from a bedroom window, "Jeffrey! Come get this, darling."

Out of nowhere, a hand struck so viciously Annette lost her dentures. She was thrown to her back, her groceries scattered. She saw handcuffs stuck in his belt—

"Grandmama, the front door is—" Elaine shrieked, and an arm seized her around the neck, lifting her, kicking, her face discolored.

Annette was stunned. The beard confused her for an instant, but then she saw his eyes and knew.

He threw Elaine against the bed, grappled her arms behind her back, and cuffed them. He kicked the child's feet away and Elaine fell to the floor.

Instantly he was over Annette, his knee in her chest, holding her by the hair, teeth bared in the bushy beard. Annette saw Elaine roll over with a groan, her nose bleeding, trying to get up.

"Do you know who I am?"

"You . . . you . . ."

"Truman Taylor," he said.

She struck up at him and he knocked the blow aside, spraining her wrist.

"I have a message for Bo Taylor."

"He's dead."

"He will be."

Jeffrey. Annette screamed, "Jeffrey, run!"

His knee pressed with his full weight and Annette heard a brittle snap; her breath locked. He jerked her head against the floor twice, then snatched her hair. "You're the bitch who played games with me, aren't you?"

"I'm sorry—"

"You want to play games with me, bitch?"

"I didn't know who you were."

He bent lower, snarling, "Truman Taylor, that's who."

Elaine shrieked, her mouth an oval in a bloody mask. He wheeled and knocked her backward with the flat of a hand. "Shut up, girl! Make another sound and I'll break your granny's neck."

His eyes, the nose—as if Bo were looking down in a crazy nightmare, furious and violent.

"I have a message for Sheriff Taylor," he said. "You tell him I will telephone in exactly two hours, and be damned sure he answers. I won't wait. Understand?"

"Yes."

"Tell him I killed Aunt Marie."

"Oh my God in heaven . . ."

"Tell him I will kill these children unless he does precisely what I say. Is that clear?"

"Not the children. Take me."

He banged her skull again. Annette's ears rang, her eyes lost focus, his knee sent excruciating pain through her chest.

"I have already confessed to one murder," he said grimly. "What have I to lose by killing the boy and girl?"

"Truman, what have you done with Jeffrey?"

"Give me the sheriff's home telephone number."

She did so.

"Tell Sheriff Taylor not to throw up roadblocks. If he does, if I'm caught, they're dead. Got it?"

"I'll tell him."

"Tell him I'll call in two hours."

"They're only children. Let's talk . . . whatever is wrong, we'll help you."

He grunted, sneering down on her.

"We're family, Truman."

"Two hours, bitch."

"We'll try to help you—I promise."

"Oh, and you shall." He lifted his knee and Annette clutched her breast, gasping for breath. She rolled to her side, groaning.

He yanked Elaine to her feet and the girl screamed. Truman pinched her cheeks to a grotesque pucker. "If you make one more sound, I'm going to hurt you."

He released his hold, patted her face hard. "Do you care for your brother?"

"Yes."

"If you want him to live, little girl, do as you are told. I expect obedience."

"Yessir."

"That's my girl." He smiled. "Everything will be fine." He turned to Annette. She reached out, and chest pains took her voice.

"Two hours," he said, dragging Elaine with him.

Annette rolled over, wheezing. She heard the slam of a car door, a trunk lid maybe.

Had to see. But she couldn't get up. The act of twisting made her cry out in short yelps, her lungs frozen by streaking pains.

Through her tears she looked at the ceiling, the walls, Bo's photograph gazing at her.

"Bo . . ."

Annette choked. "Bo . . ."

21

Denise, Vera, and Lanita worked at the kitchen counter, making iced tea, preparing deviled eggs. Bob and his son Robbie churned ice cream on the back porch. Jack iced the beer, filling a washtub as he and Bob debated a pending city ordinance. Denise could see the pool, the wild splashing of the cousins, except Elaine and Jeffrey. *Three-thirty.*

Brad popped half an egg into his mouth, nudged Lanita, and suggested, "More salt."

"Salt is optional. Add your own."

"Brad!"

Mother Taylor stumbled into the kitchen, arms clasped across her chest holding her sides. Vera grabbed the woman, lending support, and Mother Taylor cried aloud in pain. Her hairdo was mussed, one eye swollen to a puffy slit.

"The children," she choked.

Denise couldn't move.

"What happened?" Brad demanded.

"Bradley, he took the children! He has a beard," Mother Taylor wept. "His eyes . . . he looks like Bo.

Oh, he handcuffed Elaine . . . Bradley, he said he'll kill them if you stop him. He said he'll call in two hours."

"Mother Taylor, where are you hurt?" Lanita touched the woman's breast gently.

"I think he broke my ribs."

Brad was already on the telephone, calling his office. "Dispatcher," he commanded. "Conference call! Get the FBI, state patrol, city police. Call Florida state patrol, and get the chief of police in every city within fifty miles."

He halted, staring. He turned to Mother Taylor. "Did you see the car?"

"I think so. At a distance. It was red, I think. Or burgundy. I . . . Oh, Brad, I'm not sure!"

"How long ago did it happen?"

She gasped, gasped again, trying to take a breath. "Before three. Bradley, he said don't stop him or he'll kill the children! He said he murdered Aunt Marie and has nothing to lose. He said he'd call in two hours. You must answer, he won't wait."

Brad held the telephone, trembling. Finally he issued new instructions. "Get Darrell Ashe, FBI. Tell him my children have been kidnapped by Truman Taylor."

"You know his name?" Mother Taylor cried.

"Yes, we know his name." Brad sank to one knee, struggling for composore, embracing his mother. "Lanita, call an ambulance. Vera, make certain the children stay in the pool area—somebody be with them."

"What the hell is going on?" Bob questioned.

Brad was crying, clinging to his mother.

"Denise," Jack insisted, "what happened?"

"You have a half-brother," she said hoarsely. "He kidnapped Elaine and Jeffrey."

* * *

Peggy awoke, startled, as screams rent the dark.

"George?"

She fell over a sack of food, heard a can roll away. It sounded like children, hysterical wailing.

"George!" she yelled, and her whispery call brought louder shrieks.

"Who is it?" Peggy questioned. "Hello, who is there?"

"He broke my glasses, Elaine."

A boy. A girl.

"Hello? Elaine?" Peggy groped toward the sobbing, an unidentifiable noise.

"Who are you?" the girl shrilled.

"My name is Peggy, darling. I'm locked up with you. Stand still and let me find you."

"Please don't hurt us."

"No. I won't hurt you." Peggy slid her feet across the floor, feeling for the wooden walkway. "George," she reasoned, "will you turn on the flashlight, please?"

"He's gone."

"George!"

"He's gone," the girl insisted. "Oh, my arm hurts."

"Who's with you, Elaine?"

"My brother, Jeffrey."

"Jeffrey," Peggy asked, "are you all right?"

"He broke my glasses."

Peggy reached one of them, and at her touch the girl shrieked, drawing away. "It's me, it's Peggy. Come on, now, stop yelling. Let's be quiet a moment."

The sobbing could not be subdued. Peggy listened for George somewhere in the dark.

"We need a light, George. You promised to bring a light."

"I think he's gone," Elaine said. "I heard him shut a door."

Peggy felt down the girl's soft arm—*handcuffed!* Wrists behind her back. *The boy too.*

"George," Peggy said, "you can't leave them here like this. Give me the key."

Aftersobs racked their bodies, involuntary spasms. "Is either of you hurt?" Peggy questioned.

"My shoulder," Elaine said. "He twisted my arms when he threw me in the trunk of his car." Then, solicitous, "Jeffrey, did it hurt when I fell on you?"

"I don't remember."

"He beat us up," Elaine cried. "He beat up my grandmama, too."

"All right, I'll hold you and we're going to move to another place. There's a cot here, and water. Slide your feet along; we have to cross a little walkway to get to the cot. Come on."

Handcuffed. They would have to be fed. They couldn't even go to the bathroom alone! Like helpless animals, caged in a black hole.

"How old are you, Elaine?"

"I'm thirteen. Jeffrey is eleven."

Anger overriding her fear, Peggy helped them feel their way toward the cot. One of the children struck a loose can of food and it skittered aside, bringing more cries.

"We're all right in here," Peggy said. "Nothing can hurt us. This is an old refrigerator box, I think."

"We'll suffocate," Jeffrey said.

"No, it's quite large. Here we go—here's the cot. Do you feel it?"

"Yes, ma'am."

Peggy held the boy's shoulders, easing him to a sitting position, then the girl. She touched the child's face and came away with a sticky substance on her fingers.

"Are you bleeding, Elaine?"

"My nose is."

"Let me wash your face."

Peggy tore a piece of her skirt, ladled cold water from the thermal chest.

"Our daddy will get him," Jeffrey vowed. "He's the sheriff and he'll find us."

"Of course he will," Peggy said. She wiped the girl's chin, lips.

"My tooth is loose," Elaine reported. "I can move it with my tongue."

"Don't do that," Peggy said. "It will firm up if you leave it alone."

"It feels numb."

"Don't wiggle it, Elaine." Peggy felt the boy's face, ears, neck. Both of them were damp from perspiration.

"Jeffrey, do you think you could slip your hands under your bottom and pull your legs through? It would be better if your hands are in front."

"I can try."

She helped him onto his back, following the effort by touch. *The son of a bitch!* Leaving these children bound . . .

"Can you pull my hand a little farther?" Jeffrey asked. Then, grunting with exertion, he asked Peggy to bend his knees to his chest—and the cuffs were in front.

"Good for you, Jeffrey! Elaine, can you do it, sweetheart?"

"I don't think so. I'm awfully fat."

"You aren't fat!" Jeffrey snapped. "Try it."

"My arms aren't as long as yours, Jeffrey!"

"At least try it," he said.

They pulled, Elaine pushed, but indeed, her arms were too short to allow the linked wrists to pass around her hips.

"Try stepping through them, Elaine," Jeffrey said.

"I can't do it, Jeffrey!"

"It's all right," Peggy insisted. "Relax now and let's get our wits about us."

She sat between them, her arms in theirs, her voice strained and failing. "We should tell something about ourselves so we'll know one another," Peggy said. "Who begins first?"

"You," Elaine said.

"Let's see, said the blind man."

Silence. The distant drip of water in another room. Peggy took a breath. "First of all," she said, "I am incredibly beautiful . . ."

She paused for laughter.

"You are to me," Jeffrey replied soberly.

Brad sat at the dining-room table, staring at the floor. Denise held his hand. Jack and Bob were mute, stunned by the FBI report on the man who now held Elaine and Jeffrey. Telephone crews were feverishly installing new lines and equipment to record calls on the old one.

Lanita placed an urn of coffee on the table; Vera delivered a plate of sandwiches.

"An expert on hostage negotiations is flying in from Washington," Ashe reported. "He'll advise you, Brad. A Bureau psychiatrist is coming, too. He's studying everything we have on Truman Taylor. They'll be here tonight."

Brad nodded, eyes bloodshot.

"By this time tomorrow," Ashe continued, "we'll have a force of three hundred agents to coordinate law-enforcement agencies throughout the area."

"Mother Taylor is going to be fine," Vera said. "They're keeping her in Archbald Hospital for the night. Except for the broken ribs, she's only bruised and shaken."

"What kind of animal is he?" Jack asked.

"Sociopath," Darrell Ashe said. "According to the psychiatrist in Washington, he's probably working on a calculated plan designed to achieve some particular objective."

"Money . . . what?" Bob asked.

"We're not sure."

"Not money." Brad straightened. "He wouldn't hang himself with a confession about Aunt Marie if money were his motive."

"Then what, for Christ's sake?" Bob asked.

"A pound of flesh, maybe, but not money."

"Brad." Darrell consulted his watch. "If he calls on time, we have to be prepared. This first call is critical. Let him talk. Don't antagonize him. Listen to his demands, but only hint at meeting them. We need to know his state of mind. Understand?"

"Yes."

"Our specialist in these things says you should create a need for further negotiations whenever possible. Tell him he must call back and talk again for final answers. Insist on proof that the children are safe and unharmed."

Denise began to cry.

"The more you talk with him," Ashe said, "the greater our link with him becomes. Our psychiatrist believes he will be curious about you personally. He thinks that's why Truman was so specific in his demand that it be you who answers the telephone."

"Can they trace his call?" Bob asked.

"In some cases we can. If he goes outside the Bell Telephone system, that complicates matters. If the call is transmitted via microwave, that makes it more difficult. But we'll try."

Brad sat so immobile, his expression was terrifying in its intensity. *Murderous.* Denise reached to touch his face. Brad took her hand and pushed it down, holding her a moment.

"Direct lines to Atlanta and Washington are completed," a workman reported. Ashe nodded.

"The recording equipment is set up," another agent said.

"We've got people analyzing the tape your mother made of the earlier call," Ashe said to Brad. "When we get his voice again, we'll know for sure if it's the same man."

"It will be," Brad said.

The children were upstairs. They had been told Elaine and Jeffrey were kidnapped, the party was over—nothing else. They peered through banister rails, legs dangling, catching what conversation they could, murmuring among themselves.

"When the call comes through," Ashe said to the assembly at large, "everybody remain absolutely quiet."

Five o'clock. Denise fought a tremor in her hands. Her imagination cast mental images of horrible suffering, Elaine and Jeffrey hurt and weeping.

Five-fifteen.

"It's been longer than two hours, hasn't it?" Lanita asked.

"He'll call," Brad said. "He wants us to suffer."

The hallway clock ticked; the FBI agents sat at their equipment, waiting. Upstairs, Vera shooed the children into the bedrooms.

Five-thirty. Denise watched Brad sip cold coffee, glaring at the floor.

Ring . . .

An electric shift in mood. Darrell Ashe started a recording device, put earphones on his head. Denise ran to him and he gave her a set to wear also.

Ring . . .

Brad sipped coffee, unmoving.

"Brad?" Bob urged.

Ring . . .

He lifted the receiver, looked to Ashe, and the agent nodded.

"Hello, Truman."

"You got my message?"

"I got it. What do you want, Truman?"

"Aren't you going to ask about your children?"

"How are they?"

"So far, safe—but whether that remains so depends on you, my man."

"All right. What do you want?"

"The tape recorders are going, are they?"

Brad waited.

"I would assume so," Truman said. His voice was deep, rich, the delivery that of a man quite sure of himself.

Denise pressed the earphone nearer, straining for every breath.

"Who is your father?" Truman asked.

"You know who. Bo Taylor."

"Tell me about him."

"What do you want to know? The man is dead."

"Tell me about him."

"He was sheriff of Thomas County for thirty-eight years. He tried to do what was right, and in my judgment, always did so."

"Good father . . . good grandfather."

"Yes, he was."

"Gentle soul."

"He was."

"Um-hm. Loved by one and all."

"What do you want, Truman?"

"First, I would like to present my credentials," he

said. "To appreciate your situation fully, you must know certain things."

Pause. Brad said, "Go ahead."

"I killed Aunt Marie."

"Yes, I know."

"I'm not sure how many people I've killed in the last month or two," Truman said. "The names of places grow dim and repetition tends to dull the memory. Four kids in a freezer in Cuero, Texas . . . a kid in the motel across the street . . . a service-station attendant in Hammond, Louisiana . . . I'm not sure where I was in Mississippi, but two there. . . . Are you listening?"

"I'm listening."

"My Bonnie Blue-eyes and son, Chuck—they're in a wheatfield in Kansas. I'm not sure exactly where."

"They found them."

"Ah. Good. That will save time. Before her, same day, an old man and woman running a country grocery store."

"We know that, Truman. What do you want?"

"Good, good. Then you must realize the seriousness of anything I threaten. You do realize that?"

"Yes."

"Well then. Let's see. You say Bo Taylor was a good father, a good man?"

"Yes."

"You know what you are, Sheriff? You're a god-damned fool."

He was breathing harder. Denise thought she heard traffic sounds behind the man, as if on a highway.

"Truman, suppose we get down to it. What is your purpose—what do you want of me?"

"I want nothing from you, you stupid bastard. I want a confession from Bo Taylor."

"He's dead."

"No, he's not dead yet—but I intend to lay him to rest."

Denise saw Brad and Ashe exchange glances.

"If I am apprehended, your children are dead. There is no way on this earth you could find them— and time is of the essence, my man. You alone will set the limits of their suffering. If you do precisely as I say, you may reach them before they die. If you devote your time to finding me . . . well, they will die, that's all there is to it. The choice is yours."

"You son of a bitch, *what* do you want?"

He laughed coarsely. "If, however," Truman said, "you do what I say, you will have them back in good health, and that I swear."

"Tell me what!"

"I want a confession from Bo Taylor."

"Confession to what!"

"Ahhh," the man crooned, "this is where it gets interesting. I will not tell you."

"Then how am I to know?"

"If you hope to see your children again, you will start digging, my man. When you can tell *me* the substance of the confession, I will release those children. And, Taylor, it must be a public confession. I want it on the prime-time news of the television station in Tallahassee."

"The station may not cooperate."

"They'd better," he said pleasantly. "If you play your cards right, the networks will run it. This is, after all, a unique turn of events in a rather dreary world sated with humdrum antics by stupid criminals."

"Tell me what to confess and I'll arrange it."

"No, sir. No-goddamned-sir! You will confess when you know the truth, the whole truth, and nothing but the truth, so help you God."

"When can I speak with you again?" Brad asked.

"I will call in two days. That should be time enough to have begun. Remember, if you catch me, you lose."

"There are other agencies involved, Truman—"

"That's your problem, not mine."

"Call tomorrow."

"Maybe."

"Tomorrow. I want proof my children are well."

"I know about hostage negotiations," Truman mused. "I know what you will say before you say it. Believe me, the only way you can accomplish the safe return of your children is by doing what I have said."

The line disconnected. *Click. Click.*

"Did they get it?" Ashe asked his assistant.

"I don't think so. It came through General Telephone system in Tallahassee. They aren't equipped to run down—"

"Damn!" Ashe seethed.

Denise sat with earphones on her head, a dial tone droning in her ear. *Click. Click.* Silence.

"What did he want?" Bob asked.

"He wants a confession from Bo Taylor," Brad said.

"Dad? Is he crazy? Dad is dead!"

"That's what he wants."

"Confession to what?" Jack asked.

"He says," Brad said, "that's for us to uncover."

Ashe was on another telephone, issuing instructions for alerts throughout North Florida. Brad walked over and took the phone. "No roadblocks," he said.

"That isn't the way, Brad. You can't give in to the demands of a maniac."

"No roadblocks, no arrest. I want him left alone until we locate my children."

Brad removed the earphones from Denise's head

and pulled her into his arms. Holding her, he swore softly. Then, crushing her to his chest, he began to cry. "I said I loved them," he said. "I made it a joke. . . ."

22

Through the night people arrived: the hostage negotiator from Washington, a psychiatrist who was studying Truman's records. The living room and den became a center of operations which seemed to span the continent. Agents elsewhere were interviewing Truman's former wives, both remarried, both with children; neither received support or communication of any kind. Truman had abandoned them as Bo had abandoned Truman.

"That is common," Dr. Oscar Brunner explained. "We know that adults do to their children what their parents did to them."

"Bo was a good father!" Mother Taylor retorted furiously.

"I wasn't making an accusation, Mrs. Taylor." Dr. Brunner's forehead was as long as the rest of his face together, centered by a nose that began with close-set eyes and hung over a thick mustache.

"He was a good man," Mother Taylor gasped, bending forward to ease her pain. She had come home with her ribs wrapped in adhesive tape, face drawn. When she moved, she needed help. Her steps faltered, her arms trembled with the effort. Her voice had developed a rasp.

"How could the blood of my husband flow in such a man?" Mother Taylor asked.

"Perhaps to that son your husband was not the same man you knew," the doctor suggested gently.

"Look at his family!" Mother Taylor cried. "Good citizens, honest people. We give of ourselves, to our children and the community."

"Yes, you do," he said.

"That terrible man may hate Bo for sending them away," Mother Taylor said. "He may be mad, and in his madness he may blame Bo for everything, but I can tell you, my husband was a fine father, a fine husband."

"Yes, ma'am."

But the psychiatrist persisted with his questions, drawing from Mother Taylor every memory she could recall about Bo in the early years.

"Did he want children?"

"We have three."

"Did he welcome them?"

"He loved them all."

"Was he a loving man?"

"Three children—doesn't that prove something?"

"Was he strict, overly strict, in his discipline?"

"He never spanked one of them."

"Oh? How did he discipline them?"

"Firmly, verbally, with reason. Our children listened to reason."

In the dining room, an agent monitored electronic equipment, prepared to record any telephone call. Maps had been spread over a table to determine the probable distance Truman could have traveled between the kidnapping and his call yesterday. Despite

Brad's protests, Darrell Ashe had told them the FBI would continue to hunt for Truman.

"Your children are our concern too, Brad."

"Stay away from him."

"We can't allow him to run free out there," the agent said. "He's a man who kills indiscriminately. We must find him,"

"If you take him, my children are dead."

"If we contain him," Ashe said, "we will have a position from which to negotiate. But he must be contained."

Denise listened, her senses so fractured she couldn't join Brad in resisting.

"If the children are with him, we won't move in," the negotiator explained. "If they aren't with him, how do you know that he will reveal their whereabouts, Sheriff? Even if you do all he demands, how can you know?"

Brad had gone to his office, searching files for clues to the confession Truman wanted. Chief of Police Madison and several of his men were assisting. From counties a hundred miles away, deputies arrived to volunteer manpower. The area was being blocked into a grid, a net going out to snare Truman Taylor.

"The pictures of the children and their abductor will be on the evening news," an agent reported. "We'll send the story to the wire services."

"Now, then," Dr. Brunner said to Denise, "tell me about Jeffrey and Elaine. What kind of children are they?"

"Intelligent. Well-behaved. Precocious."

"Good." He made notes on a legal-size pad. When he lifted his head he seemed cross-eyed, with two tiny brown pupils peering past his enormous nose.

"Are they children you think of as self-sufficient? Can they care for themselves?"

He meant: *Do they ever have to?*

"I think they could," Denise said.

"Do they fend for themselves around the house?"

"They have chores."

"Oh? Tell me about those."

She saw what he was doing. The veiled interrogation was designed to uncover more than the children. Were they happy? Morose? *Abused?*

". . . reads constantly," Denise said. "He enjoys flaunting his knowledge to Elaine, who's two years older."

She assessed her replies before she spoke them. How did this family look to a psychiatrist? Elaine with her fears of ugliness, her refusal to attend Father Taylor's funeral, her reticence in making new friends? Jeffrey—good Lord—what must he seem to this doctor?

"Fascinating little boy." Dr. Brunner smiled.

"As I said, precocious."

Denise watched the man work, listened to oblique inquiries to Lanita and Vera, then Bob and Jack. Turning pages of his notebook, soft-spoken and never contentious, the doctor slowly compiled evidence of a family of achievers, all devoted to Father Taylor, all describing him as "stern" but never too much so.

"Um-hm." The doctor would nod, his silence inviting elaboration of explanations already given. Finally he closed his notes. "A nice family," he said.

"Yes," Mother Taylor responded firmly. "We are."

Sunday. Tomorrow was July 4. Despite the holiday weekend, the FBI phones rang constantly, information accruing, interviews reported from afar.

"We're going to bring Truman's sister to Thomasville," Darrell Ashe said. "Will that present a problem to any of you?"

"Why would you do that?" Vera asked. "Haven't we been through enough?"

"We need someone who is close to Truman," Ashe said. "So far, the only person who seems to qualify is his sister. We hope she can reason with him. It's a ploy that sometimes works, sometimes doesn't, in hostage situations."

"This is becoming a circus," Bob said. "This woman is a prostitute—isn't that what you said, Ashe?"

"It's to our advantage to befriend her," Dr. Brunner said to Denise. "If she learns to care for you and the children, as well as her brother, her incentive doubles."

"She can stay here," Denise offered.

"Denise, no!" Jack was on his feet, complexion splotchy. "We don't have to sleep with this scum."

"What the hell are you doing, Ashe?" Bob assailed the agent. "After you've gotten the glory of capturing your most-wanted criminal, there'll be scars on this family which will remain a lifetime."

"Bob, I want her here," Denise insisted.

"I think you should consult Bradley," Mother Taylor said.

"He'll agree. The doctor is right. It's to our advantage to befriend this woman. Besides, she isn't Truman, she is a sister. She is . . . family."

"That's ridiculous!" Bob said. "There's going to be a lot of publicity. Why make matters worse with a . . . a goddamned whore?"

Ashe put a supportive hand on Denise's shoulder.

"A lifetime of good reputations," Jack seethed. "A lifetime of public service—nobody is going to remember that when this is over. These federal bastards don't give a damn about any of that. We have to protect ourselves, Denise."

"I'm thinking of Elaine and Jeffrey."

"So are we!" Bob said. "Long after they're home safe, do you want them to be stared at by strangers and learn about all this from their friends? When Elaine and Jeffrey are old, this crap will still cling to them."

"Denise," Mother Taylor implored, "speak to Brad about this. She could stay in a motel as easily as here."

"I don't even want this woman in town!" Bob declared. "I don't want the Tallahassee *Democrat* running her sordid story, and they surely will."

"Every newspaper will," Jack agreed.

Lanita put a hand over Denise's, grimly. "She could stay in Tallahassee or Albany. If you wish, you could go there and get to know her."

"It's a mistake to bring this woman anywhere near Thomasville," Bob said. "Does anyone believe Truman Taylor gives a damn about her or anyone else? He's a psychotic son of a bitch, wholly selfish. He murdered his wife and son—he won't give a damn about Lana. She'll make matters worse, in my opinion."

Denise spoke to Ashe. "She comes here."

"Jesus Christ!" Jack went out the back door.

"Well," Bob said, "that's the end of us, isn't it?"

Vera sat rigid. Tears rose in her eyes and she blinked, mascara tracing her cheeks. Lanita shook her head woefully, followed Jack outside.

"Denise . . . darling . . ." Bob was down on one knee now, holding her hand. "If Lana comes here, the press will be on her. Her story, whatever it may be, will hit the papers and TV."

"The office phones have been ringing constantly," Vera added. "If it weren't Sunday, we'd have to answer."

"You see how kinky this will appear," Bob reasoned. "The media will eat this up."

"I know, Bob."

"Who knows about Lana right now?" Bob argued. "Who knows the tortured tale of this woman—and who cares? But once she is linked to us, she becomes meat for the media."

"I'm thinking of Jeffrey and Elaine."

"Oh, honey," he said, "so am I!"

"Maybe we could hide Lana," Denise suggested.

"You know better. You've chased stories. They'll get to her. It's too good, too juicy—they're going to cover page one with it."

"Bob, please, you're hurting my wrist."

"I'm sorry, I'm sorry. Jesus . . . Denise, please, tell these people no! We needn't contribute to the smear this psychopath is trying to do to us."

"I'll talk to Brad."

"Good enough. All right." He turned on Ashe. "Until then, keep her in California."

"No," Denise countered. "Until then, continue to bring her here. I am positive Brad will agree with me."

Even if he didn't . . .

An officer drew Darrell Ashe away. Vera's face was liberally striped with mascara now, her backbone erect, as if her unrelenting posture would stave off unpleasantness.

"I'm sorry, Vera," Denise said. "I have to do it."

Vera nodded, crying silently.

Mother Taylor stood, reaching for Bob's arm. Slowly, one short painful step at a time, they passed through the dining room, the kitchen, and out the back door.

"Mrs. Taylor," Ashe said as he returned, "do you

know Miss Adkins? She taught school here in the thirties and forties. She remembers Truman."

"I don't know her," Denise said.

"She wants to speak with you on the telephone."

Denise took the receiver. "Miss Adkins? I'm Denise Taylor."

"Don't you believe a word that boy says, Mrs. Taylor. He has always been vicious. He was born with a penchant to harm."

"Thank you, Miss Adkins."

"I taught Truman and his sister, I know them both."

"Miss Adkins, could I come and see you?"

"Oh, my dear, of course you can."

"Where are you?"

Denise scribbled the address, took the phone number. "I'll be there in a few minutes. Miss Adkins, I'm dressed very casually—it's been a hectic night."

"I know, I know. The man from the FBI told me."

"I'll be right over," Denise said. "If you don't mind, I'll bring a friend."

"Of course."

Driving toward the retired teacher's home, Denise asked Dr. Brunner, "Do you agree that the impetus behind all this falls in the first twelve years of Truman's life?"

"I do agree."

"He blames Father Taylor for abandoning him," Denise said. "Some years later, the mother, Renee, trying to get alimony and child support, attempted to sue Bo and the court wouldn't allow it."

"That's interesting."

"So now Truman is focusing his hatred on Bo Taylor as the cause of all his subsequent ills. Is that plausible?"

"Quite possibly."

Denise turned on Crawford Street. "I suspect that will be the substance of the confession he's demanding."

"Quite possibly, yes."

"Yes," Denise said bitterly. "Then maybe if Renee married again and the next father was cruel, Truman blamed Bo for that too. If Bo had given financial assistance, Truman thinks, his mother wouldn't have been thrown into the arms of a second father who made matters worse."

"That's possible too."

"But you think there's more, don't you?"

"I don't know, Mrs. Taylor. All that you say could be so. We should bear in mind, the cause may be no more than you say. Truman could be a disgruntled child—"

"Is he crazy?"

"His actions suggest as much."

"Can one reason with insane people?"

"Amazingly, yes. That's why I've come here."

She pulled into the driveway of a small house finished with gray asbestos shingles. The tiny yard was well-kept, the walkway neatly edged, flowers bordering the passage to a yellow front door.

"Come in, come in," a woman's voice called before Denise could knock.

"Miss Adkins? I'm Denise Taylor, and this is Dr. Brunner. He's trying to help us cope with Truman."

"He has your precious children," the woman lamented.

"Yes, he does. . . . Would you like us to sit here?"

"Come to the kitchen. I've made coffee and tea; which would you prefer?"

The table was baked enamel. The stove was gas, on legs, dust motes nesting in each support.

"Truman was one of those incorrigible liars," Miss Adkins said sadly. "In many children that's a sign of a vivid imagination, a healthy indicator of future inventions. But with Truman the lies were cruel and destructive. He lied to hurt people."

Her hair was thin, silvery, her face dotted with liver spots, but her hands delivered refreshments without a quiver. As she spoke, her pale blue eyes met Denise's gaze with assurance, compassion.

"I was a victim of his hatred," Miss Adkins said. "He and I had always gotten along so well until he came to me trying to slander his own father. When I didn't believe his story, he turned against me."

"What did he claim?" Dr. Brunner asked.

"That his father molested Lana. Lana was Truman's younger sister."

"Molested . . . sexually?" Dr. Brunner asked.

"It was a lie. I called in Lana and asked her. She denied it to Truman's face."

"Could she have been protecting her father? Afraid of him?"

"I hardly think so," Miss Adkins said. "She then went out and told everyone what Truman had said and that it was Truman who trifled with her."

The psychiatrist leaned forward slightly, an elbow on one knee.

"Oh, then he let me have it," Miss Adkins said. "He spread the rumor that I was having an affair with another teacher—a young football coach. In those days, mind you, a teacher could neither smoke in public nor ever be caught having a drink of liquor. Those were causes for instant dismissal. The idea of a liaison was scandalous!"

"He made up the story to punish you?" The doctor smiled sympathetically.

"To destroy me! The football coach was forced to

leave town to protect my reputation. Our principal, Mr. Mayhue, had a talk with Truman and warned him that we would not tolerate such behavior. At that point, Mr. Bo Taylor learned what had happened."

"How did he react?" Dr. Brunner asked.

"He gave Truman the lashing he deserved. Mr. Taylor was a fine young man. He was industrious, conscientious. He suffered greatly for having married the wrong woman. The whole community was aware of the family situation."

"Tell me about that," Dr. Brunner said.

"It isn't my place—"

"Miss Adkins," Denise said, "please . . ."

"Rumor and hearsay. It is not for me to say. Suffice *to* say, however, when the matter was resolved, Mrs. Taylor took her two children and vanished one night. Without fare-thee-well or so much as a goodbye, she up and left! Her reputation as a harlot was well-known. Those who knew Mr. Taylor closed behind him. He ran for sheriff a few years later and I voted for him, I'm proud to say."

Miss Adkins offered more tea, coffee. "It will go to waste if you don't drink it," she said. Dr. Brunner took coffee, waiting.

"Oddly enough," Miss Adkins said, "Truman was a good student. He always stayed after school, helping me clean the blackboards and pound chalk from the erasers. He was an avid reader, quite proficient at reciting verse. He would stand before the class, barefoot as a yard dog, rolling the words like a professional speaker. He liked poetry, which was what drew me to him in the first place. My thesis was on Elizabethan poetry."

"Did he have a favorite poet?" Denise asked.

"Oh, Housman! The rhythm and the simple message. Truman discovered *A Shropshire Lad* and learned to quote from memory, I recall. The sadness of it seemed to enthrall Truman. 'With rue my heart is laden/ For golden friends I had,/ For many a rose-lipped maiden/ And many a lightfoot lad.' "

"Would you say he was intelligent and sensitive?" Dr. Brunner suggested.

"Yes," Miss Adkins said softly. "He could be so endearing, so thoughtful, so manly—the contrast of his cruelty made it all the more shocking."

"Did you know Bo Taylor personally, Miss Adkins?" Denise asked.

"No. Until he came to report the children gone, I'd never spoken to him. But I had met Truman's mother often enough."

"Renee," Denise said.

"Short dresses in a day when skirts touched the calf or lower," Miss Adkins said. "Face painted as for a carnival ball. She wore black lace stockings and I remember what a sensation it caused as she flounced down the hall to assail this teacher or that."

"Assail about what?"

"Truman! Her precious Truman. She had jobs for him to do, duties to perform, things at home which required his attention. He seldom completed his homework, and his mother would come into a classroom to make a scene if Truman received a failing grade."

"How did Truman feel about that?" Dr. Brunner asked.

"Oddly, he appreciated it, or so it seemed. After his mother departed, Truman would dare anyone to say a word, his eyes a warning of hell to come if a student so much as snickered."

"Did this happen often?" Denise asked.

"Too often. To me never, although other teachers

caught her wrath in my presence. I think I was spared only because I was always careful to help Truman with remedial work."

"Did he resent that?"

"Oh, gracious, no! I thought he even missed assignments on purpose, to have an excuse to stay with me after school. I always had to chase him home. Until, of course, he got angry at me. Then came the vicious lies."

"Miss Adkins," Dr. Brunner asked with a helpless frown, "may I ask you—were you being courted by the football coach you mentioned?"

"See here, sir!"

"No offense intended," Dr. Brunner said. "The purpose of my question: could Truman have been jealous?"

"It is obvious!"

"I agree, it is."

"Several times I caught him peeking in my parlor windows! As if trying to accumulate evidence against us."

"I see."

"That boy had the audacity to repeat our private conversations to Mr. Mayhue, the principal! Oh, he was abominable, that child."

Dr. Brunner sat back, glanced at Denise.

"Miss Adkins, thank you for seeing us." Denise stood up.

"Be firm with him," Miss Adkins advised. "He understands nothing else. Be firm."

"Yes. Thank you."

As they left, the former teacher stood in her doorway, seeing them off.

"Isn't it interesting," Dr. Brunner observed, "how we are shaped by love into objects of hatred?"

23

"**W**hy doesn't Daddy come?" Elaine whimpered.

Peggy massaged the girl's shoulder and arm. The handcuffs were tighter as edema produced swelling.

"What day was it when George got you?" Peggy asked.

"Saturday."

"Morning, night—what time?"

"It was about three o'clock," Elaine said. "It was afternoon. We were in a hurry to get home to a party."

Friday. Saturday. Two days. It seemed weeks.

"Oh, I hurt so much," Elaine groaned.

Peggy felt the metal biting into Elaine's wrists. Her hands were puffy, her fingers less flexible. If the swelling continued, circulation would be blocked. Amputation could be the result, or a blood clot breaking loose, reaching the heart . . .

"We're sitting here like dummies," Jeffrey protested.

"Elaine, roll over, darling. Let me rub the other shoulder."

"I keep having cramps," Elaine said. "Do you think I'm about to start my period?"

God, please no.

"Suppose he never comes back?" Jeffrey asked. "Suppose we run out of food? Who would think to look for us here?"

"He's always depressing," Elaine said. "If the sun is shining and everything is wonderful, he finds some morbid fact to depress people."

Their first effort at a meal had been a disaster. Peggy tried to leaven the moment. "Hey, let's have a picnic!"

"We can't have a picnic in the dark," Elaine said.

"Sure we can. Blind people have picnics."

She'd fumbled with cans, unaware of the contents until opened. Odors were not true, textures seemed altered. Keenly aware of salt, which Elaine didn't need with her swelling, Peggy imagined the canned foods excessively saline. Eating required feeding, and George—that bastard—had neglected to provide utensils. She held Elaine's chin with one hand, the canned food between her knees, fingering morsels to the girl's mouth. They spilled and dripped, fumbled and wept, trying to gain strength. They suffered a waxy aftertaste and decided it was grease from a can of stew. They thought it was stew.

There was no way to mark time. Peggy tried to estimate the temperature, the hours required for their diminishing ice to melt away. She and Jeffrey had agreed to give the last few shards to Elaine.

They played word games, at which Jeffrey excelled. A kind of word association, each taking a turn adding a root: cat . . . catacomb . . . catastrophe . . . catatonic . . .

Peggy had teased and joked, but there was no humor in them. She'd learned their hopes and fears, their attitudes and opinions. The boy was a joy. Peggy found herself addressing him as an adult, not a child. They talked of their father, the sheriff. They worried that their mother, Denise, was worrying about them. Peggy pictured a warm, loving family with a spacious new home, a swimming pool and cabana, uncles, aunts, and cousins coming for a housewarming.

"We're being stupid to sit here and do nothing," Jeffrey said. "We should be trying to escape."

"How?" Elaine asked.

"Find some tools or something. Break down the door."

"The walls are steel," Peggy said. "The door is very heavy. George told me the walls are a foot thick or more."

"Yeah," the boy mused in the dark. "But this is an old refrigerator. If we could get through the steel skin, the inside is probably cork, and that tears up easily."

Peggy stroked Elaine's back, down the spine as far as the girl's bound hands allowed.

"Water is coming in," Jeffrey said. "I can hear it. If there are leaks, there is rot—even a heavy beam would be rotted after all these years."

Peggy felt him stand up from the end of the cot. "Jeffrey, don't go beyond my touch."

"I think we ought to try, Peggy. We have to help ourselves. How long have we been here now? A month, I bet."

"Not a month," Peggy said.

"Weeks, then."

"No. A day or two. When I was by myself, I thought a week had passed, but it hadn't. The food would be gone, but we still have food."

"The water is louder over there," Jeffrey said. "I'm going to find the leak."

"No, Jeffrey."

"I want to try."

"No!" Then, hesitantly, Peggy said, "I'll go with you. Elaine, stay on the cot, darling."

Together they found a wall. With that as their guide, Jeffrey led the way with cautious steps, his linked arms extended as Peggy followed, her hand on his shoulder.

"Another room," he observed.

"There are several."

"Are y'all still there?" Elaine called.

"We're here . . . everything is fine. You stay there."

"It's coming from the ceiling, I'll bet." Jeffrey advanced by inches. "It sounds deep, doesn't it?"

Glup . . . glup . . . glup . . .

"Can you swim?" he asked.

"Oh my God, Jeffrey!"

"I'm not sure I can, with my hands tied."

Glup . . . glup . . .

They groped their way into a room that felt darker in a place that was totally without light. The water deepened around Peggy's ankles. She heard Jeffrey take a quick breath.

"It slopes like a swimming pool," he warned.

"Jeffrey, let's stop here."

"I hear the water dripping, Peggy!"

"No, wait. This hole could be ten feet deep, for all we know." She raised a hand, feeling for the ceiling. *Nothing.* "The ceiling could be ten feet high," she added.

"Do you think you could lift me up and let me feel?"

The flooded concrete floor felt mossy, very slippery. "I don't think so, Jeffrey."

"Try!" he shouted. "Or let me try to pick you up. We have to try!"

"All right." *Damn him.* "All right, I'll try to lift you. But I can't hold you long."

She grasped his waist, the chain of the cuffs scraping her face as he held her head, trying to climb on one of her knees. He raked the air, extended himself, pawed the dark.

"Pipes," he said, sliding down. "Leaking pipes!"

"Let's go back, Jeffrey."

He held onto her skirt, wading out.

"Where are you?" Elaine called.

"We're coming."

"Hurry, I'm having a cramp!"

Four o'clock. What had the past twenty-four hours done to Elaine and Jeffrey? Were they hungry? In pain? Was that beast mistreating them?"

Denise refused to think: *Dead.*

At this moment, hundreds of men and women were spreading over endless woodlands, searching for the children. The radio stations had broadcast urgent appeals for help, and help came. Everyone in the county knew someone in the Taylor family.

Brad, unshaven and pallid, reported the results of his search for clues. "They must have thrown away the files prior to 1950. There's nothing in the office past that year. I went to Aunt Marie's with a couple of deputies. We ransacked the house for scrapbooks, old letters—there was nothing relating to Truman and his family."

The FBI was combing records in Atlanta. They had verified Bo's marriage, the births of Truman and Lana. They had uncovered a Pennsylvania driver's license, an automobile registered to Truman Taylor, the tag number was on the computers.

"Considering it's Sunday and July 3," Darrell Ashe said, "we're lucky to be moving so fast."

He turned teletyped pages. "Truman lost his home to foreclosure. His unemployment benefits expired and he must have gone off his rocker."

"Brad, we need to discuss this woman, Lana," Bob insisted. "She'll be here tomorrow, they say."

"About noon," Ashe confirmed. "Tallahassee airport."

"Bradley." Bob sat beside his brother, his voice low. "What earthly good is this woman to you? She's a prostitute. She's a dreg of humanity."

"She's his sister," Denise said.

"She may hate us even more than Truman does," Bob said. "She may want to destroy us too."

"Being who she is," Jack added, "her very presence will be destructive."

"What do you want me to do?" Brad asked. "Do you want me to order her away when she is the only person they've found to talk to Truman?"

"She seems genuinely distressed by what he's done," the hostage negotiator remarked. "Our agents say she's sympathetic to you all."

"Brad, she's a whore. She's scum. Photographers will be at the airport, waiting. In the last hour, two TV networks have sent crews to Thomasville from their local affiliates. Don't you see what this kind of exposure will bring? It's bad enough to have photos of the children going on the evening news. *That* is necessary, I know—but this woman!"

"She's staying here," Denise said. "Dr. Brunner believes it wise to build a bridge between us."

"I do," Dr. Brunner acknowledged.

"Then that settles it," Brad said.

"I think your father deserves better than this," Mother Taylor said hoarsely. "I think his reputation is worthy of more consideration."

"Mom"—Brad took her hand—"what else can I do?"

"Keep this awful woman away."

"I can't, Mom. I can't do that."

In the den, beside the recording equipment, a teletype whirred, paper unfolding with additional data—Missouri, Illinois, Indiana, Ohio—crimes Truman may have committed, ballistics tests using bullets found in the dead wife and son.

An agent brought several feet of message to Dr. Brunner, and he studied it, puffing a pipe.

"There won't be a country road that isn't covered by spotters," Ashe said to Brad. "We have Civil Air Patrol volunteers over the major highways, unmarked cars at every junction through adjoining counties. If they see Truman's car, they'll follow, but not apprehend, until we locate the children."

"Good."

The hostage negotiator was a squat, thick-chested man with a perpetually reddened face. His biceps bulged under long sleeves rolled to the elbows. Even when deadly serious, his expression suggested geniality. He was, Denise had learned, a psychiatrist, like Dr. Brunner. Older than Brunner, Dr. Alex Rheems had attained fame by writing textbooks to teach lawmen the intricacies of hostage situations.

"We're quite lucky to have him, you know," Dr. Brunner had told Denise. "It so happened we were having dinner together and he's between seminars."

Coaching Brad, Rheems spoke in a fatherly way, an arm around Brad's shoulder. "Pique his interest, keep him asking questions."

Dr. Brunner finished the teletyped material and put it aside. He puffed his pipe, smoke trickling through his mustache toward squinty eyes.

"What is that?" Denise touched the teletyped message.

"Bit of bad news, I fear. Truman's military dossier, the courses he studied. He has probably read everything Dr. Rheems has written. Truman said he knew what your husband would say before he said it—well, apparently he does."

"Are you going to tell them, Dr. Brunner?"

"Later, perhaps. For the moment, let's leave Dr. Rheems to his methods. Even if the attempt seems transparent to Truman, that has value. Truman will be assured he is in control."

Four-forty. Lanita delivered iced tea to the table and like zombies they stared, but didn't touch it.

"Do you think he would kill my children, Dr. Brunner?"

Brunner puffed, his pipe gurgling. "Yes, he might. He feels nothing for anyone but himself. It is the unhappy result of an unfeeling infancy."

"Oh, shit," Jack snorted.

Brunner looked at the bowl of his pipe. "Truman's mother was uncaring, unnurturing, a woman who spent most of her time away from the babies—would you agree, Mrs. Taylor?"

"Yes," Denise said.

"The military records indicate this," Brunner continued. "Sensory deprivation—i.e., a lack of touching, loving, devoid of a sense of security—the result can be antisocial behavior, an inability to love others. In the extreme, it is the base upon which a violent man constructs his view of the world. If someone is good to him, he is suspicious. *Why?* he asks himself. What does this person want from me? If he finds no logical selfish reason, his opinion of the lover deteriorates, the rationale being: How can this person be worth anything if she loves me?"

"Who gives a good goddamn?" Bob asked. "Are we supposed to feel sorry for this animal? We all have things to overcome from childhood. Learning to accept responsibility for our own actions is the final test of maturity."

"Precisely." Dr. Brunner smiled. "But Truman never attained that level of maturity. He is psychologically stunted at an emotional level comparable to a boy, say, age twelve."

Dr. Brunner puffed, puffed. "However," he said to Denise, "I am reasonably sure he will not harm your children. Not intentionally, anyway."

"You said he might."

"In rage. In retaliation. In the heat of passion. But not with forethought. That's why Dr. Rheems and I are here, to help avoid the boiling point, so to speak. We hope to give the law time to find and corner the man. In a trap, with time to think, he won't do harm, I'm confident of it. That would defeat his purpose."

"Which is?" Jack asked caustically.

"To punish your father. His father."

"He's dead."

"He is; his reputation isn't."

Mother Taylor clasped her chest.

"That's why he wants a confession." Dr. Brunner emptied his pipe into an ashtray. "The destruction of Bo Taylor's image, his ideological death, that's what this man wants. He has chosen Bo Taylor's son to do the job, I suspect, because he's convinced nobody could do it more genuinely, more surely, than a son who is known for his love of the same father. It's all guesswork, but that's what I think at this point."

"Bullshit," Bob said.

"Up to the eyebrows," Jack agreed. "This whole line of psychological crap is part of the liberal bleeding-heart mentality that has helped to produce men like Truman."

"He's saying it is Bo's fault," Mother Taylor whispered.

Bob stood up. "You pretentious son of a bitch."

"Knock it off, you guys!" Brad yelled.

"You mentioned that we all have things to overcome from childhood," Dr. Brunner said pleasantly. "Tell me what."

"I'm not falling for that trap," Bob said.

"It isn't a trap, Mr. Taylor. It's an inquiry. Please, tell me what you had to overcome from your childhood."

"Children imagine things." Vera spoke for Bob. "They always believe they are being .maligned or mistreated."

"Could you give me an example?"

"Goddamned kids all want more," Jack said. "That's the nature of a child."

"More . . . what?" Dr. Brunner persisted. "More food? What?"

"More of everything. More love, more freedom, *more—*"

The telephone rang and Dr. Rheems arose as Brad stood. The doctor's hand was on Brad's shoulder as they moved toward the phone.

Denise ran to Darrell Ashe, took earphones for herself. Brad waited; Ashe nodded: the tape recorder was operating.

"Hello?"

"Five o'clock sharp." Truman's joviality was infuriating.

Brad listened, saying nothing.

"Are you there?" Truman inquired.

"I'm here."

"What did you find out, my man?"

"I spent the day going through old files."

"Oh? What did you learn?"

"It would help if I knew what to look for."

Truman laughed, coughed aside, returned to the telephone. "Your children will be wondering why you haven't rescued them, Sheriff Taylor. If I were you, I'd get out of the office and start digging."

Brad consulted the notes he and Dr. Rheem had composed. "So you won't hit the panic button, Truman, I thought I'd better tell you what is happening."

"No fear of panic, my man."

"There are many agencies looking for you. They are outside my county and beyond my control."

"Would I be safer at your house?" Truman laughed again.

"Safer in my county than elsewhere, yes."

"You let me worry about that, my man. You worry about the confession. I'll call tomorrow at five sharp. Be there."

"I spoke to the television people today," Brad said.

"And?"

"They might not cooperate."

"Yes they will." The man sounded amused. "However, that's your problem, not mine. If you want your children to suffer, that's your choice."

"I want to speak to them, Truman."

"If wishes were kisses, we'd all have herpes."

"How do I know they're unharmed?"

"You don't know, my man. But it's the only hope you have."

"The TV station demands that—"

Vulgarities poured through the earphones. "Demands?" Truman shouted. "What do you take me for, a goddamned fool? The networks will be there! Unless you stupidly exclude them."

"They demand to know the time," Brad said.

"Seven o'clock."

"What day?"

"Tuesday. July 5. Talk to you tomorrow."

"May I tell you what I think so far?" Brad looked to Ashe and the agent made a rolling motion with a hand. *Keep talking.*

"I'll give you thirty seconds, Sheriff."

"Bo Taylor abandoned you and your sister. He should have provided support, but he didn't. You suffered for it, did without, and he deserves your low opinion of him."

Brad paused, waiting.

"Go ahead, Sheriff."

"He should have met his financial obligation. He should have done it of his own free will, but then, when your mother sued for support, he fought it and the court released him of the liability. That was unfair."

Another pause.

"Ten seconds, Sheriff."

"What more do you want, Truman?"

"Start digging. Tell me tomorrow. Five sharp."

"Truman—"

Click. Click.

An agent spoke to Ashe. "General Telephone Company. They say the call came from Franklin County, Florida, but that's all they have."

"He's moving around," Ashe fumed. "He knows what he's doing. Okay, tighten up on the Florida panhandle. Call the counties surrounding Franklin and request roadblocks."

Brad stood with a hand on the receiver, motionless.

"Brad, are you hungry?" Lanita asked.

"No."

"You have to eat." Lanita looked at Denise. "Both of you."

"Soup, then."

"Seven o'clock Tuesday," Darrell Ashe said. "Okay, we have that much." He spoke to an assistant. "Call the folks at WCTV and tell them Tuesday, seven P.M."

The phone rang. Machines started, earphones on:

"Sheriff?"

"Yes, Truman?"

"One more thing. I want you to have a telephone at your ear the entire time you talk on TV. I want it to be an extension of your own telephone line."

"I'm not sure that's possible."

"What a lummox." Truman sighed. "Just do it."

He disconnected.

"That bastard!" Brad slammed the wall with a fist. "I'm going to kill him. He'll pay for this!"

Denise saw Brunner light his pipe, puffing, listening. She went to him, shivering with emotion. "He sounds irrational, Dr. Brunner."

"Yes, but that may be a deliberate act to heighten your tension."

Dr. Rheems was reading the same teletyped message Brunner had studied. When he finished, he tapped a tooth with a fingernail.

"So he has read my book," Dr. Rheems said.

"Looks that way," Dr. Brunner answered.

"Hope he remembers the ending," Dr. Rheems noted.

Dr. Brunner chuckled.

"What is the ending, Dr. Brunner?" Denise questioned.

"The abductor is bested. One could hardly end such a text any other way."

24

Truman called after the evening news. His image had been displayed, an artist's rendition of the man as he appeared to Mother Taylor with a full beard. Then, as the drama unfolded, pictures of Elaine and Jeffrey were shown: *Have you seen these children?*

"Now, there you go," Truman crooned. "See what you can do with the media?"

He telephoned again following a late edition of televised news, and yet again after midnight, when WTBS beamed the story to satellites and TV stations nationally.

"Apalachicola, Florida," Darrell Ashe plotted the source of the calls. "Dothan, Alabama. Bainbridge, Georgia. Back to Florida. You'd think somebody would see him."

"He must be driving constantly," Dr. Rheems said. "He has to be tired. He'll make a mistake sooner or later. That's what we must anticipate."

"It would be difficult to move so freely with two children in tow," Dr. Brunner said.

The men congregated around the dining-room table, studying a map of the three-state juncture of Florida, Georgia, and Alabama.

"He's staying in the Tallahassee TV viewing area," they agreed. "That's good."

"We need ready units with helicopters." Dr. Rheems pointed to the map. "A unit here, another here, another here. The more the better, Ashe."

"I'll call Fort Rucker. Maybe the military can help."

"In the meantime," Dr. Rheems said, "let's stop trying to follow this guy around. Have your people stand still and wait—get some rest, eat, bathe—but be ready."

If the children weren't with Truman, where were they? Denise listened, watched, immobile and helpless. Vera called her family doctor for sedatives, but Denise refused to take them. Finally, with all the family gone except Vera, she went upstairs to rest.

"I'll sit beside the bed," Vera said. "I swear, if anything happens, no matter how small, I'll wake you."

Drugged by exhaustion, Denise slept at last. She awoke with the telephone ringing. It was daylight. Vera too had fallen asleep. She grabbed the receiver.

" 'Morning!" Truman's insufferable tone sent Denise's blood pressure up, her temples pounding. She heard Brad's reply. "Good morning, Truman."

"Looks like a nice day."

"How are Elaine and Jeffrey, Truman?" Dr. Rheems had urged Brad to call them by name. Try to get Truman to call them by name, establishing identity and personality to the abductor.

"Not as well as yesterday," Truman said. "This is a situation with exponential degrees of agony, Sheriff. Better get cracking!"

He hung up. A dial tone burred. Denise held the

phone until she heard an agent say, "Please hang up, Mrs. Taylor."

She sat on the side of the bed, head and abdomen aching from sustained nervous tension. The damned phone had been altered, the mouthpiece removed to prevent an outburst on her part. They had wanted to disconnect the bell, but Denise resisted angrily.

Vera was on the edge of her chair, where she'd spent the night. For the first time Denise could remember, the woman was without makeup. She was exceedingly plain.

"When I was a child," Denise said softly, "my father bought a calf. The farmer agreed to raise the calf for half the beef. On the day of slaughter, I went with my father to the abattoir. Because our calf had been fed an expensive enriched diet, my father wanted to walk alongside and be sure he got the steer he'd paid for."

Vera blinked.

"One after another, the cattle walked into a chute," Denise remembered. "They could smell their fate. I could smell it. Some went through as if to hurry and be done with it. Others balked and men used electric prods to push them forward. At a certain point, a steel frame clamped shut and pinned the steer so he couldn't move. A man stood with his legs spread, right above the trapped animal, and he hit the steer in the head with a sledgehammer. It stunned, but didn't kill. Then another man slit the steer's throat. Instantly, hooks were jabbed into the steer's rear tendons and he was snatched into the air, head down. So he would bleed 'cleanly,' my father said. The hooks moved on an overhead conveyor belt, the steer still quivering, eyes rolling, and before he was dead, they were cutting him open."

Vera was utterly still, her face the color of chalk.

"It didn't take more than a few seconds," Denise murmured. "But those few seconds seemed an eternity to me. I hadn't expected the violence. I can't remember why I was there—probably because I asked to go. I was very upset that they did what they did. I never ate a bite of that beef. I had nightmares, imagining what the steer must have suffered—struck, throat cut, jolted upside down, people tearing at his guts, the heart beating even as they snatched it out."

"Jesus, Denise . . ."

"I wondered what the steer must have thought."

"Denise . . ."

Denise took a breath, eyes dry. "Now I know," she said. "I feel so helpless, and I can see the hammer and the knife—"

"Oh God, Denise!" Vera grabbed her in a hug, holding Denise's head. "Oh God, Denise. Oh God . . ."

The kitchen sink was filled with dirty dishes, the counters sticky. Sugar crunched underfoot as Denise stepped into the room. Brad struggled to assemble a percolator, his greeting angry. "Where the hell is everybody?"

"I'll call them," Vera said.

"Brad, let me do that." Denise took the percolator. She heard Vera telephone Lanita, then make another call to her own home, where Mother Taylor was tending the children.

When she returned, Vera averted her eyes. "They aren't coming."

"Why not?" Brad asked.

"Because of Lana."

"How can they do that to us?" Brad seethed. "I wouldn't do that to Bob or Jack. If they needed us, we'd be there!"

"I'm here," Vera said.

"Shame on them," Brad cried. "Dammit . . . shame on them!"

Dr. Rheems arrived, clean-shaven, in a fresh shirt, his eyes clear as if he'd slept well. "Sheriff, may we speak privately?" he asked.

"You may not!" Denise erupted. "Talk to me too!"

"Very well. I've been thinking. We must remember the kind of man we're after." He poured himself some coffee and dumped teaspoons of sugar in his cup—one, two, three.

"Everything he does is calculated to wear us down. He's been moving about freely, so by now he knows we've guessed the children aren't with him. That can only suggest one of two things."

Brad's face drained to bloodless gray.

"Trying to think as Truman thinks," Dr. Rheems went on, "why would he jeopardize himself by moving at all? He could prevent a trace with shorter conversations. As it is, he allows us to locate the exchange, but not the number. On purpose, I think. Our deduction: he has left the children somewhere. If he is caught or slain, we suffer the loss. See what I'm saying?"

Brad's hand quivered, his coffee rippling.

"Dr. Brunner and I wish to suggest a gambit that is somewhat extraordinary, something Truman won't be expecting, if we're lucky."

"What is it?"

"With the next call," Dr. Rheems said to Denise and Vera, "I want you ladies to laugh. Talk loudly. I want everyone to talk. Jabber, jabber, jabber. Do that for just an instant after the sheriff lifts the receiver, then fall silent."

"What's the purpose?"

"Think as he thinks," Dr. Rheems said. "He hears revelry, joy—what does that mean? If he left the children somewhere safe, he may believe we've found them. If he knows they're not safe, he won't respond at all, or he'll mock us. So we hope, anyway."

"Why do it at all?" Denise asked.

Dr. Rheems added even more sugar to his coffee. "If he mocks us, Mrs. Taylor, we should assume less than the best."

In the ensuing lull, Denise heard the soft chatter of the teletype, men conversing in subdued voices.

"You'll assume they're dead—that's what you mean?" she asked. "What if you misinterpret his reaction?"

"Mustn't do that," Dr. Rheems mused.

"But what if you do? Does that mean you go rushing in on him—kill him?"

"No, ma'am. It means we've learned something rather critical. If he abducted the children at three o'clock, he had to do whatever he was going to do with them and get to a telephone by five-thirty. Assuming he drove the legal speed limit, assuming it took some amount of time to put the children wherever they are, this narrows our range of possible places to look. It proves, as an example, that they aren't two hundred miles away—probably not even seventy-five miles away. If they're well, they must be sheltered, have food and water."

"Suppose he buried them in a coffin, with an air vent," Denise argued. "Isn't that what some maniac in Atlanta did to his victim several years ago?"

"Let's get Truman's reaction," Dr. Rheems said. "Then we can debate possibilities. This will help set priorities, if nothing else."

"I don't think we should play with the bastard," Brad said. "My plan is still the safe one. When he calls the TV station with me on camera, you have time to trace the call."

"It's a good plan," Dr. Rheems assured Brad. "It's the plan we'll go with. But better that it be the *next* one than the one and only."

Darrell Ashe joined them, taking coffee. "Lana Taylor just arrived in Tallahassee. One of our agents is bringing her up."

"Good," Dr. Rheems said. "Now we'll have Lana to help, let us hope. If she can make him stay on the line longer, or even talk him out of this . . . who knows?"

Vera attacked the dirty dishes with a vengeance, flinging utensils from one side of the double stainless-steel sink to the other.

"Thank you for staying, Vera," Brad said.

"I'm staying because someone should, Brad. Not because I agree with bringing this woman to Thomasville. Bob and Jack are right in protesting. Mother Taylor is so distraught she is nearly out of her mind. This Lana woman will only make a bad situation worse."

"Thanks for staying," Brad said again.

Lana Taylor was so obviously what she was. Her hair was bleached, her lips were shocking red, her cheeks were circles of rouge. She wore cheap costume jewelry, rings on several fingers, and vivid artificial nails. What time had not marked, experience had. When she sat, her short skirt rode up her thighs. She seemed to ignore Denise altogether, playing to the men.

"Tell me about Truman," Dr. Brunner said.

"Me and him was always close."

"Are you still close?"

"More than most." She looked down to the lighted match held for her cigarette. Her eye shadow was dappled with glitter, making Denise think of the plaster dolls given as prizes in a carnival.

"Truman, he was a good brother." Lana exhaled smoke through her nostrils, digging in an oversized pocketbook for something. "Him and Mama, that was another story."

"They didn't get along?" Dr. Brunner asked.

"Like spit on a hot griddle. Mama drinks. Truman, he thinks people can do or not do when they want to. They fight about that."

"But he does get along with you." Dr. Brunner smiled.

"Better than most. He looked after me when we was kids. Take a poke at me and you took a poke at Truman. He whipped asses when he had to."

"Do you think you might reason with him, Lana?"

"Sometimes I can, other times I can't. Depends on his mood. One day he'd give me the world, the next he wouldn't lend a splinter if I was drowning. With Truman, see, it depends on what you want out of him. He ain't stupid, I'll tell you. He always could see through people."

"How does he feel about you, Lana?"

"If you're asking would he do something he doesn't want to, just because I ask—forget it. What's in it for him, see."

"All these years," Dr. Brunner said, "what has been in it for him—that you could give him, that is."

"I take him like he is and I don't make nothing of it when he's bad." She looked round as if for the first time. "Nice house."

"What I'm trying to find out—"

"Hell, sugar, I know what you're trying to find out. Am I willing to suck him in and would he fall for it. I mean, that's it, ain't it?"

"Yes."

"I might, but he won't." Lana looked Denise up and down. "My sister, I guess."

"Sister-in-law." Denise tried to smile. "This is your half-brother, Bradley."

Brad extended a hand and Lana took it, chin down, so coy it was farcical. "My God," she said, "you're the spitting image of Truman. Did you know that?"

"Yes. I saw his photograph."

"Both of you like Daddy, too."

"We're pleased to meet you, Lana," Brad said.

"Honey," Lana said, "it's like pissing on a flat rock. I may be a relief, but I'm no pleasure, and that's all right too. Good to meet you. I always been curious about you folks."

"Would you like to freshen up?" Denise asked.

"This is as good as I get."

"Have you had lunch?"

"Breakfast." Lana laughed throatily. "My work being what it is, I get up about now, usually."

"Breakfast, then, Miss Taylor," Denise offered.

"*Miss* Taylor! Call me Lana and I'll call you Denise."

It was painful. Chain-smoking, making dry spitting noises as if tobacco had bypassed her filtered cigarettes, the woman was coarse and vulgar. Dr. Brunner gently led her back to his inquiry, patiently enduring the interruptions, feeling for a chord Truman might respond to.

"He'll kill them kids in a second," Lana said. "He's got no patience with kids. If one looks at him cross-eyed, Truman will slap him straight-faced."

Darrell Ashe tried to maneuver Denise out, but she shook him off, listening.

"Let me tell you what you got to do." Lana leaned over her own knee, lecturing. "You got to do whatever he says do, and then maybe—just maybe, now—he'll do what you want. Me and him have been dumped on, you know what I mean? Hockeyed on until we're hockeyproof. There been two people in my life who give a diddly damn about me. One was Truman, the other was Daddy."

"Bo Taylor?" Brad asked, astonished.

"Your daddy! My daddy. Bo Taylor."

"Was he a loving father?" Dr. Brunner asked.

"Only man ever did love me. My mama was a whore. I had a psychiatrist tell me that's what made me one. Now, Mama got nicer to me when we were grown, but when we lived down by the icehouse, she'd go out for coffee and be gone six days! Daddy come home and he cooked and washed and cleaned house. He took time with Truman and me. Truman hated him because he loved me. He truly did. Hated him! But Daddy was nice to me. Bless his heart, he'd look after me—only man that ever did."

"Was Dad cruel to Truman?" Brad asked.

"Truman needed some meanness whipped out of him. Daddy obliged more than once. Truman deserved it, though. He won't admit it, but he was a tough little bastard. Well, he met his match in Daddy."

"To you, however, he was a good father," Dr. Brunner said.

"Damned good. And before it was over, I had had several to judge him by. Mama brought home any man with the price of Jack Daniel's. Food, not a bite to eat, but she brought home the boozers."

She lit another cigarette, blew smoke in twin plumes. Again she pawed through her purse. "Anybody got a hanky?"

Denise gave her a tissue.

"Thank you, honey." Lana dabbed one eye, then the other, examining her face in a mirror. Then slowly she lifted her head and stared at Denise.

"Your kids, they said."

"Elaine and Jeffrey."

"He won't molest her sexually," Lana said. "That is *one* thing he won't do. So you don't worry about that."

"You seem so sure," Dr. Brunner said.

"I am sure. See, Truman, he's got his morals. He's smart, too, Knows big words. Sometimes I don't understand a thing he says. He can drive you crazy spouting rhymes, too. He always could do that, even when he was going to Eastside school here in town. God, this place has changed! They shut down the train station, didn't they? We come by it, coming here."

"Yes, they did."

"First time Truman ever run away, he jumped a freight car going to Valdosta." She laughed. "That was one time Daddy let him have it. Truman couldn't walk for a week. That's what I meant. Truman asked for it!"

"Lana," Dr. Brunner asked gently, "would you try to reason with Truman? For the sake of the children?"

"I'll talk to him, hell yes. I'd like to talk to him. I reckon he's got his butt in a sling for sure, this time. I got a message from Mama, anyhow."

"What is the message?"

" 'Throw it over your shoulder and squirt it up your ass. With love.' "

"It would be better if we avoid antagonizing him," Dr. Brunner said.

"He'll think it's funny. Mama always told him he wasn't no man until he could do that."

"Nevertheless, due to his mental state right now, it would be wiser to devote our energy to pacifying him."

"You don't know Truman." She turned to Denise, then looked beyond her. "Is that my sister?"

"Vera," Denise introduced them, "this is Lana. Vera is your sister-in-law. I don't think you have any sisters."

"I wasn't sure. Truman used to imagine we had a sister—always making up godawful stories about things happening to her. He did it to scare me, and scare me it did until I was old enough to know better. Aunt Marie—he killed her, you say?"

"Suspected of it," Darrell Ashe said.

"Probably did. She never liked him, either. I always wondered if that old bitch was playing around with Daddy."

Vera was in the kitchen door, as yet not saying a word.

"All right, gentlemen." Denise stepped forward. "Lana has had a hard trip. Vera, could we get iced tea in the guest bedroom? Come on, Lana, I'll run you a hot bath and you can change clothes. These men will wear you out with questions, if we let them."

"It's okay by me."

Denise heard an agent say to Darrell Ashe, "The wire services have learned this telephone number somehow. What should I say to them?"

"I'll talk to them."

"Must be nice living in a house like this." Lana walked the stairs in awe. "Got them chandeliers like hotels have. Pretty place, ain't it?"

"Let me show you around," Denise said. "This is Elaine's room."

"It's nice," Lana said.

"Across the hall is Jeffrey's room. He's eleven, Elaine is thirteen."

"Looks like a boy's room, don't it?"

"He's such a bright little boy." Denise attempted a laugh and it caught in her throat. "He reads . . ." She fought for control. "Far beyond his age. He . . ."

Struggling for composure, she stood there with

this painted creature, this alien being who was somehow linked to Brad and Bob and Jack by blood.

An unfinished crossword puzzle was on the floor. Denise picked it up, placed it on Jeffrey's bedside table.

"Smart, ain't he?" Lana examined the neatly printed letters. "That's how Tru was when he was a kid. Too smart, really. Outsmarted hisself."

"Jeffrey is a quiet boy."

"Truman, too. They're a lot alike."

"I don't think Jeffrey would be . . . He is so . . . he tries very hard to be polite."

"Truman did that, when we lived in Thomasville. Right up until Daddy told Mama she had to go."

"Bo sent her away?"

"Said he'd kill her if she didn't go," Lana said. She sighed, nodded, looking around. "Yes, ma'am, this is nice. Sheriffs make good money, do they?"

"Let me show you the guestroom, Lana. You'll be sleeping in there."

"Canopy bed," Lana marveled. "Can-oh-pee! Don't it catch the dust?"

"I'm afraid it does."

Lana halted, staring. A picture of Father Taylor taken years ago, a Christmas gift from Mother Taylor, hung on the wall.

"That's him," Lana whispered. "That's Daddy. He was so sweet to me. I wish it could've been different."

She turned suddenly. "I'm sorry about your babies, Denise. Truman shouldn't have taken the babies."

"I love my children, Lana."

"He shouldn't of done that."

"Will you help me, Lana?"

"It ain't me," Lana said in a low wail. "It's Truman! If it was up to me, I wouldn't have took them in the first place."

Somewhere afar, people talked in the hushed tone of people waiting, as in a doctor's office.

Denise burst into tears.

Lana seemed confused a moment, then took Denise in her arms. "There, there, there," she said. "He ain't going to hurt them kids. I'll tell him he can't and that's all there is to it. Come on, now, cut off the waterworks."

"I'm sorry."

"Hell, honey," Lana said, "if I had a penny for every time I've cried, I'd be richer'n Rockefeller."

25

Forty-eight hours ago, the world was steady, the party preparations nearly complete . . .

Denise stood at her bedroom window looking down on the guards patrolling the perimeter of the yard. Protecting them from the public, not Truman. A van had arrived from an Albany TV station, feeding stories to NBC. Another from Tallahassee was doing the same for CBS.

Behind her, Vera worked on Lana. Vera had brought several of her own chic dresses for Lana to try. "To look your best on TV," Vera had said.

"In California," Lana said, "people like bright colors."

"That sort of thing doesn't photograph well." Vera combed Lana's hair into a new style. "On TV you want to be as natural as possible. You never know when a talent scout will be watching."

"You're conning me," Lana replied. "But it's okay. This looks good."

A few minutes ago, Mother Taylor had phoned Denise with an emotional recrimination, a final plea to send Lana away. Mother Taylor had seen a television account of their lives, based on speculation and conjecture. It was not complimentary. "Blood feud . . ."

"Now for eye shadow and rouge." Vera stood back to examine her work. "Something subtle, something to highlight those beautiful eyes."

"Say, you're pretty good at this." Lana flicked ashes from her cigarette into her coffee cup. "Are you a beautician, or what?"

"No." Vera took it bravely. "I learned by trying things on myself."

A tap on the door. Before Denise could reach it, Brad leaned through. "Dr. Rheems wants to see us, Denise."

In the hallway, he hugged her a moment, then held her arm going downstairs.

"We've decided not to use Lana yet," Dr. Rheems said.

"But why?"

"We want to try our idea of fooling Truman into thinking we've found the children. If he knows Lana is here, that ploy will be futile."

"Then why did we bring her here?" Denise asked.

"The more options, the better," Dr. Rheems said. "I want you to meet some people."

Three women. A police officer; a secretary from the FBI office; Darrell Ashe's wife. Dr. Rheems placed them around the room as if blocking movements for a stage play.

"I want this to sound like a party in progress," Dr. Rheems said. "Say 'Cheese and crackers' or 'Soup and noodles' or anything that come to mind—but say it happily. All right, let's try it."

He raised his hands as if to conduct an orchestra, then brought his arms down. The voices were strident and he waved them to silence. "It isn't a pep rally," he said. "It's a party. Turn to the person next to you and start jabbering. You ladies—laugh—come on, laugh!"

Again they rehearsed, the conversations more subdued. Darrell Ashe and his wife laughed raucously.

"Better," Dr. Rheems said. "Now, what we want is this: a call interrupts the merriment and we all realize it, but not suddenly, not all at once. When Sheriff Taylor answers the telephone, keep it up until I point at you, then stop. Mrs. Ashe, you have a wonderful laugh."

"Thank you."

"Keep laughing until I point at you. There's always somebody who is a little slow to catch on to what's happening. In this scene, that's you. Now, let's try it. Sheriff, you pretend to answer the telephone when I say 'Ring.' "

The bizarre rehearsal was absurd, unreal. Denise stood by the telephone recording equipment.

"Ring!" Dr. Rheems called. He lifted his arms, eyebrows raised, and the players assumed their roles. Laughter shrilled, conversation ebbed and flowed. "Ring!" Dr. Rheems played the bell.

Brad put a hand to his ear. "Hello?"

Dr. Rheems pointed first to one, then another, then all of them except Mrs. Ashe—finally even her. Total quiet. He turned up his palms smugly. "That was all right. Let's do it again."

On her hands and knees, Peggy crawled along the floor, sweeping her arms in search of canned foods. *A broken jar*—one more hazard to consider.

Elaine's condition was becoming critical. The handcuffs were now deep within her swollen flesh, the skin so taut it felt as if it could burst. Peggy had tried to pry apart the links, using a wire handle from the thermal chest. It didn't work. Elaine screamed when pressure twisted her shoulders.

The medical aspects of Elaine's predicament were frightening. She might have a dislocated shoulder and torn ligaments. The handcuffs had severely impeded her circulation. Her pain had become a torture.

"Stop rubbing me, Jeffrey!"

"I'm trying to help, Elaine."

"You're hurting me. Please stop."

Peggy felt her way through puddles, her hands and clothing so slimy she considered disrobing. But she didn't—all they had was touch.

They had all begun to see flashes of light. At first Peggy thought their eyes had become so accustomed to dark that the faintest illumination was now visible. But it was a trick of the mind, the same phenomenon experienced in a dimly lighted room when blood corpuscles floated across the retina, giving the viewer the illusion of spots before the eyes.

"Peggy!" Elaine shrieked.

"I'm here, darling. I'm trying to find the rest of the food."

"May I help?" Jeffrey asked.

"No. Stay there. I found broken glass over here."

A foul odor stopped her. It was where they took their toilet. Peggy moved away from the stench, groping for cans.

The food was nearly gone, as much wasted as consumed. The ice was gone. So, too, was most of their water.

"Want to play another word game, Elaine?"

"No Jeffrey! Leave me alone."

"I wish you didn't hurt," the boy said.

"Well, I do." A moment later, "Thank you, Jeffrey."

When they used the last of the bottled water, Peggy

returned to the room with a sloping floor where liquid dripped incessantly. She had tasted the drops from the overhead pipes. It was so rancid, it had to be rain that had slowly seeped through.

She had waded to the depth of her waist, the floor as slick as a mossy stone in a stagnant pool. Her feet slipped and she plunged in over her head. Every attempt to stand send her deeper, coughing, gasping, clawing for safety. She had gashed her arm, the gap in flesh sickening to feel. In the dark, water was indistinguishable from blood—but the cut seemed to be flesh, not artery.

In a sanctum devoid of sound, their ears began to ring. It was a medical condition called tinnitus. A secondary and more bizarre form of the same thing afflicted Elaine—clicking tinnitus, caused by the opening and closing of the mouth of the eustachian tubes, or by a rhythmic spasm of the velum palati. When it occurred in Elaine, the click was also audible to Jeffrey and Peggy.

"You sound like a cricket with hiccups," Jeffrey teased.

"I wish it would get out of my head," Elaine replied sourly.

Here and there, throughout the freezer rooms, pieces of debris indicated some of the cork in the walls and ceiling had fallen. But despite Jeffrey's efforts, with Peggy holding him aloft, they had not found a hole anywhere.

"Peggy!" Elaine screamed.

"I'm here, darling. I'm here."

The girl mumbled, lapsing into sleep or unconsciousness, her brain short-circuiting to relieve her body of the relentless pain.

Still crawling, feeling for lost footstuffs, Peggy felt her hatred of Truman grow into a white-hot thirst for vengeance. If she could reach him, she would dig his eyes out, rip his flesh with her teeth—even if he killed her, she would avenge this torment.

She prayed that Tuesday had come and gone. That Uncle Zachary had reported her missing. Then it occurred to her, Truman might have been telephoning Uncle Zachary to reassure him, to stall the inevitable. The idea evoked murderous impulses.

She crawled across a metal grid. Her fingers sore from rough concrete, she made her way back to the cot. Elaine's breathing was a liquid gurgle of short inhalations, shallow expulsions. By touch, Peggy found Jeffrey at his sister's side.

"She passed out, Peggy."

"At least she isn't hurting, Jeffrey."

"Peggy," he said softly, "we're in real trouble, aren't we?"

"Be brave, Jeffrey."

Like a puppy, he pushed under her arm, seeking comfort. "I'm wet," she said.

"I don't care."

Ring . . .

Denise jumped up from the kitchen table, running.

"Here we go, everybody!" Dr. Rheems stood in the den, arms raised.

Ring . . .

Voices rose in discordant babble. Darrell Ashe and his wife faced one another, laughing.

Ring . . .

Brad lifted the receiver. "Hello?"

In a quick but disjointed response, talk ceased, laughter faded. Breathless, Denise took the earphones and listened.

"Hello," Brad said again.

"Taylor?"

"Yes, Truman."

Silence.

"Truman," Brad said. "I'm here."

"What's happening?"

"I was waiting for your call."

Truman hung up.

Distressed, Brad turned to face the room. Dr. Rheems took the receiver from him, cradled it.

"What do you think?" Brad asked Dr. Rheems.

"He's sitting somewhere trying to figure it out," Rheems said. "A party? What the hell does that mean?"

The clock ticked. Denise could smell her own perspiration despite deodorant applied only an hour ago. Through the windows she saw uniformed men in cool pools of shade, people across the street looking toward the house.

Ring . . .

"All rightee." Dr. Rheems put his hand on the phone, speaking to Brad. "This time, don't overdo it. Try to sound as if you're trying to sound normal. Do not mention the children unless he does."

He gave the phone to Brad. "Hello?"

"You hear me, you son of a bitch," Truman shouted. "You do precisely as I say or you will pay with nightmares for the rest of your life."

Denise could hear his labored breathing, the tension curdling his words.

"Trying to play with me?" Truman screamed. "Trying to shit the shitter? You bastard, I'll give you agony you can't imagine!"

Brad waited.

"Are you ready for your confession, Taylor?"

"We need to discuss that, Truman."

"Cut the shit, you son of a bitch! No more patience, you got that? I have no more patience! Tomorrow evening at seven o'clock, you be on WCTV. Your goddamned confession had better be in full and satisfactory, because that's it—one shot—that's it! You have a telephone, an extension of your own home phone, and don't leave the line. Do you understand, Taylor?"

"I think so."

"I can't hear you!" he screamed.

"I understand."

"Loud and clear, Taylor, loud and clear! This is it—one time and that's it, no second chance."

"Truman, let's talk about you."

Obscenities poured into Denise's ears. The distant receiver slammed hard. The dial tone returned. An agent took her earphones, coiled the line.

"I think," Dr. Rheems said, "I pray, he left them alive. If he knew they were dead, he would have remained calm and mocked us."

Please, God, please . . .

Rheems turned to Dr. Brunner. "What do you say, Oscar?"

"I think he left them alive. I think he thinks they still are. I believe it worked to that degree."

The room erupted in cheering and Dr. Rheems quelled it irritably.

"Do you think he will try to find out for sure, Oscar?"

Dr. Brunner sat with long legs crossed, puffing his pipe, considering. "He may reason: if they've been found, what's the purpose in going to see? If they haven't been found and this was a trick, going to see only puts him in jeopardy."

"Then why did we do it?" Denise cried. "You should have thought of those things before we teased him."

"We did, Mrs. Taylor. But now we know the children are alive so far as Truman knows—he left them that way, at least. That gives us an important psychological edge."

Darrell Ashe tore paper from the teletype. "They found Truman's car," he said. "It was abandoned in Biloxi, Mississippi."

The agent read aloud, " 'A man answering Truman Taylor's description, with full beard, checked into a motel in Biloxi. His automobile, the one registered in Pennsylvania, was hauled to a garage for repair. The suspect forfeited the vehicle in lieu of a mechanic's lien. He stayed in the motel one week, keeping company with the niece of the motel owner. When last seen, the girl, Caucasian, age twenty-four, medical student, left with the suspect in her car.' "

He described the vehicle: "Two-door Chevrolet sedan, dark red body with cream vinyl top. We have the tag numbers."

"He's with somebody?" Brad questioned. "That woman could be holding the children!"

"With Truman's history," Ashe replied, "it's more likely he has killed her."

Upstairs, pacing the floor, Brad held a glass of bourbon. "It's only a matter of time," he said. "He can't move far; we know what to look for."

Denise sat on the bed. "What about the confession, Brad?"

"I doubt we'll go through with it. But if I do, I'll say what the bastard wants to hear."

"Which is what?"

Brad sipped liquor. "I'll say Dad abandoned his first family. I'll say he didn't follow through with financial assistance. I'll say Truman is right, Dad should have done that."

"I don't think that will be enough."

"What would you have me say?"

"Truman hasn't put his life in danger to hear what you just said, Brad."

"What more is there to say?"

"Whatever is motivating Truman is bound to be much more serious than financial neglect."

"Look, Denise." He put his drink on a dresser. "He can't make a move. If he steals a car, we'll know it. If he stays with the one he has, we'll get him. If he tries to hitchhike, he'll be spotted. There are hundreds of men out there. When they corner Truman, and they will, he doesn't have Elaine and Jeffrey with him, so his chips are gone. One wrong move and he's dead. He'll tell us where they are. These bastards are all cowards when it comes to the showdown."

"I don't think he's a coward. I don't think he's worried about being killed, either. I think he came here prepared to die, if necessary, to get what he wants."

"He isn't going to get it."

"Let me tell you what I think, Brad."

He sat beside her and rubbed his eyes tiredly.

"Truman was born to a young father married to an older woman who ran around with other men. Renee left her children in the care of Father Taylor much of the time."

"We know that."

"Father Taylor was frustrated. Angry with his wife, ashamed of her, shamed by her. Unable to cope. There he was, Aunt Marie said, washing clothes and cooking meals. Renee's reputation reflected on him. She used him. It must have been unbearable to a naive young man."

"I can believe that."

"Now let's examine the children," Denise said. "Truman became emotionally attached to his teacher, Ailene Adkins. Miss Adkins liked him, helped him complete school assignments. She taught him to appreciate language and poetry. She described Truman as sensitive, a natural thespian who excelled when reciting aloud to classmates. He memorized A. E. Housman's *A Shropshire Lad*. That pleased her."

"You've told me that, Denise."

"Of all his teachers, only Ailene Adkins escaped the embarrassing scenes created by Renee. That's very telling, Brad. It means Truman protected Miss Adkins from his mother. Then something terrible happened, something that changed his life forever. If Truman had had a woman like Mother Taylor to turn to, or if Father Taylor had been a slightly different man with more maturity, or if Truman had received compassion from Miss Adkins, he might have weathered the trauma. If any of those things had been so, Truman might be sitting in this house tonight, a welcome guest."

"Denise, for Christ's sake. We can speculate endlessly."

"What happened was child abuse, Brad."

He blinked angrily. "Are you about to blame Dad for this . . . this maniac?"

"I'm afraid it's true."

"I don't want to hear it! Goddammit, I do *not* want to hear it. My dad must have gone through hell. It's a wonder he survived. But he did, married again, more wisely, and the result was us! Bob and Jack and me."

"That's a part of the pity of it," Denise said. "Truman is the flip side of this family coin. He is what you might have become, and you are what he should have been."

"Give me another drink, Denise."

She went to her knees, holding his hand. "It's hard enough to say this without fighting to say it. Please, Brad, listen."

"Ask Dr. Brunner what kind of syndrome this is," Brad said. "Maybe it's the Stockholm syndrome by proxy, where captives become protective toward their captors."

"I think Father Taylor sexually molested Lana, Brad."

"Denise ... My God, Denise, we don't have to pander to this man's demented mind."

"I think he did, Brad. I think he did."

"Does she say that? Hell no! She says Dad was a loving father, the only man who ever loved her, besides Truman."

"That's what she would say," Denise insisted. "Her craving for love was so overwhelming she accepted sex from her father as attention she desperately needed. But the result in such cases is a horrible sense of worthlessness in the girl. That has been so all her life. When Truman tried to stop it, telling his teacher, she called Lana in and Lana denied it—that's what she *would* do!"

Denise squeezed his hand hard. "Imagine what it was like for Truman," she pleaded. "He took his terrible story to a trusted teacher and she refused to believe him. If she had supported him at that moment, how different things might have been. At about the same time, Miss Adkins was having an affair and Truman retaliated in the most cruel way he could— exposing her. The whole thing came to the attention of the principal; then Father Taylor was drawn into it and the mess became public knowledge. Truman was ridiculed by his classmates, beaten to silence by a frightened father whose very survival depended on silence. With things out of control, Father Taylor drove Renee and her children away. The entire town supported the move."

"You can't believe that."

"I do, though. I do believe it. I've thought about things Felder Nichols told me—defending Bo Taylor as 'young and naive.' Aunt Marie damned that twelve-year-old boy and she claimed Lana was a 'flirt' at nine! Lana was more concerned with keeping her father's affection than in exposing him. That is a common reaction among girls caught in such circumstances. What was her alternative? She saw Truman beaten. Her mother didn't love her. God knows what Father Taylor had threatened."

"You don't *believe* that."

"If it's true, that's the confession Truman wants."

"I will not do it. That's going too far. I'm not sure I'd believe it if Lana swore it to be a fact. But she doesn't, does she? We're dealing with delusions of a warped boy who became a psychotic man."

"Think about the books in your father's library," Denise argued. "Books about parental brutality, child abuse. He was reading them as recently as a few years ago. *Prisoners of Childhood* wasn't translated into English until 1981. Why those topics, Brad? Why the lifelong consuming interest?"

"I don't care to guess."

"Could it be Father Taylor writhed over his early years? He never cared what motivated criminals—we've both commented on it. He wasn't reading for professional purposes. But he did care about himself. Judge Nichols said Father Taylor was a man who knew what made people tick, knew what *made himself* tick."

"Dad was a gentle, loving, kind—"

"Was he, Brad? Be as objective as possible. Not like Lana, clinging to fantasies which reinforce her desire for love—but reality. He never hugged, never kissed."

"Never spanked, never once."

"Parents who punish judiciously are parents who care enough to do it. Whether punishment is correct of not, healthy parents do it out of love."

"He was a good father, a good husband, a responsible citizen."

"All of that," Denise agreed. "But in those dark days of immaturity, under the stress he suffered, was he a child molester? If he overcame that, and apparently he did, that's a testimony to Father Taylor's will to better himself. But it still left Truman destroyed by a teacher with whom he was infatuated. Destroyed by the father who must have beaten him into submission. Destroyed by a community that did nothing, then finally moved to protect the abusive father at the expense of the children. Truman and Lana were consigned to the care of an uncaring mother. The result: a prostitute for a sister, an alcoholic mother. Then came trouble with the law, according to the FBI and Lana. Finally the military. And now, as Dr. Brunner describes it, he is psychologically unable to bond to another being. He is emotionally stunted at 'about age twelve.' "

"I will not slander my father."

"Our children will die if it takes that to get the confession. I think Truman is determined to make it public."

"Then why didn't he say that?"

"Because, darling, he wanted you to believe it. He wanted you to know it was the truth—and for everyone who ever heard about it to realize it too."

"It is *not* true."

"Felder Nichols may have . . . *must* have known it. Let's go talk to him."

26

It was almost midnight when Denise and Brad rang Felder Nichols' doorbell. As they waited in the yellow light of his front porch, tree frogs burped, cicadas lending a vibrato note to night sounds.

Judge Nichols greeted them wearing a silk robe and slippers. He talked as he led the way to his den; apologizing because his servants had left for the day. "But we can have a drink," he said, going to the credenza.

"Dreadful thing this," he said as he poured liquor. "One wonders what kind of animals prowl the world, when this sort of thing occurs."

In silence Brad sat and accepted the drink, eyes glazed as if in shock. Judge Nichols wandered to subjects other than the purpose of this extraordinary visit.

"Bo was a fine, fine man," he said. "We started digging red wigglers when we had nothing but a sapling pole and a bent pin for a hook. That's when our friendship began, as children."

"Judge Nichols—" Denise cut in.

"That's us." He swiveled his chair, pointing to a photograph on a wall. "That was over at Lake Seminole. That little boy with us is Truman."

Brad stood up, went over to look more closely.

"I would say 'in the good old days,' " Felder Nichols mused, "but that's a subjective judgment. We spent two weeks over there—the bass were biting anything that rippled the water. Bo was a young deputy sheriff and I was a barrister trying to start private practice. Money was so scarce we couldn't afford a motor, so we rowed."

"Judge Nichols," Denise said, "we came to talk about Truman."

"I look back on my life," the judge said, "I look back and thank God for my blessings. Never had to go to war. Never had to kill my fellowman—not sure I could have. But as a jurist, a judge of men in trouble, I've known a few that should be killed. I believe in capital punishment, don't you, Brad?"

"Yes, sir, I do."

"Not as it's applied maybe," Judge Nichols said. "Not as 'punishment.' A dead man suffers nothing. If you want to punish, lock him up for life. But if he's like Truman has become, as the FBI described him to me—the man should be put to death. It's the only sure safeguard society has—right, Sheriff?"

"Yes, sir." Brad sat again, face gray.

"Judge Nichols," Denise said, "we need to know several things."

"Concerning the confession idea," Judge Nichols surmised. "Darrell Ashe has kept me informed. He came to see me, he and a Washington psychiatrist."

"Dr. Brunner," Brad supplied.

"Yes, Brunner." Judge Nichols swallowed liquor, poured another glass without offering more to Brad or Denise.

"Those federal boys are very thorough," he said, "trying to second-guess the fugitive, predict what the man will do. I told them what I knew of him."

"Did you tell them about Father Taylor?" Denise asked.

"His records speaks for itself," Nichols replied. "Over forty years of public service, never a hint of scandal. Fine upstanding family—except for this black sheep, Truman."

"Did you tell Dr. Brunner about Lana?"

"I never knew that girl. Truman I knew from moments like at Lake Seminole—in the picture, there."

"Judge Nichols," Brad asked, "was my father an abusive man?"

"Define that."

"Sexually abusive to Lana," Denise provided. "Physically abusive to Truman."

Judge Nichols rocked his chair slightly. "Times have changed," he said softly. "They send TV pictures from space, put a man on the moon. Who would've believed such?"

"Please, Judge, this is important—we must know. Brad is going on television at seven o'clock tomorrow evening. Truman will be on a telephone with Brad—he'll be watching. He says the confession must be true and complete."

"Years ago," Nichols said, "we never heard of psychiatrists. We didn't have much time for philosophy, and we sure by God didn't have sympathy with folks who thought you could 'cure' criminals as if they were diseased. Times have changed."

"About Truman," Denise said.

"One thing I think about as I grow older is irony." Judge Nichols smiled mirthlessly. "Irony must be God in motion when he's got nothing else to worry about. God with a wry sense of humor, God the vindictive."

Judge Nichols put a hand over his face, massaging his forehead. He sighed.

"I think of Richard Nixon, who wanted to be President so much—and disgraced himself. Nothing he can ever do, nothing his children ever do, will make the shame less."

Still massaging, face covered, Judge Nichols dug hard with his thumb and forefingers. "When a man stands before my bench, accused and convicted, I ask myself: What might he have been? He must ask a thousand times: How did I come to this?"

"We have the make and model of his car, we have his tag number," Brad blurted. "He can't move. We'll get him!"

"Yes you will."

"Judge Nichols, please." Denise sat on the edge of her chair, placing the untasted Scotch aside. "We need the absolute truth. If it comes to that, Brad must know what to say."

"Lana is in our house," Brad said. "She says Dad was a loving father. I *know* he was."

"Oh God, Judge Nichols, please . . ."

He put his hand down, pushing back in his chair, peering up at the darkened ceiling. "Bo came to me one night. Shocked. Frightened. Shaking like a loblolly pine in high wind."

The muscles in Brad's face drew taut.

"He'd lost his temper, he said. Started out spanking Truman and he lost his temper."

Denise took Brad's hand.

"He thought he'd killed the boy," Nichols said. "Hit him, kicked him, beat him until the boy wasn't breathing. Bo said he fell on his knees, praying, blowing in the boy's mouth, pounding his chest to make his heart beat again. That was the night it came to an end."

"We all lose our tempers," Brad said.

"Yes, we do, and I told myself that. I knew that gentle giant—he was my lifelong friend. I knew what Renee was doing to him, everybody did. I knew . . . everything."

Judge Nichols sighed again, a massive exhalation. He hadn't looked straight at them since he began.

"Bo told me the truth. Told me about Lana. About the beatings. How he hated Renee enough to kill her. He'd thought about it. Hatred and frustration had made him strike at people he'd arrested, he said. And at his children, he said."

After a long pause Nichols raised his brow. "That Lana . . ."

"Was there sexual abuse?"

Judge Nichols swallowed. "The beating was because Truman went to his teacher. The school knew. The town knew. Bo had to deny it."

"And Lana—was that true?"

He nodded.

"What did you do about it?" Brad asked.

"What I thought was right at the time. I told Bo to send Renee and the kids away. It was obvious the marriage was damaging to the youngsters. Bo agreed. That night he told Renee to take them and go, or he'd kill her. Wisely, she went."

Denise sat back, drained.

"I told Bo it didn't have to happen again," Nichols continued. "I found books for him to read so he'd know what made it happen at all. I introduced him to a different stratum of society, a genteel society away from the sordid professional lawman's world. When you walk in muck day after day, you begin to believe muck is all there is in this world. When you

live as Bo was living, you're positive that's all there is.
I introduced him to Annette."

"He sent them away—and that was it?" Denise
asked.

"Oh no. Renee was a grasping woman. She came
back to try to sue Bo for alimony and child support
after he won election as sheriff. Money for booze—
she sure as hell wouldn't spend it on her children.
Troy Bacon helped fight that off. I spoke to a friend
of mine who was a judge."

Brad stared at the floor, fingers tightly interlaced.

"Bo never put a hand to you boys," Judge Nichols
said. "He never touched Annette in anger. He justified my faith in him. It was Renee—more so than
Bo—she was the difference between what is and
what was."

"Then it's true," Brad murmured.

"Bo was young, virile," Judge Nichols said. "At a
certain age the glands are stronger than the mind.
It's the drive that keeps a species in existence. At a
certain age a young man will rape a briar patch if he
thinks there's a rabbit in it. It's the surest proof that
some criminals may be victims of hormonal flow."

"How long did you know?" Denise asked softly.
"About Lana and what was happening to her?"

"You see a bruised child, you wonder," Nichols
hedged. "She told her teachers she was sore. Truman was bruised black and blue a time or two. Denise, you've seen little girls crawling on the boys—that
doesn't mean incest."

Judge Nichols stood up suddenly, paced two steps,
turned and paced his way back, sitting.

"You don't know what's right or wrong until it's
too goddamned late to change it. You let one man
go on probation and it restructures his life. Another
goes free and immediately murders someone. With

your own children, you don't know! More strict, or less? More punishment, tighter reins, or more lax in your control? You don't *know* until they're grown, until it's too late."

He placed a fist in his other hand, softly. "I was wrong. Not about Bo—he proved himself for the rest of his life. But about Truman, I was wrong. I should have done something—a foster home, something. But, my God, Brad—institutionalize them? That was my alternative. Would that be better than staying with their mother?"

"Now we know what Truman wants to hear, Brad," Denise said.

"Don't blame Bo—goddammit it, don't do that," Felder Nichols said hoarsely. "Blame me. Blame Troy Bacon, who came to me twice, worried about what was happening in that family. Blame the teachers and the neighbors who did nothing. Don't lay it all on Bo Taylor. He doesn't deserve it."

Brad stood up as if exhausted. "Thank you, Judge Nichols."

"I'm so sorry, Brad. I'd have gone to my grave with that secret, had it not been for your children."

"I appreciate it."

At the door, Judge Nichols said, "I've been thinking about this and nothing else since hearing the news Saturday evening. I'd give anything to make it go away."

"Thank you."

"God help you," Judge Nichols said. "God help us all."

As Brad pulled into their driveway, his headlights swept over Deputy Smitherman, who stood waiting, hat in hand.

"Smitherman, are you working the late shift?"

"Everybody is, Sheriff. I hate to disturb you . . ."

"It's all right. What is it?"

"A waiter at the Holiday Inn called this evening. He's a kid. Been at the beach for the Fourth and only now heard the news. He thinks he remembers this Truman Taylor fellow, he says. I went out and talked to him."

"Would you care for a cup of coffee, Smitherman?"

"No, thanks, sir. Anyway, the waiter says there was a girl with him. He didn't see her too well, but she took a newspaper he delivered to the room. I had the desk check the records and this Truman made a long-distance call to Biloxi, Mississippi."

He pulled a paper from his top pocket. "This is the Mississippi number. It's a motel. I called and there was no answer. About that time, a fellow came in saying he was the girl's uncle, from Biloxi—crying . . . he saw the pictures of the fugitive on TV, he said."

Brad patted the deputy's shoulder. "Good work."

"You suppose the girl is helping this Truman fellow? Or maybe he's got her captive too?"

"We don't know."

Crestfallen, the deputy realized his news was not a revelation. "The FBI don't tell us shit—excuse me, Mrs. Taylor."

"Maybe this won't last long enough to worry about fouled communications," Brad said.

"The uncle, name's Zachary Stephens, is begging to see you, Sheriff."

"Not tonight."

"He's been on me every step. He's in the car."

"Tomorrow—"

"Brad," Denise said. "I'll see him."

Brad trudged up the steps into the house. Denise waited for Smitherman to return. She saw shadowed figures of guards walking the perimeter of the yard. The media vans were dark, but a glow of cigarettes proved people were there.

"Mrs. Taylor, this is Zachary Stephens."

"Mrs. Taylor, I'm sorry about coming so late. They wouldn't tell me where you lived."

He was a short man, completely bald, his eyes bloodshot as if for want of sleep.

"Come in, Mr. Stephens. We'll have a cup of coffee."

He sobbed, stumbled on the first step, then followed Denise into the kitchen. She looked at the pile of dirty dishes, the counter filthy again.

"It'll only take a few minutes, Mr. Stephens."

"Peggy is all I have," he said. "I lost my wife. I lost my Donna, and now Peggy . . ."

Denise washed the parts of the coffee percolator, angry that the men who used this room didn't take the trouble to clean up after themselves.

"I left people in the motel and came at once," Stephens said. "I drove as fast as I could."

"Mr. Stephens, would you like to stay here? I could have a bed made for you."

"I couldn't do that."

"You may, if you wish. I would want company. I'd want to be near the people who are staying on top of all of this."

"The FBI is in it," Stephens said. "That's good."

She abandoned the coffee, pouring a glass of milk instead. "Drink this, and take four Bufferin," she said. "We're so exhausted, we both need sleep. I'll show you to your room and we'll talk tomorrow. Is that all right?"

"I know she's dead."

"No, you don't know that. Neither do I. Come along, let me show you the room. . . ."

*　　*　　*

After she closed the door to Jeffrey's bedroom, Denise paused. Lana's light was on, the door ajar. When she looked in, the woman was in full attire, putting lacquer on her fingernails.

"Lana, may I get something for you?"

"Oh, hell no, honey. I'm all right."

"Would you like to go down and watch TV?"

Lana waved a hand at her. "Hell, honey, if I had a penny for every slow night, I'd be a millionaire."

Trembling from tension and the long day, Denise shut her own bedroom door and stood in the dark. Brad's silhouette was etched against the window. Going to him, Denise watched the men patrolling the yard.

"I asked Zachary Stephens to stay here overnight, Brad."

"I don't have time to baby-sit, Denise."

"He's as worried about his niece as we are about Elaine and Jeffrey. I couldn't bear to have him alone in a motel."

"All right."

She massaged his shoulders, her own back and arms throbbing.

"Can you imagine what this would do to Mom?" Brad said. "To go on TV and say my father was a child molester. To destroy him and Mom—Mom would suffer the rest of her life. I don't think she would ever fogive me."

"It wasn't your doing, Brad. It was . . . You know it wasn't you."

"None of us will ever see two people whispering, that we don't wonder."

"Brad, you need sleep. So do I."

"I can't sleep."

"Lying down is restful, even awake. Come on to bed."

"They've got to catch him," Brad said. "They've got to get him before the broadcast."

"But be prepared in case they don't," Denise said.

"I'm angry," he said. "Angry with Felder Nichols and Troy Bacon and that teacher, what's her name?"

"Ailene Adkins."

"I'm angry with Aunt Marie—she must have known too. She and Dad were close."

"I think she did," Denise said.

"I'm angry with Dad," Brad said. "How could he have done this to us—to everybody?"

Denise unbuttoned his shirt, easing it off as if he were a child.

"All the years of creating a good reputation, gone if this comes out. His name, our name, our children, and maybe even their children . . ."

"Sit down, so I can take off your socks."

"I keep asking myself: why?" Brad said. "Then I ask myself: what made Dad as *he* was? What makes any of us the way we are?"

Denise urged him down on the bed, stroking his chest.

"You've been right all along," he said.

"About what?"

"About my abuse of the children."

"I didn't say *abuse*, Brad."

"Why didn't I want to hug and kiss them? I'd get off alone and think about it. I know now—because my Dad didn't kiss and hug me. I'm doing to them what Dad did to me."

"To a much lesser degree," Denise said. She kissed his chest, his neck.

"I hope I have a second chance," he said. "I hope I have a chance to be different."

"Yes," Denise said. "But don't you think, no matter what Father Taylor did, maybe he too prayed for a second chance? You and Bob and Jack are evidence that he changed."

"Too late, though. Too late for Truman."

27

Denise heard laughter as she descended the stairs. *Lana.*

An FBI agent sat at the recording equipment. Male laughter rose from the kitchen. When Denise entered, the men fell silent and Lana greeted her with a cheerful "Good morning!"

The kitchen was clean. Vera was loading the dishwasher. Lana was at the stove, dressed in fashionable slacks and one of Vera's blouses. She wore high heels.

"What do you want for breakfast, honey?" Lana asked.

"Only coffee."

Dr. Brunner, Dr. Rheems, Darrell Ashe, Deputy Smitherman, two city policemen in uniform, all sat with Zachary Stephens at the breakfast-room table, eating.

"Lana, thank you for helping," Denise said.

"Hell, honey, if I had a penny for every breakfast I've cooked . . ."

The smell of bacon frying, the crackle of grease in

a skillet, eggs "cooked to order," and Lana entertaining the troops—Denise felt oddly out of place.

"Anyhow," Lana resumed telling an interrupted story, "somebody told the guy he could freeze corn on the cob that tasted like fresh corn on the cob in December—if he put each ear in a prophylactic."

The men shifted nervously, enjoying the old joke.

"So he goes to the drugstore and orders a thousand prophylactics," Lana said. "Over the weekend he sticks corn in the rubbers and when he finishes he only had nine hundred and ninety-seven rubbers. He goes back to the drugstore on Monday and says, I'm the guy who bought a thousand prophylactics on Friday—remember me?' The clerk says, 'Yes, I do.' 'Well, there were only nine hundred and ninety-seven rubbers in the box, you owe me three more.' The clerk says, 'Gee, I hope I didn't ruin your weekend.' "

Laughter roared. Vera worked at the sink, face averted. Denise walked out and found Brad in the den.

"Anything?" Brad was asking an agent.

"No, sir. They're chasing down reports of sightings here and there, but who knows?"

Denise gave Brad a cup of coffee and said, "Lana is in the kitchen with Vera."

More laughter.

Brad used an FBI line to call his office. A moment later he hung up. "Nothing. He's got to be holed up somewhere."

"Sheriff," Dr. Rheems said, entering. "The TV technicians need time to prepare for this evening. It's become complicated. All three networks have representatives, as well as CNN out of Atlanta and the print media. They would like to do the program here in your home."

"No."

Dr. Rheems scratched his eyebrow. "There are logistical advantages to doing it here," he said. "Our equipment is in place. Your telephone is ready. We can control the premises more efficiently—our men are out there."

Four vans were now parked out front. While some men climbed telephone poles, others were erecting a portable microwave tower which extended above surrounding obstacles. They had blocked off the street just beyond the driveway. People milled about, curious.

"All right," Brad said. "Do it here." He turned to Denise. "I'll have to talk to the family. I've been debating when. If I don't go through with this, what's the point in telling them what we found out? If I do go on, they should know beforehand."

"They would have to know sooner or later anyway, Brad. Tell them this morning."

"Yes," he said grimly. "I suppose I'd better. Will you call them?"

Laughter in the kitchen rose sharply. "What the hell is going on in there?" Brad demanded.

"I'll get rid of them," Dr. Rheems offered.

"No, it ... it's all right." Brad peered out the window at the preparations in progress. "Denise, call Bob and Jack. Tell them they must come."

"Mother Taylor too?"

"Yes. Mom too."

The atmosphere in the breakfast room became more businesslike with Brad's presence. As Denise used the FBI telephone, television men began their work around her.

"That's no good." A director surveyed the den, Brad's desk. "It ought to have more of the flavor of the house."

"We could open with exterior shots, cut to the stairway, pull back and fade, cut to the desk."

"Yeah, okay, that would work. Have somebody get some footage—all angles. Show the pool area too."

They were setting up lights, laying cables.

Mother Taylor's voice on the phone was weak. "Denise, what will we do with the children?"

"Bring them with you, if you must."

"Into that . . . that attention? There are several policemen here to keep reporters away, and still they managed to talk to Robbie through the fence."

"Brad says you must come, Mother Taylor."

"I don't see what good it will do. Vera is over there night and day—"

"Mother Taylor," Denise said, "the message is, *be here*! I must hang up. I have to call Jack and Lanita."

A hand touched her elbow. "Excuse me. We need to get to that electrical outlet."

Lanita answered at their office. "Brad says come over," Denise said without amenities.

"I'll find Jack," Lanita said.

Behind Denise, Darrell Ashe questioned a fellow agent. "What about that report from Perry, Florida?"

"Right car, had a beard—but it wasn't the man."

"He has probably shaved."

"The various composites went on TV this morning," the agent said. "With mustache, with sideburns, with shaved head—it's his eyes and nose that'll nail him."

The TV director huddled with his coworkers. "Southern aristocracy, see. Mansion from Civil War days. Get some fill on the town too: City of Roses, landed gentry, quail hunts . . ."

Brad studied maps at the dining-room table. At strategic locations, tabs identified available equipment—automobiles, helicopters—and the men on hand.

"The family is coming, Brad."

"How much should I tell them?"

"At least what you'll say on television."

"If I can avoid it, I won't say anything on TV."

"So tell them *that*. But warn them that you will say if forced to do so."

In the breakfast room, Lana was alone with Zachary Stephens. "Truman, he can be so sweet sometimes. Then something makes him unhappy and—"

Brad spoke without looking up. "Can you get rid of her, Denise?"

"I don't think we should."

"Do it anyway."

"Brad, the family needs to see her. See her as she is. It isn't all bad. She's been washing dishes, cooking breakfast—"

"She is an affront to Mom."

"She's the truth," Denise said. "She is what this is all about, or a good part of it. I won't send her away, Brad. Bob and Jack and Mother Taylor must accept reality."

He slammed a hand to the table, wheeled, stalked away.

"It sounds real nice," Lana was saying. "Forty rooms right on the water?"

"Across the highway . . ."

When Jack and Lanita arrived, newsmen swarmed their car, cameras thrusting. Police officers tried to clear passage to the driveway. Standing at the back door, Denise watched. Voices shouted, flashbulbs flared. Jack emerged like a consummate politician, hands lifted to signal for order. Lanita slipped through as he spoke.

"They've been at the office all morning," Lanita

said. "There were pictures of us on the news—did you see it, Denise?"

"No."

"They're using telephoto lenses to shoot at a distance. We don't even see them. God knows what they've seen."

"Lanita, this is our sister-in-law, Lana Taylor."

Lana hesitated, then presented a hand. "Hi, Lanita. I sure am sorry what's happening."

There was a repeat of the same pandemonium when Bob arrived with Mother Taylor. The children broke free, running in their bathing suits to the swimming pool. A deputy blocked newsmen, but cameras caught the splashing and laughter.

Her shoulders rounded, each step an effort, Mother Taylor was assisted up the stairs by Bob and Jack.

"Bob, Jack," Denise introduced them, "this is Lana Taylor. Mother Taylor, this is Lana—"

Mother Taylor walked past Lana without response.

"Close the dining-room doors, Smitherman," Brad said. "Keep everyone out. Dr. Rheems, we need you and Dr. Brunner in here, if you will."

Without invitation, Zachary Stephens joined them. He and Lana sat beside Vera. Deputy Smitherman shut the French doors and posted himself in the hall, hands behind his back, facing the den.

"There is no word on the children," Brad began. "We believe Truman left them alive, but there are thousands of acres, tens of thousands of acres—we haven't found them."

Mother Taylor's head shook as if she were palsied.

"Lana is here," Brad said. "If all else fails, she will talk to Truman. We hope it will keep him on the telephone long enough to trace the call."

"I'll talk to him," Lana confirmed.

"Truman is demanding Bo Taylor's confession,"

Brad said. "He says I have one chance only, tonight on television, and if it is complete and true, he will let the children go."

Brad cleared his throat, cleared it again. "We have discovered some unpleasant information. I wish I didn't have to tell you, but I must. I may have to say it tonight. I won't, unless I have no other choice . . . but then . . ."

"Get on with it, for God's sake," Bob said. "It's all supposition anyway."

"I'm afraid it isn't," Brad said.

"Bradley," Mother Taylor said harshly, "please be done with this."

He began much as Denise had begun last night. He revealed the troubled family history, the emotional duress, Father Taylor's youth and immaturity. He told them about Truman's infatuation with the schoolteacher, the poetry, and Truman's need for an adult who cared for him.

Then, looking at Lana, but not accusingly, Brad said, "Dad was having sexual relations with Lana. She was nine years old. Truman knew it, tried to stop it—"

"It's a lie," Mother Taylor said.

"Truman went to Miss Adkins, his teacher—"

"It is a lie!" Mother Taylor cried. She glared at Lana. "It is a lie, isn't it?"

"Mom, the lives of Elaine and Jeffrey depend on truth. Truman knows the truth!"

"You tell me it's true," Mother Taylor challenged Lana.

"Daddy was nice to me," Lana said. "Him and Truman, that was different. But Daddy loved me."

Mother Taylor glared at Brad. "It's a lie."

"Mom, Troy Bacon suspected it," Brad said. "He

went to Felder Nichols several times, worried about the abuse. Aunt Marie must have known about it."

"Marie was so much in love with Bo she didn't see the world around her," Mother Taylor said. "She resented me, she resented anybody else who held Bo's affection. But she wouldn't lie to destroy them."

"Dad beat Truman until he thought he'd killed him," Brad said softly. "He had to use mouth-to-mouth resuscitation. He couldn't feel a pulse. Judge Nichols told us this. Dad went to him the night it happened. Dad admitted he'd sexually abused Lana. He was trying to force Truman to remain silent."

Lana sobbed, hands limp in her lap.

"Felder Nichols would say no such thing!" Mother Taylor said.

"He didn't," Brad agreed, "until the lives of our children depended on it. He didn't say a word until he had to."

"I knew your father better than he knew himself. He had character, Bradley. Character!"

"Mom, I wish I didn't have to say this."

"You don't have to say it," Bob replied. "Especially on television."

"You'd better not say it on TV," Jack said.

"Truman was jealous." Lana spoke to Vera and Zachary Stephens. "Him and Daddy had a fight because Truman was jealous."

Brad explained Truman's desperation, asking them to imagine that twelve-year-old boy, beaten, ridiculed, his only adult confidante unbelieving.

"Tonight," Brad said, "I will do all I can to avoid saying what I've said here. But I cannot risk the lives of three people—"

"Three?"

"Elaine, Jeffrey, and possibly this man's niece." Brad indicated Zachary Stephens.

"That your father should suffer this . . ." Mother Taylor's voice quavered. "That his good name should be smeared when he isn't here to defend himself . . ."

"Mother Taylor." Vera was on her feet. "What would Father Taylor do if he were here? Would he shake his head and worry about his good name? Would he refuse to go on TV and say this? If he did, he wouldn't be the man you thought he was. And you—would you run and hide? If you did, you wouldn't be the woman Father Taylor thought. He would go on television. You would stand beside him."

"Perhaps if it were true," Mother Taylor said.

"Especially if it were true!" Vera shouted. "What's the matter with you people? You, Bob, and you, Jack—you are being so selfish I can't believe it. Brad is sheriff, the hostages are his children. He has no choice. You're leaving him to suffer the whole load of this, beating the messenger for bearing bad news. If this were us, he'd be there. He'd stand by us if it ruined him!"

She turned full circle, tears in her eyes. "We must stand together in this. All you're thinking about is the shame. Well, yes, there will be shame. But there will also be people who refuse to believe. If Brad swore to their faces, they wouldn't believe it. Then there will be those who do believe it but who will have compassion for us, for Father Taylor, even for Truman. Our enemies will relish this, that's true. But they're our enemies already."

Vera sat beside Lana, who took her hand.

"Dr. Brunner," Brad said, "will you comment, please?"

He puffed his pipe, nodding. "I agree with everything you've said, Sheriff. This is what Truman wants to hear on television. This is what he came for."

"So Truman gets what he wants," Bob argued.

"What have we gained? Does this public confession guarantee the return of Elaine and Jeffrey?"

Dr. Brunner shifted his pipe from one side of his jaw to the other. "This man came to kill Bo Taylor," he said. "Not only physically, but ideologically. Bo Taylor is dead. But the community's high esteem of the man remains. Truman selected Bradley Taylor as both his target and his weapon of destruction for a variety of reasons—physical resemblance, the office of sheriff, emotional transference. To Truman, Bradley is the very essence of Bo Taylor. He strikes the face of this living man, and in his mind the dead man feels the pain."

"Will he release the children?" Bob asked.

Brunner sucked his pipe pensively. "In my opinion, if you fail him tonight, Truman will certainly allow the children to die."

"And if the goddamned confession is made?" Bob pressed.

Dr. Brunner crossed his fingers for all to see. "Truman is totally selfish. The most selfish act imaginable is what he *will* do. In this instance, the most selfish act happens to be one of generosity. He will let them go."

"What kind of double-talk is that?" Bob asked.

"Look at it this way," Dr. Brunner said. "Truman's purpose is the destruction of an image. If the children should die, people will remember that Truman killed helpless children. He will let them go, not because he cares about them—he most assuredly does not—but because he wants people to concentrate on loathing Bo Taylor. Releasing them will be his final attempt to excuse himself and focus instead on the sins of his father."

"He will have destroyed us," Jack said. "Destroyed my father, who damned well doesn't deserve it. Destroyed my mother—and he comes off a sympathetic cult hero."

"I hardly think that," Dr. Brunner replied. "There may be some pity for him, but sympathy—no."

Brad looked at his watch. "The broadcast is at seven this evening. If they catch him, it won't go on the air. If Lana can convince Truman to quit, I won't have to speak. If they can trace the line and trap him, that will end it. But if not, I have no choice."

"I wish I were dead," Mother Taylor said. "I wish I were with Bo."

There was one can of food that defied the opener. Peggy had tried repeatedly, both ends of the tin, without success. She felt around her feet for another can, found one, and opened it. *Damn.* Sardines. Very salty, sure to increase thirst.

"Let's not eat that one," Peggy said.

"It smells good," Jeffrey said.

"We'll save it for later." Peggy felt for yet another can. All the water was gone now. The last few drops had been applied to Elaine's cracking lips. The girl's shallow breathing was frightening.

"Is Elaine diabetic, Jeffrey? Or allergic?"

"I don't think so."

She was hot to the touch, her skin dry in places, seeping perspiration elsewhere.

"Except when she sunburns," Jeffrey noted. "Then she breaks out."

Peggy felt arms, legs. "Could she be burned?"

"Mama said she was."

Elaine's wrists had enveloped the handcuffs like a tree growing around a wire fence nailed to the bark. Her fingers were rigid, the flesh so tight the hands felt like rubber gloves.

Peggy put a hand on the girl's neck. Her pulse was

strong, but erratic, beating rapidly one moment, slowing the next. Occasionally she muttered incoherently, or awakened with whimpered cries for her mother. She had soiled herself and Peggy struggled to clean her and the cot, but the odor remained.

"She's going to die," Jeffrey whispered.

"No, Jeffrey, she is not!"

But she might. . . .

She'd held the boy tightly, stroking his hair, soothing him with lies and hope and fervent prayers without mention of God.

Elaine's condition was deteriorating despite everything Peggy had tried. Was it already too late? Should she get the girl to her feet? Should she leave her alone, turning her only to prevent sores? How long had they been here?

God, Peggy thought, *we could use some help*

If He heard, His only response was silence.

Peggy severed the top from a tin, sniffed it. More beans. *That son of a bitch.* Jeffrey had first complained of constipation, then diarrhea. Their prison had become increasingly foul.

Logic told her they hadn't been here *weeks*. Days, yes—not weeks.

"Peggy . . ." Jeffrey's voice rose, alarmed. "She isn't breathing, Peggy!"

Peggy dropped the can, groping for the girl's body. Heart . . . beating. She bent near, her ear to Elaine's mouth. A whispery sigh . . . silence.

"Elaine, darling . . ."

Suddenly a gasping inhalation. Another. *Apnea.*

"She's all right, Jeffrey. People do that sometimes when they're asleep. My Uncle Zachary used to be scared to death because I'd go several minutes without breathing. She's all right."

"Are you sure?"

"Yes." Peggy felt for the can. Some had spilled. The juice, the precious juice, was gone.

"Eat this, Jeffrey."

"What is it?"

"Surprise."

He tasted it. "Beans," he said. "Some surprise."

Why didn't George return? Why didn't he bring more food and water? They needed toilet paper and spoons with which to eat—bowls, so nothing would be wasted. Elaine's handcuffs—take them off! *Please, George . . . please.*

"The rest are yours, Peggy." He put her hand on the can.

"Have you had all you want?" she asked.

"I never want another bean as long as I live," he said.

As she ate, he added, "Which may not be so long."

28

The den was brightly lighted, a desk placed before the drapes. Cables lay like sleeping serpents down the hall. In other rooms, TV monitors had been set up, chairs brought in. From the desk, Brad could see himself on another monitor off to one side.

"The tragedy of this American family . . ." an announcer intoned. Another newsman spoke nearly the same words in his report.

A technician touched a monitor. "This one is in-house, Sheriff. What you see here is what the camera sees, but not on the air." He touched another TV set. "What you see here is on the air." WCTV's evening news was drawing to a close.

Face drawn, Brad sat at the desk. The immediate family was across the hall in the dining room. Men with portable shoulder-borne cameras had already captured images of the silent, morose mother, sons and daughters-in-law. Pictures of Thomasville flashed on the television sets as crews set up a sequence of shots they intended to use before or after the broadcast.

Six-forty-five.

They pinned a microphone to Brad's lapel. Another microphone was on a boom over his head. Lights were adjusted to eliminate a shadow. Other microphones were clustered like sterile bulbs on the desk itself.

"It isn't necessary to lean toward the mike," the technician was saying. "Speak in a normal voice."

"Give us a test on the lapel," a voice called from the shadows. Brad cleared his throat. "Testing . . . testing . . . one, two, three."

Perspiration oozed in Denise's palms, soaking a tissue she held for that purpose. When their eyes met, Brad attempted a smile but it fell apart with a quiver.

"When you see a light on the camera—see that red light? That means it's on."

"I see it."

"Look directly into the lens. To the viewer, you are looking him in the eye."

"It's hot as hell in here," Lana said. "I'm starting to sweat."

"Nothing you say is going on the air, remember that," Dr. Rheems said. "Not until we tell you; then and only then, the conversation will go on WCTV live, and be taped by everybody else."

Dr. Brunner sat in a corner, pipe unlit in his mouth, observing. When he noticed Denise, he closed both eyes tightly in a double wink, nodding assurances.

"Stall as long as you can," Dr. Rheems continued. "Keep him talking. Remember, he's worried that you've found the children. He isn't sure this is going to happen at all. The moment he balks, turn it over to Lana. Then he'll know he has the edge again."

Ring . . .

A man behind the camera murmured into his headset, "Roll tape."

Ring . . .

Dr. Rheems backed away from Brad in a stoop, urging, "Stall . . . stall . . ."

"Hello?"

Brad's face on the screen seemed strained. He adjusted an earphone plug. "Hello?"

"Yes or no?" came Truman's voice on the monitor.

"This is Brad Taylor, Truman."

"Yes or no, my man?"

"Truman, you're asking me to blemish my father's reputation. I think I deserve proof of your intentions."

"Anything you get, you must earn," Truman said.

"I want assurance that the children are all right."

"You stupid son of a bitch," Truman said. "Trying to play me like a fiddle, and now you want rosin for the bow. Are you going on the air or not—yes or no?"

"Is Peggy with them, Truman?"

He swore softly. "Last time, my man—yes or no? No more games."

Dr. Rheems pushed Lana into the lights, handing her a telephone receiver.

"Truman?" she asked.

Silence.

"Truman, honey, it's me."

"Hello, sugar babe."

She turned to face the cameras and saw herself on the monitor. "Hey, I'm on TV, Truman." She raised a hand and wiggled the tips of her fingers. "Can you see me?"

"No, sugar babe, I can't."

"There I am!"

"Not here, not yet. Lana, why did you come?"

"Hell, they paid for it, Truman. Free ticket on the airplane, free food. Look at these clothes—do you like my hair fixed this way?"

"You're beautiful. You always were."

She laughed, posturing, watching her image.

"How's Mama?" he asked.

"She says throw it over your shoulder."

He laughed and Lana stooped to see Denise beneath the glare. She nodded gleefully, pointing at the receiver.

"Remember the time we went to Disneyland, sugar babe?"

"Sure I do."

"Rode all the rides, ate hot dogs . . ."

"Yeah," Lana said wistfully.

"And the time we went to Colorado to shoot the rapids?"

"That was scary."

"But fun."

"It was, but it was scary."

A long pause. Lana chewed her lip, blinking into bright lights a moment, before staring at herself on the monitor again.

"We've had some good times, Lana."

"Sure have, Truman. I wish I could see you."

"I wish that too."

"If you give yourself up, I'll visit you."

"I want you to remember the good times, sugar babe. Remember the cabin we stayed in, up in the mountains, when the snow was still there in July?"

"Mama is going to be mad with you, Truman."

"Yes. Well . . ."

"You shouldn't ought to have taken the babies."

"Remember that time we went to the Grand Canyon? I fell off a burro, remember?"

"He bit you, too." Lana laughed.

"Took a plug out, didn't he?"

"Truman, why did you take the babies? They never hurt us, did they?"

Darrell Ashe whispered to Dr. Rheems, "The call is coming from Panama City, Florida. We're alerting the helicopter groups now."

". . . took a picnic basket and camped near the geysers, remember that, Lana?"

"I remember, Truman. Truman, they aren't going to let me talk very long. This is long distance, ain't it?"

"Oh, they'll let you talk, sugar babe. Talk as long as you like, I promise you."

Seven-fifteen.

The director turned to Dr. Rheems. "Control wants to know if they should pick us up."

"Not yet."

A cameraman relayed the message.

Denise listened to the familiar voice of Truman Taylor, now so tender, so sweet to Lana.

"That's where we bought you the Chinese dress, remember that?"

"I still got it."

"You look good in it."

"I'm too fat to wear it now."

"All the more to love."

"Truman, can I talk to you now?"

Minutes ticked away. FBI men talked in hushed tones on the telephone.

"Motel," Darrell Ashe muttered. "Panama City Beach."

"How long will it take?"

"Twenty minutes, thirty, maybe."

"Truman," Lana said again, "can I talk to you?"

". . . to the top of the Empire State Building and you spit over the side . . ."

Lana looked at Dr. Rheems and lifted her shoulders in a helpless shrug.

". . . took the Circle Line cruise around Manhattan Island . . ."

"Truman," she said, "if they do what you want, are you going to hurt their babies?"

Denise could hear him breathe.

"If they do what you say, will you let them go?" Lana asked more sternly.

"I love you, Lana. I wish it could've been better."

"These people have been real nice to me," she said. "Denise is sick about her babies."

"Let me speak to the sheriff, sugar babe."

"Truman, don't you hurt those babies, you hear me?"

"Tell Mama I love her too, and I wish it could have been different."

"Truman! I want you to promise!"

"Well, sugar babe," he said, "it all depends on the sheriff. If he does exactly what he must, everything will be fine."

"You promise?"

"I promise. Let me talk to him."

Rheems was on the FBI phone. Distressed, he shot a glance at Brad, then turned his back, talking into the receiver.

"Lana," Truman warned, "tell the bastards I won't wait."

"I'm here, Truman," Brad said.

"Let's get it going, Sheriff."

"Are they all right, Truman?"

"Less so every minute. Get on the air, you bastard."

Brad wavered, watching Dr. Rheems and Darrell Ashe for a cue.

"My man," Truman snarled, "I'll give you thirty seconds and then I'll hang up."

"They're having some technical problems, Truman."

"Jesus, you think I'm stupid, don't you? Twenty seconds."

In a hallway, Rheems and Darrell Ashe were conferring. Rheems wrote a message on a large card and held it up for Brad to see: "NO TRACE. CALL FORWARDED FROM PANAMA CITY MOTEL."

"What does that mean?" Denise demanded.

"Truman paid a clerk to accept his call and dial us from the motel," Ashe explained. "The two calls were patched together through the switchboard. We traced the call to the motel, surrounded it, but he isn't there. Now they're tracing the call from that point."

Dr. Rheems pulled his hands apart as if extending space between his fingers, signalling "Stretch it."

"Ten seconds," Truman said. "Then I'm hanging up, Sheriff. Don't expect me to call again."

"Okay, put it on," Dr. Rheems told the director.

"Five," Truman counted down, "four, three, two— ah, there you are."

Denise stood with Ashe and Dr. Rheems, both men stricken.

"Coming from Continental Telephone Company of the South," Ashe reported. "It's a small independent company in Donaldsonville, Georgia."

"Can they trace it?" Dr. Rheems asked.

"It won't be quick. They cover a sparsely populated area but it extends to the Florida line south and the Alabama line west. They say there are thousands of remote cabins around Lake Seminole and along the banks of the Chattahoochee River."

Dr. Rheems selected a cue card prepared in advance. It was one of two: "YES" and "NO." He held up "NO"—trace not possible.

"Quit playing with me," Truman said, his voice coming over the TV. "Get on with it, or get off it."

"Yes," Brad said. "All right, Truman. Where do we begin?"

"It's your show, my man. But get on with it."

The television audience saw what Denise saw: a perspiring and anguished figure, so tormented that his very posture commanded attention.

"The lake is formed by the Jim Woodruff Dam," an FBI man reported to Ashe and Dr. Rheems. "It'll be dark in another hour and a half. By the time we get men there, he could have taken a hundred routes, by land or boat. There is no way to encircle the entire county."

"My father was Bo Taylor," Brad said huskily. "He was a quiet man. A man known for gentleness and compassion. He had strong principles. He upheld the law and served as a respected officer of the court for over forty years. To his wife and children, Bo Taylor was a man of moral character. Never once did he shame us in any way. He was, I think, the perfect father."

Brad paused, head down for a second or two. Only then did Denise see notes he'd made for himself.

"I think the people of Thomas County will agree with my assessment of Bo Taylor," Brad said. "They elected him for nine consecutive terms. And as a family friend told me recently, there was never a hint of scandal."

"Get on with it," Truman said, his voice on the air.

"It is nearly impossible for a child to judge his parents," Brad continued. "We see them through a veil of our own making. They are, to the children, either better or worse than reality."

"Cut the psychology," Truman said. "Get on with it."

"To my brothers and me," Brad said, "perhaps my father appeared better than real life. Like all public servants, he had his enemies. His detractors accused him of racial bigotry when he locked up Dr. Martin Luther King's followers during the civil-rights struggle. But at the same time, the black community helped reelect him to office."

Eyes downcast, Brad paused. They could hear Truman breathing evenly, waiting.

"The point is," Brad said, "no man is what he seems to any one person. Every man is a complicated pattern seen in different light by different people in a different way. That was the case with my father. The loving way we saw him was not the way others may have seen him."

"Get *on* with it," Truman said.

Brad jerked his head up, glaring at the camera. "Either shut up and let me do this my way, or hang up! Which is it going to be, Truman?"

Silence.

"Don't interrupt again until I'm through," Brad ordered. "When I finish, say what you will, but until then, keep your damned mouth shut!"

Truman chuckled softly.

"My father," Brad said forcefully, "was no better nor worse than any of us. He was to *me* an ideal, a model by which I fashioned my entire adult life! I entered law enforcement because of him, because I admired him so much. I accepted his unexpired term as sheriff as a living testament to my father's strengths and his good character."

Brad twisted before the camera, face contorted. "But to the man on the telephone—to you, Truman—my father was somebody I never knew. Truman Taylor was the firstborn son, by a prior marriage, before Bo Taylor ever met my mother, Annette. His first wife was Renee—"

"I didn't come to hear about my mother," Truman said.

"You're going to hear it all—or nothing!"

Denise could imagine the men glaring at one another across the void of space, linked by sound and image. Brothers. She thought of Cain and Abel.

"Renee was six years older than Bo when they married . . ."

Darrell Ashe and Dr. Rheems received another report: "A small fishing town on Lake Seminole, a place called Fairchilds."

". . . under duress, marital problems . . . a son, Truman, a daughter, Lana . . ."

Stoic, attentive, Dr. Brunner leaned forward with an elbow propped on one knee, listening, watching Brad.

". . . Truman had no adult to whom he could turn . . ."

"You son of a bitch, get on with it," Truman shouted.

Brad shot a glance at Dr. Rheems. His fingers trembled as he pushed aside a page of notes.

". . . a teacher who befriended him, taught him to appreciate poetry and language—"

"Okay," Truman interrupted. "Okay, you bastard. I'll give you exactly three minutes more. Then I'm hanging up. Tell the truth, the whole truth, or kiss your kids good-bye, you hear me?"

An agent approached Ashe and Dr. Rheems. "It will take hours," the agent said. "They won't get him tonight."

Rheems nodded, faced Brad. He lifted his hands, palms up, resigned to failure. Brad gave a single nod, exhaled, rubbing his face with both hands, oblivious of his smearing makeup.

"Imagine this boy, twelve years old . . ." His voice broke and Brad halted, staring at the microphones, trying to regain self-control. "Imagine how it must have been," he said. "He discovered something that . . . that we could hardly believe . . ."

Mother Taylor stood up slowly, legs trembling. Bob reached for her arm and she waved him away. One small step, pause; another, pause; another—she walked toward Brad.

"Bo Taylor was having sexual relations with Lana, age nine."

Mother Taylor faltered, stepping over cables.

"Truman realized it and tried to stop this terrible abuse . . ."

Mother Taylor moved into the sphere of lights, inching her way toward Brad, tears streaking her cheeks.

". . . beat him until he thought Truman was dead . . ."

Mother Taylor stood behind Brad, her back straight, eyes forward. The camera pulled away slightly to include her image. She put her hands on Brad's shoulders, her chin high.

". . . a terrible, terrible thing," Brad sobbed. "I don't know how such a thing could happen."

Jack and Lanita rose, walked into the light, and stood beside Mother Taylor.

". . . the teacher didn't believe Truman . . . the mother uncaring . . . isolated, ridiculed, beaten almost to death . . . sexually abusing his nine-year-old daughter . . ."

Bob saw Vera going and joined her. They took their places on the other side of Mother Taylor.

"I'm sorry, Truman," Brad wept. "I wish it had

not happened. I wish I could suffer what you have suffered and you could have known my father as I did."

Silence. Brad stared at the camera, his tears spattering on the desk. Behind him stood his mother, a frail symbol, and both brothers with their wives. Denise stepped into the light, joining them.

"The truth is . . ." Brad wiped his eyes. "The truth is, this could have been any of us. What Truman is, that could be me, or you, or anyone. The tragedy is greater than my father's acts alone, although they are the paramount tragedy here. The horrible thing is, the teacher did nothing. A judge who *knew* did nothing. Other people in the community suspected or knew, an aunt most certainly knew—and they did nothing. To protect my father, they sacrificed the children."

Brad accepted a tissue from Denise and blotted his eyes.

"There is no way I can reverse what happened before my birth," Brad said. "To me, the monster Truman knew never existed. But I know now, it is so. I didn't want to believe, but I do. What I have said here is all true. I have no intention of ever retracting even one word."

He looked at Denise. "We know it's true, don't we?"

"Yes," she said.

"It is true," Vera added.

"Yes." Jack and Lanita nodded. Bob made one quick nod and stared straight ahead.

"Truman?" Brad looked into the camera. "Where are my children, please?"

Silence.

"Truman, I've told the truth. I have confessed in the name of my father."

Nothing.

"Truman . . ."

His voice came wearily: " 'The night my father got me/ His mind was not on me;/ He did not plague his fancy/ To muse if I should be/ The son you see.' "

A camera moved slowly across their faces, transmitting their expressions for millions to see.

Truman continued softly: " 'For so the game is ended/ That should not have begun./ My father and my mother/ They had a likely son,/ And I have none.' "

Brad settled his body in an involuntary act of submission. "Truman, please, where are the children?"

Truman's long sigh whispered through the TV sets. " 'If it chance your eye offend you, Pluck it out, lad, and be sound: 'Twill hurt, but here are salves to friend you, And many a balsam grows on ground.' "

Lana's quiet weeping was a low moan in the shadows.

" 'And if your hand or foot offend you,' " Truman recited, " 'Cut it off, lad, and be whole; But play the man, stand up and end you, When your sickness is your soul.' "

"Truman," Brad said, "the children . . ."

The man's voice rose. "I love you, Lana. Remember the good times, sugar babe."

"Truman!" she yelled. "Truman!"

"Bradley?"

"Yes, Truman."

"You know the old icehouse?"

"Here in Thomasville?"

"I left food and water."

Men ran for the doors. Denise stumbled over cables, following.

As she passed a television set, she heard Truman

say, "Could have been you, my man, and I could have been . . ."

Car doors slammed, revolving lights flashed, cameras tried to catch their faces.

The icehouse.

29

Truman slumped in an overstuffed chair, the bluish glow of a black-and-white TV his only light. He watched reports from Thomasville, updates being issued by a Tallahassee TV station. When they interviewed Lana, he chuckled softly, sipping beer gone warm in the can. Beside him, loaded, lay his pistol.

No hurry.

He had heard a warble of sirens earlier, the whack of copter blades somewhere afar. But now the night air was a harmony of fiddling crickets and throaty frogs, chirps and tweets that conjured conflicting emotions—of Vietnam, of childhood days spent in a nearby cabin on fishing trips, of lost time and wasted dreams.

". . . reports that the hostages are weak, but alive . . ."

He didn't care one way or the other. It was academic now.

". . . bruises and contusions . . ."

The whump-whump-whump of helicopter blades

stilled night creatures momentarily, but the machine
flew over and away. Again the amphibian sopranos
and baritones rose in good voice.

It had to end somewhere. Better here than in a
godforsaken battlefield. He downed the last of the
warm beer and went for another, stepping over the
body of the man who owned the cabin.

He hadn't killed him. Heart attack, maybe. The
old fellow just sank to the floor and never moved
again.

Truman opened a can by the light of the refrigerator and bumped the door closed. He sat in the chair
again, kicked off his shoes, and peeled away socks to
air his tired feet.

> *Shot? So quick, so clean an ending?*
> *Oh that was right, lad, that was brave:*
> *Yours was not an ill for mending,*
> *'Twas best to take it to the grave.*

His eyes burned for lack of sleep. The beer tasted
green. He wished he'd thought to buy cigarettes.

More helicopters.

Truman sighed wearily, staring at the television,
listening to the whir of insects outside.

> *Oh you had forethought, you could reason,*
> *And saw your road and where it led,*
> *And early wise and brave in season*
> *Put the pistol to your head.*

They were getting closer. Truman could sense the
armed men in flak jackets, creeping from dwelling to
dwelling, narrowing their search, eager to embrace
the danger of combat—afraid, but giddy with the
fear.

Of all the emotions life offered, fear was the one passion he had come to savor. He had learned to create it, appreciate it in others, and to enjoy it in himself.

But now he wasn't even afraid anymore.

Men's voices. The almost indistinguishable burp of a shortwave radio transmission. It wouldn't be long now.

> *Oh soon, and better so than later*
> *After long disgrace and scorn,*
> *You shot dead the household traitor,*
> *The soul that should not have been born.*

He heard the metallic slam of automobile doors, the scuff of booted feet in the dark. Truman reached out with a bare toe and pushed the off button, extinguishing the TV light. He watched the final bead of light in the center of the screen as it burned a few moments longer, then evanesced to black.

He drank the beer quickly, set the can at his side. The pistol felt cool—the grip was comforting, even now.

How many of them could he get? Four, five, six?

He had no zest for it.

The hiss of portable lights broke the dark, the floods coming on one after another.

"Taylor? We know you're in there!"

He put the barrel in his mouth, sucking the flavor of burned powder as if it were sweet.

"It's over, Taylor!"

A lone tree frog carried the final notes of the symphony.

Shot? So quick, so clean an ending?

He drew the trigger slowly, surprised by the slight quaver in his hand.

Oh that was right, lad, that was brave:

"Taylor, we want you to come out with your hands on your head."

Yours was not an ill for mending . . .

He paused.

"Taylor! We're asking for the last time!"

'Twas best—squeeze—to take it to the grave.

The shot rang out.

The tree frog fell silent.

30

Oak leaves curled like cats' tongues, licking here and there as they fell with a sigh. Denise stood at the kitchen sink, motionless.

Dr. Brunner said time would heal.

Yes.

But unexpectedly, shockingly, the scene thrust into her consciousness, overriding all else for a few vivid moments.

The black pit of the icehouse, the foul stench when they broke the padlock and threw wide the heavy portal. Flashlights carving dark with light. Peggy hysterically attacking the first man to reach her.

"Police . . . police, miss . . . police . . ."

Yes, she would live it again and again—and she knew the children would too. She'd seen them halt in play, caught in thought, held by the memory until something tore them free.

The telephone brought her back to the moment. When Denise lifted the receiver, she heard Brad talking to Bob. "We'll be at the Plaza Restaurant at seven o'clock."

Going out tonight. Dr. Brunner had told them they must. For the children, but also for themselves, he'd said. He had warned of emotional scars which deepened in isolation, the tendency to become reclusive, afraid of strangers.

Through the open kitchen window came an autumn air, the leaves rustling groundward as breezes stirred the boughs.

Brad came in buttoning his shirt cuffs. He kissed her, took a step, returned and kissed her again. "Where are the children?"

"They're dressing. They'll be down in a minute."

He sat at the breakfast-room table, gazing out the back door. "I don't want to go," he said. "It's been difficult enough going to work every day."

"I know."

She hadn't had the courage even for that. Putting off Bob's repeated pleas, she had invented excuses to stay home.

For the children, Dr. Brunner had counseled. "Go out together; something social, something public."

Tonight was the night.

Jeffrey's footsteps clumped on the stairs. He presented himself for inspection and Brad adjusted the boy's necktie.

"I don't see why we're going to a restaurant," Jeffrey said. "There's a pizza in the freezer."

"It will do us good to get out," Brad said. "Where's Elaine?"

"You know how women are."

"Um." Brad grinned at Denise. "I do."

They had received a long letter from Lana a few days ago. It was filled with misspellings and atrocious grammar, but had not a hint of sadness. She'd signed it "Aunt Lana."

"Do we know that aunt?" Elaine had asked.

"Maybe someday . . ."

The nights were the worst. Elaine often screamed in her sleep until they reached her. Most of the sensation had returned to her hands. Her therapy included squeezing rubber balls and swimming. For several days she had stayed in the hospital, the doctors fearful lest clots form and break away to vital organs.

Elaine came into the kitchen, green eyes blinking rapidly. She had yet to regain her full pudgy form—or maybe the weight of childhood was gone forever.

"You're stunning," Denise said.

"Yeah," Jeffrey acquiesced, "you look okay."

Brad took the girl in his arms and hugged her long and gently. "I think you are ravishing," he said. "I want you to sit beside me tonight."

"I don't want to go, Daddy," Elaine said.

"Neither do we," Brad said. "But we should. We will."

"People will stare."

"We'll stare right back."

"I really don't want to go." Elaine's lower lip trembled.

"Hey, hey." Brad held her at arm's length. "Come on, Elaine. You can do it, baby. The first time is hardest, the next will be easier. This is something we need to do for ourselves."

As they left the house, passing the swimming pool, Brad commented on the changing season.

"Maybe we could ice-skate this winter," Elaine said.

"It never gets cold enough here for that," Jeffrey said. "Besides, the expansion of freezing water would be deleterious to the structure. There would be cracks and—"

"I was joking, Jeffrey."

In the car, they locked the doors. Brad looked at Denise and forced a smile. "Here we go," he said.

Mother Taylor would meet them there with Bob, Vera, Jack, Lanita, and all the children.

In silence Brad drove toward town.

When they had found Truman, there was no note, nothing to explain further or to justify his actions.

But it wasn't over. Would never be over. When Denise went shopping for groceries, she felt people watching, imagined whispers of her name. Elaine and Jeffrey had complained of the same thing from their classmates.

"Time will mend all," Dr. Brunner had assured them. "If you go forth bravely and pick up a normal routine, the day will come when this will seem remote, like a dream, ended."

"I don't want to do this," Elaine wailed in the back seat.

Denise twisted to see her, but said nothing. Jeffrey stared out the window at the streetlights and sparse traffic.

"Here we are," Brad said, his cheeriness that of an intern wheeling them to surgery. "Now, I want us to go in here as if we owned the place. I want us to smile and talk and act like we belong here!"

"Yessir."

But as he locked the doors, Brad looked about, frowning. The lot was filled with cars, but not Bob's, not Jack's.

Denise took his arm. "Smile."

"Could we take the side entrance?" Jeffrey asked.

"Hell no," Brad said. "We're going through the front door with heads high. Come on, gang, let's get 'em."

Elaine and Jeffrey walked as close to Denise as possible, without actually clinging. The diners seated at the front tables saw them coming. Denise felt them react, turning to one another. A young girl pointed.

"Heads up," Brad whispered. "Smile!"

He held open the door as Denise entered, then Elaine, then Jeffrey—and finally Brad.

"Sheriff Taylor!" The owner stepped from behind the cash register. The room fell quiet as people stared.

"It's an honor to have you, sir."

Elaine took Jeffrey's hand, straightened her back.

Brad held Denise by the arm, urging her to follow the maître d'.

A man stood up, blocking passage. Unsmiling, he clapped his hands once, drew back, clapped again, slowly. Clap . . . clap . . . clap . . .

Another patron rose, joining in: . . . clap . . . clap . . .

Then another, and another, the clapping rising in a slow swell as more hands met, the cadence quickening. Chairs scraped, people came from other rooms, adding applause until it was thunderous.

Elaine and Jeffrey slipped into their chairs. "Why are they doing that?" Elaine asked.

"Because," Denise said, "they understand."

About the Author

C. TERRY CLINE, JR. lives in Fairhope, Alabama, with his wife, author Judith Richards. His previous novels include *Damon, Death Knell, Cross Current, Mind Reader, The Attorney Conspiracy,* and *Missing Persons.*